SOJOURN

AN

ACCOUNT of the

Queen's Bench

Behaviour, Confession, & Dying Words

Of SIR JOHN LEVITICUS WILLOW QC MP

Who gave an Accounting

On the 26th Day of May 1904

BY:

J L HAZEN

Eastbourne :

PRINTED FOR J. H.WILLOW, BY A. WAKEFIELD

[Price 6p.]

iUniverse, Inc.
New York Bloomington

Grateful acknowledgment is made to Conan Doyle Estate Ltd. for permission to use the Sherlock Holmes characters created by the late Sir Arthur Conan Doyle in this work.

iUniverse books may be ordered through booksellers or by contacting:

iUniverse
1663 Liberty Drive
Bloomington, IN 47403
www.iuniverse.com
1-800-Authors (1-800-288-4677)

ISBN: 978-1-4401-9519-8 (sc)
ISBN: 978-1-4401-9521-1 (hc)
ISBN: 978-1-4401-9520-4 (ebook)

Printed in the United States of America

iUniverse rev. date: 06/04/2010

‘LAW is not order for a gentle world. Law is threat, a threat of penalty directed at those who did not keep it. The threat of punishment, the threat of prosecution, the threat of one’s very life being taken from him. Order comes only after the threat has been acted upon, the execution of the law and the punishment that walks hand in hand with it.’

—Harold A. W. Stratford LCJ

Prefatory Remarks

It must be explained that, in Scotland, the Court of Session is Scotland's supreme civil court. It sits in Parliament House in Edinburgh as a court of first instance and a court of appeal. The court consists of judges who are designated 'Senators of the College of Justice' or 'Lords of Council and Session'. Judges take the courtesy title of 'Lord' followed by their surname or a territorial title. The court is headed by the Lord President, the second in rank being the Lord Justice Clerk.

The decisions of the Court of Session are reported in Session Cases. Session Cases takes precedence over all other case law series in Scotland. A session case is an account of the trial or proceedings resulting in a summary of the decision. The accounts of the Queen's Bench and of the King's Bench, as my time upon this earth spanned both, are so typed and stored among my papers by my clerk.

I might begin my story when I was a small boy. Perhaps it might give insight into how events have shaped my life. But my life did not being there. Indeed one might say it ended there, and this is not an account of my life, but of another's. To tell my story I must tell you all, and there is no better place to begin than the long sojourn we embarked upon that fateful October and the year to follow.

J Willow

Darley Rd
South Lodge
King Edward's Parade
South
Downs

The

LAW JOURNAL REPORTS

FOR

THE YEAR 1904:

COMPRISING

REPORTS OF CASES

IN

The House of Lords and in the Privy Council,

IN

The Court of Appeal and the court for Crown Cases Reserved,

AND IN

THE HIGH COURT OF JUSTICE

VIZ.

Chancery; Queen's Bench; and Probate, Divorce, and Admiralty, Divisions.

MICHAELMAS 1903 TO MICHAELMAS 1904.

The Appellate Cases, in the House of Lords and in the Court of Appeal, are with the Reports of Cases in the respective Divisions and Courts from which the Appeals come. These Cases form five distinct Volumes, having separate Indexes of Subjects and Tables of Cases; viz., the Privy Council Volume; the Chancery Volume; the Queen's Bench or Common Law Volume, including Bankruptcy Cases; the Probate, Divorce, and Admiralty Volume; and the Magistrates' Cases.

THE CASES RELATING TO THE POOR LAW, THE CRIMINAL LAW, AND OTHER SUBJECTS CHIEFLY CONNECTED WITH THE DUTIES AND OFFICE OF MAGISTRATES, ARE SEPARATELY ARRANGED, AND FORM A DISTINCT VOLUME OF REPORTS, VIZ, THE MAGISTRATES' CASES.

THE PRIVY COUNCIL CASES, INCLUDING SCOTCH AND IRISH APPEALS IN THE HOUSE OF LORDS HAVE THEIR OWN INDEX AND TABLE OF CASES, AND FORM A DISTINCT VOLUME OF REPORTS.

THE REPORTS ARE EDITED BY

JOHN LEVITICUS WILLOW, Q.C., M.P.,

AND

LORD HAROLD STRATFORD, C.J.,

QUEEN'S BENCH DIVISION, VOL. LXII.

{CONTEMPORARY WITH LAW REP. [1904] 1 Q.B. : [19040 2 Q.B.}

EASTBOURNE:

PRINTED FOR J. H.WILLOW, BY A. WAKEFIELD

[Price 6p.]

CASES

ARGUED AND DETERMINED

IN THE

Queen's Bench Division

OF THE

HIGH COURT OF JUSTICE,

REPORTED BY

JOHN LEVITICUS WILLOW, Q.C., M.P., LORD HAROLD STRATFORD, C.J., MYCROFT HOLMES, SHERLOCK HOLMES, AND OTHERS

AND ON APPEAL THEREFROM

IN

Her Majesty's Court of Appeal,

REPORTED BY

JOHN LEVITICUS WILLOW, Q.C., M.P.

AND IN

The House of Lords,

REPORTED BY

LORD HAROLD STRATFORD, C.J.

EDITED BY

J. H. WILLOW, BY A. WAKEFIELD, Q.C.

MICHAELMAS 1903 TO MICHAELMAS 1904.

SESSION CASE

QUEEN'S BENCH DIVISION

LORD JUSTICE

HAROLD A. W. STRATFORD

FIRST SESSION,

HELD AT

JUSTICE HALL, IN SUSSEX COURT,

ON FRIDAY, THE 27th DAY OF OCTOBER, 1903,

AND FOLLOWING DAYS.

TAKEN IN SHORT HAND

(BY AUTHORITY OF THE CORPORATION OF THE CITY OF EASTBOURNE)

BY A. WAKEFIELD

Eastbourne :

PRINTED FOR J. H. WILLOW, BY A. WAKEFIELD,

No. 74, MEADS;

AND PUBLISHED BY G. HERBERT, COUNTY COURT

1904

OPINION OF LORD STRATFORD
in the cause

1904 } THE CROWN v. SIMON BALLARD et al
October 24 }

[1] Holmes made his way wearily up the stairs to his well-worn rooms. Not for the first time, he felt the ache of old wounds and the accumulating years weighing heavily upon him. At nearly fifty years of age he was hardly an ancient, but age definitely had its disadvantages in his rather active line of work. Even he had to admit that his age asserted itself more strongly than by the presence of a few grey hairs and aching muscles. The tall thin frame that had cut so striking a figure five years earlier now appeared gaunt and his angular features were creased with care. The great detective stood on the landing and drew in a deep breath, releasing it slowly in the manner of the Tibetan monks whose self-control and asceticism he so admired. The tension and the aches in his body receded like an ebbing tide. Silently chiding himself for letting such a trifle occupy his mind, he unlocked the door and entered his lodgings.

The mail upon the sideboard contained nothing of great importance, only invoices to be paid and a circular advertising the great efficacy of a patent medicine in the prevention of influenza. Holmes draped his coat over the sofa and made swiftly for his pipe and Persian slipper full of tobacco, propelling the remnants onto the floor. Lighting it, he drew deeply upon the long thin clay pipe for a moment, his face relaxing as the tension he had begun battling on the landing receded still further. It had been a long week, and yet the task he had fixed for himself was not yet complete. The moment enjoyed, he went for the note on the mantel, which he had affixed some days prior with a knife to be sure he could find it upon his return. It was not there. Mrs Hudson had removed it in her cleaning, no doubt disturbed by his maltreatment of the woodwork.

Calling out to her in frustration, his impatience forbid him to wait and he rummaged through drawers and files without success to find it. The sound of a rapid tread of feet upon the stairs distracted him briefly from his search while he considered the source. When the footsteps fell silent at the threshold, Holmes addressed his concealed guest with confidence.

'Watson, would you be so kind as to ask Mrs Hudson where she put the note I had on the mantel?'

Holmes returned to his search, his anxiousness increasing every moment he could not find the note. He rifled through books and notebooks within seconds, dumping out the contents onto his desk. Sitting, he wrenched open drawer after drawer, slamming each of them in turn when they failed to reveal his prize.

'You are slipping, Mr Holmes,' the voice of a young man replied, causing Holmes to stop in his tracks and turn around. 'But then again, I half suspect the key to that trick is having a fair idea of who is most likely to be coming up the stairs at this time of day.'

Holmes stopped abruptly for a moment to give his attention, but resumed without turning around. 'Hardly. Observation and deduction is a precise science accentuated into an art.'

'But you were wrong,' James insisted with a pernicious grin.

Holmes turned to the boy with the utmost seriousness. 'I am never wrong,' he said, returning to his search. 'I merely made the observation that there were two footfalls upon the stairs, one younger and another older, the latter with a distinctive tread.' Slamming the drawer shut in frustration, he called out again. 'Watson, do you mind awfully? It is rather important.'

Watson stepped out from behind the door and leaned over the banister, calling down for Mrs Hudson before taking his place among the familiar artefacts, of which he had become a part. James paced the floor, his arms folded and his expression dim at the failed attempt to fool Holmes, running through the exercise in his mind.

Perking up at a singular thought, James addressed Holmes again. 'You knew my father's tread, but you didn't know it was me. I see now that it was clever of you only to address the known quantity, deliberately bypassing the unknown. It made it appear as if you knew everything. Clever, but not good enough. I have you this time.'

Holmes leaned back in his chair, giving his full attention to the youth and regarding him with arms folded and expression blank. Allowing a few seconds for the young man to bask in his victory,

Holmes drew from his smouldering pipe a few mouthfuls of the remarkable tobacco, savouring the gaseous calm that descended upon him. James took his seat in complete confidence, smirking with youthful pride. Holmes fixed him with a amused eye and gave his reply.

'You came by carriage. I know so because it had just rained, allowing me to hear the distinctive slowing. I heard it stop for a moment in front before continuing to the end of the street. It was then you formulated your plan, which by then was already known to me, for what other reason could you have for continuing on to the end of the street and walking back? You came in together using a key, because the bell did not ring. Mrs Hudson did not announce a visitor so it dictated a familiar person to this house. You paced your steps as you walked across the tile downstairs and began up the stairs in step. Your mistake'—Holmes imparted a grin—'was when you approached the upper portion of the stair. In your anxiousness you fell out of step, allowing me to hear two sets of footfalls, the heavier one being quite distinctive of my old friend. If I had any doubts in my theory, you dispelled them when you walked alone along the landing,' Holmes revealed as he watched Watson take a seat near the fire and James flop onto the sofa.

Before another word could be spoken on the matter, Mrs Hudson appeared in the doorway. Her frail features paled in striking contrast to her expression of grave displeasure.

'What…?' she began in a trembling voice. 'Mr Holmes, you are the very worst tenant in all of London.'

Holmes winced in embarrassment. Overturning his rooms without thought of consequence was a bit much to put the long-suffering woman through. She was very proud of her house and not a little assertive in her disdain for ill treatment of it.

'Yes, I'm sorry, but it is all important that I find the note I had placed on the mantel.'

Mrs Hudson tightened her lips and negotiated her way around the mess to the fireplace. Retrieving the unopened mail and the note from a small letter holder at the edge of the mantel, she made her way over to the slouched figure and stretched forth a hand, along with a stern reproachful look. An embarrassed 'thank you' was all

Holmes could manage as she stormed out of the room, leaving the mess behind.

Watson chuckled at the undeniable consistency of his friend, silently relighting his pipe, which he had allowed to grow cold for the deception.

'You are on a case, I see,' Watson said, tossing the paper from under his arm onto the footstool.

'It is a simple case; nothing that would interest you. Child's play, but he is willing to pay handsomely for it.' Holmes grinned in satisfaction. 'It is a mere matter of intercepting the sale of a stolen artefact. I've traced it to Sussex and have arranged to draw him out this evening. It was a dull matter indeed, until I learned of the silent funds behind the intermediary. Does the name Stratford mean anything to you?'

'Lord Justice Harold Stratford, the High Court judge?'

'The same.'

'I know that his is one of the noblest households in England and he is a fair seaman. He races at the Sydney-Hobart yacht race on occasion and often wins. He has been decorated by the queen twice.'

'And a personal friend to King Edward and my brother Mycroft. A well-respected family, with many secrets,' he added softly. 'I have been in Sussex all week. I was actually disappointed in my investigation until today. This new information convinces me that there just might be something in it after all.'

'Then I should assume you shall be engaged for a while? Elisabeth did so want you to come before sending James back to university.'

'I shall be home tomorrow, two days at the outside.'

Holmes sprang from his seat and arranged himself in an attitude of confidence for the benefit of his guest who, by the jingle of the bell downstairs, would be arriving any moment.

'Now, unless I miss my guess,' said Holmes, 'there is my client at the door.'

In that brief moment Watson saw Holmes thrust the note into his pocket with a trepidation that had not been there before the man arrived downstairs.

'Do you need my help?'

Holmes shook his head. 'The case is a trivial one, as I have said. I am more interested in the man behind it than the immediate players. It should be an interesting find. Either way, it should not take long to find out the real mystery behind the acquisition of this stone. We will find out in a couple of days. I would not dream of taking you away from your family for so trifling a matter. You know I will call upon you if I need my strong arm.'

'Are you quite sure?'

'Quite sure. I have been known to solve a few cases on my own,' Holmes chuckled.

Pulling on his coat, Watson collected his things and paused for a moment in the doorway trying to dispel the sense of foreboding that came upon him suddenly as he looked at his friend. Holmes did not look worried as he stood masterfully by the fireplace, nor did his confident posture suggest an attempt to conceal any hidden problem. Yet, in that briefest of moments, Watson found himself trying to decipher the cause of his growing anxiety. 'Are you sure you are all right?'

'Quite! Now if you are going to stay, Watson...' Holmes returned, dispelling Watson's last hope of discovering what was at stake in this case.

'Then I'll see you in a few days.'

'I shall be there, save death or imprisonment.' Holmes winked, seeing Watson and his son out the door as his guest breached the bottom stair.

Having much to do and little time in which to do it, Holmes was eager to begin, and eager to have this case at an end. There was more on the mind of the noted detective than this one small case, however, things he preferred not to share with even the closest of companions. His mind was full, too full for the case at hand. Perhaps it was this that he sensed his devoted friend and partner felt as he departed their old rooms.

Watson trotted down the stairs after James, passing a well-dressed young man under a smart-looking Humbug. Watson slowed his pace as the man passed, straining to get a better view, but the gentleman kept his pace. He was obviously in some anxiousness to see Holmes. In the next moment the door closed behind him and the matter passed. There was nothing to do except to trust that Holmes knew what he was doing.

'Mr Holmes?' the man addressed.

Holmes turned around to face his client with a nod.

'Do you have it?'

Holmes turned back to the fireplace and, taking his time, took a cigarette from a box and lit it. 'Not yet, but I will; tomorrow.'

'If it is a matter of money ...,' the man began.

Holmes cut him short with a nod of his head. 'I just need you to clarify a small point before I leave. Might I presume you are not the primary principal in this transaction?'

A subtle nod saw Holmes pressing the mark. 'And might I also presume your benefactor is a well known High Court judge?'

'I am sure, Mr Holmes, you can understand why I must decline to answer. Had my partner wanted his involvement known he would have come to you himself.'

Holmes granted the man a conciliatory smile. 'Quite so. Then shall we say tomorrow evening, six o'clock?'

Holmes gestured toward the door. The interview was over. It mattered little what the man wanted. If he could not provide answers, he rendered himself superfluous to Holmes.

With all arrangements made in advance, Holmes packed a few things that might aid him in his quest and hurried out the door. Mrs Hudson had prepared tea only to be run down by Holmes as he was rushing by.

'But your tea, Mr Holmes!'

'No time! I shall return in a day or two,' he said as he fled out the door and into the discomforting cold of the late fall winds.

[2] Settling himself in the sheltering embrace of a hansom, Holmes directed the driver to take him to Marylebone Street. With little of interest to capture his intellect along the way, Holmes turned his restless mind to the matter at hand. The case was well beneath his powers, but mental stimulation was not on his agenda. He had already compiled a plan of action, which only needed the conclusion of a previous affair to set him into action. Indeed, he had received

word from his contact while in Sussex to return to London to retrieve the information that would lead him to his man. At the time, a former investigation had demanded his attention, but free from those bonds Holmes could devote himself entirely to his new charge, or so his arrogance allowed him to think.

Holmes arrived at his destination, a small marketplace on Marylebone Road, where the driver pulled to the curb in front of an age-battered shop. An old boisterous merchant in the midst of giving advice to one of his favoured customers nodded his head to Holmes as he entered.

'I'll be right with you, Mr Holmes,' he said.

The woman turned to look, straining over the shelves to see. 'Is that Mr Holmes, the detective?'

'Yes, Mrs Evarts, but not to mind him. You know you can't have pepper spice. It upsets your stomach. How about this?' he asked, handing her a mild blend.

Having attended the woman, the avuncular old merchant turned back to Holmes. 'I have your order nearly ready, Mr Holmes: a loaf of rye, some rice, high tea, and Indian curry. I see Mrs Hudson is making you up a nice vindaloo for supper. Now mind me; there is a place that makes a fine vindaloo, real hot and spicy. It is exactly what you need to taste authentic cooking. I'm getting older and my memory fails me on the exact address, but it is worth the trip if you just have to have it. There is a little pub by the station. It's somewhere around there. Not too many people know where it is and you must be precise in the directions or you will not find it. Sometimes the landlord of the inn makes a nice stew, as well, but only when the mood strikes him. Mind you, it takes a bit of patience to get him to make it, but he's a fine one, a little odd perhaps, but a good man. Sometimes he gets into these moods where all he'll make is exotic and dangerous foods, but if you approach him just right, you will find what you are looking for.'

'Thank you,' said Holmes, laying down a ten-pound note for a tuppence ha'penny order.

The portly man's cheerfulness slipped a bit as he looked out the window. 'Looks like a bit of rain out tonight, Mr Holmes. I'd button up if I were you, especially if you're going out.'

Holmes followed the man's gaze and tried to hide a smile at the notice of a man across the street, trying to look inconspicuous.

'A little rain has never bothered me,' Holmes assured him.

'I think this one could turn into more than a bit of rain, my friend. Neither Dr Watson nor Mr Mycroft would be happy if I let you catch your death. I hope that old coat of yours protects you well enough in this storm. I fear that one day it will not. You put it too much to the test and I think it has become a little threadbare of late. I think you need to go on back home and have Mrs Hudson make you a nice pot of tea. Put your feet up and curl up with a good book. Let the storm blow outside while you are tucked safe near the fire. It isn't worth getting caught out tonight. Come, let me persuade you. I beg of you.'

'It is just a case; simpler than most. What harm is there in this?' Holmes whispered.

'If I knew there was harm in it for you, not even a hundred pounds could buy my information.'

'What then?'

'This man you are after tonight'—he paused—'you just be careful. I hope you have not inadvertently stepped on any toes for him to be waiting for you, or not even Mr Mycroft's protection will be enough to save you. Please, go home, Mr Holmes. Consult Mr Mycroft on this matter before you go, for the rain has already arrived.'

'What connection does my brother have with this business?'

'Nothing. I just mean I think Mr Mycroft is a smart man,' the old merchant quickly diverted with reticence. 'Sometimes he sees things the rest of us miss, even you.'

'I'm not interested in the man, only what he has. It is a simple transaction. I won't be long. I'll make it home long before we see a storm from that rain.'

'I hope you are right. Here, take this with you. You might want it with that spicy supper of yours,' the old man insisted, the cheerfulness once again returning to his face as he handed Holmes a bag of mint candies.

Holmes took the bag and gave a nod. 'Watch your back,' he said, pulling up his collar and walking out the door.

'I always do, with you,' the shopkeeper muttered to himself, watching Holmes retreat down the street. The man across the way followed after. The old shopkeeper dispelled the worried look from his face before returning to Mrs Evarts with boisterous good cheer. She still looked with longing at the tin of pepper spice.

[3] Holmes looked into the small bag of mints and stopped for a moment in front of a store window to put one covertly in his mouth. The man across the street was still following him. Ducking into several more stores to pick up a few things and dislodge his follower, Holmes hailed a cab and headed to Victoria Station. After glancing briefly at a map, he stepped up to the stationmaster and purchased a ticket to Rye, discarding the groceries before he boarded the train.

The long train ride unfolded without incident, but Holmes took every precaution, never once forgetting that he had been followed so soon after taking the case. Sitting alone in the compartment, he leaned back and cleared his mind of all thoughts save for how he was to approach the man he was to meet later that evening, and the warning the old merchant had given him. At the fourth stop, a woman and child stepped into the compartment and sat quietly across from him, allowing him to slip back into his reverie, a curious mixture of light slumber and meditation. For whatever reason, he turned his mind away from the case and onto the woman and child, studying them. The child was remarkably well behaved and the woman graceful, mindful of her child's actions at all times, which was evident in her occasional correction of the child's spelling.

For an instant, an undeniable sense of regret flooded his consciousness, forcing from his mind all other concerns. How pleasant it might have been to follow Watson's path or the path taken by so many other men: a wife, a child, a comfortable home; to be taken care of in the years ahead, once his body began to cheat him. With Watson gone, his house had become inexorably lonely.

Turning back toward the window, he stared out at the rolling English countryside. With a nearly inaudible sigh, he took out his Bradshaw, his only bit of paper, and jotted down his thoughts on the case, which filled his mind for the duration of the trip.

[4] The train arrived promptly in Rye at seven-thirty o'clock. Stepping onto the platform, Holmes made for the small public house as instructed. It was crowded and moderately noisy, with the landlord bustling about tending bar while his wife rounded the floor serving food to the patrons seated at tables throughout. Holmes took a table in the corner, pulling out the bag of mints from his pocket and setting them on the edge of the table in plain sight.

'What will you have?' the harried wife asked.

'I'll have a glass of your local ale. I have heard there is a nice Indian restaurant that serves an excellent vindaloo somewhere in the vicinity.'

'Don't know of any around here.'

'That is too bad. I was in the mood for a good curry.'

'How about the stew? It's not spicy, but it will fill you up nice.'

'That will be fine.'

She returned with ale and, some minutes later, a dish of hot stew, which he sampled but was not fond of. Minding what he had been told, he managed to choke down a few more bites before dismissing it, noting a tall lean figure with tattered country boots and worn trousers coming into view. The man was middle aged and rough looking, with a pint of ale in his hand and a smouldering pipe in his mouth.

The man sat down and peered into the bag on the table. 'Mint.' He frowned. 'I'm not sure I like mint this time of night.'

'My name is Sherlock Holmes.'

'I know who you are, Mr Holmes. You live up to your reputation and more. I don't know how you found me, but you must leave at once.'

'If you know who I am, may I presume you know why I'm here?'

'You may presume what you like, but you have to leave now, this instant. It is not safe.'

'What game is this?'

The man leaned in close to Holmes. 'A very deadly game, sir, one in which you have been played as a pawn to find me. You have just forfeited my life,' he said in a serious tone, taking on a sombre expression as he continued, 'and most regrettably, your own, as well.

However, I am bound by oath to protect you, and fortunately for you I never have yet broken a promise.'

'Protect me?' Holmes questioned. 'From whom?'

'From the man behind the person who hired you,' he said, looking carefully around before he took a seat opposite.

'Lord Justice Harold Stratford, perhaps?' Holmes probed, receiving a repressed laugh in response. 'Then who? Who wants this stone?'

The cheerful expression slipped from the man's face. 'I am quite sure the stone was a ruse. He must know I would never turn it over to him,' he said, shuffling in his seat as he sized up his companion, 'if it existed.'

'If it does not exist, why bother to hire me?'

'To find me,' the man said, his expression again turning sober. 'They will be coming now. We should leave,' he added as he looked at his watch, and again looked around. 'He's late back. I don't know how much longer we can remain without them closing us in.'

'Who are we waiting for?'

'The only man I trust to safeguard your life. He hates us, but his holy vows keep him honest.'

'A priest?'

'Yes. I mean, well, it is complicated,' he started before withdrawing. 'I have no time to explain. Our guests have already arrived and we can no longer wait for him. Listen to me very carefully and do exactly as I tell you and we may yet survive this night. Two men just walked in. Don't turn around; use the lid of the pot. Do you see them? We are going to take a little stroll. If I'm right, they will follow. We'll start in my room. I have some things I need there, and if we are lucky we'll see our man en route. We can talk a little along the way. Now rise as if we have no knowledge of their presence and walk out with me casually. Oh, and leave a generous gratuity; the people here are friends of mine.'

[5] Holmes did as he was told, not so much because he was convinced the man's story was true, but because, for the moment, he had no other choice.

'We're going to walk down to the end of the second block and turn left,' the tattered itinerant continued. 'We'll pass by a shop window on the corner. Don't be obvious, but glance into it as we pass by. If you see someone there, they will be the men who will follow us next. The pair behind us will step back. They are too far back to make a move now and so they will let the next pick up the trail.'

'You're being followed?'

'No, my dear naïve pawn, they've been following you! Until now my identity and position have remained concealed. Sometimes one or two will get clever enough and come too close to my general location, but it is difficult to identify a man whose face is never the same twice. Even this face I wear tonight is but another mask. That is why they needed you.' He chuckled to himself with amusement. 'Out of all the people to betray me it would have to be you. Come, let's go. We can't wait for him any longer. I'll have to take you myself.'

'Who is this priest?'

For a moment the man did not seem to understand Holmes's confusion over such an obvious thing. Perhaps reluctant to reveal too much in the open, he abandoned the conversation and slowed his pace. He stopped and tapped Holmes for a light, pulling two cigarettes from his inner pocket and handing one to Holmes. He glanced at the glass and then, with a coy sleight of hand, turned Holmes to see the reflection.

'What do you see?'

'One man in the shadows of the building across the street and another two coming up behind him.'

'Three? They are anxious. Our man is certainly hedging his bets. We'll see more before we're away.'

'Perhaps this was not the path we should have taken.'

'I don't think it would have mattered what path we took. There would have been others in any other direction. I believe we are not to live out this night, so our adversary will send all that he has. I've found a little misdirection helps, or has at least until now. Here is my room. Are you as good as I hear? If you really jumped the falls and lived to tell about it, this should be easy for you.'

'What should be easy?'

The man gave no answer, but pressed through the door in the back. Glancing back once more before entering, he pressed up the stairs. At the top he unlocked another door and turned up the gas.

'Is that wise, to announce ourselves, if we are being followed?'

'You threw wise out the window when you contacted me. We can discuss how you managed it later. Right now we can assume they already know we are here and that I will be protecting you. I should prefer, however, that we do not give away that we are ahead of them. Stay away from the window and keep an eye on the stairs,' he ordered as he grabbed a small sack with straps from under his bed. Striking the floor with his fist, a board popped out of place, which he then removed while Holmes peered down the hall through the small opening he left in the door. Between the floorboards lay a revolver and a box.

Holmes motioned for the man to hurry. 'Someone is coming up the stairs.'

'That was quick. Time to jump, little brother.'

Grabbing Holmes by the arm, the man thrust him through the window and followed without hesitation, landing on a sloped roof where the pair rolled down without direction and fell from the precipice to a wagon full of straw, then onto the road. Before Holmes could gain his bearings he was being dragged down the alley through one turn after the other, through alley doors, upstairs and down, until he had no sense of where he was. Finally the man stopped for a moment, and pushed Holmes smartly up against the wall, out of the light, as he glanced around the corner.

Holmes made light of the rough treatment. 'Do you always keep a wagon of hay in the alley?' 'No, but Mr Vanderbilt does. The constable has warned him more times than I can count. He never listens. He drinks too much and does what he pleases. I'll have to thank him for that.'

'That was taking a great risk.'

The edict seemed to affect his host, who withdrew his hand along with the tense and abrupt treatment. 'Was it? What was the worst that would have happened? We'd have landed on the floor?

Come on; you fell over the falls and lived to tell about it. What are you afraid of?'

'I wouldn't recommend it.'

'Do you believe me now?'

'No,' Holmes replied. 'A clever ploy by an extremely quick-witted opponent.'

'You don't trust me. Good. Hush. There's the train,' the man insisted, inconspicuously looking around the corner at some distant noise. 'We're going to make that train. I hope you are in good health. It's going to be a fast run followed by a dangerous jump, and that will be the easy part.'

'Where are we going?' Holmes asked.

'To get help,' his companion replied, starting out of their concealment in the shadows.

'Why?' Holmes halted him, beginning to see that there was more to this matter than he had first supposed.

Though the moment was grave, the tousled rogue stopped a moment, turning to Holmes with serious eyes. 'Because you just made my life infinitely harder, little brother. I don't like harder. Someone just pulled the coup of the century, setting you straight in the middle of it. I don't know why, but you are a very important piece in a very dangerous chess game. We have to get you to Eastbourne, but you can wager all the paths will be covered.'

'You—' Holmes barely got out before his odd companion interrupted.

'Quiet. It is time to go. Listen to me carefully, for it means your life. Don't stop for any reason. If I let go, you keep up. If we get separated, get yourself to Eastbourne. The westbound train will take you there. Go to The Camberley at 29 Elm Street, opposite the pier. You'll see the road from the watchful soldier. Give them any name save your own. If I'm not there by the following morning, go to the Greek at the desk and say you are in need of the Templar without delay. He'll ask you your name. Tell him this time. Whatever the Greek says to do, do it without question. Any deviation would mean certain death for both of us.'

'Templars?'

'Look, I'm getting on that train and so are you, willingly or otherwise. We've been marked for death. I've been dead before, but if they kill you...' He stopped as if reluctant to finish the thought. 'Well, if I have anything to say about it, they won't. Do as I say, exactly what I say and we may both come out of this alive.'

With that he peered out around the corner. Before Holmes could say another word, his host grabbed him by the arm and bolted out through the streets towards the train. By the time they came into view, the train had already started to move. The rogue did not slow, but urged Holmes to keep running. As they approached the train Holmes saw four men dart out of the shadows. Whatever the peculiar man's paranoia, the immediate danger was real.

'Grab the rail!' he called out to Holmes as the train began to move faster.

Holmes grabbed the rail of the caboose just as one of the men closest to the train pulled out a revolver and fired. It echoed like a child's popgun, losing its potency over the noise of the train. The two men stood trying to catch their wind as the train sped down the tracks into the night.

'Now what?'

'Up,' his host announced.

Holmes climbed upward, swinging himself around to climb the rail to the roof, at the man's heels as he motioned for Holmes to move forward on the carriage. Halfway, the man stopped and knelt down on one knee, pulled off his sack, and opened it. Against the wind, covered by his coat, he lit a cigarette and puffed on it for a moment while looking at the sky. Drawing out another, he lit it from the first and handed it to Holmes. Letting a moment go by, the man pulled at his hair, revealing it to be a wig. Another moment saw him removing a false nose and eyebrows. Unfettered, he was a magnificent-looking fellow, propped up against a moonlit sky, dedicated and sharp. Even in the low light the most unobservant creature could tell that his mind was working all the angles.

'What could have kept him?' the man muttered to himself again. 'Something is wrong. Something must have happened.' Thrusting the spent cigarette over the side, he sat down. 'I wonder what big brother will have to say about all of this in the morning.'

'Your brother is in Eastbourne?'

'You're joking, right?' the man asked, as if astounded by the response. Not for the first time, the man stopped and looked at Holmes with confusion. 'You really don't know, do you?'

'Know what?'

'Your family, your …' He trailed off as if reluctant to continue further. 'You listen to me. You keep your head down and do as you're told. You're pretty good for an old man. I wasn't sure you were going to make it.'

'What's this all about?'

'Gluttony, power, greed; why does any man kill his brother?' he said, returning to his stance. Pulling out a flare gun and loading it, he looked at the sky as if making some mental calculation. He fired off three rounds; one yellow, two red. 'I just pray nothing else goes wrong. I insist, if it does, you do not take the time to question or argue. The Camberley is not far from the station. Head to the sea, to the pier and the soldier. Make your way there as fast as you can. Speak to no one along the way.'

'And ask the Greek for the Templars,' Holmes scoffed.

'Do you know what they are?'

'Stories have been circulating for four centuries. It is said the Crusaders took up the holy cause after the French Templars were burned alive. By the fifteenth century they too were hunted down, but escaped to Scotland. They are a myth, stories to excite little children who still believe in knights and holy wars.'

His host cocked his head at the chary answer, kneeling down to light another cigarette. 'Well, not quite. They are the ultimate force of reckoning. If not too simplistic, they are the king's men, sworn to hold that England never falls. When needed they will guide and protect those on a holy sojourn. For our purposes, we will call upon them to safeguard our journey, to South Lodge, at least,' he added as he handed Holmes another cigarette.

The destination struck Holmes sharply, suddenly uncomfortable. 'South Lodge?'

'We'll call in reinforcements from there and get you back to London. Your brother is not going to be pleased.'

Holmes leaned back, not knowing what to make of what he was being told. It was the second time that evening a reference had been made to Mycroft and South Lodge. Everything told Holmes that his opponent was insane, yet everything about the case thus far had made him uneasy. If the man was not as mad as he sounded, he was the most masterful con artist he had ever met. At the very least, he was the most intriguing man Holmes had met in some time, which caused a grave, uneasy feeling to seep into his bones.

SESSION CASE

QUEEN'S BENCH DIVISION

LORD JUSTICE

HAROLD A. W. STRATFORD

SECOND SESSION,

HELD AT

JUSTICE HALL, IN SUSSEX COURT,

ON FRIDAY, THE 27th DAY OF OCTOBER, 1903,

AND FOLLOWING DAYS.

TAKEN IN SHORT HAND

(BY AUTHORITY OF THE CORPORATION OF THE CITY OF EASTBOURNE)

BY A. WAKEFIELD

Eastbourne :

PRINTED FOR J. H. WILLOW, BY A. WAKEFIELD,

No. 74, MEADS;

AND PUBLISHED BY G. HERBERT, COUNTY COURT

1904

[6] It was October 25, 1903, at precisely 6:23 in the morning when Sergeant Doherty stepped into the large foyer, with its great oak coat hanger benches and gleaming brass hooks. George, a trusted and faithful servant of long standing helped the young sergeant off with his coat and led the way down the cold marble hall. Doherty's damp police-issue boots sounded on the white and dark green marble floor, echoing hollowly throughout the great hall like the mournful cadence of a funeral drum. George's footfalls were silent, amplifying the tapping of the sergeant's boots as they made their way past the portraits, the closed doors, and the polished wooden wainscoting.

Midway down the long hall were two massive white doors secured with brass handles. The servant's white-gloved hand neatly turned the knob and the doors were drawn aside to allow passage. The room was large, yet warm in atmosphere and divided essentially into three primary parts. The centre was welcoming, with two sofas that faced each other to divide the room. Comfortable chairs accompanied them and commodious tables set with lamps and small collections of books. One's eyes, however, were first drawn to the life-size portrait of a woman and child, which hung with pride above the sitting area, ever watching, ever a part of the atmosphere that encompassed the great hall. The portrait had been commissioned many years before, for the young toddler who posed so angelically with her head and hands in her mother's lap was now a young woman, keeping only the angelic smile which she portrayed at the age of four.

Following the natural flow of the room, Doherty's eyes traced the bookcases, filled from floor to ceiling with law books. A master's desk sat out from the walls of books with its leather and wood chair pulled back as if the old judge had been working even at this early hour. He was not at his desk, nor at the ladder, which had obviously been used recently, for a small stack of books lay on the bottom rung. Coming nearly full circle, Doherty turned to face the old jurist lifting his eyes from a dusty old book to greet him.

Doherty took a deep breath, drawing himself up to speak. 'Good morning, my lord.'

'Sergeant, I trust that this is of grave importance, for you to disturb me so early at home?' Stratford asked as he put down the fine leather-bound book and glowered at the intrusion.

Clearly, by the sight of him, Doherty had little to fear for his own person. Yet, the words that needed to be spoken made him hesitate.

'Yes, sir. The matter is,' he stammered, 'well, sir, it is of a peculiarly serious nature and one where, I am sure you will appreciate, the outcome may have grave and far-reaching consequences for those involved.'

'I understand. Pray, have out with it then and mind your facts,' Stratford granted as he took a chair, lighting a cool pipe.

'Late last night there were discovered three amber lights in high places. It was Stanton, sir; you know the one, with the wife who was taken ill. Well, sir, he chanced to look up at the tower. He saw a light. Odd as it may seem, he saw a second light upon that same street. Viewing only one, one might tend to ignore it. Viewing two he felt compelled to search for a third. He found such a lamp.'

'I presume you have performed the necessary geometric manipulations?'

'We did.'

'Recount them to me.'

'Each location was plotted on the map and a triangle drawn between them as prescribed. The triangle's sides were bisected on the square and the intersection of the lines revealed that which was concealed.'

'And the result?

'The bisector pointed to the old abandoned Snowden house upon the Downs. We arrived to find the manor in flames. Quite by chance I noted a man inside lying on the floor. My men and I went in to pull him out. We were able to rescue him, but he was barely alive.'

'Burned?'

'No, sir. It looks as if he fell through the floorboards. The fire brigade managed to subdue the flames well enough for us to pass through, but it was too late. We found a second man near the hall and two in the front room, all dead.'

Stratford found himself leaning up against the chair for support at the news, greatly disturbed at the horror of the thing. 'Good lord.'

'The men upstairs were...' Doherty paused. 'Well, sir, they were murdered. One was stabbed in the chest, another in the gut, and the other was...' Doherty hesitated again, abruptly halting what he could not bring himself to say.

'Was what?'

'The man was shot in the head,' Doherty stammered again, his voice losing its strength and vigour. 'We searched through their belongings and found only one to have identification. His coat lay on the chair next to him and, well...' He faltered again.

'Well what, Sergeant? Out with it!' Stratford rounded on the man, his jaw set with impatient fury.

Doherty was a strong man and not one to dally about the business, but whatever it was he was trying to relay found its way to obscurity. Doherty handed the judge a billfold with its contents intact. Stratford opened it and instantly sank back into the armchair as the blood drained from his face. 'Dear God! Tell me you are mistaken!'

'I'm afraid not.'

'Give me some hope, Sergeant! This news bears too great a weight. Of all the men in the world to be killed here! What was he doing here? What motive would anyone have to kill him?'

'I don't know, sir.'

Stratford's nerves soon precluded him from sitting still for too long, and he rose again to settle himself. He paced back and forth, trying to absorb the full meaning of what he had been told, trying to find some clue as to its purpose. In the absence of any logic, he looked back toward his friend, and seeing his lost expression, felt compelled to make apology for the lack of strength in his own person.

'Forgive me. Tell me about this man you saved. Can he tell us anything?'

'We took him directly to hospital, but I'm afraid he is in a bad state. I doubt we will get much from him anytime soon. Dr Teixeira does not expect him to live.'

'Ben Teixeira?'

'Yes, sir. He was the surgeon in residence at the time. They worked on him all night, but when I checked this morning, the news was not good.'

Stratford put his arm around Doherty and walked him to the doors. 'Get every man we have back out to that house. Take a hundred men if you have to. Search every inch of it. I want to know what happened out there. I want to know why he was there, whom the man is that he met there, and why. I want to know who dared to kill Sherlock Holmes on our ground. I want the precise details of the incident on my desk before I leave for London. Inform me of every inquiry, no matter how small, and keep what you find to yourself and me alone, for the moment.'

'I shall see to it,' said Doherty, replacing his hat and closing the doors behind him.

[7] It was a vicious blow, to be sure. Lord Stratford gazed wearily at the painted crest above the fireplace mantel. It depicted a sword so masterfully drawn that the cold, impersonal menace of sharpened steel was communicated with frightening realism. The illuminated glory of pure white and blue around the sword seemed to imbue it with a supernatural radiance: the fire of divine judgement and sure retribution. The brilliant silver of the sword stood in bright contrast to the deep azure field surrounding it, which caused it to stand out so vividly that one might think to pluck it from the painting. The sword hung there suspended, unwavering over the blood-red sanctity of a naked heart, which spoke of the ever-present possibility of swift and terrible judgment, even unto death for those pitting themselves against the law. The careworn corner, smoothed from the recurrent touch of a human hand, spoke of many long hours in supplication, many instances of the need for guidance and petition from so masterful a delineation of justice.

He placed his hand once again upon the cold, coarse surface of the portrait as if drawing strength from the iconography depicted there. Law was not order for a gentle world. Like the sword, law was threat, a threat of punishment directed at those who did not keep it: the threat of punishment, the threat of prosecution, the threat of one's very life being taken. Order came only after the threat had been acted upon, the execution of the law and the punishment that walked hand in hand with it.

Stratford clenched his hands into fists, tightly clamping them together until his nails sunk into the flesh of his palms. To embrace law was not an easy thing. One could spend a thousand years upon the bench hearing the petty cases of men: the theft of a loaf of bread, a dispute over a neighbour's land, a woman suffering at the hands of an abusive husband. This, the murder of an innocent, of a sacred heart bound by a still higher law, this was no ordinary task. This was not the law of the bench; this would require the full retribution of the highest justice, a task fallen upon his own hand to perform. Stratford muttered something softly to himself and then drew back. 'Damn!' he shouted as his soul cried out from the very depths of despair and anguish, no longer able to look up at the painting.

[8] The difficult task ahead could not be attempted with sketchy information. Facts needed to be precise if Lord Stratford wanted to approach his old friend with the news. Mycroft Holmes would expect no less. While Doherty collected information at the old Snowden house, Stratford dismissed the idea of breakfast and drove directly to hospital to look in on the unknown patient who might hold the only clue to the dreadful affair.

His condition was poor, and upon seeing the nearly lifeless body lying on the cot near the nurse's station, the full import of events began to sink in. It was a pitiful sight. The prostrate figure was swathed in bandages. Even without the aid of a physician to explain, it could easily be inferred that the man suffered from massive injuries.

Stratford turned sharply to the nurse's station. 'Nurse, how is our patient this morning?'

Immediately responding to the judge's request, the nurse closed her duty book and sprung into action. 'I'll get the doctor for you.'

Thanking her, he noticed that even as she stepped away from the desk, another nurse took her place so that someone would be in attendance at all times. Yet, even with a nurse on hand, it did not guarantee the man's safety, only his health. The more he turned it over in his mind, the more it became obvious that whoever took such drastic measures to ensure the man's death would not stop at an attending nurse. Stronger measures would have to be taken. As he stood planning a better means of protection, a familiar face appeared in the doorway and approached him.

Stratford extended a warm smile and welcoming hand. 'Teixeira, I heard that you were attending our patient. I could not be more pleased.'

Teixeira broke out in a grand smile at the compliment, shaking his old friend's hand. 'Stratford, how's the shoulder? Is the tincture of laudanum I gave you helping at all? I hope you are remembering to take it in the dosage I prescribed.'

'Not as well as I would like, but that is not why I came to see you. The man they brought in last night: how is he doing?'

Instantly, Teixeira took on a sombre countenance. His duty to Stratford sometimes conflicted with his duty as physician, but it did not sit any easier. 'Stable, for the moment.'

'Will he live?'

'That's difficult to say. Most of the wounds will heal; it's the blows to the head I worry about. Have you seen the report?'

'No, not yet. Doherty gave me a brief overview.'

Teixeira walked Stratford over to the bed and pulled back the patient's sheet. 'I've seen quite a few accidents in my time, but none where the bones of the hand were broken like this. I'm not convinced our man merely fell. The breaks and lacerations are too straight and too many.'

'You think him tortured?'

'That is for the police to decide. I can only offer you my opinion. You might also want to note that his head injuries were to the front, not the back. The injuries to his back were consistent with a fall. His head injury, however, is not. Someone struck him three times with something thin, heavy, and cylindrical.'

'Such as a lead pipe? Sgt. Doherty found a pipe with blood on it,' Stratford said.

'Yes, something like that.'

'When will he be able to tell us something?'

Teixeira glanced toward his patient in a physician's hope that the man might suddenly prove him wrong.

'It is just not something we can predict. He could live in a coma for years, die, or suddenly wake up tomorrow and call for his dinner.'

'Can he be moved?'

'I wouldn't recommend it. You could severely decrease his chances.'

Stratford put his hand on Teixeira's shoulder, gently turning him in confidence. 'What have you heard about the incident last night?'

'Nothing outside of three men brought in dead and this one in critical condition.'

'On the square, Sherlock Holmes was one of the men brought in dead last night. He may have been on a case. Three lights in high places were found.'

The blood drained from Teixeira's face at the implications. 'That was bold! What does Mycroft say? He can't be pleased.'

'I haven't gone yet. But I can guess what he will say: protect the last man at all cost.'

Teixeira gave a nod. 'I already spoke to Doherty. We have a nurse watching him round the clock.'

'That is not enough,' Stratford insisted. 'I want policemen here with him.'

'I can't have that! This is a hospital!'

'Ben, I need this.'

'What you ask is impossible. I cannot have a policeman here among the patients. It would present the wrong impression to visitors and staff. Besides, they'd only get in the way.'

'Then let us take him away from here.'

'If you move him, he could die.'

'You leave me with no options. At least allow me to put Doherty on him.'

Teixeira thought for a moment and then gave a nod of approval. Doherty was young, but subtle and polite. 'We'll keep him in a ward alone, off from the others. It will be easier for Doherty to hear someone coming down the hall and easier to protect this man if something does happen. If he so much as stirs, we will call you.'

The compromise was less than what he wanted, but Stratford reluctantly agreed.

[9] Stratford made his way to the constabulary to inquire after Doherty, who had just arrived back from the house and had not yet changed. Stratford was willing to wait. It had been a long time

since he had visited the halls of a police station. Court had kept him busy at the other end of the law. Sitting and watching the officers perform their respective duties reminded him of days gone by. He had forgotten how dull and institutionalised the station seemed with its stone walls painted a sickly bottle green and white, offset only weakly by the austere wooden desks. Stratford rose and paced the floor, inadvertently causing a young constable to insist the sergeant hurry for his visitor. Presently, Doherty emerged from the back, still buttoning his clean tunic.

Stratford could hardly contain himself. 'What did you find?' he asked, putting a friendly hand on Doherty's arm.

'Nothing more than I told you this morning.' Doherty shrugged him off, taking his seat behind the desk.

'How many men did you take back out with you this morning?' Stratford inquired, already knowing that Doherty had taken less than a handful, from other sources of information at his disposal.

'All I could spare,' Doherty answered, clearly treading carefully.

For Stratford, who had known Doherty for some years, it was a simple matter to see that he was holding something back. There was something on the mind of the sergeant that had not been there two hours earlier. Doherty dismissed the notion, stating only that he had been working long hours without a break. Stratford knew better, but could hardly call the man out for no more than an assumption. He had faith that Doherty would reveal all when his facts were straight.

'Inspector Sanders wants us to follow protocol on this one.'

'Does he understand the ramifications of this case?'

'We could...' Doherty started to say before he realised his voice was rising in excitement and frustration. 'We could take him into our confidence.'

Stratford shook his head. 'No, not yet.'

Sanders was a middle-aged man who had worked his way up through the ranks of the police department from the rank of constable. His methods were archaic and often wrong, but he tried hard and had influential relatives.

Stratford looked away from Doherty, who seemed unable to look him squarely in the eyes. 'What about the other men; have you identified them yet?'

'No, sir. That is the odd thing about it. None of the other men had any identification on them, no clue as to their identities, as if...' Doherty strayed off.

'What?'

'As if we were not meant to know. I know how it sounds, but what other explanation can there be? Whoever did this is extremely clever and knows us.'

Stratford quickly assessed the possibilities. 'Keep an eye on Sanders while I am gone. I want more details of the incident on my desk by the time I get back from London.'

Stratford collected his things and Doherty walked him out. Doherty paused just ahead of Stratford, not turning around but addressing him discreetly.

'We missed you at the policeman's ball last night. You are usually always there. Other plans, sir?'

'I'm sorry to have missed it. I was unusually tired last night and retired early. I did send Sam with my usual contribution.'

'I must have missed him, having been called out to the house,' Doherty said, still unable to face his old friend. 'Your contributions are always welcome, as you are. You enable us to help a lot of people. I cannot express enough how grateful we are,' he reiterated, moving to go once again.

'Ian,' Stratford called after, waiting for him to turn around before continuing. 'Is something on your mind?'

Doherty stood fast. 'No, sir, I was just thinking. You wouldn't happen to have the time, would you? I was wondering if I had time to stop by the house and change before I go back out.'

Stratford started to push back his coat to reach for his watch before recalling it was not there. 'I'm sorry, I don't,' he answered before realising Doherty had only just changed. His prevarication was a weak one.

'What happened to your watch? I don't ever recall a time when you did not have it on your person.'

'I lost the cursed thing! I must have bent the clasp on the chain, allowing it to break free.'

'Recently? I thought for sure I saw you with it the other day.'

'Yesterday. I'm not sure when, but I am sure I had it in the morning before court.'

Doherty gave a nod of acknowledgement, but continued to shy away from facing him. 'I should get back if we are to have those reports for you to take to London.'

Stratford stopped him again at the bottom step. 'Ian, I want you to do something in addition for me. As soon as you have dispatched your men, return to hospital and remain with our man. When you are on guard, remain vigilant and maintain a ready stance at all times.'

'You suspect an attack?'

'I hope not, but what I hope and what I expect are two different things. If you are with our man I have every confidence that his safety is assured. There is too that, should someone attack, you are the man best qualified to capture him. If you must have someone relieve you, ensure that he is most qualified in both body and in trustworthiness. Let him not stay too long in your stead, but return to your post with haste.'

Doherty gave a nod. 'You may rely on it.'

'And Doherty, tell no one what you do, not even the one who may relieve you. Don't let down your guard for a single instant. Trust no one.'

'And Teixeira?'

'We have him in our confidence, but reveal nothing of our conversation and pray tell no one else. These are dangerous times, Ian. If this is anything of what it looks like, we are at the brink of war.'

Doherty put his hand on Stratford's arm with more confidence than he had in the moments previous. 'I shall not fail you; I swear it.'

'There's a good lad. Take your rest by day. We shall make ready by supper.'

'No, it is too dangerous for you. I will be there. No one will pass.'

Stratford again let his insistence show. 'We can trust no one! A day or two will see us through to the truth. You are my strongest ally in both body and fidelity. I doubt he shall get past you and then we will have him in hand.'

'If you will permit, I would like to take Carter with me. He is a good man. I should recommend him to be one of us if you are agreeable. We will see that no man gets by while we remain alive. Pray remain at your house. Let them believe us to be off our guard. I shall die before I let anything happen to the man.'

'You are a good man, Ian. What would I do without you?'

'We will bring an end to this, sir. I will find out what this is all about and who has done the thing. I swear it on my life.'

Stratford examined the young man's face closely, and in the determined set of his jaw and the resolute look in his eyes he knew that anyone attempting to get the better of him would have a difficult time. Yes, he thought, a very difficult time indeed.

[10] Stratford returned home and made ready his plans for London, a heavy burden he would rather set aside than bear. By noon Doherty had his men send over the preliminary results of the investigation. Crude and swiftly constructed, they painted a picture of the events that transpired over the preceding twelve hours, enough to begin a full-scale investigation.

His daughter Helena met him in the foyer as he prepared to leave. She was quickly distraught, for he had not informed her of his intended departure, a thing he would never do under ordinary circumstances.

Taking his daughter in arms, Stratford tried to give her a consoling smile to hide the burden of his task, as well as his anguish. 'I must go to London. I should not be long.'

Helena leaned in and hugged her father. 'Something is wrong, isn't it, Father?'

'Yes.'

'Please tell me. You look as though your very heart is aching. Is it John?' she asked, pulling away from him at the unpleasant prospect. 'He's all right, isn't he?'

'I'm sure he's fine. No, it's just that ...,' Stratford found himself struggling to utter the words. 'Sherlock Holmes is dead.'

'What? Are you sure?'

'He was found shot to death at the abandoned Snowden house last night. I'm on my way to London to break the news to Mycroft. I don't want him hearing it from the police or, God forbid, the newspapers. I need to tell him in person.'

'Do you want me to go with you?'

Stratford stroked his daughter's cheek. 'No. I want you to take over my casework today. Have Judge Norris take the bench in my stead.

Kissing his daughter good-bye, Stratford took his leave and picked up the box that sat desolate on the table in the foyer. He picked it up and carried it out to the motorcar as if it contained the last remains of his own child. Removing the lid, Stratford ensured that all the personal effects and files were packed neatly and carefully within, resettling it as George came up behind him.

'George, it is a heavy weight that we carry today. If only this cup could pass from me. How could we have let this happen?'

Giving a nod of acknowledgement of the hardship, George opened the door for his master, waiting patiently for him to enter. 'It will be all right.'

'Will it? I don't know that I have the strength to tell him.'

'I am sure my lord has the courage to carry out his duty. It will be better for Mr Mycroft coming from a friend.'

Stratford gave a consenting nod as he got into the back. 'Yes, I'm sure you're right. I just wish John were here to go with me. Mycroft would take it better coming from him.'

[11] The journey was long and taken in silence, partly in reverence and partly in mental anguish. It was just past two when George pulled the motorcar to the curb outside the great doors of the Diogenes Club. Stratford looked upward, toward the towering columns of white, with the glass reflecting the sun from a dark pane above. He found himself pausing to wipe away a solitary tear that escaped at the thought of his commission.

Within, the halls were long and quiet, and he heard only the tapping of his own shoes as he made his way up the stairs and down the corridor to the rooms of his old friend, a founding member and patron. His strong heart seemed to turn to water as Mycroft waved him in happily, not having seen his friend in some time. Stratford stepped in and quietly closed the door behind him.

'Stratford!' Mycroft smiled. 'Come in and sit down. What brings you to London? I perceive your health has improved since I saw you last. You've been spending a good deal of time on your new boat, which begs the question of why you are so deeply distressed. I should think a new boat would keep all distressing thoughts from you. If the boat cannot, surely Norfolk should.'

The momentary diversion provoked a smile from the old judge. 'Good heavens, Holmes! Is there anything you don't know in advance of my arrival?'

'Since your arrival, Harry, since! Everything I have just named can be perceived from your general appearance. When last I saw you, you had suffered from an injury that occurred on your boat, a broken shoulder, as I recall. When I saw your hands healing from recent rope burns and cuts, I made the logical conclusion that you replaced the boat which had caused your injuries, and purchased a new one which still requires breaking in: the remnants of a well-spent summer after so difficult a spring. The signs of a well-seasoned tan still visible on your face confirm my hypothesis.'

'Astonishing! And how is it you know I've just come back from Norfolk?'

Holmes tapped on the box, taking a seat opposite Stratford. 'The box you carry has a label from Blakeney Point. I should very much doubt you would keep a box from Australia for seven months, and so I concluded you have been recently sailing in Norfolk. And since your accident happened nearly a year ago, what else could I conclude? As you have your new boat and have spent many long hours at sea in the warm summer breezes, I may take it that your heartsick expression comes from elsewhere. That box has been opened and resealed, suggesting that its original contents no longer reside within. The box you have not yet deigned to set down suggests its contents are valuable and your mood subject to it. Taken in conjunction with your hasty departure from Sussex to see an old dog like me, I would say you are troubled greatly by the contents of that box.'

'Oh my dear friend, I hardly know where to begin,' Stratford said as he finally agreed to take the seat offered.

'Would some fortification help? Brandy?'

'Thank you; I think it would.'

Mycroft rang, and moments later a servant appeared with refreshments, departing as quietly and unobtrusively as he had come.

'Now to your box,' Mycroft said, anxious to assist, only to be halted suddenly by the pained expression on Stratford's face. For one who noticed even the smallest details of any situation, Stratford wondered if he would notice his increased heart rate, as well.

'Something has happened, hasn't it? I beg you to tell me about it.'

'My dearest friend, my heart is crushed under the weight of it. I would gladly take the world itself upon my own shoulders if it would allow me to turn away from what I have to relay.'

'Tell me. Whatever it is, I assure you, we will set it right.'

Stratford nearly broke at the invitation, clutching onto the box so tightly it was evident that his hands were shaking. 'Were that but possible, I would give my life for it,' said Stratford, gulping down the contents of his glass. 'Last night there was an incident upon the Downs. Four men were discovered, taken from a burning house, purposefully set, we feel. All died save one. The last man had been severely beaten. It is possible this man was tortured. He is in hospital presently and not expected to live. Sergeant Doherty pulled him from the flames, half dead. You met him once; Doherty. He is a good man. He risked his own life in the hope of saving even one of the four. We do not yet know the identity of this man, but we remain diligent. The police found no identification on most of the men, but it is still early yet. The fire was swiftly suppressed, enough for Doherty and his men to enter farther into the house. The fire, however, was not the cause of their demise. The men upstairs had been murdered. One was shot and the others stabbed, one as he made his way to the stairs. We aren't sure why these particular men had come together on that night, or what they were doing. They were,' he stammered, 'killed quickly. Only the last man, the man in hospital, seems to have suffered. I doubt any of the others had time to react, especially the first man shot. He would have felt no pain.'

Holmes sat forward in his chair. 'That is an odd statement to add. It is hardly necessary to know that the man did not suffer, unless it will play a part in the mystery you have yet to unfold to me?'

'What I have to say I feel does me great disservice; admittedly I feel not unjustly so. I feel responsible that it was permitted to happen at all.'

'Don't wander, Harry. Come to the point before I end up recounting the matter to you, instead of you to me.'

'Mycroft, Sherlock is dead. He was at the house. He was shot in the head and died instantly. The damage to his face was not extensive enough to hide his features; tall, thin, middle-aged, dark hair. Doherty recognised him from a likeness in The Strand Magazine.'

Mycroft's cheerful interest instantly faded away to silence as Stratford pushed the box across the table toward him. With enormous restraint and strength of will, Mycroft opened the box and examined the contents. Enclosed he found a black felt hat with silk ribbing, a long black wool topcoat, a black frock coat, white shirt and thin black tie, all charred and singed on the left side. Stratford watched as Holmes carefully examined the buttons and noted the tailor. They were those used by his younger brother. Examining the inside pocket of the overcoat, Mycroft's face blanched as he fondled a tear in the fabric.

'Sherlock tore it last week, and mentioned that it would have to be repaired,' he said.

Setting it aside, Mycroft moved on to a piece of paper beneath. It had an odd cut near the top corner.

'Ireland; Phoney Profits, Fraud, Penalties and Equity, Random Field of Bond Returns. BF £5000,' Mycroft read aloud. 'What is this?'

Stratford examined the paper. 'I don't know.'

Reaching into the box, Mycroft retrieved the train ticket and a black leather billfold containing all proper identification, several pound notes, and a Bradshaw, which had strange scribbling on it, one pair of black boots, and a pair of old ruddy socks, which made him frown.

'Robbery does not seem to be a motive,' Mycroft finally pronounced analytically, struggling to maintain his composure. 'The autopsy?'

'It's in there. The official coroner was not on duty at the time. Lewiston did the initial exam so that I may have something to report. He's a good man, younger, but very fond of your brother's methods. I should hope the official report confirms his findings.'

Mycroft flipped through the report, stopping at a diagram drawn hastily by Lewiston. 'You noted the angle of penetration?'

'I did, but did not wish to make assumptions.'

'Do you believe it is an assumption to conclude that my brother was kneeling on the ground, unarmed at the time of his murder?'

'I...,' Stratford stopped, at a loss for words, finding himself unprepared to face a superior master in the art of observation and deduction.

'What is in your mind, Harry? He was assassinated, along with his companions. His killer knew he would be there and raised no alarms as he entered. How else do you explain how the killer or killers took them unawares? Why did you deliberately omit these details?'

Stratford recoiled at the berating. 'I'm a judge, Holmes, not a detective!'

'You don't need to be a detective to come to the conclusion that this was an execution! What else aren't you telling me? His body was found on the Downs, outside of Eastbourne, yet his train ticket puts him in Rye. How do you account for the discrepancy?'

'I cannot! We found no ticket to Eastbourne.'

'Then how did he arrive? What was he doing there? Who knew he was there? What about this paper you seem to know nothing about? Was he investigating someone in Eastbourne?'

'We don't know yet.'

'Did you view his body for inconsistencies yourself?'

'No; I thought it best to send him here.'

'Did you photograph the elements of the crime? Did you perform an analysis of the surrounding grounds? Do you know anything of the matter?' Holmes asked, his voice shaking. Snatching up the police report, he found little more than rough notes, which were handwritten. 'You've come to me in haste, Harry! You barely have your facts in order.'

'I thought the news would be better coming from me, rather than you seeing it in the news headlines or hearing it from a police inspector. I'm sorry, Mycroft. By God, I am sorry!' Stratford began to realize that Mycroft's grief had already begun to seize him. 'We were there. We were warned, by three lights in high places, but too late to save him. If only he had told someone he was in trouble. I would have sent the world to his aid.'

'Told someone? He gathered several men in assistance, set the lights for even more of our brethren to come to his aid, and you tell me my brother should have told someone he was in trouble!' Holmes shouted. 'Preposterous! Next you will be telling me he knocked on your own door to tell you he was in need of you!'

Gathering himself, Holmes drifted over to the window and gazed out over the streets below, perhaps collecting his thoughts. The day was bright and busy, not yet revealing its cold heart to the coming winter. Stratford sat quietly, allowing his old friend time to take hold of his welling emotions, quite unable to help. For the longest time, as Mycroft faced away from him, Stratford could not tell what he was thinking. He was simply quiet and still.

'If Sherlock did not arrive at Eastbourne by train, then discover how he arrived. My brother has always been impetuous, always running headlong into the petty problems of the police. Find out if this is one of those times. Someone knew enough to draw on these particular men to help and I can quite guarantee you that Sherlock did not place those lights. It is my belief that someone lured him there. I want to know why. My brother is dead! Someone knew he was coming, and knew he would be on the Downs at that precise time. The very people overseeing his safety forewarned his enemies. We have been betrayed!'

'Not necessarily,' Stratford quickly insisted, fearful of this very conclusion.

'The lights are an unmistakable sign! Pray, what is this theory in your mind?'

Stratford put down his brandy glass and leaned forward in his chair, anxious to propose a possible theory. 'The man who was injured was tortured for some time and then his skull fractured at the conclusion. Sherlock was killed instantly. Would it not make more sense that this other man was the intended target? Perhaps this man is the one that was in danger and Sherlock, along with the others, came to assist. We could easily be wrong that Sherlock was killed first. They may have witnessed the torture of this unknown man. I beg of you! Do not let this come to civil war before we know all of the facts! Your brother may have been there to find this man, to protect him. Even in his cleverness he does not fully know our ways. He may have been killed for no more than his attempt to intervene on behalf of this man's life. The report says the only other injury to your brother was a broken leg, which he could have suffered earlier. His presence there got him killed. I would not deem it assassination, but more likely a murder for having witnessed the crime of them torturing this poor man. Do not jump to the conclusion of betrayal. I beg of you, as your faithful servant!'

'There is still a barrister in you after all,' Holmes said with a calmer, more jovial attitude. 'So tell me, what do you make of these other men with my brother?'

'They were older gentlemen. They did not appear to have dirt on their clothing, outside of the soiling caused by falling onto the floor.'

'Suggesting?'

'They drove a carriage out to the Downs from Eastbourne,' Stratford answered, following the line given him.

'And?' Mycroft led, as master to student, expecting that the answer was obvious.

To Stratford, however, the answer was as obscure as the murders themselves. What could one derive from the men's appearance, outside of the fact that they had not been engaged in activities forcing their clothes to be soiled? Holmes had already seen clues missed by the police, but whatever else he observed he kept to himself, save for a few daunting details.

'They knew each other!' Mycroft revealed as if it were child's play. 'How else do you explain that at least three men out of the four went willingly with my brother to the Downs at so late an hour? What do you suppose; that he met them on the street and invited them to their deaths?'

'Of course not,' said Stratford.

'Then they must have known him, or someone with him, to call upon them at so late an hour. Sherlock is fond of using the telegraph office. I would start there. He is also fond of assisting the police with their problems. I shouldn't be at all surprised to learn that he was on a case. Start with his partner, Dr Watson.'

Holmes seemed hopeful about this tactic. 'Before you leave, stop by Baker Street and speak with my brother's landlady. Dr Watson usually attended my brother's more dangerous and noteworthy cases. Make sure he was not one of the men out there. And let me know at once.'

Stratford took Mycroft's tone as his leave, collecting his hat and cane. 'Of course.'

'Go; make your investigation. Show me that the evidence does not speak of betrayal. I want to know about this man who lived.

Who he is, why he was there, and why this cost Sherlock his life. Keep him alive at all costs.'

Holmes turned back toward the window when he had given Stratford his formal leave. It took little observation to see clearly that he was crushed by the news. In some way, Stratford had secretly prayed that his old friend would find some fault with the evidence, some reason to hold out hope that it was another of Sherlock's tricks of investigation, but to no avail. It lay with him now to find the killer of Sherlock Holmes and to let his brother bury the dead. There could be no greater pain than this, that his old friend's brother should meet his end while in Stratford's keeping.

[12] Seeing the full enormity of the situation, Mycroft Holmes knew he would never see his brother again. With trembling hands he rang the bell, causing a servant to appear. Scribbling something down on a piece of paper, he handed it to the servant, who read it at once before replying.

'He is reported to be out of the country. I am not sure we can reach him.'

'I did not ask for the difficulties, I said to bring him here!' Holmes cried out in a tone never before heard out of him. Without another word, Mycroft turned once again to the window, looking out over the people passing by.

[13] Stratford sat quiet and dejected across from his partner's empty chair in the study. The police had struggled to find any bit of information in an attempt to make sense of such a shocking waste of life, but every clue, every lead turned cold. Inspector Sanders had been put in charge of the case, but had made very little progress in the first days of investigation. Entering the dimly lit room, Helena Stratford made her way over to her father, putting a tender hand on his shoulder. At the lack of response, she leafed through the various telegrams on the reading table beside him.

'There is nothing,' said Stratford. 'They have found nothing at the house, no evidence Sherlock hired a carriage in Rye, no witness—nothing.'

'It takes time.'

'Doherty is holding back. I can see it in his face and there's not one message from him.'

'Ian is a good man. If he knew something, he would tell you.'

Stratford shook his head in scepticism. 'I don't know. I'm sure he knows something. Sanders is making a mess of things and my last hope has turned me down,' he said, handing her the telegram.

The autopsy on Holmes revealed evidence of a fractured tibia and remnants of acid scarring. The fire damaged the skin, but the conclusion was that the body was that of Sherlock Holmes. Watson had taken the news badly, turning down the request to come to Eastbourne to investigate.

Helena caressed her father's shoulder. 'He's right. He's too close to the problem right now. Give him time.'

'Time is something we don't have any more of than we do evidence. Doherty is holding out, Dr Watson can't investigate, and Sanders believes our survivor could be one of the killers.'

'What evidence does he have?'

'He says the placement of the bodies and that our survivor was dressed differently. He's reaching. It is no more than an attempt to have a conviction before the funeral. This is going to hurt Mycroft.'

'He'll understand. He always does.'

Stratford looked sharply up at his daughter. 'Do you understand what Sanders is saying? Sherlock and his companions beat a man half to death. I have to tell Mycroft that his brother and his companions committed a heinous act which resulted in their deaths. How sensible does that sound? Mycroft will have my head at the very proposal.'

Helena set down the stack of briefs in her hand and sat next to her father. 'It does seem a little out of his realm, but we don't know what happened out there.'

'You are forgetting that Sherlock did not know his way around the Downs. Mycroft is right. Someone took him there. And what about the motive? We are not talking about a beating, this was torture. There is a decided difference. The evidence suggests this man was tortured for some time before he was struck down. I don't care what Sanders says. Sherlock would never do that. I want the truth about what happened that night, not just a conviction.'

'Why does this trouble you so?' Helena asked. 'You don't think the man did it, do you?'

'What I think is irrelevant. You know better than anyone else he cannot be retained or let go on one person's feelings. This unknown man has the answers in his head and if it is all within my power, I must retrieve them. People want to know the truth, and in the light of insufficient facts they will seek to place blame at the nearest convenient doorstep.'

'How can you be so sure this man did not kill Sherlock and those men?'

'There is something about the placement of everyone. If Sanders is right then our unknown man was outnumbered three to one when he walked into the room. Sherlock was, according to this new theory, killed last. That means that our man, armed only with a knife that cannot be found, overpowered two men to reach a third who was armed with a revolver. How did he wrestle the revolver away from Sherlock with two men to prevent him from doing so? Why did Sherlock not shoot him before he stabbed the other two? And how did Sherlock's leg come to be broken? Not even Mycroft's theory explains that. This theory implies a quick-witted fighter, a novice boxer, was so helpless he could do nothing; yet we are to believe that, in his helpless state, he tortured a man. No, it will not do. We are missing something.'

'He may have been kneeling because of his leg and perhaps he was not in possession of his revolver at the time. You are assuming they knew they were in danger.'

Stratford smiled at his daughter's reasoning. He had taught her well. All the facts seemed to lead to the inevitable conclusion that Holmes and the man in hospital had been enemies, and that a fight had caused the death of one and the near death of the other. Still, it nagged at the old judge, but what troubled him was not yet clear in his mind.

'Perhaps,' Stratford continued, 'but it still leaves questions that aren't readily being asked. There is too much pressure for this case to be solved, to assign blame. It is a sign of much anguish and pain. People cry out for justice, and in the light of too few facts, they will hang the first available man who comes close. There is one more thing that bothers me. If Sherlock and his companions were dead and our unknown man unconscious on the floor below, who set the fire?'

'Maybe he fell as he was setting the fire,' Helena proposed.

'Nay, for evidence clearly suggests he was in no condition to do anything. If he had set the fire prior to an hour's torture the house would have been entirely consumed. If it was set after his torture he would have been unable to set the fire. Where is the knife used to kill two of the men? There had to be someone else there, but whom?'

'You speak from emotion and supposition this time, Father. The fact that this was Mycroft's brother has tugged at your heart. We may not have all the facts in the case. Perhaps there is something that brings this last man into question. Be careful, Father, that you do not allow your feelings for Mycroft to taint your judgment in this case.'

Stratford turned to his daughter with pride, which etched its image in her face as he looked at her. 'You argue admirably, and I must concede, which is why we must find out. There are far too many people who want a quick conviction. That's not justice, it's revenge.'

SESSION CASE

QUEEN'S BENCH DIVISION

LORD JUSTICE

HAROLD A. W. STRATFORD

FOURTH SESSION,

HELD AT

JUSTICE HALL, IN SUSSEX COURT,

ON FRIDAY, THE 27th DAY OF OCTOBER, 1903,

AND FOLLOWING DAYS.

TAKEN IN SHORT HAND

(BY AUTHORITY OF THE CORPORATION OF THE CITY OF EASTBOURNE)

BY A. WAKEFIELD

Eastbourne :

PRINTED FOR J. H. WILLOW, BY A. WAKEFIELD,

No. 74, MEADS;

AND PUBLISHED BY G. HERBERT, COUNTY COURT

1904

[14] There could be no doubt that Holmes's death had affected Watson deeply, for he had closed their rooms on Baker Street and withdrawn from public life, but the difficulty of Lestrade's case necessitated intervention. A telegram with the details had Watson taking the next train out to London. Lestrade was sure there were points about the strange business that would appeal to Watson, and in the absence of the noted detective there was no one else he could turn to. Watson had once before attempted to employ Holmes's methods but met with indifferent success. However, one particular peculiarity of this case brought Watson back to London with great interest.

The facts as they were known were simple. Charles Grace was the assistant to the curator of Egyptian arts and antiquities at the British Museum. His duties included the authentication of antiquities and valuing them. The young man moved in the best society and had, so far as was known, no enemies or vices. He was a second degree Mason of the Whittington Lodge in London and had been engaged to Miss Ashley Lavigne, of Crawley. Grace moved in conventional circles, his habits were normal and mature, yet upon the evening prior, he had met his end violently between the hours of eleven-thirty and one.

Grace and his fiancée had plans to attend an evening gala. They met outside the museum just after six o'clock and took supper in a small café around the corner. Miss Lavigne described his behaviour as unusual, worried and particularly nervous, though he insisted all was well. Afterward he escorted her home and left by ten o'clock. He headed home on foot, his apartment being no more than a quarter hour's walk. He arrived at his apartment shortly before ten-thirty where, according to his landlady, a visitor had been waiting for him. Though the lighting in the hallway prevented an accurate description of the man, she believed him to be a gentleman of average height and weight wearing a distinctive fur coat. Grace stated that he knew the man and admitted him willingly. The visit lasted no more than half an hour with no shouting or loud noises of any kind. The landlady saw Grace walk the man out, and appeared perfectly fine. No sound was heard from his room for the rest of the evening, and yet the following morning Grace was found beaten to death in his apartment without ever having left again.

Lestrade had left the apartment just as he had found it. Grace lay stretched out on the sofa as if he had fallen asleep. An empty whiskey bottle and a glass lay next to the sofa near Grace's fingertips. His eyes, lips, and hands were bruised, making it appear as if he had been struck by something, yet no weapon of any sort was to be found in the room. Examining the man carefully revealed additional severe bruising on the body, but no apparent explanation. His clothes were not dishevelled in any unusual way, which was odd for a man who had so obviously been attacked. There were no open wounds or markings to suggest what was used to strike him. Some of the wounds were large enough to suggest a fistfight, yet the wounds did not show the distinctive shape of a fist. Blood vessels were broken in the man's eyes, again with no apparent cause.

Pulling out a handkerchief, Watson picked up the glass on the floor and took a strong whiff of the contents. It was odourless. Walking over to the windows, Watson examined the sills for signs of entry. There were none. It was too high to scale the wall with no ladder or drainpipe near. Belgravia was a frequented thoroughfare and several storefronts faced the window. And yet there was the dead man with injuries that should have produced some sound loud enough to alert the other residences or people passing by. Squatting at the fireplace Watson examined the ledge, which bore a faint black mark and remnants of spent tobacco in the grate. Taking out a piece of paper, Watson took a sample and replaced the folded paper in his pocket before continuing on. The bedroom revealed signs that the man did not have a maid in each day. The bed was not made and several shirts were strewn about with a pair of trousers and two ties. The kitchen was neat, but his floor had not been swept.

Returning to the sitting room, Watson picked up his bag. 'All right, Inspector; if you arrange to have our friend brought round to the mortuary I will have a look at him.'

Somewhat surprised, Lestrade felt compelled to ask, 'Didn't you see anything?'

'I should hope I saw several things, but I'm not sure where they fit at the moment.'

Lestrade gave a sigh. 'Good heavens, doctor, you're as bad as he is…was.' His tone softened. 'What is it you found?'

'I'm sorry. I'm just tired. It's been trying of late,' Watson explained, gaining a nod from Lestrade. 'Your visitor is your murderer.'

'But the landlady said Mr Grace closed the door after his visitor left.'

'No one could have climbed up to the window without leaving traces so the man had to have come through the front door. As we know, Grace only had one visitor last night.'

'But how did he beat the man without being heard? And why did Grace see him out?'

'Grace saw him out because he did not realise what had happened.'

Lestrade perked up with interest. 'How can that be?'

'Because he was not beaten, he was poisoned.'

'Are you sure?'

'We'll know more after the autopsy, but look at the way he is lying upon the sofa. He wasn't feeling well, so much so he could not bring himself to walk into the bedroom. He slumped over where he sat. His killer wished us to believe Grace had been drinking alone, but the glass was clean. If Grace had been that ill, he could not have got up to clean his glass and replace it near the sofa.'

'He could have drunk directly from the bottle,' Lestrade pointed out.

'Then why procure the glass?'

'Then the poison was in the bottle?'

'I doubt it, but send it along as well. Our man is very clever. I doubt he is going to leave behind clues that he doesn't want us to find.'

'I don't think cleaning a glass and replacing it was very clever.'

Watson packed up his things and turned to go. Chancing to look down, he saw several bits of crumpled paper in the trash bin. Removing them, he noted drawings of what looked to be a project Grace had been working on, a translation of old text from a stone tablet. It must not have gone very well, for the remnants of long, hard effort had been discarded. Watson had seen more, but felt reluctant to mention anything before confirming his facts.

All day, as he drove upon his rounds, he turned over the case in his mind, endeavouring to hit upon some theory that could reconcile all the facts, and to find that line of least resistance that his old friend had declared to be the starting point of every investigation. It had been some time since he walked down the streets of London past Baker Street. And as he did so he stopped outside those now dark rooms and gave a thought of the man he felt sure would never inhabit that house again. It was an odd thing, he thought as he looked up at the stone front. It wasn't like before, when Holmes had feigned his own death. This time there was a body. And then there was Mycroft. He had not looked well at the viewing, clearly shaken. Watson pushed the image from his mind, turning back to the last day he and Holmes spent together in the old house. It seemed an odd coincidence. Watson was sure the murdered man was the same man he had passed on the stairs.

SESSION CASE

QUEEN'S BENCH DIVISION

LORD JUSTICE

HAROLD A. W. STRATFORD

FIFTH SESSION,

HELD AT

JUSTICE HALL, IN SUSSEX COURT,

ON FRIDAY, THE 27th DAY OF OCTOBER, 1903,

AND FOLLOWING DAYS.

TAKEN IN SHORT HAND

(BY AUTHORITY OF THE CORPORATION OF THE CITY OF EASTBOURNE)

BY A. WAKEFIELD

Eastbourne:

PRINTED FOR J. H. WILLOW, BY A. WAKEFIELD,

No. 74, MEADS;

AND PUBLISHED BY G. HERBERT, COUNTY COURT

1904

[15] The first nights at the hospital came and went without incident. Doherty was better than his word, placing Carter outside of the patient's room and himself within. By the end of the first week, Teixeira was convinced that Stratford's fears were unfounded and begged for his hospital to return to normal. Yet, Stratford would not yield, not even to reason. He refused sleep and ate but a few bites of food until Teixeira insisted he would have the judge and Doherty on his hands next if Stratford kept it up. Teixeira could not fathom such single-minded efforts at security for a man who would most probably die without ever saying a word. Yet Stratford felt sure that the man was extraordinary, even if he could not name the reason for his importance. Only time would tell, and at the close of the week, each of them grew weary and began to doubt whether anything would ever happen.

[16] At home, Stratford sat back in his chair, looking out of the window, wondering if he had missed something, for no one had inquired of or approached the unfortunate man, outside of one man earlier this evening. Doherty thought he was a detective from London. He had insisted on seeing the patient, but Doherty turned him away for he lacked proper authorization. The entire affair may have been suspect, save the fact that when Doherty offered the option to return with paperwork or to seek permission from Stratford, the man made an appointment for first thing in the morning to see him. It would be another dead end with some detective trying to make a name for himself by solving the unsolvable, or someone sent by Mycroft or Inspector Lestrade.

The long hours of the day had passed yet again without event, with no more than a passing motorcar or carriage in the streets to interrupt his thoughts, but he still found it difficult to concentrate. As the hour drew late, Helena Stratford turned down the lamps in the unused rooms and settled in the study with her father.

'What is the matter, Father? You look so tired.'

'I'm fine.' He shrugged.

Strolling by his desk to pick up a shawl, Helena noted the Dawson question had remained open on his desk all day. A question of law had been raised and Stratford had adjourned court to review. He had come home, closeted himself away in his study, and picked out several key books to answer the question. Yet the books remained closed on his desk and the paper blank. It spoke not of the difficulty of the question, but of the state of Stratford's troubled mind. He was clearly tired and despondent, no longer able to keep up with even the most mundane of his duties.

'Why don't you go on up to bed?' she urged.

Stratford shook his head slowly, partly in answer to her question and partly in sufferance. 'There was a time,' he said, pausing to relight his pipe, 'that I held Sussex in my hands. Nothing transpired in this town or any other that I did not know about. You could not steal a loaf of bread nor pay your rent late without me knowing'— he paused at the thought— 'without John or me knowing.' Taking another few draws on the pipe, he turned back toward the window. 'I regret every day that I argued with him.'

'I wasn't aware that you argued with him.'

Stratford reluctantly shook his head. 'He left because of me.'

'Nonsense. John allows no one to dictate his actions. Nothing you could say or do would force him to leave your side. He loves you so.'

'I hurt him.'

'You love him just as much as he loves you. What could you possibly have said or done to hurt him? He is a fortress of strength and impenetrable in that he is just.'

'Do not make him out to be a saint, child. There are things, things that if I ever dared speak of...' Stratford began, and cut himself short.

Stratford looked away under Helena's withering gaze, unable or unwilling to continue. The arduous recovery from the accident had left him requiring daily medicines to control the intractable pain, but they often had the undesirable effect of dulling his reason, as well. His mind still seemed keen to the casual observer, but the uncharacteristic harshness of his tongue gave away the game.

'I miss him,' Stratford added, reclining back into his chair as the drug bore him under.

'Me, too,' she granted softly. 'It's all right, Daddy.'

Draping the wrap over him and gently kissing his troubled brow, Helena drew the curtains aside and peered out of the window. It was a clear beautiful sky. It was always clear when the night was cold. The stars seemed to dance in the heavens while the moon shone like a lantern hung in the velvet evening sky. Closing and stacking the books on her father's desk, she swept them up in her arms along with the file and quietly made her way upstairs.

[17] At hospital, Doherty looked at his watch, noted that it was running slow from the three-quarter-hour bell, and took the time to wind it. Carter had stepped out for a stretch, but the footfalls in the hall told Doherty that he was still nearby. As the one o'clock bell struck, the head nurse walked quietly down the hall to the ward to offer the duty nurse and policemen some hot tea to take away the evening chill. It had been a frigid evening, and promised only more of the same. Teixeira had ordered extra nurses on staff for the week, but she had seen little evidence of it in regards to service or staff on her floor. Too often they would disappear at the very moment their assistance might have made a difference. It might have been cause for concern, had Teixeira's reputation been other than what it was. He was a fair doctor and an able administrator, but had a great weakness for the ladies, especially impressionable young nurses unfamiliar with his practices and dazzled by his charm.

Peering in quickly to take the order, she noticed that the nurse's station had been left unattended, raising a flutter of nervousness. She knew how important it was to keep a staff on duty in the east ward. Though the nurses were not given details, Doherty had made an issue of the matter and that was enough for her. It was nice having him at hand. It helped to pass the hours, for he was not only handsome but intelligent, and unlike Teixeira, who sought evening companionship of an easier sort, Doherty preferred substance in a relationship. He regarded the courting of a woman as seriously as he took being a policeman. It was a job for life, both challenging and fulfilling.

Irritated that she would now have to spend her time tracking down the missing nurses, instead of enjoying the company of so refreshing a young man, and having to confront Teixeira to get her nurses back, she stormed down the hall in annoyance. Stepping up to the desk, he saw the papers and charts laid open alongside a cold cup of tea and half a sandwich. Looking in all directions, it slowly began to dawn on her that more was amiss than the absence of the duty nurse or Teixeira spending the evening having his way with the nurses. Carter was not standing at his post outside the curtain, either.

'Ian?' she called out to Doherty, receiving no reply. 'Ian, its Sharyn. Are you awake?' She raised her voice slightly, but was met again with silence.

A hand touched her shoulder, causing an outburst quickly extinguished by her own hand covering her mouth, so as not to wake the patient. Snapping around, she relaxed her stance, now feeling her heart pounding in her throat.

'Oh, thank heavens, Ian. You scared the life from me.'

Doherty looked back over his shoulder at the enclosed stall of his charge before addressing her. 'What are you doing?'

'I didn't see you or Constable Carter,' she said.

'He's on guard inside with the patient.'

'Where is the duty nurse?'

Doherty put a reassuring hand on her shoulder. 'It's all right, I sent her for an extra blanket for the patient. It is rather cold in here.'

'I'll put more coal on the fire. I have to go downstairs for an hour or so. I'll be in the children's ward if you need me.' Quick footsteps echoed at the darkened end of the corridor. 'That must be Emily returning now. I shan't be long.'

Giving a reassuring smile and a nod, Doherty waited until her back was turned before he glanced back at the doorway, straining to see down the hallway. Seeing that all was clear, he resumed a seat in the hall, watching the pleasant stride of the nurse as she made her way to the children's ward.

[18] The situation had returned to normal, or so it seemed. A dark cloaked figure stopped long enough to stare back down that same hallway. He too had been interested in the placement of the staff. With his companion waiting for him at the bottom of the stairs, heavily burdened, he turned to join him until a shadow appeared out

of the corner of his eye, causing him to pause. A man wearing a long, rich coat and a trilby appeared around the corner of the opposite stairway, casually making his way down the corridor. His face could not be seen, but his garb was unmistakable.

'Harry?' the tall dark cloaked figure muttered to himself, straining vigorously to confirm or deny the vision as the man made his way down the hall.

'Come on,' his companion whispered loudly, urging him to give up the exercise. 'We have to go, now!'

The advice was sound, and whisking back around the corner, the dark hooded figure disappeared down the stairs into the gloom below.

[19] Sharyn returned to the east ward as quickly as she was able, carrying a tray of hot tea and biscuits. She smiled to herself, looking forward to spending the rest of the evening in the company of her handsome sergeant. Setting the tray on the narrow counter of the nurses' station, she saw with annoyance that Emily had disappeared again, this time with Doherty. She walked down the length of the ward, quietly pulling back the curtains surrounding each stall, stopping outside the cell of the guarded patient. Her eyes widened as she looked down and saw a growing pool of thick, dark red liquid slowly forming on the floor beneath the curtains. She put her hands tightly over her mouth, stifling a scream.

Drawing upon every ounce of courage she possessed, she drew back the curtain. Constable Carter was dead at his post, his throat cut from ear to ear. Doherty was slouched over the lifeless body of the guarded patient, as if he was using his body as a shield. Emily's feet protruded from the adjoining stall. She saw with horror how Doherty and the patient had met their end. The steel of a dagger had been thrust deeply into the chest cavities between the second and third ribs, piercing their lungs. Death would have been instantaneous; there would have been no time or air to cry out. Sharyn felt a cold numbness spreading through her, and let the merciful blackness embrace her as she slipped silently to the floor.

[20] The following morning the headlines heralded the news: 'Attack at Hospital Ends In Four Dead. Police Baffled.' Stratford let the newspaper slip from his fingers, shaken to the depths of his very soul. He knew that Sanders would play the fool and make a dog's dinner of the investigation. He had too much clout and not enough brain. With Doherty dead, Stratford felt unsure of whom to trust. The investigation had to proceed, yet it would take far more than a second-rate police inspector to gain any real progress.

[21] Sanders stood before Stratford, unimpressed at the summons.

'Why wasn't I informed of this last night?' Stratford asked Sanders, who stood confidently before him with his hands in his pockets, unaffected by the berating.

'Sometimes, my lord, you forget whose police department it really is,' Sanders returned. 'I am aware that your friendship with Sergeant Doherty has afforded you much in the way of information, but that's all over now. You may own half the town, but not my police station. Are we clear on that point, my lord?'

Stratford's face reddened with rage. 'You insolent . . . Let me make something perfectly clear to you, Inspector: without my contributions there would be no police department. Every crime, no matter how small, that passes through your doors, passes over my desk. I don't care who you married. I want this investigation to be flawless. I want to know who killed Doherty, Carter, and the man he was guarding. I don't care what it costs. I want answers!'

'I don't think you are in a position to dictate, my lord. I came here because an eyewitness put you at hospital last night, just before the murders, not because you summoned me. What were you doing there?'

'I saw Teixeira for my shoulder, but that was earlier in the evening. I was home all night.'

'Can someone corroborate that?'

'If you need corroboration you can ask my daughter.'

'I will do that!' Sanders said, picking up his hat and brusquely taking his leave.

'Sanders!' Stratford called, allowing him to reach the inner doors and no further. 'I am still waiting for legitimate results on the Holmes murders. I am not pleased with your conclusions thus far. Cross me again and you will wish that you had not.'

Sanders paused briefly, regarding the judge, and then strode through the door. Stopping outside, he ran the exchange once again through his mind. Sanders knew the little display of power he put forth to Lord Judge Stratford was wasted effort, but with Stratford's hold slipping, it was best for each man to make a stand, letting all know on which side he stood.

[22] As the weeks passed and the December snows began to fall, it brought with it cheerful shoppers and carollers, as if to say that life still continued, even in the midst of death and despair. Helena Stratford stepped out onto the street from the law office, looking up at the embedded stone inscription of 'Stratford, Stratford, and Willow' to hear the echoes of the paperboy on the corner, still sensationalizing the events of the Holmes murders. The editor was now making a connection to the most recent murders, speculating boldly.

With Willow gone from the house, the bells of Christmas tidings rang hollow in her ears, and the festive spirit of the season was dulled by the absence by his jaunty demeanour. There had been no word from him since June, when an argument with her father saw them part ways for the third and longest time. He had sent only a card in early November, saying no more than that he was to prolong his stay and could not say for certain when he would return.

The snow began to fall heavily, clinging to the indentations of the inscription no less than the girl clung to her loneliness for him. He had been a second father to her, with a lighter hand and a softer touch. Generally a rational woman, she was not given to flights of fancy nor irrational thought, though the nagging feeling that something was terribly wrong could not be dispelled. Pulling herself away from the sight of his name so prominently displayed above her head, she slid onto the cold leather seat of the Vauxhall and turned over the motor. She wretchedly made her way down the streets toward home only to find herself compelled to turn onto Lewes Road, then onto Wannock, then to Old Mill Lane, and then to Jevington, finding herself still driving. In half an hour she found herself in Friston, turning down Willingdon Road and onto that small, hidden, familiar drive until she stopped in front of a quaint little villa set back from view of the main road.

Stepping up to the door she found it locked, but that had never stopped her before. She had always been welcome there. Willow had given her a key during one of the several times she had run away from home as a child, seeking the hand of justice, in her mind rather than the cold impersonal law of her father. She had been crying the day she had made it all the way from Eastbourne to Friston on foot one rainy afternoon, her tears flowing as freely as the rain, only to find the door bolted against her. Only nine years old at the time, and weary from her journey, she took up residence in the doorway, awaiting the second father she knew would always be there for her. Having been called away to Liverpool on a case, Willow arrived some twelve hours later to find her drenched and feverish, still huddled in the doorway of her sanctuary. Stratford had been panicked looking for her, sure in his mind that so young a child could not make it as far as Friston, especially knowing that Willow was away. After three days of influenza bordering on pneumonia, she opened her eyes to find Willow fast asleep in the chair next to her bed, one hand upon hers and the other on a small cross attached to a chain. The key to his door was never to leave her possession from that day forward, nor had there ever been a time a spare had not been upon the lintel for her use.

Slipping the key into the lock, she stepped inside into the warmth of his house, which was like the affection of his arms in all its character. His small house suggested a woman's touch. No man would take such care to place lace doilies over the headrests or the arms of chairs, nor would a man choose such a flowery pattern for the cloth. Yet, clear as it was that a woman's touch had once adorned the house, it was equally clear that her presence had long since passed. He kept no maid or servant, but kept the place in a neat style to which he had become accustomed.

Even with a chill in the air from the lack of a fire burning, the house filled Helena with the sense of warmth she missed in his absence. Sitting in his chair by the fireplace she almost felt his presence easing away the new troubles on her mind. They slipped from her as did her consciousness, giving herself over to that world of dreams where warm sunny days and Willow's tender arms embraced her. Snug within the soft wrap, she slept soundly as she had not for days. She awoke to find the hour growing late and well past the time for her to depart. Grabbing her coat and replacing the wrap neatly back over the chair she noted something quite singular, which presented a most complex enigma.

Willow had departed for his holiday abroad in the summer, and yet there was a small blue spruce upon the table, showing no signs of aging from lack of water. It was a puzzle, but one that would have to wait as the snow had begun to fly and the dark of night approached.

SESSION CASE

QUEEN'S BENCH DIVISION

LORD JUSTICE

HAROLD A. W. STRATFORD

SIXTH SESSION,

HELD AT

JUSTICE HALL, IN SUSSEX COURT,

ON FRIDAY, THE 27th DAY OF OCTOBER, 1903,

AND FOLLOWING DAYS.

TAKEN IN SHORT HAND

(BY AUTHORITY OF THE CORPORATION OF THE CITY OF EASTBOURNE)

BY A. WAKEFIELD

Eastbourne :

PRINTED FOR J. H. WILLOW, BY A. WAKEFIELD,

No. 74, MEADS;

AND PUBLISHED BY G. HERBERT, COUNTY COURT

1904

[23] The month passed away, melting into a new year and with it new hope, but nothing within the forbidding stone walls of the estate gave evidence of this rebirth. For a week the masterful judge paced the floors in uninterrupted thought, stopping only long enough to refill his pipe. Life demanded attention and stubbornly refused to make accommodation for human grief or frustration.

Samuel Damon had been the judge's ward since the death of his parents when Samuel was fifteen. Law was his passion, though not his forte. He had come to a point in his research where he needed the careful guidance of a teacher and mentor, for in the practice of law a mistake could, quite literally, mean a man's life. To press on without sufficient knowledge was no less a crime than a physician cutting into a patient without first settling upon a full and proper diagnosis. If it was beyond one's means to do so, he was obligated to consult with colleagues and superiors to determine the proper course. Time and again Stratford himself had stressed the concept of responsibility in such matters of law. Damon most assuredly would have been served better in this instance, however, to have consulted someone other than the learned jurist, for in answer to his innocent inquiry came a most vehement and unexpected response.

Stepping over to the large oak desk in Stratford's study, Damon waited until Stratford set down his tea before intruding, handing him a book of statute. 'On the Bromwich case tomorrow, should the actus reus and the mens rea be combined or kept separate? It might be better played if we combined them. Such a distinction could—' Damon started before being abruptly cut off.

'Combine the actus reus and mens rea?' Stratford echoed. 'It is a question for a first-year law student. Why do you persistently hound me with your childish annoyances, expecting others to correct your mistakes? Can you do nothing right? Have I raised an imbecile in the law, incapable of the most perfunctory of tasks? Get out. Get out of my sight!'

Frustrated beyond endurance, Stratford tore the book from the lad's hand and thrust it violently against the wall, the impact rending its binding before it plummeted to the floor. Damon had never been given so much responsibility before, yet he was hardly the imbecile Stratford insinuated in his tongue-lashing. Damon had taken over many of the judge's duties since Willow's departure with efficiency. But now the judge took him roughly by the arm and expelled him from the room, slamming the massive doors forcefully behind him.

Damon gathered himself and, still shaken by Stratford's behaviour, sought out the younger Stratford to seek her counsel.

The demonstration of anger spoke more of the frayed nerves in the house than it did any frustration caused by Damon's questions. Helena Stratford, as well, conveyed a sense of unrest. The wealth of knowledge she held was even greater than her father's, though no one would dare openly admit it. Yet she sat staring down at the same brief she had begun proofing two days prior. Looking at it from over her shoulder, Damon could see that she had made no corrections of any kind.

'Stratford?' Damon tried to capture the girl's attention to gain his answer, but she seemed unreachable. 'What is it with the two of you lately? What am I supposed to do with this property issue?'

'What property issue?' she asked, rousted from her daze.

'The Bromwich case. The original survey of the property lines places Bromwich's building on his own land. After the resale, the survey places his building a foot within Remington's land. You remember; there was a serious assault over the matter. The case is due to be heard today.'

'Father has no hearings today,' she said, staring through the papers before her.

'Stratford,' he pressed, beginning his own course of frustration at her distant response. 'What am I supposed to do with this? A case of assault with intent has been added to the charge. Do we file under separate litigations or combine it? I need to know!' He waited. 'Helena? Good heavens! You would think the whole damned world had suddenly stopped over a few deaths. People die every day in the world. The rest of us have to keep living!'

This singular statement broke her dreamy trance. She found the whole idea that he did not understand unfathomable. Helena Stratford turned to face him, incredulous at his apathy.

'Sherlock Holmes offered the most promising gift to the law that we have seen in fifty years or more. Think of what Mycroft must be going through at this very moment. Sherlock was Mycroft's brother and Mycroft is a dear friend to this household. How can you be so callous?'

'He was just a man, Helena, a man whose head you have often said you'd pay to have served up on a plate for his disregard for the law.'

'Yes, but he also cleared up more cases than all of the police forces and courts in England combined. Look at the Moriarty trials; over twenty hangings resulted from his investigations. The man was insufferable, but effective. And what of Doherty and Carter? You went to school with Carter. You courted his sister. Do you feel nothing for these men?'

'Of course I care, but I'm not going to sulk day after day neglecting my work, and neither should you. You and I have to be strong for Father,' he added, using a gentler tone. 'In a perverse sort of way, perhaps it was best, for Sherlock Holmes, at least.'

'What do you mean?' she asked.

'Well, the man was a spent force, an anachronism, proven by the fact that he couldn't even see the obvious danger in the case he took! He missed that little fact and it killed him! He shouldn't have been out there at his age. He was too old and too slow! At least he was spared the embarrassment of his negligence in the papers. He died a legend!'

Angered at the callous nature of his opinion, she stood up, slamming the file closed. 'He was forty-nine. You really are a complete imbecile. And you spelled habeas corpus wrong again!' she added as she pushed past him with indifference.

[24] The holidays eventually came to a close and Helena Stratford returned to her father's offices downtown. She welcomed back members, both new and old, to the New Year. Though saddened by Willow's absence, Helena was eager to greet the small handful of legal minds she had engaged for various purposes of law before the holiday. She quickly found her way back into the routine of work, finding its complex problems preferable to the stagnant chessboard and an increasingly distant father who buried himself in ancient law books until the conversation both in the morning and the evening grew nonexistent.

[25] The second Monday morning in January brought with it a bright warm day, prompting an early awakening at the intrusive sunlight. Stratford pulled back the comfort of his blankets and stepped onto the floor, his feet feeling their way around to find the warmth of his slippers as he drew on his robe, tying it tight around him on his way over to the wash basin. Even the warmth of the day and George's meticulous habit of warming the morning water did not seem to stave off the shock against his face. Dipping the shaving brush into the water and whipping it into lather over the soap, he painted his beard in preparation to shave, hearing the hope of his life stirring in the other room.

Unlike her father, who tested the waters before braving the morning air, Helena Stratford lay in bed until the last possible moment, and then leapt from bed to floor with blankets still wrapped tightly around her, rushing to the fireplace for a warmth while slipping on undergarments and stockings. She readjusted the blankets as she tiptoed across the floor to face the water. Her rooms, even when she was young, always faced the sea. The rise of the cliffs negated a perfect view, but it was the best view in the house.

Finding herself lost once more in straining to see the movement of the waves, which was quite impossible, yet always attempted, her eyes fell upon a massive, elegant black landau making its way up to the house. It had a delicacy of line that spoke of fine craftsmanship, sporting a black lacquered finish that was buffed to a high gloss, and embellished with gold appointments offsetting a red, white, and gold coat of arms. Two fine horses, driven by a dour coachman dressed in the finest livery brought it round the circular drive to a gentle stop in front of the house. Seeing the door open and a thin elderly gentlemen depart, her heart instantly soared. Whatever sorrow she had locked within her heart dissipated as she ran swiftly down the hall to descend the stairs with the enthusiasm of an energetic child.

Stratford, hearing the commotion in the hall, put down his razor and stepped into the hall just in time to witness the girl running down the stairs and then quickly whirling around to head back to her room, having forgotten to draw on the rest of her clothes.

Reappearing in under a minute's time, she tore through the upstairs like a wildebeest.

'What is this?' asked Stratford with an air of authority that clearly denoted displeasure. 'We now bound up and down the staircase like a monkey?'

'John is back!' Helena replied, unable to conceal her delight.

Her smile was so broad and radiant he could hardly admonish her, and thus his hesitation allowed her to escape, the way she had done when she was five. Her wide, bright blue eyes melted his heart like the first day he held her in his arms, bringing her into the world. Her innocent smile broke past all anger of infringement of his steadfast rules. A kiss saw her running past him and out the door. Shaking his head in defeat, he reached into his pocket for a matchbox to light his pipe. Lighting it, he resigned himself to follow, forcing his own excitement to be kept at bay and wiping the remnants of the soap from his face.

Willow had barely stepped from the carriage before he was attacked by warm hugs and kisses in affectionate welcome without restraint. Lord Stratford appeared in the doorway shortly thereafter, still only half dressed beneath his robe, straining to withhold his own delight at the view. He wished in his heart that he, too, could spring about in such open display. It was obvious that Willow had missed Helena, for so touched was his heart that he had nearly forgotten his guest, who sat within. Seeing George bring forth the staff, Willow motioned for someone to collect the luggage, but held fast to George as they approached the house, whispering something in his ear. George nodded and called out to two younger servants to go to the other side of the carriage.

Stratford watched as Willow, unable to release himself from Helena's grip, escorted her to the other side of the elegant landau to lend aid to the unseen guest. The tall lean figure stood just over six feet when he emerged, but was quite lame in his walk. Willow, like the dutiful father to an injured child, waited patiently to cover the man with a shawl. Stratford's interest was as keen as his daughter's, as he observed her looking on in curiosity as well as pity. What sort of man would inspire such affection from a man who had previously confined his affections toward her, her expression seemed to say. A tight beard and moustache covered the man's strong Anglican jaw line and high cheekbones, giving him a slightly emaciated look. His dark hair accentuated his grey eyes, distracting from his pale complexion.

Slowly ascending the stone staircase to the top, they were met by Judge Stratford, who stood towering over them like a giant. Willow stopped on the landing and faced his friend, whom he had left harshly and in haste some months prior, only to find Stratford so moved by his friend's return that he was inspired to embrace Willow, too emotional for words.

'It is good to be back, my friend, truly,' Willow said. 'I am eternally wretched to have left so abruptly.'

The judge, taken aback by a reversal of blame, faltered in his stance. He was eager to take up the olive branch held out for his reception. 'You hold no blame. I do not know what possessed me to hurt you. It is I who beg you for forgiveness with all my heart.'

Willow placed a caring hand atop Stratford's, melting away all barriers between them.

Stratford faltered and embraced his friend again. 'I have sincerely missed you. Whatever punishments you would have heaped upon me for what I did to you could not begin to compare to the torture of your absence,' Stratford whispered, regaining his composure and placing the pipe back between his teeth, trying to remain dignified in an emotional moment.

'We'll speak no more of it. This is Myles Whitmore, the man I spoke of in my letter,' Willow said. 'Myles, this is Lord Justice Harold Stratford, probably the most powerful and intolerable man in Sussex. He takes some getting used to, but he is a harmless enough fellow if you do not mind unadulterated law.'

'You are very welcome, Mr Whitmore. May I present my daughter, Helena?' Stratford held out a proud hand to introduce his daughter.

'Mr Whitmore,' she said, finding him an intriguing and curious specimen.

Taking her hand, Whitmore brought it to his lips and kissed it. She observed that his hands were soft, yet strong, though now debilitated by some unknown cause. Whitmore held fast to her hand, unwilling to yield to her sympathy. She broke free of his grip reluctantly; unsure of what she was feeling. Much to her relief, Willow took him in hand and led him inside. Even in his absence, the air of mystery attached to the man remained, and clung to her like a palpable force as the others made their way to the dining room.

[26] George poured out fresh coffee and tea, while Stratford and his daughter pressed Willow with excited questions about his long absence and his intriguing companion. Willow brushed them off with grace and charm, answering only that his business had consumed his every waking moment, and that Whitmore was the son of a friend he promised to take care of.

It wasn't long before the two old friends settled onto the topic of the murders. The unsolved case of Sherlock Holmes's death could hardly be taken lightly. Word had reached Willow that Sanders had bungled the case, for lack of any real evidence. It was as if the murderers had come, accomplished their task, and left the invisible way they had come, unceremonious and quiet as the night. Interviews with Holmes's landlady and partner had revealed little. Holmes had relayed nothing more than that he would be home in two days. Interviews in Rye revealed little more than the facts they already knew. The only thing that seemed clear was that Holmes seemed quite ignorant of the danger he was in.

'If we could even learn what he was doing here it might guide us in how to proceed,' said Stratford.

Willow sighed. 'You have learned nothing new at all? That does seem strange. Did you send everything to Mycroft?'

'I have, but there has been no word from him since that awful day. I tell you, old friend, I have paid handsomely for the smallest bits of information, none of which has borne fruit. We have lost.'

'I don't recall you ever giving up that easily,' said Willow. 'If all avenues are closed, then we shall make new ones, you and I. How is Mycroft holding up? I have made several attempts to contact him, but have heard nothing.'

'He is not well. He was doing remarkably well at first. Even at the funeral he held up, and then it was as if the life just drained from him. The change seems to have taken place right around the time the survivor was murdered. You heard about Doherty?'

Willow's face suddenly lost its vigour. 'Yes. I would have thought Doherty was capable of taking care of himself. He was nearly two hundred pounds and all of it muscle. There was a constable with him as well, I understand. How could anyone get past the two of them? Are we dealing with a ghost, a man who walks through walls?'

Willow's frustration was shared by more than Stratford. The entire police department was helpless to explain the attacks.

SESSION CASE

QUEEN'S BENCH DIVISION

LORD JUSTICE

HAROLD A. W. STRATFORD

SEVENTH SESSION,

HELD AT

JUSTICE HALL, IN SUSSEX COURT,

ON FRIDAY, THE 27th DAY OF OCTOBER, 1903,

AND FOLLOWING DAYS.

TAKEN IN SHORT HAND

(BY AUTHORITY OF THE CORPORATION OF THE CITY OF EASTBOURNE)

BY A. WAKEFIELD

Eastbourne :

PRINTED FOR J. H. WILLOW, BY A. WAKEFIELD,

No. 74, MEADS;

AND PUBLISHED BY G. HERBERT, COUNTY COURT

1904

[27] In the days following, life returned to normal and Stratford found himself able to relax for the first time in months. With Willow in residence once more, Stratford found comfort in sharing the responsibility of the great burden placed upon him by the investigation into Holmes's death and the inexplicable murders attending it. Work had been his only solace for many months, but at the close of his last case he headed home with a lighter heart.

Crossing the study to his bookcase, Stratford removed one of the many books within whose pages he had found comfort so many times before. His strong hands caressed the rich binding and he breathed deep the smell peculiar to fine leather. He traced the exquisite tooling that chased its way across the book boards, sighed, and opened the volume. All sense of time and worry passed from his mind, just as another might lose himself in a book of adventure or romance. This book's pages were thick and delicately milled, the colour of fresh cream. The finely formed type, like the laws and codices of the great society that it described, stood proudly against the page, communicating order, solidity, and inviolable purpose.

Willow had taken up residence in the study, as well, with a good book in the comfort of his wingback next to the fireplace. Occasionally he would lean down to stoke the fire and retrieve a bit of coal to relight his pipe, but on the whole sat lost in a reverie of his own.

Samuel Damon knocked gently on the study door and stepped inside.

'I'm home.'

Stratford looked up. 'Everything go all right?'

'It went extremely well. I am quite pleased with the results.'

'Good,' Stratford replied, turning his attention back to his book.

Damon was used to it and did not take Stratford's brush as a slight. As the judge's ward, he understood that there was a quiet distance between members of family. Often the rare volumes of Stratford's books took precedence. He settled himself at his desk and leafed through the mountain of paperwork that had been neglected during his trip. A subtle movement from behind his wing chair informed Damon at once that Willow had returned. He felt a slight irritation at the prospect, for it meant a demotion, in both place and value to

Stratford. He had worked hard over the past year to prove his worth, but with Willow back he could easily find himself discarded.

Damon was twenty-seven years of age now. For ten years he had been reared and groomed for the law, having been afforded a clear and concise path by his new association and position. Coming from a modest family with only an elementary education, Damon did well under Stratford's tutelage, graduating college at London's most prestigious law school in the top ten percent of his class. Like so many other young lawyers of the day, trying to find their place among the legal community, Damon started at the bottom as an apprentice. His progress was consistent with his age, though perhaps slower than he might like, having an ambitious nature. Careful to associate himself with the promise of future power, such as Brandon Faulkner and Maynard Wickers, Damon went far quickly. He mastered his mentor's understanding of alliances, but not the rudimentary concepts behind the political agendas, hindering how fast Stratford would allow him to climb. Stratford believed that only a culmination of political awareness, legal awareness, and responsibility of both should dictate how quickly a man came into his own, much to the lad's disappointment. Still, Damon was eager to learn, idolizing Stratford and eager to take on additional duties. Even as a young boy, Damon set his feet upon Stratford's path, modelling himself after Stratford in hopes that one day he too would carry greatness.

Having spent a week in Wales, Damon would have to work twice as hard to catch up on old work. The cases were long and tiresome and, unlike his mentor, he was not enamoured of their tedious complexities. He was a dreamer of great accomplishments through the law. The inglorious research required to scour ancient opinions and to apply them to the tawdry criminality of modern times held little value to the impatient young barrister. His concentration broken, he rose and walked to the study doors leading to the patio. Standing within the cool shadow afforded by the house, he watched Helena walk lightly into the sunlight near the far side of the brick fence. She was not alone. Turning to Stratford, who was eagerly engrossed in his book, Damon made mention of the sight in the garden, having not yet been introduced to the new guest of the house.

'Who is that person with Helena?'

Stratford grumbled some unintelligible sound, not giving him attention or bothering to look up from his book.

'That is not Brandon she walks with,' Damon said, gaining no response from the engrossed judge. 'The man is obviously an invalid.'

'It must be Whitmore,' Stratford responded finally, looking up from his book to view the yard. 'Myles Whitmore, John's friend who is staying with us for a while. You'll meet him tonight at dinner, if you are staying. He is a remarkable man. I was quite impressed with him over a delightful conversation about law, quite impressed.' He trailed off and returned to his book.

'Barrister or judge?' Damon scowled, sure it had to be one of the two for her to take such an interest in so grotesque a creature.

'Neither,' Stratford returned, replacing his volume only to pick up another one, searching for an elusive passage. 'He is a chemist. He gave our Helena an argument though, I can tell you.' He chuckled as if the moment had come back to him. 'He is quite a fellow, if he can impress our Helena.'

Damon made a face. It seemed, to such young eyes, a strange and monstrous thing for so dainty a flower to walk beside anything so deformed. More hideous was the fact that she seemed happy and eager to be with him. It was not that Damon had any romantic feelings toward her; all such feelings were reserved for what he felt were greater things than mere flesh. Still, it did not fit with his idea of the perfect order.

Turning from the sight, Damon resumed his seat, paused at the lofty surroundings, which spoke of the grander things of which he dreamt, and then took to his work once again. Even with Stratford leaning heavily upon Damon's research and case compilation, his favour could not be taken for granted. Damon took each case, each opportunity, as a chance to prove his worth.

Yet the vision outside twisted in his mind until he could no longer concentrate. Glancing once again at the figure in the garden, Damon felt sure the young beauty must be moved to pity to be seen in public view with a crippled middle-aged man who was as far removed from perfection as he was the law. Even if Whitmore had made a momentary impression upon Stratford, the sight still found its way to a dark part of Damon's heart. While Stratford concerned himself with matters of ancient law, Damon repeatedly forced himself to return to work, but could not tolerate the unpleasant image pervading his mind. Such a disruption would provoke more than unsavoury whispers in public, it would create conditions upsetting to his ambitions. Though the young lady might be naive in her understanding of public perception, Damon's position in the family meant he could hardly stand by and do nothing.

[28] Having enough of research and troubled engagements, Damon turned his attentions toward the particulars of their monthly closed dinner. There would be issues to discuss, which would require a deeper level of understanding in order to speak with any insight. The Holmes case would bear out naturally, each knowing as little as the next, though it would probably be the foremost topic on the agenda. It would be wise to have in one's pocket other interests that could possibly be addressed. It would not do well to walk in unprepared, or to omit the issues out of ignorance of the details. To do so would suggest disinterest, possibly slighting the interests of those depending upon him. It was a delicate balance of friendship, food, and politics, but these men could collectively make or break a man. It had been done before, with one word from that prominent figure mulling over antiquated law books in the corner.

Damon closed his books and addressed Stratford. 'We should prepare for opposing discussion tonight. I will have the details and background of Comte de Guernon ready for the meeting before I return. Recall that he died this past week on British soil. Anglo-French relations may be affected, so we should be prepared for some debate. Having answers would strengthen our position. Martin Granger is an equivalent legal counterpart in America. He is doing well. We might want to consider the possibility of an alliance between him and the presidential cabinet.'

Damon's suggestion of agenda may have been well intended, but it did not fail to capture the attention of the eldest member of the household, who rose to face the insolent boy.

'Tell me you did not just dictate his lordship's venue and course of action this evening.' Willow confronted him with a soft but undeniable tone of power seething from his lips.

An instant rush of nervous fear crept over Damon until he faltered, fumbling around with increasing ill ease in hopes of Stratford's intervention. 'Harry?' Damon turned, looking for Stratford to back him.

But before Damon could receive anything from his ally, Willow forced the confrontation by moving toward him. If Damon had the arrogance and audacity to take on the duties of one of the most powerful and influential men in Sussex, Willow felt that he should easily be able to take on an opponent questioning the authority. Damon may have inveigled his way into Stratford's trust, but he would not have so easy a time with Willow.

'You impudent pup! Mind your place,' Willow chastised him, and Damon squirmed.

'I am just trying to help him here, John,' said Damon, feeling out on a limb without Stratford's aid.

'Don't call me John, laddie. You'll show respect in this house!'

'His grace asked for my help,' Damon whispered.

In six short words Damon had silenced Willow, and captured Stratford's attention as Damon continued to press the point. 'He is a busy man with a lot on his mind. He can't afford to miss anything or the dogs will be at his heels. You know that! Don't strike at me for assisting him when you spend seven months abroad. He is still trying to recover and you left him!'

Damon spoke boldly and without thought of consequence, and clearly Willow's mood had shifted.

'Sam!' Stratford intervened, knowing Willow would tear the boy apart in the next move. 'Why don't you take a break? You've been working too hard. Helena can pick up on the Townsend research. I'll see you this evening.'

Damon picked up his things and stormed out the door, letting his feelings be known by his actions. He had worked hard to prove himself to Stratford, finally making headway. It was a slap in the face to be berated by Willow as if he were no more than a schoolboy.

Willow waited for his friend to speak, trying not to jump to any harsh and unjust conclusions. This was a serious matter. Stratford could be dismissed from his position if found incompetent. Even an unintentional movement toward the suggestion might be enough to bring a vote of no confidence.

'He is just trying to help, John. He's ambitious; I'll give him that, but don't chastise him for it.'

'Is he telling the truth? Did you ask him to help with your political duties? You can tell me. You know it will go no further.'

Stratford turned away with embarrassment. 'I am just a little tired of late. He offered to help out with some of the paperwork in court, answer a few letters, and make sure I keep my appointments. He assists me. That is his job. He is just a little overanxious to please. He knows what is discussed and what is involved in keeping abreast. It shows initiative and intelligence to try and keep up.'

Willow suddenly felt uneasy, realising he had spent too much time away. 'That did not sound like keeping up, it sounded like an order of action,' Willow explained with delicate concern. 'Are you well?'

'Just a little tired and at times a bit grumpy. I'll be fine!'

Willow stood at bay as Stratford turned away. It was not the first time that Willow felt the rift widen between them. It was obvious that Stratford felt sick about the thing. He could not even bear to look at Willow.

[29] Placing a brotherly hand on Stratford's shoulder, Willow proposed a way to ease tensions.

'You know, it's been months since I have had the opportunity to take up the sword. You might stand a chance at beating me.'

Stratford chuckled silently with relief, but he was secretly afraid. 'I don't know.'

'Come on. It will do us both good to stretch our legs. We don't even have to suit up fully if you don't want to. We will use the battle swords.'

Stratford began to take to the idea. It had been months since the two of them had played together. Near the north wing, South Lodge held a large gym and pool house, equipped for a king, with ancient and modern swords, flails, axes, hammers, pole arms and more, all dark woods and training equipment. The young men especially enjoyed the room, but yielded to the two old warriors who still preferred to take to battle in full armour.

Willow opened the double doors to grant additional light and breeze before making his way over to his partner. 'Do you remember what to do?'

'Try me,' Stratford returned, pulling down the shield of his helmet.

'Might I suggest, sir?' George interrupted them, appearing as if out of thin air and holding Willow's chainmail and armour.

'Old woman,' Willow mumbled under his breath.

Stratford motioned for George to continue, feeling easier for its placement. Once more in position, Willow waved Stratford on.

'Again,' Willow demanded.

Stratford took the sword, but found his hands shaking as he grasped the handle.

'I can't do it, John. My shoulder won't hold the weight.'

'Good heavens, man, we're not a bunch of old women. A man's sword is his blood.' Willow walked over to the wall and replaced his sword with two lightweight battle swords, tossing one to Stratford. 'Now try again. Your shoulder is fine.'

[30] Hearing the clanking of sword to metal and raised voices, Whitmore took an interest in the strange exercise. He watched through the open door, as Willow appeared to take on his partner practically unarmed.

'What are they doing?' Whitmore turned to Helena.

'Practicing, or just having fun.'

'Practicing for what?'

'They do re-enactments and ceremonies. I think there is a ceremony coming up. They always have something going on in one lodge or another. I think I heard them saying something about John receiving some sort of honour or promotion soon. They will, no doubt, put on an over exaggerated display. They always do.'

Helena could see that Whitmore seemed very much the pacifist, preferring only the action and reaction of chemicals in warfare.

[31] Damon stood for a moment, observing with distaste the close proximity of the pair. Having had enough of the display, he turned on his heel and made his way to the front foyer. He called to the under-butler, scribbling something down on a piece of paper.

'Take this note to the telegraph office and have them dispatch it right away.'

[32] Finding the shadows starting to lengthen, Willow checked his watch and made his way over to the door. The night had grown cool under a pink and red sky. Releasing the straps on his armour, Willow turned to face his old friend, who was slouched and overheated in the corner.

'I have to go out for a while. I won't be long. Will you be all right?'

Stratford looked up. 'Of course.'

'Helena said you have been looking tired of late. She's right, you know. You do look tired. How's the shoulder?'

'Continually reminding me I'm not as young as I used to be. I really have missed you,' Stratford said, looking away. 'You never wrote, not one letter, not even to Helena.'

Willow put a reassuring hand on Stratford's shoulder. 'I know.'

Given the hour and the task he had set for himself, Willow let the matter rest. Extending a helpful hand, Willow helped Stratford to his feet and into the bath.

[33] Settling himself into the landau, he set off for Naomi Close, stopping in front of a whitewashed brick semi-detached. A round-faced woman answered the door and showed him into the parlour.

A pleasantly excited voice broke the silent air. 'John, I heard you were back.'

Taking the seat offered, Willow reached into his coat pocket and retrieved three photographs, laying them on the table. His host picked them up and granted an uneasy acknowledgement to his guest.

'Do you know them?'

The man examined them carefully, trying to see past the death mask each of them wore. The first was easy enough. Outside of a pale meaningless expression there was no damage to the face. The others were more difficult.

'This one,' he said, handing it back to Willow, 'is Phillip Worth, a retired doctor over on Orchard Road. I knew him slightly. It is rumoured he was quite a hell-raiser in Buckinghamshire, in his day. This one'—he hesitated—'I believe is, or was, Nicholas Megaw, late of Her Majesty's Royal Sussex Regiment. He fought at Meremere and Ngaruawahia in 'sixty-three. I'm not sure, but I think he lived at Ravens Croft.'

'A brave man,' Willow acknowledged with regret.

Tapping the last photograph, the man finally tossed it on the table between them. 'I've never seen this man before.'

Willow sat back, pulling out a cool pipe. 'So at least two of these men were hell-raisers and not easily put down.'

'You might say that.'

'Ours?' Willow asked, leaning forward in some hope.

The man gave him an understanding grin. 'Dunno 'bout Megaw, but I'll check Buckinghamshire for Worth.'

Willow gave a nod and moved to go, replacing the photographs in his pocket. 'Talk to the family. Find out who came for them, but keep it quiet. I want this between you and me,' he said, shaking the man by his hand.

'For God, King, and Country, I am yours,' the man said, and gave a small bow.

SESSION CASE

QUEEN'S BENCH DIVISION

LORD JUSTICE

HAROLD A. W. STRATFORD

EIGHTH SESSION,

HELD AT

JUSTICE HALL, IN SUSSEX COURT,

ON FRIDAY, THE 27th DAY OF OCTOBER, 1903,

AND FOLLOWING DAYS.

TAKEN IN SHORT HAND

(BY AUTHORITY OF THE CORPORATION OF THE CITY OF EASTBOURNE)

BY A. WAKEFIELD

Eastbourne :

PRINTED FOR J. H. WILLOW, BY A. WAKEFIELD,

No. 74, MEADS;

AND PUBLISHED BY G. HERBERT, COUNTY COURT

1904

[34] Lord Stratford looked out of the window at the guests who paraded into his home with genteel elegance. They were eager to embrace the warmth of Stratford's hospitality once more. Willow's absence had cast a long shadow over South Lodge and its effect on Stratford had been noticed. Adjusting his tie, Stratford made his way downstairs and greeted them with a welcome heart as they filed through the doors. For the moment his weariness fell away. John's absence now seemed a distant memory and all was right in the great hall.

As the dining room began to thicken with cigar and pipe smoke, Stratford eased into and away from conversations with ease. At the first hint of weariness all it took was to glance down at the end of table at Willow and his strength returned. It was Damon, however, who finally asked the question on everyone's mind.

'So, Mr Willow, are you going to bring in this extraordinary man you brought back with you?'

'And perhaps more importantly is there some intent behind his presence at this precise time?' Brandon Faulkner added.

Stratford, startled at Damon's remark, shot a thunderous look in his direction at the indiscretion.

'Extraordinary? Intent?' Willow echoed back the questions with an air of innocence. 'Whatever would make you apply such words to such an ordinary fellow?'

'Then why is he here?' Faulkner pressed.

'My dear boy, you read too much into things,' Willow said blandly.

'But you are looking to keep him here, are you not?' Damon asked.

'He is here for no more than our hospitality. If he chooses to stay I will endorse him. If he chooses to go I will not hinder him. For the moment, he is on holiday.'

'On holiday in the middle of winter?' Damon pushed.

Stratford gave Damon a halting and disapproving look before shifting the conversation. 'My ward has a marvellous gift for diplomacy.'

A sudden uproar of laughter filled the room, clouded in a haze of cigar smoke.

Judge Faulkner looked up from lighting a fresh pipe to lend assistance. 'He's just curious. Boys at that age tend to forget themselves.'

'You're not nurturing him properly, Stratford,' Stackhurst teased.

'You're too hard on him, Stackhurst. Stratford has a great capacity to nurture'—Bridgewater paused—'horses, that is.'

'Maybe Helena should try her hand with him.'

'Helena, mothering?' asked Crampon with a jovial laugh.

'I think Helena has a great capacity to nurture,' Brandon Faulkner remarked.

'She might surprise you and find motherhood quite enjoyable. I think she will make a fine wife and an excellent mother.'

'Well said, my boy,' Caldwell remarked, taking a break from his odious cigar. 'Women take to motherhood like ducks to water.'

'When will we find out, Harry? Has she, at long last, decided?' Judge Faulkner asked with eagerness.

Stratford hesitated at the uncomfortable question. He wanted dearly to answer yes, but Helena had been difficult on the matter. Willow had sided with the girl, creating a full standstill on the matter until tension between the two friends came to blows.

'It is difficult to know the mind of a woman, especially our Helena.'

Damon pressed the envelope of Stratford's patience as he alluded to new developments and growing concerns, all designed to arouse questions. 'We might have to wait now that she has taken to the role of nurse. Mr Willow's friend is a cripple.'

Stratford, at the height of frustration, forcefully placed his hand on the table. 'That will be quite enough.'

For the first time during the evening, Dr Stoner joined the conversation. 'Should I be looking in on him? I could make it a working visit on Mondays.'

'Quite unnecessary, Doctor,' Willow replied. 'I assure you, he is not ill.'

'Forgive me,' Brandon interrupted, taking on his adversary directly, 'I was just wondering; I understand he is a chemist and shies away from crime and law, so how did the two of you meet? I didn't think you had an interest in test tubes and chemicals.'

Willow deduced unequivocally that the pair of youths had allied themselves earlier to bring some devious plot to light, totally forgetting their opponent. Willow drew on his pipe in preparation, allowing the moment to build before he tore his adversaries down.

'You know, I was wondering myself; with South Lodge perched at the heart of Sussex where some of the best legal minds congregate'—he motioned to the present company—'how it is there has been no progress made on the Snowden house case and Doherty's case, of course. Now I know. Having a legal mind does not endow it with the qualities of a detective. You miss the obvious, gentleman.' Willow motioned to the two young men. 'You look at the son when you might be better served to look at the father. While Myles is not a student of law, his father has an incredibly acute legal and political mind. His business, however, takes him abroad most of his time. I thought we'—again he motioned to the members of the room—'could watch over Myles for awhile.'

'Are you sure that is all?' Judge Faulkner asked.

'You really do make too much of my absence.'

'Well then, we have our answer. I, for one, wish to raise a glass to the return of the prodigal son!' Judge Crampon extended his arm in a toast.

Hear, hear!' The entire company raised their glasses in agreement.

'Stratford was becoming unbearable without you, Johnny!' Paul Faulkner added.

'Was becoming unbearable? Oh, Paul, speak the truth. Stratford passed intolerable months ago,' Bridgewater heckled.

Paul Faulkner shook his head. 'Seriously, now. When do we see this man of yours, John?'

Judge Paul Faulkner had been a long-standing friend of Stratford's and shared hopes of their two children marrying. With continuing delays, his interest in the comings and goings of the house was a priority. His interest was not unique, however. Dr Stoner was a local physician, specializing in diagnosis and surgery, who tried his hand at chess every Monday afternoon with Willow in hopes of spending time with the young Helena. Stoner had been in love with the girl from the moment he first laid eyes upon her. It was a love not likely to fade over time, nor waver upon indecision. Though he was several years her senior, she seemed to prefer his intellectual company to that of the younger and more favoured Brandon Faulkner. Much to his chagrin, however, Helena made it clear that she had no interest in either man outside of friendship. She kept everyone at bay. Perhaps it was the fact that the girl had lost her mother at so young an age and had only aging men to tend to her while growing up that caused her to feel more at ease with a more mature man. She had once revealed that younger men had nothing but one thing on their minds and consequently little of interest in their heads. Whatever the reason, she refused a suitor; the young lady had found her true calling outside of marital constraints. She had been reared in a house of men who practiced and argued law and, though she was unable to practice, she had become the prodigy she was meant to be at the feet of the best of them. This, too, might have had something to do with her decision.

Willow, too, found his calling outside society's expectations. Though repeatedly encouraged to take a judgeship, Willow preferred to remain the best barrister England had to offer. Though he was among the eldest of the company, he rivalled the best of the younger class in nearly everything, as any defeat seemed to him a step toward the final days of his life. Still, it would not do to close the door too quickly on the questions of the present company. Willow knew that unanswered questions often resulted in unreasonable investigations, investigations he preferred directed elsewhere.

Ringing for George, Willow gave a nod that the congregation would receive his guest, instantly quelling jest for curiosity. Whitmore was shown in by the young lady, who escorted him to a place prepared for him. The meetings were not generally open to women or guests, but the arrival of Willow with an unusual guest made for an exception. 'I hope your wit and knowledge is better than your humour, gentlemen,' said Miss Stratford as she walked into the room, causing the men to quickly arise from their seats, for though she was reared independent of her sex, she was still very much a lady and everyone knew it.

'My dearest child, just a bit of fun. We'll get them later for it,' her father insisted.

'Helena, your cheeks are flushed. Are you feeling well tonight?' Dr Stoner noted in a concerned, but tender-hearted manner.

'Now if you are going to tease me about my ability to apply make-up, doctor, I shall have to refrain from taking tea with you later.'

'You're in it now, old boy,' heckled Bridgewater.

'Mr Whitmore, a pleasure.' Brandon Faulkner offered the first hand of welcome. 'I do hope you will not mind our little quirks. Our Helena never takes us too seriously, do you dearest?'

'I never take you seriously on anything, Mr Faulkner.'

Helena Stratford had a man's wit, a sharp tongue like the most seasoned of opponents and charm second to none. She was adored by all the company and her talent for the law was readily acknowledged, at least within those walls. Without, the rules of engagement were entirely different. Legally she could only solicit, prohibited from arguing in court as a barrister by her gender. Even her position as assistant to her father was possible only because her father was placed so far above his colleagues that none would dare challenge him. His small legal firm was her only outlet for the law outside the debates held at the estate. She ran the firm from behind her father's name and played the dutiful typist and assistant, but behind the scenes it was she who ran everything. Even the lawyers and solicitors in the firm were mere masks from which her words issued.

Brandon Faulkner had long held one desire and one focus aside from his ambition; he desired Helena Stratford. She was symbolic of the pinnacle of all that he dreamed of attaining: power, position, wealth, and a beautiful wife who would bear him his heirs. To align himself with her would naturally put him in line to inherit all. The idea of Willow placing Whitmore in residence where he would be constantly under foot, and the concerned focus of Helena's attentions, interfered with his finely drawn plans. Any show of dislike or contempt, however, would keep his rival at a distance. He needed to keep the man close, for all men had weaknesses. All men had something to hide. To hold that knowledge was to hold advantage, and with it the ability to set yourself between the two sides, playing ally to both, and insuring that the spoils go, not to the victor, but to the man with the power and control. Judge Stratford had enemies, who sat at his table along with his friends. To ally himself with those enemies as well as remaining close to his friends could well return the balance to his favour.

The present company gave all the impressions of a jovial and innocuous gathering, but the moment the formalities of introduction had concluded and the pleasantries to ease into conversation passed, the barrage of questions commenced, eager to learn who this man of Willow's truly was and, more importantly, why he was there. It may have gone easier on him had it not been for the fact that unsettled tides rose and fell in great swells of late, generating many suspicions. Willow was a quiet man, but when he spoke, there were few rebuttals, and when he decided to move, he moved mountains. By no more than the fact that Willow had brought him, it eased the minds of some and struck fear in others at the prospect. All, however, moved to find out his true purpose. The cross examination went smoothly only in so much as everyone was well aware that, should Whitmore be a key player in Willow's plans, he would be well versed in how to answer. Willow was nothing if not thorough in his fifty years in law. If Whitmore was revealed to be of a benign nature, saying too much could warrant repercussions.

'May I ask you, Mr Whitmore, why you decided to take holiday in Eastbourne at this time of year? We are known for our shores during the summer months, but in the off-season there is very little to do,' Brandon Faulkner said, feeling sure Whitmore and Willow were hiding something. It was a good question, for there was little to do at the seaside during the winter months. Even walks along the beach offered cold winds and freezing temperatures, hardly conducive to holiday.

'It may seem somewhat irregular to so energetic a man such as yourself and Mr Damon to understand, but I just want the quiet— to rest.'

'Then no long walks upon the South Downs?' He intimated boldly that Whitmore might be interested in the Holmes murders, angering Willow, almost unreasonably so.

'No,' Whitmore answered. 'As you may have noticed, I am not about to take long walks anywhere, and as you have intimated at the recent murders,' he openly challenged, unnerving Willow who began formulating ways to end the conversation, 'I have no such interest. I am not a man of law and neither am I an aficionado of crime or mystery.'

Brandon Faulkner tried not to fidget at the ease by which Whitmore seemed to handle the questions, forcing Faulkner to try and corner him. 'I am intrigued, Mr Whitmore. If you have no association with law or crime, how did you and Willow meet?'

'You know, gentlemen, you have given quite a barrage of questions for our guest,' said Willow, offering a stopping point. 'And we have questions to discuss of our own. I would hate to think it consumed our conversation for the evening when I am eager to learn of what has happened in Sussex in my absence. Besides, Myles is looking rather tired. I think he will be here long enough for all of you to learn about him.'

'Shall I walk you upstairs, Mr Whitmore?' Helena asked, picking up on Willow's ploy to end the conversation.

'Gentlemen, it has been a pleasure, but Willow is right, I am tired.'

Rising from the table, Whitmore's action caused the girl to quickly arise to assist him, which in turn caused the entire company to rise and take their leave of him. Almost unseen and certainly unnoticed in his mild manner, Willow shuffled after, closing the doors behind him and allowing the meeting to continue.

After seeing Whitmore to bed, Willow and Helena strolled slowly a few steps before Helena stopped.

'Why did you bring him here?' she asked.

'Now do not tell me you are getting as paranoid as those old men downstairs?'

'Well, it is rather odd. You were not exactly honest in everything you said about him, where you?'

Willow cast his eyes away at the suggestion, hitting far too close to truth. 'I don't know what you mean.'

'I can see right through to the back of your collar button, John Willow. You brought him here for a purpose, and I think I am beginning to see a crack in your scheme, a little light shining through to the truth.'

'He is a man who wants to rest, without being riddled with questions and tormented by work. I did not realise that bringing him here would make his life harder. It was my intention to make his life easier.'

'Can you tell us nothing of the man, outside of what we already discovered?'

Seeing that his reaction was unwarranted in the end, Willow put a gentle hand on her back, leading her away from Whitmore's door. 'I can tell you that he is a good man. I did not bring him for political reasons or to find answers to our little problems. He is here for me to look after and hopefully I can receive some help from my family. I beg you, do not read too much into this. I know you are, for you bombarded him with questions heavily his first night and well into the next day.'

'He ran to you, did he?'

'No, to his disloyal credit, he said nothing. But you forget, little one, I know everything,' he said with a kiss.

Helena backed down. 'I'm sorry. You present a mystery and dare none of us to solve it. It is too much of a temptation, especially in this house. I will behave myself from now on,' she promised, stepping into her room. 'And yes, you are right: he is a good man, and rather handsome in an odd sort of way,' she added, closing the door behind her.

With a satisfied grin, Willow put his pipe neatly between his teeth and lit it, chuckling to himself as he made his way back to the dining hall. It was certainly a modicum of success.

[35] After a long night it was time to get back to work. Stratford stepped briskly into the hall precisely at the sixth bell, checking his pocket watch against the clanging of the grandfather clock. At a minute past, Stratford looked at Willow's door with an air of impatience, eager to quell the morning tremors with some coffee. Years of habit saw the two men descend the stairs together. The morning edition of the *Times* offered a reward to the early riser, and

Stratford's anxiousness, in recent months, had him chomping at the bit. Yet, at five past the hour, Willow had not emerged.

Stratford finally tapped on Willow's door. 'John?'

Willow emerged, still slipping into his coat and gently closing his door behind him. He stood beside his partner as if preparing for the commencement of a parade.

Stepping into the dining hall, Stratford paused at the sight of Brandon Faulkner, who had stayed the night and was already seated at table.

'My word, son, you are up early. I should have thought you would have come down with your father.'

Brandon hesitated at the obvious forgetfulness, assessing how he might gently recall the facts to Stratford's mind without causing embarrassment. 'I think you had already gone to bed at the time, but Father decided to go home last night.'

Stratford turned his eyes away, having remembered. He picked up the coffee pot and mechanically poured himself a fresh cup of coffee.

'I like to get an early start on the day and read of the world before I enter it,' Faulkner continued, sliding his cup toward Stratford.

Stratford smiled wanly and inclined his head in a nod of approval. 'Very admirable, my boy. Very admirable indeed.'

Nigel poured out fresh coffee as George presented the freshly pressed early editions of both the local and London morning papers. Willow briefly shuffled through a few pages, setting it aside for a sip of the soothing liquid before him. Stratford, on the other hand, sipped his coffee and briskly turned page after page with vigour, reading aloud occasionally with great enthusiasm.

'Hmmm, I see the campaign for women's suffrage is intensifying. The government has failed again to reform the voting laws and it is turning violent. Several women were arrested. They opened the Gloucestershire County canal from Stroud to Daneway,' he continued. 'Here is something. It turns out that those seven boys who came down with typhoid did not get it from food. The ship they were on was filthy and full of disease, not to mention that the blankets acquired were from a hospital. No doubt they had not been thoroughly washed first.'

'That was the Caldwell, wasn't it?' Faulkner asked.

'The Cornwall,' Stratford corrected him. 'The training ships can be a wonderful opportunity for the young lads. I heartily endorse it. They return more fit and better educated than if they were left alone, but sometimes these commanders don't think. Well, well. Old Baron Grenfell was finally promoted. He has been put in charge of the fourth Army Corps.'

'Good morning, my lord.' Damon trundled in with his usual flare for interrupting. 'Brandon, Mr Willow. What's for breakfast? I'm positively starved.'

'Eggs and quail,' Faulkner responded. 'Baron Grenfell married this year, I believe, and Edinburgh University granted him an honorary LLD, too.'

'Yes. It has assured him a clear shot to full general now. What do you think, John?' asked Stratford.

Willow looked up absently. 'I'm sorry, what did you say?'

Stratford looked at him with concern, noting the second inconsistency of the day. 'Is everything all right? You seem distracted this morning.'

Before Willow had a chance to respond, Helena entered the room, her hand delicately on the arm of Myles Whitmore.

Faulkner stiffened. 'Good morning, my dear. I'm glad to see you could join us.'

'We are not late, are we?' she asked. 'Myles had another one of his bad headaches this morning.'

'I'm dreadfully sorry to hear that,' said Faulkner. 'I sincerely hope it is not serious. You seem to have taken a turn for the worse in your health. Perhaps the household presents too many opportunities for overstimulation.'

'I have taken something for it and have no doubt that I will soon be better. I do thank you for your concern, however.'

'Yes, Brandon, how thoughtful of you to inquire as to our guest's health,' said Stratford. 'What is the saying? The quality of mercy is not strained.'

'It is a quality you yourself exemplify, my lord, and one of many qualities of yours that I try to hold up as my exemplar.'

In the next moment, as Helena poured out coffee for Whitmore, Damon called out, 'Good heavens, Mr Whitmore, you are a very fortunate man indeed to be served your morning coffee by the lady of the house.'

At this, Faulkner swung his head about to see Helena bending solicitously over Stratford's guest, pouring coffee into his cup as if she were his loving bride.

'Helena, really!' cried Faulkner. 'The man is capable of doing some things for himself, I'm sure!'

'Eat your breakfast, Brandon. It is getting cold,' Helena dismissed him as she finished pouring the coffee and set the pot back upon the table. The gaze that she then turned upon Faulkner seemed to stop the breath in his throat. 'Mr Faulkner, I will remind you that as a grown woman I will do as I please in my own house. It is no business of yours to whom I present my affections, and I am growing doubtful that it ever shall be.'

Willow, quite unprecedentedly, remained silent in his seat. George appeared with the later edition of the paper and laid it before him, who barely had it in hand when he turned to an article, as if expecting it.

Placing it down again, Willow announced, 'Sanders has closed the Holmes case. He makes the argument that the last man to die was or was among the perpetrators of the murders.'

Helena instantly leapt from her seat and burst out in denial. 'No! It cannot be! Father, you cannot allow this! John!' She turned to Willow for reinforcement.

Faulkner jumped up from his seat, as well. 'It's all right, dearest. It is just a formality.'

'Tell him he cannot do this,' she persisted.

'He can't keep the case open forever. Sit down!' Faulkner told her.

'Father, please. This is not only a wrongful conviction, it is an unlawful conviction.'

Stratford patiently corrected her point of law no less than he would an outraged barrister before him in court. 'No one has been convicted of the crime; the case has merely been closed. Brandon is correct. The police have the right to close any case that has not produced viable leads and probably will not.'

'How can you say that when by this act we condemn a man without trial merely because his clothes were torn and tattered? A man is innocent until he is proven guilty in a court of law. John, you taught me this is the golden thread of law. The facts need to be duly argued by prosecution and defence, deliberated by judge and jury. You cannot decide the facts outside of the walls of justice and apply them after a man is dead. It is unheard of! It is madness! It goes against everything you believe in. How can you condone this?'

'He has not been charged or convicted,' Stratford defended. 'Sanders is merely stating his opinions on how he believes the crime fell out. He is not holding court or pronouncing judgement.'

'He is, Father! He says this vagabond was responsible for the murders of Sherlock Holmes and his companions. Murder! We don't know that this man murdered anyone!'

'Murder is with the intention to kill or cause grievous bodily harm. I should say this man certainly did intend bodily harm! He shot Sherlock Holmes without hesitation in cold blood and instructed that the others did not escape,' Damon argued.

Helena turned on him. 'We don't know that this man committed those acts, and if it was him, he may well have been under duress. We don't know what happened out at that house. We don't know the facts enough to make any assessment, let alone convict a dead man of murder.'

'What other reason could he have for going there?' Damon interjected.

'Any reason. Perhaps he was cold and saw the light. It doesn't matter. No court of law proved or disproved this man's innocence in this case. If you condone this, Father, you will be as guilty as the killer.'

Willow finally spoke out, quashing both the argument and Helena's hope. 'Enough! What is done is done and cannot be undone.'

Helena stopped short, her lip quivering as she tried to hold back tears. Out of all the people she had expected to turn a blind eye to the law, it was not Willow. The world had lulled itself to sleep. Life had settled back into the routine existence of the everyday, taking with it all sense of reason. In many ways the mundane turnings of everyday life had become an escape to avoid the horrible truth from which not even a cunning and observant mind was safe. Politically it was a good move. Sanders had milked the case dry and secured his career in the doing. Yet the unsolved mystery had been an open wound for the public, who cried out for justice. Closing the case, after months of no leads, had been the only choice.

Yet they were not in court and Helena was still innocent to the harsh reality of law, still holding to the belief that law was flawless in its nature and that its sword could right any wrong. The disillusionment of this ideal, if only for a moment, struck her hard, and she stormed from the room without taking proper leave.

Her abrupt exit in such an obvious state of discontent prompted those assembled to close off conversation and follow suit, until only Stratford and Willow remained. Lighting his pipe, Willow stood, placing the spent match on the plate.

'I am sure you had a good reason,' Willow remarked in a placatory tone. 'There will be no peace in this house for at least a month.'

Stratford wiped his mouth and threw down his napkin. 'We have taught her well. I am pleased, if inconvenienced. It will pass, if for no other reason than she could not abide the man.'

'Is that what we want, simply for it to pass?' Willow probed. 'I am not sure I agree with that. Forget for a moment that the brother of a dear friend has been murdered in our jurisdiction. The law has been violated. Justice has gone unanswered. We took an oath to uphold that law and to secure those in our territory, not to grow tired or to pacify political needs.'

Stratford kept his peace, taking a leisurely approach to cleaning his pipe before reaching into his coat pocket for fresh tobacco and a match as Willow waited for some response.

'Which do you respect more, my position as your friend or my supreme judicial position? You see, not all questions can be answered without distilling it down to a choice between the lesser of two evils to be revealed, neither of which will solve the problem.'

'There was a man looking into the Holmes case,' Willow said, changing the subject. 'He was at hospital the night Doherty and the witness were murdered. He was asking for you! What did he want with you, Harry?'

'Permission to see the patient. I had Ian deny all visitors without my express authority.'

'Why?'

Stratford's face reeled in frustration at the persistence. 'I was trying to save his life!'

'What did he want, this detective? It wasn't Inspector Lestrade of the London police; he was in Bristol at the time.'

'I don't know. I never spoke with the man. Why the questions, John? It's not like you to cross-examine me.'

'I...,' Willow began to tell him, but quickly thought better of it. It was not wise to reveal what he knew until he was certain of his facts.

'I was just thinking. I was hoping there was something in it.'

[36] Helena ran full speed to the stables and flung open Myth's stall. She drew him close, clinging to his muscular neck for comfort. She would never openly allow anyone to see her cry, but with the two-year-old Arabian, her best friend and confidante, she could let her tears flow.

Faulkner knew right where to find her. She had always been a spirited girl, but this time however, her actions had disrupted his plans.

'What the hell was that display?' he asked. 'Come out of there this instant.'

'Go back to the house, Brandon. Just leave me alone.'

'Your behaviour was nothing less than disgraceful. Your father was appalled and I will not stand for it.'

Helena turned to him with the last remnants of fight left in her. 'He should be appalled.'

'Stop this nonsense. You didn't like Holmes any more than the rest of us.'

'That's not true.'

'You've said on many occasions that you'd like to have his head for his disregard of the law. I don't see the necessity now to make a fuss over him. I, for one, am not sorry to see him gone. I say good riddance to the man and his methods. He was a nuisance.'

'Why does everyone dismiss him so? You and Father, and even Sam, have no heart at all.'

Faulkner scowled. 'I see that you are deliberately leaving Willow out of all of this. Oh yes, I noticed, my dear girl, again. Did you honestly think your displays of affection would go unnoticed?'

Helena recoiled as if struck. 'How dare you!'

'I do dare, I do, and I will remind you of your place. You will apologize to your father this instant,' Faulkner insisted, grabbing her by the arm.

Helena struggled to free herself from his grip but Faulkner tightened his hold until it physically pained her. 'You will do as you are told.'

'Let her go.' A voice rich with soft conviction came from behind them.

Faulkner relaxed his grip and spun about to face the intruder.

'Step aside, Whitmore. This is none of your business. As my future bride she is my responsibility, and that includes her behaviour.'

Whitmore leaned heavily on his walking stick and with calm dignity he repeated the request, this time more firmly.

'Unhand the lady.'

Faulkner released her and moved within inches of Whitmore. 'You have no authority in this house. You are on my territory now, old man.'

'Nevertheless,' Whitmore returned.

'This isn't over, and I would warn you not to cross me again,' he spat.

Faulkner looked at Helena with a dismissive smile. 'Enjoy your afternoon, my dear. We will continue our discussion later.' Faulkner forcefully pushed by and disappeared around the corner.

Helena dropped her gaze. 'I'm sorry for that. Brandon is a good man, but he has to maintain control.'

Whitmore nodded in acknowledgement.

'He spoke out of turn,' she said. 'I never promised to marry him.'

'I require no explanation.'

'I know, but my behaviour must seem somewhat contradictory. No doubt you have heard things from Sam and Mr Faulkner. It is not what you think. Last year, not long after Father's accident, Brandon asked my father for his blessing to marry. My father obliged by setting a wedding date. He announced the plans over dinner one night, almost as an afterthought, never thinking to consult me to see if I was agreeable to the idea. I was so mortified that I left in tears. I don't think I had ever before seen John so angry. It was the first time I heard anyone ever raise a voice to Father. That is where it all went wrong. They were still arguing a week later. One day I came home and John was gone.'

Helena turned away to shield her emotions.

'Are you in love with him?'

'I beg your pardon?'

'It is a simple question. Are you in love with him?'

'That is not a suitable question to ask.'

'I would imagine, given his age and closeness to your father, the idea would not be one your father would embrace. I am surprised, though, that there was never anyone else. You are very beautiful.'

'How do you know there wasn't? You dismiss Dr Stoner.'

'No, not Stoner. He is too eager and too much in love with you.'

'How rude!'

'And then there are the men your father parades through the house for your inspection,' he continued. 'They might offer a choice, but I suspect you would not want to give up the attention, or Mr Willow.'

'My father does not parade men through the house. I'll have you know that most of those men are married. I cannot believe your impertinence!' She tried to stand tall, but found herself unable to meet his gaze directly, and turned away to hide the colour rising in her cheeks.

Whitmore took her hand and pulled her uncomfortably close. He placed his hand gently upon her cheek, brushing back the loose strands of hair, which had fallen to obscure her face.

'You don't need attention,' Whitmore breathed softly. 'You thoughts, your wants, your desires need to be respected. A man cannot condescend to you.'

She felt his arm encircle her waist, her breathing becoming more rapid as her confusion mounted.

'You're trembling.'

'No, I'm not.'

Whitmore leaned in close until she could feel his body against her. He put his hand gently upon her cheek, brushing back the loose strands of hair, which had fallen.

'Do I frighten you, Miss Stratford?'

Closing her eyes against the heat rising within her, she allowed herself the idea of a tender kiss, putting her hand out against the rough wood of the stall to steady herself. She did not feel the slight prick of the wood splintering into her hand, but it was enough to force a small drop of blood. In the next moment Myth reared up and whinnied uncontrollably, stamping forcefully on the floorboards. Helena forced her mind to clear and noticed a stinging sensation in her hand. The small trickle of blood ran down her palm and she realised the danger they were in.

'Get out quickly,' she told Whitmore. 'Go!'

Helena wrapped her handkerchief around the tiny wound and instantly tried to soothe the animal. With the blood now hidden from the animal's sight and his mistress caressing him, the horse calmed and quieted. A carrot and a kiss saw him right as rain and she slipped from his side unnoticed. Away from the danger, Helena closed her eyes, her heart beating wildly against her chest with a fear felt deep in her soul, but not for herself alone.

Whitmore started at her appearance, putting his hands on her shoulders to emphasise the point. 'You could have been killed.'

Overcome at the sound of his voice, Helena threw her arms around him and held him tightly against her. His strong hands unconsciously found their way around her waist and she surrendered to his caresses. Helena looked into his eyes, so beautiful yet somehow so sad, so filled with longing and loneliness. Standing there, trembling at the mere touch of his hand she faltered. She plead softly for mercy to a higher court, afraid that to utter a word out loud would betray her weakness. With no answer to her entreaties she closed her eyes and allowed herself the idea of a tender kiss.

Whitmore pulled back, leaving the moment tense and unfulfilled. Whatever had possessed him to encourage her affections now gave rise to unease. It was more than propriety and respect for Lord Stratford. Her very touch seemed to stir conflicting feelings within him with no basis for them.

'Ride with me,' Helena proposed suddenly. 'Let us be late for work today.'

'Where?

'Anywhere. Across the Downs.'

Helena took him by the hand and gleefully took him down to the open portion of the stables. With a wave of her hand two stable boys appeared and got to work. The horses saddled, she headed off to the Downs with Whitmore close at hand, whisking freely through the cool early spring breeze, riding past the Gables and onto the entrance to the Cow Path as the temperamental steed fussed wildly at the quick slowing of the pace. The sun held long in the sky, seeing their journey favourably across the South Downs. The rays of twinkling light danced over the water like gold stars on the waves, rushing in toward the lower lighthouse of Beachy Head in the distance.

Atop the cliffs, set back from the only path down to the shore between Meads and Birling Gap, sat a small villa, dilapidated and careworn with age and disuse. Whitmore dismounted at the site, breathless at the beauty of it. Its seclusion and serenity were protected by the surrounding hills. It was completely hidden from all sides. Even from atop the hills, one would literally have to know what to look for in order to see it. Like the beach below, which only revealed itself at low tide, it was as if an enchanted cloak covered it, keeping it safe.

Whitmore spanned the incredible view. 'What a lovely place this is.'

'When I was a child I used to think this was a magical place, only visible to me if my heart were true. The beach below is like that, as well. Before I understood the ebbs and flows of tides I was convinced that only magic could make the beach appear. John made it so, telling me fantastic stories. He would bring me here right when he knew the tide was about to go out and then stand on the top of the cliff, stretch his arms forth and say, "*Omnipotens Deus, duco tergum unda per vestri validus manus manus quod ostendo sum quicumque est occultus...* So mote it be," calling upon God to draw back the sea and reveal the sands. I would stand next to him with eyes wide and watch the slow miracle. He was a god and I was in awe at his feet. As I grew he taught me that the natural recession of the tide revealed it twice a day, but the magic never died for me. I will forever see him in my mind conjuring up the beach from the depths of the ocean by the power of his will alone.'

'You love him very much, don't you?'

'With all my heart,' she said softly, without thinking, adding to it the moment she realised what she had revealed. 'Of course, I love my father, too. They are both great men.'

'Of course.' Whitmore let the matter be, seeing more than she could have revealed with words. 'Who owns the house and grounds? It appears to be abandoned, and for many years from the condition of it.'

'I don't know, but you are right, no one has set foot inside it in my lifetime that I am aware of. John used to bring me here since I was a young girl. We would come out with a rug and a picnic basket, sitting or walking for hours taking in the splendour of it. I always wanted to go inside, but he would not hear of it. It was a time I shall always look back upon with fond memories.'

'What happened?' he asked

'I don't know. One day he stopped coming, with no word of why or any obvious regret.'

At the hearing of it, Whitmore moved toward the front of the house, peering through the window, straining to see inside through the clouded pane. Trying the front door, he found it to be bolted, but only against him, for Helena was granted access by way of the lower side window coming to the front door to grand him admission through more conventional means. Obviously it had not been her first time inside. The faded curtains were bronzed with dirt and age, skewing the true delicacy of the white lace they once must have been. As they fell back into place from the removal of Whitmore's hand, the room revealed that same dark and dingy colour, marring the dainty comfort it once held, fading the flowered wallpaper now pulling apart at the corners and seams. In the bedroom, a bed stood out as the most prominent fixture, reaching out to two night tables, a bureau, a washstand, and a table covered with cloth, books, and other various items. The floor was littered with dust so that each footfall made its mark.

'The sitting room is filled with books, all sorts. I tried to find a pattern in hopes of revealing whom might have lived here, but concluded only that the person or people who lived here must have been very intelligent and well rounded. The kitchen is sparse, but clean—well, it was. The real oddity is the room next to this one. It is entirely empty, without furnishings or even window dressings. I have long since concluded that he was a single man, perhaps young, just starting out. He probably had just purchased the house and had not yet finished furnishing it when he disappeared, never to be seen or heard of again.'

'Impossible.'

Helena broke into an excited smile of enthusiasm. 'Precisely! Perhaps he met with a violent end born from something he saw, and his family holds the deed in trust until the murder is solved, or perhaps he met a woman who was leaving abroad suddenly. He had to make an instant decision.'

'Do not be dramatic. He did not meet with a violent end. He left here because his family died, probably suddenly. He remained for a while, but eventually could not bring himself to return for the pain of it,' Whitmore announced with confidence in his conclusions.

Helena looked at him as he spoke, the dim sunlight accentuating the features in his face as he spoke. There was a clear presence of empathy in his expression, revealing his own loneliness in such quantities as to touch her heart with every word. She stepped toward him, desiring to comfort him, only to see it did not take away his pain.

'How do you know that? How do you know he was married? There is no evidence of it,' she asked, receiving only his gesture of tapping on the covered table cluttered with books and nondescript items. Her confusion must have been self-evident, for his next move was to remove the top portion of the cloth, revealing an attached mirror. The table was not just any table, but a woman's vanity cleverly hidden from plain view.

'Are you married, Mr Whitmore?'

'No.'

'Were you ever?'

Whitmore shied away. 'Not to my knowledge.'

'Not to your knowledge?' Helena chuckled. 'I wouldn't think that would be something one would forget.'

Oddly, the statement invoked no response, not even a wry look.

'The house seems so sad,' Helena finally diverted.

'It's perfect,' Whitmore replied softly, engrossed in every detail of its splendour.

Looking at him, the thought seemed to strike her with a morose pain hiding something underneath. 'Come, I have something to show you.'

The barn was a few meters away, behind the house. Two large doors were held fast by a lock and the windows were securely boarded shut. Producing a key from behind a loose board, Helena slipped it into the lock.

'You must promise me, Mr Whitmore, before I open the door, not to tell a living soul what you see,' she insisted before she would remove the lock, conveying a most serious nature of life and death. 'My father would, most assuredly, disapprove.'

Helena opened the lock and pushed back the heavy doors burdened with age. It was dark at first, shielded from the light by means of large tarps suspended from the rafters, concealing its inner secrets. As she opened the door wide, the tarp took on a peculiar shape, which did not register fully in his mind until she began to pull them back. Hidden beneath was a motorcar, green with silver trim. Unlike a traditional design, the small gem possessed a larger engine and a smaller storage capacity. The bonnet was strapped down with leather belts and the gear levers were inside the compartment instead of on the side. The windscreen was smaller, sporting a curved design rather than a rectangular one. Whitmore recognized the design immediately from similar pictures in magazines. It was the vast 8.7-litre Dutch-manufactured Spijker race car, with a twenty-eight horsepower engine.

'My friend Charles took on a new partner, Henry. He says their new designs will revolutionise the automobile industry. I had him make a few modifications to the suspension and the chassis in exchange for a loan. He showed me a new design that he and his new partner had come up with to make the ride smoother. I was impressed and offered to finance a model made by his own company in exchange for this model he had modified. You see, a traditional frame is designed like an *I*, allowing the two axels to yield when going over a bump. Charles's design is shaped more like an *X*. He calls it a wishbone design, allowing each wheel to move independently allowing for an even smoother ride. The more aerodynamic and smooth the ride, the faster it will go. I've made it to London in under an hour. Charles promises the Ghost will go faster, but it won't be ready for another couple of years.'

'You frighten me, Miss Stratford,' he said, amazed and impressed. 'What else do you have hidden away that the world does not know about? I wonder what it is that you cannot do.'

'Would you like to drive?' she offered with a broad, excited grin.

The temptation was almost too much to bear. He worried that the decrease in mobility in his right hand and leg would hinder his ability to handle the vehicle, but Helena quickly assured him that he was more than capable.

She had obviously done this routine before, as the barn was equipped with fresh hay, oats, and rope to secure the horses. She needed no help to open wide the doors and push the glistening motorcar from its position in the barn to the drive without. Closing the doors behind, the engine turned over with extraordinary ease. A quick lesson of the operation of the vehicle proved again to be simple in design. It was not clear if the car had been modified for the use of a woman, for racers, or for the hoi polloi. Whatever the case, everything about it suggested that it was a remarkably well-designed vehicle. Putting it into gear, Whitmore eased off the clutch, edging the car forward with grace. Turning onto the main road, he found the changing of gears of no hindrance, propelling the motor forward to increasingly higher speeds. The exhilaration could not be compared to anything yet known, but only imagined. It was the equivalent to spending one's life on an old mare, suddenly being transported across the Downs by a two-year-old champion thoroughbred unmatched in his class. It was what one would imagine it to be like to fly through the air without constraint.

The ride was gentle, even over the rugged terrain of the dirt roads. Before long they found themselves flying by houses, horses, and other motorcars, receiving envious stares at every turn. Soon all traces of worry or doubt passed away, replaced completely with laughter and vivacity.

SESSION CASE

QUEEN'S BENCH DIVISION

LORD JUSTICE

HAROLD A. W. STRATFORD

NINTH SESSION,

HELD AT

JUSTICE HALL, IN SUSSEX COURT,

ON FRIDAY, THE 27th DAY OF OCTOBER, 1903,

AND FOLLOWING DAYS.

TAKEN IN SHORT HAND

(BY AUTHORITY OF THE CORPORATION OF THE CITY OF EASTBOURNE)

BY A. WAKEFIELD

Eastbourne :

PRINTED FOR J. H. WILLOW, BY A. WAKEFIELD,

No. 74, MEADS;

AND PUBLISHED BY G. HERBERT, COUNTY COURT

1904

[37] Eventually the snow melted away, until there was nothing left of that grey nothingness found amidst the dreary months-long death that was an English winter. Whitmore had found a home among the long pebble beaches and kind old faces of Eastbourne, that dear town. It had embraced him with warm and welcoming arms, no less than the house of Stratford and Willow had welcomed him with its love of family. Unable to pace the floors unoccupied, Whitmore found employment as a chemist at District General Hospital. Angus Porter headed the laboratory and eagerly welcomed another pair of hands. Soon he was a part of a collective whole, nestled in a community, which closed its doors to all save its own. By spring he had become a fixture.

Lost in a world of bubbling concoctions, various coloured liquids, and prepared samples, Whitmore sank into blissful disregard of the problems besetting the household. While the rest of the household dealt with crime and conviction, Whitmore found challenge within a different realm, and it consumed many long hours each day and often on into the night. Strolling amongst the haphazardly stacked columns of books and odorous beakers, Whitmore leafed though the various boxes and bins for something more elevated and challenging to stir his mind than the routine experiments of the day. Seeing a stack of files that had been placed aside, he took the time to look through them. Cases of cancer, advanced diabetes, and typhoid filled the pile, offering a plethora of agony but little in the way of mental stimulation. One, however, stood out. It was thicker than the others, clearly denoting that someone had devoted great effort to the case, but had now abandoned it. Sifting through the contents, his curiosity and his interest grew. There was something compelling about it, drawing him into clearing the table of its current projects and settling down to the recreation of the experiment. A woman's life hung by a thread in a hospital room upstairs, while her husband continued to pray for answers.

The first physical examination showed bruising around the mouth, nose, eyes, and ears. She was brought in unconscious and did not regain consciousness during her stay. The second examination, given the following day, reported the pattern of bruising had increased, suggesting deeper wounds. It was at this point that the police were called in and a number of tests were run in a short period of time. The patient was reported to be deteriorating, rejecting all known anti-venoms and serums. Doctors had given up hope of a cure. Captivated, Whitmore began the first of many long nights and unrelenting weekends, sleeping at times in the laboratory; unable to give up something that compelled him beyond reason.

In the week preceding the Easter holiday, Porter and the other chemists were filled with festive cheer, and invited wives, children, family, and friends to a party in the laboratory before closing early that Friday. Porter was an easy man to work for, marrying late in life to a pretty wife who found infinite ways to please and serve him daily, often bringing to the dull laboratory delicious treats that were proof of her baking skill. Cavendish had two young children, happy always to see him and rendering upon him sticky kisses of sugared spice and liquorice. Somers was married with a new baby, his wife always patiently waiting for him in the hall to finish so that they might walk home together. Even the young assistants rushed home to wives and girlfriends.

Finding him the only bachelor among colleagues with family, the women never ceased to ensure that Whitmore wanted for nothing in the way of food or drink, feeling the man to be helpless in his dysfunctional life without a woman of his own. A half-hearted smile hid the truth of the matter, for he was not without regret. In the midst of their daily comings and goings, their careful solicitude and dedication, Whitmore found himself still alone, pressing himself harder each day to avoid that one unmistakable conclusion. Whatever his life was or had been, he currently had no such intentions. Watching the women dance merrily with their husbands, twirling around the little children with bright shining faces, a pain seemed to start low in his chest, working its way upward to his head until the room faded into a loud pounding of agony.

'Another headache?' Porter asked, reaching for a white powder Whitmore kept on the shelf as Whitmore subtly rubbed the pain from his chest. 'What did Dr Stoner say?'

'To forgo wild parties and festive women who stuff a man with food past his endurance. It is nothing.'

'It is clearly something. You push yourself too hard. I wish I had ten more who worked as hard as you, but I would be amiss to ignore the toll it has taken upon you. I have noticed the headaches are getting worse, and more frequent. Say the word and you can have as much time off as you need.'

'It would not help. I am sure it would make matters worse. I have the Stanton case I just started on and—'

'It can wait. She has been lying there for six months. She isn't going anywhere. It is a holiday. No more work today, or this weekend!'

Whitmore shook his head in denial. 'I am close to an answer, I am sure.'

'You still believe she was poisoned?'

'It is not a matter of belief, but science,' said Whitmore.

'Should I involve the police?'

'No. We have yet to determine the substance, let alone how she came by it. Let me find the antidote. We may decide then how best to serve her.'

'We are all leaving early today, and I insist you do not stay again tonight. Go home!' Porter handed him the headache powder and a drink, and with a pat on the back he returned to the celebration.

[38] The steeple bells rang out half past ten o'clock in the blink of an eye. Whitmore arose from his seat, fumbling in the cold for the keys to unlock the cabinet for another wick for the lamp that had slowly faded during the evening hours, as had the coal stove. His hands, stiff from cold, shook as he disassembled the lamp. The temperature had caused even greater affliction in his weakest hand, causing heightened frustration at both his inability to solve the problem with his experiments as well as fix the lamp. Clutching the matchbox tightly, he struck match after match unsuccessfully until he threw the lot on the table, returning to his work in half-light.

Scribbling down the corrections he had made in his head in the dim light, he reformulated his calculations one more time in hopes of an answer. It had been his custom for many nights, unwilling to concede defeat. Ignoring the low light and the dying fire, Whitmore pressed on until the fatigue began to cloud his judgment, and was startled by a warm hand that caressed his aching back.

'It is time to go home.'

That tender, soothing voice calmly insisted, like a violin calling to through the darkness. Whitmore's tired eyes found their way to Helena's face, adjusting in the light to see that she was still clad in work dress. It took little deduction to realise she had come directly from her father's offices, working past a reasonable hour. Helena's dedication was equalled only by his own, gaining a certain amount of respect from the overworked and unyielding chemist.

Whitmore sat upright. 'A difficult case?'

Helena nodded. 'Difficult enough when an innocent man faces the end of a hangman's rope.'

'You don't have to work so hard. You have every available resource at your disposal. Would it not be better for the barrister handling the case to do this?'

Helena Stratford took on an immediate air of defence at the offer of an easy way out. 'It is the life of an innocent and I don't want to leave matters to a man who retires the case at five.'

'How can you be so sure he is innocent?'

'It argues out that way,' she said, waving her arm as if in conclusion of a court argument.

She had not meant to be humorous, but in her fatigue the wording came out skewed, causing Whitmore to find the whole matter funny in relation to her singular demeanour. She was a woman known for her command of law, rather than her powers of observation and deduction. Present her with the physical scene of the crime and Whitmore was convinced she would find nothing in it. Present her with facts gathered both for and against a suspect and she would find every angle in which to argue the point until the truth could not help but find its way to the surface. She was an excellent barrister, who under different circumstances would have made a first-rate judge, but she made a poor investigator and would have disgraced the profession of the official police.

Reaching over to turn down the gas burners, Helena brushed past the weary chemist, who found her fragrance of lilac and honeysuckle soothing to the senses. Staying her hand, he dismissed everything diverting him, lest a moment of loneliness move him to another indiscretion.

'I have to work,' said he, pushing all other thoughts from his mind.

'No more tonight, you are too tired.'

'I will be along shortly.'

His abrupt treatment ended all conversation and Helena took her cue. She picked up her coat and without argument took her leave. A woman was both soothing and a vexation, bringing a man to forego his own convictions.

[39] Easter weekend brought an unusually high temperature for the year, finding the residents of Eastbourne active for an early walk before services. The House of Stratford was no exception. Cheerful faces with dispositions to match greeted the breakfast table, in keeping with a ritual that rarely deviated. Even the early edition made no mention of ill-fated demise or declining fortunes. God had granted a stay from plots of vengeance, damnation, and intrigue, allowing a momentary breath before returning to the dark. Putting aside issues of law and forced marriages, the family took to the beach, bringing with it only that which they could carry in the family motor. All of Eastbourne and as far away as Kent and London had arrived with picnic baskets and lounging chairs to bask in the early celebration of warmer weather.

Cold water greeted the eager and not faint of heart until every boat ashore was cast. It had been the custom, in the warm weather, to walk along the beach each afternoon, settling at the end of the pier after a lunchtime sonnet or chapter had been read, while Stratford and Willow reclined in lounge chairs, curled up for a nap or the thriving adventure within the pages of a book. The day could not have been more perfect, melting away all thoughts of unsolved crimes or chemical mysteries. The pier was bustling with visitors and vendors. Even a puppet show appeared by the café for the children.

Returning to the party with tea, Whitmore paused at the table as Helena crouched, pacifying a young child who lost his balloon. How tender and natural she seemed with him, her smile unlike any expression he had seen before on her face. Wiping away the child's tears with her delicate lace handkerchief, she was the image of maternal perfection, raising again the question of why she seemed adamant not to marry. Exchanging a half penny for a balloon, she had not noticed the puppeteer had made her part of the play, swatting the puppet's stick first over the police puppet's head and then back toward the balloon, causing wave after wave of laugher from children and adults alike. Whitmore chuckled at the way her dedication and focus to a task completely negated the surrounding world, this time in the form of the stick striking and bursting the balloon at the precise moment she turned around.

Whitmore broke into laughter as the little child's tears were instantly dried at Helena's expression. Yet, it was not her startled expression or the general laughter that drew the sudden attention of an inconspicuous observer across the pier, who strained to see them through the crowd. The interested party shuffled his way through tightly packed children and busy adults to get close enough to bump into Whitmore. It took but a moment to confirm his suspicions, allowing him to withdraw, veritably unnoticed, to return to his observations from a distance. Arms stretched out in joy, Miss Stratford pleaded for respite from Whitmore as the children made her a pole to prance around in delight, finding the slight incident completely removed from Whitmore's mind.

The day was far too bright and warm to sit when the water called with fervent summons. Unwilling to make the day upon the shore, Helena Stratford pulled at the weary chemist until they reached a large covered object nestled near the water's edge. Peeling back a tarpaulin to reveal a finely crafted sailing skiff, and with pleading eyes that could not be ignored, Whitmore was persuaded to join her with a basket of food and books.

Opening his eyes long enough to check on his companion, Willow noted Stratford was intent on something he was viewing through the spyglass.

'What do you see?'

'Bridgewater and Crampon on the new Kippford. The man has no business being on a boat, let alone sailing one,' he muttered disagreeably, much to the amusement of Willow.

'Can you see Helena and Myles? What are they doing?'

Stratford scanned the edge of the horizon until his view came upon the tiny skiff, drifting at will.

'It looks as if Whitmore is throwing a book into the Channel.'

'Gaston Leroux,' Willow muttered as if he could see the discussion between them in his mind's eye, knowing Whitmore's aversion to detective novels. 'What is our Helena doing?'

Stratford steadied the glass, peering into it intently. 'Laughing,' he said. 'What on earth are they doing out there?'

'It is called having fun. You remember fun, don't you, old darling? It is that thing we used to do at their age.'

'We have fun,' Stratford replied, putting down the glass and easing back into his chair, returning to his book, but grumbling over the notion for some little time.

Taking a seat at Stratford's side, Brandon Faulkner sat brooding over the vision off shore, despite repeated urgings from Willow and Stratford to occupy himself better. He found that the girl's softening nature toward the repulsive and defective chemist was becoming intolerable. Ambition would soon demand that something be done about it. He paced the shore for hours, stirring the fires of hatred as he scanned the water for the bright yellow, blue, and white skiff, which did not appear back at shore the whole of the afternoon.

[40] As cooler winds spoke of the hour growing late, Whitmore opened his eyes and noted that his companion was fast asleep. With compassionate regard for her slumber, he raised the sail and positioned himself to tack the skiff back to shore. It was a fine wind that saw them swiftly through the waters, touching the points of the reef until safe shores welcomed them in. A gentle caress alerted the girl to the coming shore, where she awoke cheerfully and jumped from the side to pull in the boat without thought to the cold water. Whitmore shook his head at her childlike spirit. Putting the boat away, the couple strolled back to the pier for a hot cup of tea, laughing at how eagerly and prematurely it had been to bound into the water without a change of clothes. Their smiles faded rapidly, however, as they saw Brandon Faulkner striding angrily toward them, accompanied by his faithful friend and watchdog, Samuel Damon.

'Where have you been?' Faulkner demanded of Helena possessively, glaring at his rival. 'Look at you. You look like a drowned sea urchin.' He took off his coat and wrapped it around her in protection from the cold, and from Whitmore. 'Come, I will take you home to change. We barely have time to make it to dinner. Your father expects us to help greet the guests, you know that! What were you doing all day?'

Helena struggled against him. 'Brandon, please, do not make a scene. I was with Myles and perfectly safe.'

'We will talk about that later,' said he.

'Don't make it sound illicit and immoral, Brandon; we were just reading.'

He was about to assert his authority, making it clear who it was that held control and who it was her father intended her to marry, when a friendly and familiar sight altered the state of affairs with his presence alone. Willow had arrived, pipe tucked between his teeth, lighting it against the wind. He said nothing, merely stepped among them as any friend might do. Faulkner felt nothing akin to fear, but stayed himself, as chancing Willow's wrath was a fool's errand.

'Mr Willow,' said he. 'I am taking her home.'

A nod from Willow gave momentary approval, and with a look of impending vengeance from Faulkner that spoke far louder than any words he might bestow on Whitmore, he spirited Helena toward the carriage with Damon close on his heels.

'Why does he treat her so?' asked Whitmore, watching them depart as Willow ordered tea. 'Why do you allow him to continue? She does not love him.'

Willow took the two cups of tea from the counter and began walking toward a table. 'Adding a little sugar to one's tea for the first time often makes you wonder why you never discovered its sweet taste before. Then again, too much sugar at any one time can severely trouble the senses.' Willow wandered, fussing over the tea. 'It is good to sample both and come to a measured preference of taste in one's tea. Don't you think?'

Whitmore stopped sharply, taking hold of Willow's arm. 'What exactly is that supposed to mean?'

'I need more sugar in my tea. Do you mind awfully?' Willow asked, handing Whitmore the cup in an unspoken gesture to oblige.

Throwing up his hands, Whitmore made his way back toward the counter, while Willow fumbled for another match with a smile, having let his pipe go out again.

SESSION CASE

QUEEN'S BENCH DIVISION

LORD JUSTICE

HAROLD A. W. STRATFORD

TENTH SESSION,

HELD AT

JUSTICE HALL, IN SUSSEX COURT,

ON FRIDAY, THE 27th DAY OF OCTOBER, 1903,

AND FOLLOWING DAYS.

TAKEN IN SHORT HAND

(BY AUTHORITY OF THE CORPORATION OF THE CITY OF EASTBOURNE)

BY A. WAKEFIELD

Eastbourne:

PRINTED FOR J. H. WILLOW, BY A. WAKEFIELD,

No. 74, MEADS;

AND PUBLISHED BY G. HERBERT, COUNTY COURT

1904

[41] Willow sat unmoving at the chessboard for several minutes. Not even a gentle prodding from his opponent seemed to stir him at first.

'John? It is your turn.'

Willow glanced up and pulled his attention back to the board, but noted that Stratford was sweating. The immediate transformation in his expression prompted Stratford to grant a smile of diversion.

'What's on your mind, Johnny? You've been in check for the past twenty minutes.'

The announcement came as a small surprise, prompting Willow to check the board. Finding it true, he gave a nod of resignation. His mind was otherwise occupied and any continuation would forestall the inevitable.

'I have to go to London for a few days.'

'Is there anything wrong?'

'No; I have a case to attend to at the Courts of Justice and I'll be away all week.'

Stratford offered another smile, though the idea did not appeal to him.

'Well, I'm sure we will all struggle along without you. Helena can handle the office and we'll make sure Whitmore is taken care of.'

'I thought, since Myles has been working relentlessly of late, that I would take him with me.'

Stratford nodded.

Willow hesitated at the second half of what he had to say, but put it forth as gently as he could under the circumstances. 'Well, I thought I would take Helena, as well.' Willow chuckled. 'Remember how she would sit all day in court listening to one judge after another waffle on when she was young? She would sneak off whenever our backs were turned. She never tired of it. You don't mind if I take her, do you?'

'Why should I mind? I doubt any of us will be able to stop her once she hears where you're going. She does love London. It will be good for her.'

Willow dropped all pretence as he broached the true concern foremost on his mind. 'What's wrong, Harry? You don't look well.'

'I'm fine, just a little tired.'

'I don't like to leave you. You've not been yourself since I've been back.'

'I'll be fine. Sam is here.'

'Hardly inspiring. Why don't you come? I have a fancy for that nice little Indian restaurant we went to when we were last in London, then perhaps a trip to Piccadilly for that imported tobacco you introduced me to.'

'I thought you did not go in for imports, John, strictly New Castle or Stonehenge.'

'Once in a great while it does not hurt to change. What was the name of that brand?'

'Seaport Rum, from Virginia, in America, or they have that nice Turkish blend.'

'Bah! It is no different than our own Cavendish blend.'

'I'd like to come,' Stratford granted him with a sigh, 'but I can't. I have certain things to regulate here.'

'Will you be all right?'

'I'll be fine,' Stratford insisted. 'You three have fun.'

[42] London welcomed the trio with blue skies and cool breezes as if expecting them. The gentle pace of the carriage ride allowed an instant review of the splendour and majesty of the place, culminating in their arrival in Kensington. It was a marvellous little hotel overlooking Hyde Park near Queen's Gate of which only the privileged availed themselves.

Settling into a quiet supper and relaxing evening, it seemed the perfect solution to deflect the young lady's mind from the questions of crime and murder that Willow knew still plagued her mind. She had been strangely quiet since the announcement of the closing of the Holmes case. He knew she quietly bore her father's decision with discontent, but there seemed far more to her silence. A change of activity seemed just the solution, and it was time his plan included outside intervention.

With the change of venue her countenance softened with each passing hour, opening the door to put Willow's plan into action. After supper he released her to Whitmore and into the nightlife of

London. It would not serve him to have them hanging about with what he had to do, and turning them over to the gentle night afforded the perfect solution.

[43] The street lamps afforded an amber glow, imparting a new dignity on the tired, soot-covered facades of the old buildings. People walked casually through the warm streets, enjoying the refreshing qualities of the new spring air or strolling down to the theatre to take in a show. It was a different world at night when at last the ledger books were closed and the errands and exigencies of the day were cast off. It was almost as if, with the coming of evening, old Mother London wrapped herself snugly in her finest coat, determined to appear in her best for the millions who walked her streets. The grand streets of upper West London hid well the dark evil that lurked in the back alleys and opium dens.

Strolling past the Albert Hall toward the park, time was suspended. The park was aglow with light and busy with all manner of festivities, people passing, huddling together as they walked along. It was hardly a picture which would lead one to assume the presence of dark motives and even darker crimes. Yet, this was the very heart of Sherlock Holmes's territory, Baker Street being no more than four kilometres away, on the other side of the park.

'Mr Holmes must have walked these streets a thousand times,' Helena remarked in childlike awe at the thought.

'If you mention that name one more time,' Whitmore admonished with sufferance, 'I shall be forced to throw you in the Thames.'

It was a response she had not expected, conveyed without the slightest hint of expression or emotion, leaving her doubtful as first of his intention.

'You wouldn't!'

'I would.' He grinned.

'Seriously now, does it not interest you in the least, even after all you have heard? Does it not interest you that his very presence in this city and the fear of his involvement decreased the surplus of crime? That he walked these streets at night when he could not sleep, and that because of that criminals would think twice of their deeds?'

Whitmore thought about this for a moment, its ramifications, and then made his pronouncement with due consideration. 'No.'

'You're impossible!' She laughed, holding fast to his arm as they walked briskly along the path.

It was refreshing in many ways to have a man whose interest in crime was confined to the laboratory instead of the continual debate in law. Helena's life had been filled with every aspect of discussion upon the subject from her first words to her education at university to her stewardship of the firm. Myles Whitmore cared little for the criminal world. His life revolved about the actions and reactions within Petri dishes, flasks, and test tubes. It was alchemy as controlled and logical as the man himself.

The city teemed with life after dark, affording anything and everything to do or see. After seeing Frank Bridge give a violin concert at the Royal Academy of Music, the couple took a walk to Devonshire for a cup of coffee and stimulating conversation. It was a paradise for every conceivable kind of nature or temperament.

Away from the subjects of crime and law, Whitmore found a side to the young lady he had not witnessed before, like the moment on the pier. Her breadth of knowledge extended well past the mundane topics of precedence and statute. She changed topics with ease, being well-versed in music, art, and philosophy. Her logical mind coupled with an equally curious nature allowed her great diversity across the range of any subject he cared to name. Even if she could not readily understand it she would not shy away from contemplating it. When he found himself rambling on about the intricate problems of his work, she never once lost a beat in the conversation.

'Have you tried inquiring at other hospitals and laboratories to see if they have had any recent cases similar to Mrs Stanton?' Helena asked.

The question took Whitmore by surprise, not only in that it demonstrated her attention to the conversation, but an interest.

'You surprise me; really, you do.'

'How is that?'

'Your knowledge suggests some scientific training and yet you've never mentioned anything before.'

Helena broke out in a wide grin. 'No, I'm afraid I was never very good at chemistry. But then again you are not conversant in law and yet you bested me upon a legal question the first night we met. Perhaps our professions are not so dissimilar after all.'

In the pale lamplight of the streets and in the atmosphere of elevated conversation, the child-like image he had carried of her seemed to melt away into a portrait of seductive womanhood once again, creating a feeling that sat uneasily with his inherent nature. The hour had grown late and gave good cause to head back to the hotel and retire for the evening. They passed by the bridge at Clarence Gate, where she paused to gaze uneasily in the direction of Baker Street once more, but Whitmore's tender hand took her arm and hurried her on her way.

[44] With each passing day Helena's countenance softened, granting Willow the ease of mind he had hoped for. Breakfast brought with it healthy appetites and warm conversation. The vitality of the city lent excitement to the mellow beauty of a fine English morning. The London Times heralded great reviews for the popular rendition of John Bull's Other Island, captivating the young lady for quite some time. Her reverie was broken at intervals only by her enthusiastic commentary about the piece's content. Listening to her, Willow waited patiently for her to come to the climactic disappointment that, though she may have wanted to see it, the play had been sold out for weeks.

Ah, she's reached it, he said silently to himself just as her face lost its childish exuberance. Willow retrieved two tickets from his vest pocket with a Cheshire grin, sliding them across the table. Her face lit up once again as if it were Christmas. Once Helena had been used to his singular talent for obtaining whatever it was he sought, but this was a newly gained talent, wholly unexpected.

'But there are only two tickets here,' she observed immediately upon inspection, her elation subdued.

'I regret that I am unable to accompany you, my dear. There are unavoidable engagements I must attend to. I'm afraid I will have to be satisfied with your review of it.'

'But I thought we would all spend the week together.'

'There will be plenty of time for that. I have some things I need to do.'

'Are you going to the Royal Courts of Justice?' she asked hopefully.

'No, I'm not in court. And don't go running off there wasting the day. I don't want you sitting around all day listening to cases you've heard a thousand times. I want the two of you to enjoy yourselves. There will be time enough for court and work when we return home.' He chuckled.

Signing off on the bill for their meal, Willow stood and kissed her good-bye, keeping a watchful eye on his charge to afford himself that last bit of comfort before leaving.

[45] Across the room a man surveyed the trio intently, watching their every move as he nonchalantly sipped his morning coffee. The morning edition of the *Times* he held limply before him would not have convinced even a novice observer that the man behind it was but casually looking in their direction. However, it was hardly necessary to conceal to any great extent his real endeavour. An old barrister was unlikely to be of any interest, less so his companions, and yet when they departed the man watching them changed in an instant from a languid dreamer to a man of action. He rushed to draw on his frock coat and hurried down the stairs and into the street after them. Miss Stratford and Whitmore were still visible as the observer broached the walk, turning in the direction of Hyde Park.

He quickened his pace until he had decreased the distance between himself and the couple, yet he kept a comfortable distance so as not to be seen. Then, still keeping a hundred yards back, he followed them into the park, past the Round Pond and toward Kensington Gardens. The silent observer felt a slight flutter as the pair turned onto Sussex Gardens, which ran all the way up to Marylebone Road and then to that most famous of streets. The couple huddled unusually close as they walked along, but it wasn't until the young lady stopped and looked around that, suddenly unnerved, their follower ducked into a shop entrance. A cautious glance was rewarded with the view of an indiscreet kiss before the pair slipped down Eastbourne Terrace.

Here, within a stone's throw of Piccadilly, shopkeepers exhibited galvanized dustbins on the pavement. A small china shop on the corner sold little floral teapots of the kind that spinster ladies procured for Saturday night garden parties. Old women walked stiffly round with pearl-handled walking sticks, a swarm of Affenpinschers, Griffons, and spaniels rolling affectionately at the hems of their tailor-made skirts. The couple worked their way through the buskers and the crowds and turned into Piccadilly Station, where their pursuer watched as they boarded an outbound train.

[46] If the evening of the first day demonstrated the loveliness of London, the second day refined and exemplified it, serving as a venue for a full selection of activities and culminating in a flawless performance of John Bull's play. The political overtones of the play incited an animated conversation between the couple upon its conclusion, traversing every topic from the debate over Irish home rule to the portrayal of the lovers as touchingly romantic.

Helena tucked her hand into the crook of Whitmore's arm as they walked along the sun-drenched streets. The cold stone exterior of the building gave no indication of the cheerful busyness of Apple Market, Coventry Gardens within. The green-painted iron steps revealed a queer warren of little shops packed with vendors whose onions overflowed upon the floor and whose kiosks were crowded with patrons haggling over bits and bobs and shiny trinkets.

Down King Street, bald heads in club windows, pretty sandy-legged ladies, and children with stockings and short trousers greeted each soot-ridden ray of London's afternoon sun. Lords in red robes with fine white fur walked in procession outside of St Paul's, up the Strand. The heart of London was filled with maypoles and gallantry, of coaches and inn parlours. As the couple stopped to peer into a shop window, a man nearby snapped an ivory snuffbox closed to wave a fine batiste handkerchief at a good-looking chambermaid. Eastbourne and murder found no place in those hours, which instead were spent in passionate discussion and companionship, drawing the two of them ever closer.

Not another moment could Whitmore bear as he wavered on the walk, too weary to take another step. Even the offer of a fine dinner could not tempt him away from a desired hot bath and a comfortable bed. Standing outside of his door, Whitmore fumbled for his keys, his fatigue revealing itself in an inability to manipulate his fingers. Offering simple assistance, Helena favoured him with a tender smile as she swept up the keys and slipped them into the lock. Gently forcing the tumblers over, the lock clicked open. Fatigue was not the only cause of his discomfort in that seemingly eternal moment as she stood between him and the door. She was a beautiful and desirable woman. Her perfume and wondrous beauty intoxicated him. Her soft delicate hand moved to caress him in such a fashion that would force any man to crumble, and made Whitmore struggle against his own desires.

SESSION CASE

QUEEN'S BENCH DIVISION

LORD JUSTICE

HAROLD A. W. STRATFORD

ELEVENTH SESSION,

HELD AT

JUSTICE HALL, IN SUSSEX COURT,

ON FRIDAY, THE 27th DAY OF OCTOBER, 1903,

AND FOLLOWING DAYS.

TAKEN IN SHORT HAND

(BY AUTHORITY OF THE CORPORATION OF THE CITY OF EASTBOURNE)

BY A. WAKEFIELD

Eastbourne :

PRINTED FOR J. H. WILLOW, BY A. WAKEFIELD,

No. 74, MEADS;

AND PUBLISHED BY G. HERBERT, COUNTY COURT

1904

[47] The solitary week at South Lodge lent itself to lonely nights. George meticulously waited table for Stratford no less than he would upon a full complement of guests, foregoing no formalities in his routine. He stood mechanically aside as the old judge made his way through the soup placed before him. The hollow sound of Stratford's spoon against the side of his china bowl echoed the loneliness in that great house, for all his friends and company throughout the day could not compensate for the absence of his family at night.

His house had been lonely during the week of their absence. Time seemed to move inexorably slower until the singular thought of their return became his sole fortification. Though he was not wont to freely admit it, Willow's guest had granted a sense of wholeness to the house, adding symmetry and balance Stratford had failed to previously recognise. The supplement was subtle, yet in his absence, undeniable.

Setting aside the soup, it occurred to him that his house would miss Whitmore's presence when he returned to his home. Just as George made an attempt to serve the main course, Stratford dismissed dinner. He sat back in his chair, overwhelmed by a singular thought. Willow was fond of the man, protective and nurturing, like a father. If Whitmore were to leave, Willow might choose to return with him.

The relationship between Stratford and Willow had been an agreeable one to all concerned, providing companionship for the two confirmed old bachelors and stability for the girl in her nurturing years. Willow would, from time to time, depart for his house in Friston, but always returned. He never could stay away for long without the young lady recalling him. She was the child he might otherwise call his own and, like any father, he could not refuse her.

But Willow and Stratford's relationship had been strained by argument of late, and she was often caught in the middle. The aftermath left an overwhelming sense of loss each time Willow departed. It had been especially desolate during his absence in the midst of the Holmes affair. The thought of another continued departure removed Stratford's appetite completely. There was, too, the added enjoyment his daughter seemed to take in the man's company, though at times it countered Stratford's own plan for her to marry.

Stratford had no more than waved his dinner away at the thought when Nigel appeared in the doorway announcing an unexpected visitor. David Malone awaited him in the drawing room, having come unannounced. The intrusion was welcome and Stratford met him well, receiving him warmly, only to find Malone unmoved. In response, Stratford offered a multitude of amenities, noting Malone was deeply troubled by whatever was on his mind.

'Tell me what it is that I may offer you to ease the telling of your troubles to me,' Stratford finally pleaded at his old friend's struggle. 'Is it money that you need? Anything, just tell me.'

'I need,' Malone said, 'for you to restore my position. Give me back my right to be in good standing and to be a solicitor again!'

'You know I cannot do that,' Stratford said reluctantly. 'You used your position both in legal matters and as a Brother for personal gain. You betrayed your oath. I offered you your freedom, but I cannot offer you absolution.'

'You gave your word!'

'I would not give such a word, even if it were in my power to bestow. You broke the law, David! What were you thinking?'

'I bent the rules a little and made a few of us many thousands of pounds, you included. I brought no harm to anyone. Good heaven's man, no one died over what I did.'

'The law is the law!' Stratford insisted, slamming his fist onto the table.

Malone waved his arm. 'The punishment does not fit the crime. You deprived me of my livelihood!'

'I sent you to three of my friends, who would have offered you employment for the asking.'

Malone huffed at the insult. 'Writing patents and advising ignorant businessmen how to write proposals? I was the best solicitor in Sussex! You offer me no more than to hold the hands of ignorant fools as a two-pence clerk! You promised me restoration and I come to demand it.'

Stratford turned in adamant force. 'I made no such promise! I will help you in any way I am able, but I cannot put you within arm's reach of the law again.'

Malone took a threatening stance. 'You have the power and you have asked much of me. Live up to your word or I shall reveal all.'

Stratford's voice matched his stance, throwing off the threat as easily as he would squash a bug. 'Do not presume to threaten me? I have been your greatest ally, but I can just as easily become your greatest adversary,' he warned before he could regain his sympathetic disposition. Malone had lost much and his anger was understandable. It was difficult to remain harsh with him. 'I am sorry. I understand your anger, but you must realise what you ask is quite impossible.'

Malone paced the floor in thought, as if sizing up his worthy opponent's options before rendering his decision. Malone stopped squarely before Stratford and gave his verdict in a calm, determined voice.

'I've risked everything for you. Restore what you took from me or I shall tell Mycroft Holmes the truth of how you came to murder his brother. I will tell him everything.'

'Are you so unimaginative that you believe him not to know?' Stratford asked with morose guilt pouring from his heart at the thought. 'Do you believe it is Sherlock's death alone that broke his noble heart and sent his mind into eternal torment? He knows, David; he knows. I pray every day that God grant me the power to turn back the hands of time to undo that terrible night.'

'You may pray, Harold, but God cannot undo what the devil has done. He may or may not know of your hand in his brother's death, but I will wager all he does not know that Simon Ballard was in that tally of deaths.'

Stratford staggered back at the name, knowing well the consequences for any man responsible for that particular death. Ballard was marked as an untouchable, for any duty to crown and country. It included the undesirable tasks a diplomat required, but could not condone. Ballard's position, by its very nature, required immunity. Every country had an equivalent, an agent protected by international treaty, cleaning up political indiscretions left behind. To avoid war, an entire village might be sacrificed. To avoid embarrassment, a woman or unwanted child might disappear. Many sought the demise of these men, who performed these distasteful tasks, but only the brave or foolhardy dared make the attempt. The mention of Ballard's name alone, in conjunction with that of Sherlock Holmes, spoke of an even deeper involvement than first suspected. It also meant that anyone involved in the man's death would be forfeit, as well as any who were connected with him. For Stratford's name to be linked to the death of Simon Ballard meant certain death for him and the removal of his entire family. No remnants of that night would ever remain. They would send another, like Ballard, to clear away the debris, leaving no man alive to speak the name of Stratford ever again.

Stratford shook his head in violent denial. 'No! Every man was accounted for; every man except—' He stopped in mid-sentence; realising there was one man whose identity was never revealed. 'My God! How do you know this?'

'Do not play games with me, Stratford. I will not be put off. Fulfil your promise or I will fulfil mine.'

The panic of Malone's words had dulled Stratford's quick wit. In the next moment the door opened to reveal Samuel Damon who, hearing the raised voices, stepped up quickly to add numbers to his mentor's defence.

Damon set upon Malone. 'What are you doing here? Get out.'

'I'll not play games with you,' Malone said as he poked Stratford in the chest to emphasize the point. 'You have two days.'

Damon stood fast against his opponent, at the ready to end the matter quickly, only to be cut to the quick with ease as Malone made his way to the door.

'Get your horrid creature out of my way and mind well my words,' he said, pushing Damon aside as he bounded out the door.

Stratford sank into a chair, causing Damon to rush to his aid with all due haste.

'What did he say?' Damon asked, seeing the state of his master. 'I heard him shouting at you—threatening you.'

'It is nothing,' Stratford insisted, carrying the full weight of the burden alone, in part for the protection of his young charge and perhaps out of fear. Whatever his motive, he was unwilling to go further with it. Even the young man's usual subtle twisting and prodding to draw out information had no effect. Stratford waved him out of the room, shutting the door behind him for nearly an hour.

At half past eight precisely, Stratford emerged, and descended down the hall to the sitting room where he was sure he would find his ward. Damon was well into a book of outback adventure when Stratford approached him. He stood for a moment fondling a sealed envelope in his hands.

'I want you to take this to David Malone. Now, tonight,' he insisted as he put forth the envelope with his seal embedded in wax.

'What is it, money? Is he blackmailing you?'

'Just take the envelope, Sam. Take my carriage and do not let the envelope leave your sight for a moment. Put it directly in his hands and his hands only. Do not leave with to his servant or his wife. Wait there. He will give you his reply. When he does, bring it directly to me, stopping nowhere en route.'

[48] Damon did not understand, but obedience required no understanding. He took the envelope and set off for Malone's house at once. Striding up the stairs, Damon rang the bell and waited until Malone appeared in person.

'What the devil do you want, monster?'

'I wouldn't be so hostile if I were you. I can help to soften or harden Harry's heart.'

'What do you want?'

'His lordship is a reasonable man. He wants to settle this matter.'

Damon handed him the note. 'He told me to wait for your answer.'

Malone read the note and the expression on his face began to relax.

'Tell him I will be there. But he had better be prepared to keep his word or I will keep mine.'

With a nod of acknowledgement, Damon went swiftly back to the estate. Stratford had been pacing, but stopped and gave his full attention to Damon as he came in.

'He said he agrees, but he begs it to be at five.'

Stratford breathed a sigh of relief and gave Damon a pat on the back as he made his way past. It seemed Malone's answer was most satisfactory.

[49] Chattering voices in the hall, trailed by a woman's obnoxious laugh, finally rousted Whitmore from a sound sleep. Reaching for his watch he strained to adjust his vision to see the hour. It was just past seven. Fumbling through the objects on his bed table, he found his cigarette case and a match. As he grew more alert it suddenly captured his attention that the room was inordinately quiet and he was distinctly alone, with no sound from the adjoining room.

Drawing on his robe, Whitmore stepped into the front room, toward the door to Helena's suite. Pulling the robe tighter around him, he knocked on the adjoining door. He stood for a moment or two, allowing his mind to come alive along with his apprehension. Her evening gown lay outstretched upon the bed, but her closet was open, as was her bureau drawer. It was her empty coat rack, however, that suggested that she was no longer in the hotel. As he began to close the door, resigned to waiting for her eventual return, he noted a magazine, well thumbed, on the desk. It was folded back to an article that she had apparently been reading. Picking it up, a chord struck in his mind, recalling a comment she had made during their walk together on the first night in the hotel.

Letting out a verbal expression of frustration, Whitmore rushed back into his rooms, thrusting off his robe and pulling on a shirt and trousers with as much haste as his mobility would allow. Slipping on his coat and shoes, he thrust coins in his pocket and bounded out the door. Dishevelled and untied, he hastened out the front doors of the lobby into a waiting cab; tapping the roof of the carriage to drive on, he gave no more than 'Baker Street' as an address before the door was even closed. In hindsight, it might have been wiser to wait until the carriage was in motion to give an address, for in his haste he dismissed the man, propped up against the side of the building, who took note of the address.

Within minutes they had arrived, with Whitmore a little tidier for the time. Handing the cabbie a coin, he stepped onto the curb and waited for the driver to pass on before crossing the street, hoping to see the young lady in full view. Finding his hopes unfounded, he made his way around the back by way of a small alleyway at the end of the street.

Coming to the centre, he stepped onto the back stoop of 221B and found that the door had already been forced. Checking around him before entering, he removed a handkerchief and wiped the knob of any fingerprints. Inside he found that the passage led directly into the kitchen, which was immaculately kept though covered by a thin patina of dust, suggesting that it had been some time since anyone had been in the house. A quaint dining room lay just beyond the kitchen, leading to a larger sitting room with a door to the bedroom and another door, which appeared to lead out into the hall. Following the natural course of the house to the upstairs, Whitmore turned the glass knob and stepped out into the hall. The floor was littered with mail, forced through the mail slot, building into a small hillock on the floor in the absence of its owner. He bent down and picked up a handful, sifting through the letters and bills in the fading light of the window in the foyer.

Now that is odd, he remarked to himself.

Whitmore picked up the remainder of the mail and sifted through it with increasing speed. The stack contained a variety of bills, letters and advertisements, all addressed to one Mrs Martha Hudson.

Whitmore carefully rearranged the mail on the floor in front of the door. He looked at the table and coat stand against the wall, feeling as if there was something about it he should see, but for the life of him he did not know what it was. The illumination admitted by the fanlight above the door afforded a meagre light by which to ascend the stairs.

In the gloom enshrouding the upstairs landing was a shorter hallway to the right and another flight of stairs. To the left was a corridor, which housed a closed door along its wall. But it was the door facing him at the head of the staircase that again filled him with the same feeling of unease and dread that he had experienced below. Flanking this door was a wooden coat rack from which a long, thin, pale grey top coat, a trench coat, a top hat, and a deerstalker cap hung limply from various hooks. Two walking sticks leaned disconsolately within a ring near the base of the stand and a heavy black woollen coat hung like a shroud from the hook behind.

A large plant sat in the corner near the window at the end of the corridor, now brown and dry from lack of water. He drew in a breath, opened the door, and stepped inside. The room was large and airy, and was filled with warm furnishings, pictures, and books. It seemed a comfortable room to him, one where he might find a relaxing moment among the books, papers, and trinkets. A half covered chalkboard sat near an ornate sideboard beside the entrance, shielding a bookcase and a filing cabinet.

Hearing footfalls in the hall behind him, Whitmore quickly concealed himself behind the door and waited, lest the approaching visitor be someone other than whom he suspected. As the door opened, Helena Stratford stepped through and Whitmore caught it.

Helena jumped violently backward with a short scream of panic. 'Oh God, Myles! How you startled me!'

'What on earth are you doing? You have broken into the man's house!'

'I'm looking for something,' she said.

'What? What could you possibly risk jail and disgrace to find?'

'I'm looking for what Mr Holmes was working on before he left. It has to be the clue to what killed him.'

'Your father and Willow said to leave the case alone, and expressly forbade you in particular to take it up. Do you realise you are committing a felony? You cannot burgle a man's house!'

'Holmes is dead. I doubt that he will be pressing charges any time soon, making it a misdemeanour at best.'

Whitmore gasped in disbelief. 'Do you hear yourself?'

'You heard what they did. It is unforgivable! They closed the case without having ever done what the law was set down for. The law was there to protect Holmes, and failing that it was to have punished the guilty for having broken that law. The police are not even looking for the murderer, Myles! I swear to you, it is as if no one wants this case to be solved.'

Whitmore took her by the arm. 'You are coming with me this instant.'

'Please, just ten more minutes. It's here, I know it!'

'No!' Whitmore shouted in frustration, pushed to the very edge of his nerves. 'No, Helena, no more!'

He tried to keep his voice calmer, repelled again by the start of her typical barrister's urge to argue the point, defending the position of why the case should be solved.

'Do you care at all for the people who love you? Your father is a prominent High Court Judge, and Willow...' He paused at the thought of Willow finding out. 'Willow, good heavens, what will he think? I want a life, Helena,' he said, taking her more gently in hand, 'a life away from crime, death, and pain. I don't want to feel afraid and sick all the time. I want to walk along the beach or sit with nothing more to do than close my eyes, falling asleep in the grass. I want a life, but equally I do not want to sacrifice yours. I have no desire to attend your funeral over the answers to the death of a man who could care less if you solved the mystery of his demise or not. I beg of you to leave this. We do not have the skill required for this investigation.'

Helena's face lit up with excitement. 'I've read everything about his methods. I can do this.'

'If your famous detective could not solve this case unscathed, who are we to attempt it?'

'How can you just let it go, Myles? How can I? Where is the justice in that?'

'I am not prepared to concede your life.'

'You won't have to.'

Whitmore stood unmoved. 'Then you leave me no choice but to go to Willow to stop you.'

Whitmore moved to go, but Helena quickly grasped his arm

'No; it will break his heart. I will go.'

Whitmore turned her towards the door and moved to go, but just as he put his hand on the knob, he saw something that caught his eye. A blackboard sat next to a well-equipped chemistry table with an all too familiar compound formula. Like an automaton, he drew closer to it, reading through the derivatives and the equation at the bottom. Letting his eyes drift onto the table, he spied Holmes's Bradshaw laid open to a page of notations, and next to it a small notebook, which housed nearly the entire formula. Captivated by the intricate work done on it, Whitmore lost all track of everything around him.

'Are you coming?'

'Was this detective of yours a chemist?' Whitmore asked.

'Yes. Well, no. I mean, Dr Watson never really portrayed him as such, but did note he studied it and even used it on some of his cases. Why?'

Whitmore continued to read through the various compounds and notations, losing all sense of his surroundings.

'What is it?'

'Unless I am mistaken, the answer,' Whitmore responded sluggishly, still reading and trying to understand the logic.

'The answer to what? It's just letters and numbers.'

'He's stayed with the primary elements, only distilling it partially, taking him down an entirely different path,' he said, leafing through the notebook and comparing it to the blackboard.

'Come on, we should go.'

Scooping up the Bradshaw and notebook, Whitmore noted the mail open on the table. An uncomfortable feeling swept over him like a cold wave, as his mind began to put together the pieces of his agitation. The mail was open and obviously had been read. Looking over the chemistry table he noted there was no dust anywhere. Rushing over to Holmes's desk, he noted that it too was devoid of dust, as was Dr Watson's desk, and yet the windowsill, mantel, and sideboard were laden with a thin layer.

Whitmore took a careful view of the street below, trying not to be seen. There was a man standing in a doorway across the street reading a newspaper.

Whitmore took Helena's arm and moved her swiftly toward the door. 'We have to get out of here.'

'Why? What is the matter?'

'Unless I miss my guess, we have company.'

Whitmore goaded her to move fast down the stairs and through the house. He closed the door behind them and moved her quickly down the back alley, not feeling safe until they were around the second block.

SESSION CASE

QUEEN'S BENCH DIVISION

LORD JUSTICE

HAROLD A. W. STRATFORD

TWELFTH SESSION,

HELD AT

JUSTICE HALL, IN SUSSEX COURT,

ON FRIDAY, THE 27th DAY OF OCTOBER, 1903,

AND FOLLOWING DAYS.

TAKEN IN SHORT HAND

(BY AUTHORITY OF THE CORPORATION OF THE CITY OF EASTBOURNE)

BY A. WAKEFIELD

Eastbourne :

PRINTED FOR J. H. WILLOW, BY A. WAKEFIELD,

No. 74, MEADS;

AND PUBLISHED BY G. HERBERT, COUNTY COURT

1904

[50] Walking down the length of the Diogenes' parlour, the slipper-toed servant quietly opened the door and made his way over to Mycroft Holmes, who sat slouched in a chair near the fire. Holding out a fine silver tray containing an envelope, the man waited patiently until it was received before disappearing in the manner he had come. Turning it over for an address, Mycroft noticed there were no markings of any kind upon the envelope outside of his name. Opening it, he found it to contain a series of photographs, which he leafed through slowly. Stopping at the last, his face drained of all colour as he tried to absorb the image before him.

[51] As the hour chimed half past five, Stratford stopped pacing long enough to pull out his watch from his vest pocket to recheck the time. He clicked open the tiny door of the delicately etched watch only to be frustrated at his inability to see it clearly. Though it was elegant and stylish, it had smaller features, making it difficult to read. With a huff, he reached inside his inner pocket and pulled out his spectacles, glancing around at any audience within sight before slipping them onto his face. It was perhaps a little vain to care how strangers might view his weakness, but Stratford had few scratches in his well-polished armour and his declining vision marred the pride of his perfection. Snapping the lid closed, he wasted no time in removing the spectacles from his face and returning them to his pocket.

Continuing his vigil, Stratford tried to relax, committed to wait as long as he had to. Rubbing his shoulder, which ached in the damp cold, he noticed that his hands were shaking. He was sweating and found his concentration strained. By quarter till six, his body was gripped in pain to the point of nausea. He would be of no use to anyone if he did not find relief. He was careful to keep the alley in sight as he slid into the seat of the Daimler and picked up a small black leather case. Inside lay a vial and a syringe. It was all he could do to remove them, clenching both tight at the sight of the empty vial. He was almost frantic searching through his dispatch box for another.

'Sam, where did you put it,' he rambled to himself.

Finding a fresh bottle, he thrust the needle into the clear liquid and pulled back the piston. It was not an easy task, for his hands refused to obey his commands. Exposing his arm, he searched for a thick vein and pressed the needle upward until it broke the skin. Depressing the plunger, a rush of uncomfortable warmth spread over his arm. The sensation radiated outward over his body until it engulfed him completely. Stratford sank back onto the seat and let the drug overtake him. Within minutes he felt better, though an odd sensation, stronger than he had felt before, lingered.

[52] In Eastbourne, Damon made his way across the rear yard to the house and entered the study through the French windows. He looked around for Stratford, but he was nowhere in sight. He stepped into the hall and looked one more time before bolting for the foyer closet to discard his coat, boots, and bag, making himself more comfortable before returning to the study. It was late, just past seven.

Damon walked along the hallway towards the kitchen and called for George, who appeared from around the corner to greet him.

'Is his lordship not home yet?'

'He came home, but went out again.'

'What time was that?'

'About four-thirty,' George replied, making a move to return to his duties.

'Did he say when he would be back?'

'No, sir, he did not.'

'You don't think he would mind if I had dinner now then, do you?'

'I will set a place for you in the dining room.'

George disappeared and Damon checked his watch again. Upon replacing it in his vest pocket, he made his way over to the window and drew back the curtains. It was nearly two hours before Stratford returned, coming through the front and removing his outerwear in the closet before coming entirely within. Not seeing the post on the table, Stratford called out for George, pulling the bell cord hard as he did so. George and several others of the staff hurried down the hall to see what the matter was. Even Damon stepped out to see why Stratford was in such a temper.

'George, where is the post?'

'I had left it on the hall table, my lord.'

Stratford tensed as his eyes scanned the tabletop again, secretly hoping it would not suddenly appear as if by magic before his entire staff.

'Obviously it is not there now. Therefore, we can reasonably assume someone has taken it!'

George tried to abate the situation; hoping reason would overtake Stratford before things got out of hand. 'I am sure I placed it there earlier. If you would like to retire to the study I will check to see if anyone has moved it.'

George shuffled the staff to the end of the hall and questioned them to the point of interrogation. One by one they each denied having gone near it. Damon stood in the doorway of the study, watching from a distance. Stratford was not one to make mistakes. He was a man who loathed inefficiency and negligence. To have it in his home was intolerable. Damon offered no intervention, nor assisted in embarrassing the man who had made him. Stratford's patience wore thin and he lashed out again before stepping into the study.

'I want an answer and I want it before dinner is on the table tonight.'

Stratford slammed the doors behind him, not realising that the hour for dinner had already past. As George rallied the staff, Damon stepped aside to allow passage for the judge. Seeing Stratford head to the fireplace for his pipe, Damon disappeared as quietly as he could. Finding a nice blend of tobacco to soothe his nerves, Stratford began to realise what he had done. The hour had grown late, past eight-thirty, and it would have been presumed that he took nourishment along the way, as was his customary habit on late nights. His frustration at the missing post had caused him to dismiss both the hour and the trust he had placed in his staff. Stratford tossed the match in the fireplace in disgust. Some of his staff had been with him before his daughter had been born, others since she had been a child. To call them out for so trifling a matter weighed on him. Taking a moment to clear his mind and take refuge in the soothing taste of tobacco, Stratford closed his eyes against a weary day, opening them to his protégé, who had a small bundle in his hands.

'It was in your overcoat pocket,' Damon announced calmly, setting the post on the desk with no further incrimination.

Stratford took the post with reticence, grasping at any memory of having picked it up. 'Thank you.'

The moment past, Stratford swept the matter from his mind, and began to sort through the correspondence. It was only at the sight of a small envelope swirled in delicate handwriting that his impassable disposition mellowed, melting away thoughts of weakness. He reached for the letter opener with renewed vigour, eagerly running through the tender words of warm greetings. Unable to read it without his glasses, his mood was not altered in the chore of pulling them out and settling them onto his face.

Helena opened with the very words he longed to hear, that he was missed in every corner of her heart. Reading on, her words spoke of enjoyment and discovery, but they carried with them an undertone he could not quite place in his mind. He had never witnessed it before in her writing. It left an impression of uneasiness within him, as if some event had forged an invisible wall between them, a wall not easily torn down. At the conclusion she gave notice of their arrival, taking him by surprise. They were due to arrive on Saturday by the noon train, negating any plan he had been formulating in his mind for the weekend. It would have to wait.

[53] The long majestic train of the Southern Line pulled slowly into the seaside station of Eastbourne like a proud parade. A sister city to Brighton, Eastbourne offered magnificence. The grand seaside hotels, miles of beach, and a prodigious pier offered a quiet sanctuary unlike any other place in the world. Unlike Brighton, however, Eastbourne announced its grandeur the moment you turned the bend to the station. Mustard brick walls, bright whites, yellows, and electric blues greeted its guests with open arms, welcoming them to the seaside with a myriad of indoor and outdoor shops, trinkets, coffee or tea, and uniformed coachmen. Its magnificent glass ceiling revealed the sky with enormous wonder.

It was virtually impossible to stand in proximity and feel anything but delight. People poured from the train into the welcoming arms of a team of staff waiting to tend their every need in disembarking. It was Helena's custom to be the first off the train. Today would be her father's turn to be met with the open arms and affection allowed only by her youth. Faulkner and Stoner stood by, marking the slowing of the train and waiting for the bouncing young woman to spring out of the carriage into their awaiting arms. Lord Stratford stood undemonstrative and dignified as always, a mien which opened him to sport by his juniors. He consoled himself with the fact that, among all of them, Helena would come to his arms first.

A loud hiss of steam marked the confirmed arrival of the train, with carriage doors opening and people departing spiritedly to convivial arms. The feeling of Stratford's impending embarrassment was but fleeting as the passengers departed without any sign of the energetic girl hurrying towards her father and friends. Momentary trepidation overtook him, thinking some ill fate must have befallen them, sparking him to turn in several directions to find a porter. Happily his fears were overturned by the sight of a familiar, handsomely weathered old man, pipe tucked between his lips and hands in his pockets, turning round to face the train. Next to depart was Whitmore, his beard gone, with only fashionable mutton chops remaining. He wielded a mahogany cane with a silver handle instead of his ordinary one. The changes dramatically altered his appearance, adding dignity and an air of mastery to the man.

Whitmore paused after stepping down, turning to offer a gentleman's hand, not to a child, but to an astonishingly beautiful woman wearing a close-cut gown with a large-brimmed white hat and face netting. She was a breathtaking vision of elegance, transformed from that brash young child who had left little more than a week earlier into a beautiful woman. A hint of a smile escaped Stratford's lips upon the sight of her, all grown up, more beautiful than her mother, poised with grace and elegance.

Helena stepped up to her father, coyly looking back over her shoulder at Willow and Whitmore behind her. She delicately put her hands on her father's shoulders and kissed him properly on the cheek. His slight flutter of disappointment was instantly relieved by her whispers of how much she missed him.

Turning to Stoner, who could hardly contain himself, she granted a smile and a warm verbal welcome, no longer turning away from his lustful eyes. To Faulkner she presented two distinctly different approaches. The first was to address him formally, by way of her reference to him as Mr Faulkner. The second was to give him a kiss on the cheek, much as she had done with her father, then draw away as if it meant no more than a societal greeting, appropriate for public display. Taking her father's arm, they continued on through the station to the waiting motor across the street. She sighed with contentment and held her eyes tight shut to absorb the full brunt of the moment's impact on her.

'How wonderful it is to be home!' she enthused.

She had not meant it to be amusing, but Willow and Whitmore could not help but laugh. 'Is this the same girl who only hours before had been so reluctant to leave London with all its glittering charms?' Willow said softly to himself. 'It hardly seems possible.'

The suitcases in back, they headed back to the estate with the hood of the cabriolet down and Stratford at the wheel.

[54] Back at South Lodge, Helena daintily removed her hat in the foyer and placed it gracefully on the table. She took a moment to look over the great house as if with new eyes, while Willow and Whitmore accompanied Stratford into the den to smoke. Pulling out a bag of Stratford's favourite tobacco, Willow handed it to him in recompense for the sorrow of his absence. The weary judge accepted with thanks, though more for Willow's return than the gift. He struggled a bit, as if the task of opening it were difficult. Though he made a turn to conceal it, his sluggish movements had already been noticed.

Stratford looked exhausted, which was unusual for the old lion who usually exuded strength at all times. His concerted attempts to subtly conceal his weakness only served to announce it further. He passed through dinner only lightly engaged in the conversations taking place, allowing the others to set the topic and tone. It was most unlike him, who had the tendency to dominate every tête-à-tête. After dinner, as he settled into his accustomed pose at the chess table, he did so with little enthusiasm and seemed uneasy when faced with Willow's stare.

[55] Whitmore stepped on the back patio, watching Helena rock gently in the comfort of the dying sun. He had been there but a moment when the gardener came around the side with a basket of bulbs and tools, taking to his knee on the ground just off to the side. He said nothing, but took such care with the new plants that it seemed as if he had been born to it. It was an interesting endeavour with far more involved than one might first suppose. The man first dug out the weeds and dead plants. He then took the trowel and delicately overturned the rich soil to bring it to the top for the placement of new plants. It was a long process requiring patience, and the gardener seemed to have plenty of it.

His pipe grown cold at his inattentiveness, Whitmore retrieved a box of matches from his coat pocket. At first, still lost in his thoughts, he forgot his limitations and pressed through one match after another until his full attention was engaged upon the commission. The combination of the lack of full muscle control in his hand and his agitation made the task of lighting it notably demanding. It was pitiful to behold, both from the aspect of his ailments and his fear of exposure, for it quite incapacitated him.

Coming to his aid, the gardener struck a long Lucifer and held it steady for him. So genuine was the offer that Whitmore accepted it, reaching out with his favoured hand, inadvertently exposing the pattern of scars on the weaker one, trembling at the tension.

'You have been injured!' the kind gardener exclaimed in surprised concern, though without formality, causing Whitmore to quickly withdraw his hand and place it in his pocket.

'Old wounds.' Whitmore shrugged it off. 'I have not seen you around here before.'

'I have been here, in and out, in case you needed me.'

'Me?'

'The estate.'

Whitmore found the conversation unsettling, though for no apparent reason. The tremors he usually suffered in times of distress, cold, or strain, suddenly flared up at his uneasiness. Coming to the point of intolerance, Whitmore shoved his hands deeply into his pockets, gnawing on his pipe.

'You are a chemist for Mr Porter I hear,' the gardener continued, replacing his gloves.

Whitmore took an unconscious step away. 'You are very inquisitive, for a gardener.'

'I meant no offence. Are you sure you are all right?'

Whitmore tried to control his anxiety with the cold light of reason, but he was certain that even to the most unobservant creature it could be seen that he was unduly and inexplicably afraid.

'It has been a long day and I should get back to work.'

'Quite understandable. I will leave you in peace and return to my duties. If you need anything, my name is Avondale and my room is the last door on the left in the servant's quarters.'

It was problematical, especially after recent events, for Whitmore to trust anyone, but to accost a humble gardener allowed even Whitmore to see how tense matters had become. Deciding that his unwitting paranoia had got the better of him, Whitmore resolved that there were more important issues to serve than to fear ghosts and shadows. The compounds written on Holmes's blackboard had proved difficult and flawed. In the grip of a need he did not fully understand, he turned his mind to solving them.

SESSION CASE

QUEEN'S BENCH DIVISION

LORD JUSTICE

HAROLD A. W. STRATFORD

THIRTEENTH SESSION,

HELD AT

JUSTICE HALL, IN SUSSEX COURT,

ON FRIDAY, THE 27th DAY OF OCTOBER, 1903,

AND FOLLOWING DAYS.

TAKEN IN SHORT HAND

(BY AUTHORITY OF THE CORPORATION OF THE CITY OF EASTBOURNE)

BY A. WAKEFIELD

Eastbourne :

PRINTED FOR J. H. WILLOW, BY A. WAKEFIELD,

No. 74, MEADS;

AND PUBLISHED BY G. HERBERT, COUNTY COURT

1904

[56] It was just past ten when Stratford made his way downstairs to secure the house. By eleven, however, he had not returned. Helena listened for his footfalls upon the carpet outside her door, but heard nothing. She watched the hour growing older without relief of his presence. Willow had taken the evening out at his club and was not due back until late, so when the hour approached eleven-thirty, she drew on her robe and made her way downstairs. It was quiet and dark with a draft sweeping through that chilled to the bone. It was clear not all the windows had been shut. She could see a faint glow down the hall, which told her the lamps in the drawing room had not been doused. It was on her mind to investigate when she heard a strange noise, heightening her anxiety at the eerie atmosphere, and she ran back upstairs.

Helena tapped on Whitmore's door, hoping he would still be awake. Receiving no answer, the sliver of light beneath the door coupled with her growing concern was enough for her to take the liberty of opening it. Whitmore lay half reclined against the pillows with the open Stanton file fallen against his lap. He had nodded off while studying it. Kneeling beside the bed, Helena placed a gentle hand upon his arm, stirring him from slumber. He struggled to wake as if in a fever dream, and she saw by confused expression that his mind was slow to adjust to a conscious understanding of what she was saying. The look upon her face, however, must have been unmistakable. He blinked at her and rose up on his elbow and spoke to her with concern.

'Is there trouble?'

'Father has not returned from locking up. The servants always do it, of course, but it is a ritual of his. He went down well over an hour ago to secure the downstairs and he has not come back,' she said, almost pleading with him in her tone to investigate.

'Did you go down?' he asked.

'I walked through the downstairs a little, but silly as it may seem, when I did not find him, I became frightened. There was a strange noise and it was very cold. It is silly, I'm sure.'

'Has Willow returned?'

'No, not yet, and Damon won't be back until tomorrow,' she said, now almost embarrassed at her own childish fears.

'Nothing is wrong, I promise you. I suspect he is sitting up for Willow somewhere, no doubt engrossed in a law book and totally unaware of the hour.'

Whitmore pulled back the covers and retied his robe as he drew on his slippers. He opened the top drawer to his bed table, retrieving a small revolver. The precaution unnerved Helena, but she resigned herself to say nothing of the matter, trusting him to know best.

[57] Whitmore descended the stairs with caution. He could see that parts of the downstairs were still lit, though scantily, and there was no sound at all save a peculiar tapping noise coming from a room in the middle of the hall. Taking the thorough approach, Whitmore began a search of each room, starting with the morning room, which was closest to the stairs. The room was lit only with the light afforded through the windows, which were closed and locked, though the curtains had not been drawn. There was no sign of the judge or of trouble.

Moving down the hall, he searched each room, and each time he found nothing amiss save an occasional open window, sparking his senses to stay alert. Coming to the study, Whitmore quietly checked the revolver for readiness. The distinct pronouncement of the tapping sound grew louder upon his approach, signifying his initial hypothesis was correct: the sound had originated here. Stepping inside he saw nothing immediate. His attention was drawn quickly toward the window and the source of the sound. A metal clasp to the curtain tie struck against the windowpane in the breeze.

The room was not disturbed otherwise. It was precisely as it had been left before they all retired for bed, save the undoing of the curtain. The room was cold, affording it an eerie feeling of death, accentuated by the beating of the clasp against the open window, hammering out a message of doom. The warm atmosphere of rust-coloured law books, fine burgundy leather, and the expiring fire gave off a cosy glow to light the chess table, now dissipated into a tomb of featureless shades of grey.

Whitmore hoped a gentle inquiry would settle the matter of the judge's whereabouts without alarm, and to such an end unobtrusively called to Stratford without revealing a hint of anxiety. It was the still quiet of the night that returned his call, which raised his sense of fear. Stepping to the large desk, he readied his weapon, moving around to the side to see what might lie on the floor. There was nothing. Feeling his heart release, Whitmore suddenly noticed, as he wiped his brow, that his hands were shaking.

Moving steadily toward the open window, his mind began to let go of the fear of what he might find, and in doing so, realised that something aside from the window had been out of place. The high wing-back chair, which generally sat beside Helena's desk, had been moved. It now faced the open French windows, concealing whatever it contained. The vision informed him that he had found the judge. Cautiously stepping into view, Whitmore hid the revolver from sight, though keeping it close at hand, lest there be any surprises.

'Your grace?' Whitmore questioned, for he saw at once that all was not well with his host.

Stratford looked up at him and addressed him sluggishly, as if in a fever dream. 'You ... look familiar to me,' he said, as if trying to puzzle out the problem.

'Alex? Is that you?'

'It is Myles Whitmore,' Whitmore replied, releasing the cock from the revolver and letting it drop into his dressing gown pocket.

Stratford strained to focus, but his voice came out in a sleepy manner. 'I came down for something, but somehow I seem to have forgotten what it was. It happens of late when I am taken off the subject.'

'Something distracted you? Outside, perhaps?'

'Creamed rice,' Stratford replied as if the explanation were obvious. 'Yes, that is what it was, but I have lost the desire for it now.'

Whitmore contemplated the situation for a moment as he glanced around the room for some clue to Stratford's condition. It was odd that the open window did not strike the judge's memory, almost deliberately so. Whitmore chanced to look down and noticed a tiny bottle of clear liquid next to a syringe on the table. It was obvious that it had been used. It contained the laudanum prescription Whitmore had been told he had been given after his injury. There was also a newspaper folded on the floor as if dropped from his hand as he sat melting away from reality, reeling from the drug. The paper had been turned to an article about a killing in Seaford, a pilfering of the man's wallet turned fatal at resistance.

On first inspection, the article seemed to have little to do with Stratford's condition, as he was routinely interested in crime. Stratford followed such articles intently to monitor how justice was being served in his county. It wasn't until Whitmore picked it up, when he went to help shuffle Stratford off to bed, his interest in the article was rekindled, and he granted it more significance than on first glance.

The newspaper made little of the matter, quoting the police to have believed the struggle began from behind. The bruising around the man's neck suggested an attempt on the burglar's part to strangle his victim. There were also other bruises found on his person, which the police believe were due to resistance. When the victim fought back, however, he was stabbed. It was reasonable, but Whitmore found it too much of a coincidence to the Stanton symptoms.

Taking Stratford in hand, Whitmore noticed Stratford's eyes seem tired and dark, but a closer inspection left doubt. Taking a moment to slip the vial and paper inconspicuously into his pocket, he closed the windows and directed the judge to the stairs where Helena took him over. He took care not reveal all that he had found, stating only that her father had nodded off during his rounds of the house, no doubt due to the lateness of the hour.

Seeing her on her way, Whitmore held off following, as Willow had stepped through in time enough to witness part of the scene.

As soon as Helena was out of earshot Whitmore turned to Willow. 'How long has it been going on?'

Willow took off his coat and thrust it on the table along with his hat and cane. 'I do not know what you mean,'

'The restlessness, sluggishness of mind, inability to concentrate, forgetfulness. The laudanum would explain some, but I suspect not all. What else is he taking?'

'Just what are you implying? He is a tired man, nothing more. Do not make more of this than there is, son, I beg of you. He is a busy man with a busy schedule. It would make even a young man tired. Now, it is late. Try to get some sleep.'

Willow's explanation would have been reasonable without Stratford's daughter routinely sorting through his work. She prepared and wrote most of the lengthy briefs. It was a custom Whitmore had observed for months. The old lion's health and relentless perfection had been slipping for some time, growing worse with each passing week. Though it was admirable of the family to compensate for him, it allowed them to deny the inevitable.

[58] Whitmore stood at the large French windows overlooking the garden. It had been a sleepless night. The prospect of symptoms appearing in a case as far away as Seaford, and now possibly Stratford, instantly raised the importance of Whitmore's success with his experiments. He had worked tirelessly on it all evening, using Holmes's notes in the notebook taken from Baker Street to augment his calculations, but he had hit a snag. A page had been torn from Holmes's notebook, a page containing the last portion of the solution. Though riddled with errors, the new insight provided avenues not yet considered by Whitmore.

He stood mulling over another wasted evening until he saw the gardener walking slowly about the grounds, staring intently at the grass. It was intriguing to find Avondale out on the lawn so early on a Sunday morning. More peculiar was the fact that his interest seemed confined to the area between the study patio and the lower wall. Finding the coincidence unsettling, Whitmore took the long way around to breakfast, placing himself in the path of the inquisitive gardener and his duties.

Avondale did not seem disturbed by his presence. He stood at the edge of the patio as if waiting for Whitmore to speak.

'Curious, to find a gardener working on a Sunday, on his lordship's private patio.'

'The stone,' Avondale replied, as if his meaning were self-evident.

The particular wording unsettled Whitmore, who forced himself to keep from making unwarranted associations based on fear.

'It seems to be misplaced. I'm afraid it may require a mason to fix it,' Avondale continued.

Not for the first time, Whitmore had found himself unreasonably uneasy in the presence of Avondale. Avondale continued on his way and Whitmore stood for a moment, chastising himself for his unwarranted paranoia. It bordered on compulsive obsession. For whatever reason, Whitmore found himself afraid of the gentle gardener, but he could not, for the life of him, figure out why. Turning to go into the house, Whitmore noticed depressions in the grass where someone had crossed the lawn from the far corner of the garden, and ending where that person had entered the house through the French windows. Either Stratford had a late visitor or Stratford had taken an evening stroll entirely unaware of his own actions.

Measuring the length and width of the footprint, he could tell nothing, save that the man appeared to be in no hurry. What seemed even more intriguing was that Avondale had walked the course multiple times. Whitmore had preferred to keep a distance from such matters, but in truth something disturbed him about it all. The notion seemed to reach in his imagination, filling him with that same ominous feeling he had before, in London.

Returning to the dining hall, Whitmore found Damon to have joined them. There was no mention of the evening's events. Each member of the family kept to themselves. Stratford sat dutifully with a cup of coffee, pouring over a brief, or rather staring at it, for it could not be said that he made any progress. Helena picked at her food, brushing aside most of it with an occasional glance up at her father. Willow, on the other hand, seemed unaffected, mulling over the morning paper as if all were as it should be.

Where Stratford took great offence to any incident forcing him to appear less than perfect, Whitmore found his own faults less damaging to his social agenda. His cup dropped from his hand, spilling upon his plate, causing Helena to rise from her chair within seconds of Willow's instinctive habit to attend, motioning for the others to remain as they were. It was not a bad spill, provoking more surprise than anything else.

The tense moment not yet over, a fierce knock came upon the main door, causing each to stop what they were doing. Even before George could reach the foyer the boisterous knock came again. Opening the door seemed to expose the house to a tempest. It came in the form of an older woman, her voice raised, loud enough for the company within to hear pieces of the conversation.

'Get him! Get that coward out here! Harold!'

'His grace is taking breakfast, madam,' George tried to soothe her.

'He doesn't want me to leave, I can tell you that! Get him out here or I will go to whoever I have to. I won't take no for an answer.'

Helena peered with interest at the dining room door. Stratford closed the file and took one last sip of his coffee before making his way to the source of the commotion.

[59] 'Come into the drawing room,' Stratford motioned to the woman.

'You beastly coward. You murdered him!' she spat at him, no more than inside the room.

Stratford pressed her forward and hurriedly closed the door.

'You monster! You killed him.'

'Betty,' Stratford started before being cut off.

'No, damn you! Do not play ignorant with me, Harold Stratford. I know your secret. I know what you did. David told me everything. He told me why you gave him the money, what you made him do all for the price of hope; hope that you would give him his life back. The life you stole! I told him you would never keep your promise, but he believed you. You coward! You killed him to keep him from talking.'

'What are you talking about? What is this promise you believe me to have made?'

'You lured him to that alley,' she said.

'I tell you I did no such thing. I did not meet with him.'

'Do you deny you sent him there? Because I have the proof.'

'I do not deny that we had a meeting, but he never arrived.'

'Never arrived? He was murdered in the very place you prescribed! You killed him. You murdered your friend for nothing. He would do anything for you, anything to practice law again. You took that from him.'

'He took that from himself. I did what I could.'

'You are such a coward! You monster! Even now you tremble faced with the truth.'

'I know you are grieving, but blaming me will not bring David back.'

'No, not even your mighty hand can do that. You can rob him of his livelihood, you can sentence him to live in hell, but not even you can bring him back, and for that I will see you hang.'

'Betty, I swear to you, I had no part in his death. On my honour!'

'Honour? Your honour means nothing! You cannot lie to me, Harold Stratford. I have the proof of your horrid deeds. You may have stopped him from testifying, but you cannot stop me.' She thrust a piece of paper into his chest. 'I applaud him for denying you your prize, though it cost him his life in the end. Do you hear me? I applaud him. What were you afraid of, that David would betray you? You need not have killed him for that. He loved you, even after all that you did to him; he still loved you and would never have brought harm to you or your precious career.'

Watching her as she stormed out of the house and toward the street, Stratford stood unmoved until she was out of sight. Opening the tattered blue bit of paper, Stratford read the contents, but his mind could not justify what he saw. Unable to reconcile his mind to it, Stratford walked to his desk, unlocked it, placed the paper inside, and relocked the drawer. He tucked the keys back into his pocket and returned to breakfast. No one would dare discuss the issue with him save some cursory questions he would naturally stave off answering. One man alone could be so bold as to open the matter for discussion and he would only do so in his own time.

[60] Outside, Whitmore placed his right hand on the starting handle of the Vauxhall and his left on the bonnet. Helena turned on the petrol tap, admitting a measured quantity of fuel into the carburetor and gave a nod. Whitmore pulled the handle sharply upwards. There was a chirping sputter to the start, but it was taken over by a smooth purr. Whitmore stepped away at the smooth chunking of the engine, turning his head toward the street as he came around the side only to note that they were being watched. A carriage passed only for a

moment, but in that time the spectator had vanished without giving away a clear image of him.

Continuing on their way, Whitmore took care to look diligently for any hint of the man. Failing to see any signs of him, he turned back to the road, but never once allowed himself to relax. He had suspected they had been followed in London, but he had not thought they would have been followed home.

Had his little stratagem inadvertently brought the killers to their door? It had not been his intent. Like the young lady, Whitmore had gambled that a small peek into a nagging question would do no harm, forgetting his own words and advice. There was, too, that growing question in his mind, a hint of doubt that all had transpired as it had been told that fateful night upon the`South Downs. One thing was for certain: the man following them was no amateur. It posed several questions of which he could not be sure of the answers. A cold chill ran through his bones at the thought. Helena had gone alone to Baker Street at first, and he could not be sure, even at her word, that she did not attempt to look into the matter further after their discussion. She had insisted that she hadn't been observed, but a lawyer was no detective or even an observant scientist.

Once ensconced in his dark world in the basement laboratory, Whitmore tried to put the incident from his mind. He sat before the myriad of chemicals and experiments in process, the light pouring in through the one upper window, highlighting the dust partials in the air as if tiny angels were dancing their way from heaven to earth in a dusty attic. He stared through the individual colours of various liquids and effects without conscious awareness of their reactions. His mind sifted through the events of the prior evening with scrutiny, trying to decipher their meaning. Stratford was a strong man, not only in bearing, but in influence. He maintained control of every situation, from the flowers planted in his garden to the lives of those who came pitifully before him, seeking mercy. No pebble upon the beach or speck of dust settled in its path without his command.

Yet, to see him seated helplessly in the chair, staring out the window like some mindless creature of incompetence, spoke clearly of the power he once so masterfully commanded slipping from his fingers like grains of sand, exacerbated by the powerful accusations made by a determined woman. The cause could only be speculated, but the effects were cumulative. Even his own daughter had begun to pass beyond his control, to what extent could only be conjectured.

Reaching into his coat pocket for the vial retrieved from Stratford's table, Whitmore opened a bottle of solvent before him and poured it into a large beaker. He added in turn one element after another, noting the reactions.

At long last, Whitmore withered back in his chair at the answer to the solution in the vial, confounded by the significance of the implications. It would take another day or two to solidify confirmation, but it was enough to render an opinion. The vial of laudanum was diluted with a sixty percent solution of cocaine. Relaxing his shoulders, he resigned himself to the fact that no more answers could be had for the rest of the day. The knowledge that Stratford's prescription of laudanum had been tainted weighed upon his shoulders. It would not do to approach the judge on the matter, for if the cocaine had not been added with malice, it would impose upon the man's privacy and perhaps his own private shame. Such an intrusion would be too bold. Even approaching the matter would suggest foreknowledge and thus be an insult. All he could do was watch and wait. Concerning him greater still was the article of the slain man in Seaford, which contributed to the judge's condition. With little details it would be quite impossible to make a firm connection, but it never strayed far from his mind. The symptoms were too similar to the all-consuming problem that had been perplexing him for weeks.

Trying to focus his mind on the problems at hand, he found himself continually diverted by the article found at Stratford's feet. The pattern of the victim's bruising bore a striking resemblance to the bruising Mrs Stanton had sustained in the initial days of her confinement. The doctors and chemists could find no cause for it, crediting it to the injuries the woman had sustained at her husband's hands, but Whitmore was unconvinced. The bruising bore no resemblance to fists or objects, but rather a pattern formed from the inside out. It was impossible to derive anything without data. Speculation would not help the unfortunate woman prostrate above, and neither would it answer the nagging question of why Stratford had taken the matter of the Seaford victim so hard. A walk was, without a doubt, most necessary for the brain, as well as the nerves.

Stopping at the newsstand, Whitmore purchased every newspaper that might carry mention of the crime. Finding the day a pleasant one, he sat down on a bench facing the shore and flipped through the individual papers looking for any piece to the puzzle. Surprisingly, the widespread mention of the murder the evening before was now remarkably suppressed. The few papers carrying the story stated less than the original. The article in the local paper about the murdered man in Seaford was frustratingly vague and general, but it was obvious in its lack of mention of the swollen and bruised membranes described in the previous article.

An unsettling thought gave rise to great concern. There was a disturbing coincidence between the suppressed information about the murder and Mrs Malone's accusations. However, speculation without evidence gave way to tricks of the mind. If Stratford were somehow involved, it would not do to ignore such facts. If he were in trouble, tied within a web he could not free himself, ignorance and time would be too great an enemy. It was not good. Some answers had to be had, if no more than to know how deeply his host was involved in the matter. Thrusting the papers into the trash on his way, Whitmore hailed a hansom to the station.

SESSION CASE

QUEEN'S BENCH DIVISION

LORD JUSTICE

HAROLD A. W. STRATFORD

FOURTEENTH SESSION,

HELD AT

JUSTICE HALL, IN SUSSEX COURT,

ON FRIDAY, THE 27th DAY OF OCTOBER, 1903,

AND FOLLOWING DAYS.

TAKEN IN SHORT HAND

(BY AUTHORITY OF THE CORPORATION OF THE CITY OF EASTBOURNE)

BY A. WAKEFIELD

Eastbourne:

PRINTED FOR J. H. WILLOW, BY A. WAKEFIELD,

No. 74, MEADS;

AND PUBLISHED BY G. HERBERT, COUNTY COURT

1904

[61] Opening the door to the long narrow corridor of the Seaford hospital laboratory and morgue, Whitmore followed the white tiled wall to the closed room at the end, past various laboratories and closets. It was not unlike the dimly lit halls and dark doors with opaque glass of his laboratory. The intermittent carpet, thin upon the hardwood floors, did little to muffle the sound of his boots against the flooring, which seemed to disturb the quiet. A discoloured metal plaque, screwed into the door panel, informed him that he had arrived. The prospect of seeing dead bodies scarcely made an impression on him, yet he harboured a sense of foreboding about his visit that caused him to hesitate at the door. Grasping the handle, he entertained the idea that his imagination had overwhelmed him, for the handle itself seemed to convey the chill of death. Steeling himself, he turned the knob and entered, finding only a young man with an apron sweeping the floors.

He exhaled with relief and looked about the room. Two long wooden tables stretched forth before him, with trays of instruments and large jars at the head. The gas jets afforded a dim view of the various paraphernalia about the room, but it was not for its provisions he had come. Glancing around the room, he saw no body in evidence and felt his hope for an answer retreat.

'May I help you?' a dusty little voice accompanying a thin frame and wire-rimmed glasses asked, scrutinizing his guest as he leaned heavily on the broom handle.

'My name is Myles Whitmore. I am looking for the coroner.'

'That would be Dr Forbes,' the young man answered, returning to his duties with the broom. 'He's not here. If you leave your name and address we'll send someone around to collect the remains.'

'No!' Whitmore quickly tried to correct him with a wave of his hand. 'I am in no need of his services, not in that way. I have come about an autopsy recently performed on Mr David Malone.'

The name seemed to strike a familiar note, causing the man to again stop his duties to review Whitmore with a sense of curiosity.

'What is your interest?' he asked.

'There was mention of unusual bruising on the body. I was hoping to view the corpse before it was removed and possibly acquire samples of blood and tissue for analysis in reference to another case

I am reviewing. May I presume you are Dr Forbes's associate? I see you are completing reports for him.'

'No. Not that he would notice anyway.' The young man shied away with a smile at the compliment. 'I just clean up around here and finish off the reports he leaves unfinished, which is most of them. You won't find Dr Forbes here often. After lunch he seats himself at The Red Lion around the corner and doesn't stagger back usually until ten o'clock the next morning.'

'Then I trust you handle most of the preliminaries? Would you happen to know what was determined to have caused the phenomena?'

The young man set down his broom and walked over to a large filing cabinet.

'My name is Daniel Trevor,' he said as he sifted through various names on the folders, removing one marked 'MAL647'. He drew back towards the autopsy tables and laid the folder open for inspection.

'Dr Forbes made a preliminary exam, noting the odd bruising, but he said it wasn't worth doing a full autopsy. He felt the cause of death was obvious. The man was stabbed and death was a result of a loss of blood. But he was wrong.'

Whitmore shuffled through the file, noting that there were additional notes written in another hand.

'Are these your notations? They are quite impressive.'

'I wrote them, but they are not my findings. I just took dictation. I would lose my situation if I ever dared to correct the doctor's work, but they're not Forbes's either. Yesterday a man shows up and asks to examine the body. Forbes turns him away, tells him the autopsy is already done. Next thing I know the man hands him a note and Forbes turns over the body. He wasn't happy. After the man left, he went round to the Inn and hasn't come back.'

'What time was this?'

'I don't remember the exact time, but it was early, nearly first thing. This man'—Daniel paused in residual amazement—'he was amazing. The man took one look at the report and knew right away that Forbes had not looked at the body. The man gave Forbes a disgusted look and took a magnifying glass from his pocket. He examined the mouth, nose, and ears first. He was interested in the same as you, the bruising. He grabs me and has me assist him. Forbes didn't like it much, but it was the first time I was able to earn my wages around here. Then he started recounting his findings like no professional I had ever seen, telling me to take notes. He observed not only the bruising and swelling, but vascular haemorrhaging inside of the various cavities. We never would have even thought to look.'

Daniel continued with an air of excitability tinged with admiration, 'This man examined the man's hair follicles, fingernails, and eyelids. He examined the man's feet! I never saw anyone examine a man's feet before, not unless they were disgusting or torn off or something. He examined the wound and asked Forbes what it was he was thinking when he declared the stab wound to be cause of death. He said the man could not have died from the wound because the blade wasn't long enough. The incision was no more than a few centimetres, the length of a small pocketknife, traversing no vital organs or capillaries. He said the placement of the wound suggested the assailant was unfamiliar with how to kill a man, which left the question of why he died.'

'Was this man a policeman or medical examiner?'

'No policeman I've ever seen. He used a scalpel to cut around the wound, pulling away the fat and tissue to prove the depth and damage. I would have marked him a medical man, except his knowledge of post-mortem diagnosis was exceeded only by his knowledge of crime. He recounted the murder as if he were there! I tell you, the man made it all sound so simple, a child could have figured it out. Malone was definitely murdered.'

Whitmore studied the report as Daniel recounted the incident, finding scattered notes rushed through as if in afterthought, putting it down only at Daniel's next statement.

'Do you want to see the body?'

Whitmore stood bolt upright. 'I thought the body gone by now.'

'It's behind you.' Daniel smiled proudly. 'The cabinet behind you near the door is a large ice chest, room enough for two bodies,' he said, explaining both the temperature of the door handle and the conspicuously empty autopsy tables.

Daniel moved the trolley over to the cabinet, motioning for some assistance, and revealed the bluish-grey cadaver within a whirl of fog teeming out of the open doors. Pulling the body onto the gurney, Daniel quickly closed the doors and wheeled Malone under the light.

'I was told that if a man came to examine the body looking for the same thing he was, I was to turn it over to him and give him anything he asked. When you walked in and asked to see what he asked for, well, I guess you'd be him then, wouldn't you?'

The notion struck Whitmore as supremely odd. Seeing the oddly formed swelling and bruising around the mouth, lips, nose, and parts of the eyelids, Whitmore retrieved a magnifying glass from the chemical table and examined the bruising carefully. Under close examination the haemorrhaging was visible, following similar, though more extreme, patterns as Mrs Stanton. It was difficult to conceive of how a man could walk freely about with such damage without being ordered directly to doctor by his wife. Only one hypothetical explanation came to mind, and he requested extractors from Daniel to open the wound. Holding skin and muscle apart, Whitmore examined the area of the wound finding something not noted in the autopsy report or Daniel's account. The deepest point of the incision seemed to be massively bruised, haemorrhaged, and damaged, to the point where he was hard pressed to explain the cause. Confirming that no mention was made of the massive devastation, Whitmore retrieved a jar from table and took samples of the affected area.

'This man who visited the body, did he give his name?'

'It must have been on the paper, but I didn't see it.'

'And he wasn't a physician?'

'He made no claim to it, but for the life of me I tell you he was better than any physician I had ever seen. He referenced everything as if it was a criminal investigation, but he acted as if he had knowledge of medicine, at least enough to examine bodies. This man was astonishingly thorough and precise. No policeman I ever knew used a magnifying glass to look in a man's mouth, or possessed the skill to use a scalpel in dissection like he did. I don't know who this man was, but he was good.'

A remote and unfathomable thought traversed Whitmore's mind, causing an internal chuckle at the impossibility of the idea. There was only one man ever reported to possess such powers, and ghosts did not have a penchant for performing autopsies.

'He didn't happen to have a sinewy forearm, all dotted and scarred with innumerable puncture marks, did he?'

The reference eluded the young assistant, who responded with a bemused look and a nod, taking care to place the body back in its frozen cabinet. 'I beg your pardon?'

'It is nothing.'

The whole of the matter did not settle well in Whitmore's mind, and he bit off a sarcastic comment just short of it leaving his mouth. With a well-placed compliment to the young man's attentiveness, they parted favourably, although Whitmore was left questioning impossibilities in his mind. He had obtained what he had come for, but in the doing had discovered more questions which begged to be answered.

[62] Whitmore returned swiftly to the station, but found that he had just missed the outgoing train, making his return time well past tea. He paced the outboard platform looking at his watch, glancing up occasionally at the local map displayed behind a pane of glass. Curiosity, if nothing else, prompted him to mark out where High Street was located in reference to his current position. It would have nothing to do with his experiments, nor would it solve the complexity of the unknown equation. Still, it was not devoid of interest. It could explain certain aspects of how the poison had been delivered.

Just the very thought caused a wave of nausea that forced him to find a bench on which to rest. His head rested on his hands as he leaned heavily on his cane, Whitmore beat the message home. Trying to reason it out, he knew it was his own brain rebelling against whatever force had brought him to his fate, yet knowing the reason did not seem to quell the effects. The answers were on High Street, possibly the answer as to how Mr Malone came by the undetected poison before his demise. Had he ingested something at the Inn or had it been slower to fruition? All answers lay out there, on High Street. Whatever he might find within the fluid and tissue samples in the jar, it would not explain the reasoning behind it. Forcing himself to brave the journey, Whitmore pressed on to High Street.

The Red Lion public house was nestled in an alcove in Pelham Yard, just off High Street. It was a quaint little place set back from the main road. Around back was a delivery entrance, cornered off by buildings and brush. It was just visible from the road. Whitmore walked over the area, first along High Street turning onto Pelham Yard, and Pelham Yard to South Street, confirming that there were very few places one could be assured of complete privacy.

The ground was soft, not like the cobblestone around front. Even after days there were faint traces of footfalls and disturbed dust. There was nothing obviously chemical which could have caused Malone's wound to become tainted, or anything on the ground that might have tainted something sharp, which might have inflicted the wound. A brownish stain, which he took to be Malone's blood, told of the man's fall with no other markings for several meters. It would have been in the evening, before dusk, when Malone had met his end. There were no signs of scuff marks to suggest Malone had been dragged to the centre of the lane. Therefore he must have walked willingly, either to wait for someone or to meet someone already there. There was evidence that several men had walked about the alley since then, but two distinct sets of footprints stood out above the rest. One seemed to wander aimlessly, settling along the wall where he had obviously stood for some time, for there was a pile of ash and several cigarette butts. The other set of footprints, however, seemed very deliberate in nature.

The footfalls seem to have started at the entrance of the alley, moved toward the centre where the stain was found, and then moved off toward the wall. Staring at them for some time, Whitmore forced his mind to connect the pieces of the puzzle. Unable to see the connection, he searched his pockets for a pair of reading spectacles and crouched on the ground, using the lens to magnify the bloodstains, first the small spattering, then the larger pool, and finally back to the spattering. The blood had been scraped from the ground and disturbed with the tip of a sharp knife, as if someone was examining it. Embedded within the dried blood were stands of brown and silver hair, and evidence of another small scraping of the blood with the tip of a sharp implement. It was clear that whoever had investigated the crime knew what they were doing.

Whitmore took out a bit of paper from his inner pocket and placed a few strands of bloody hair into the fold. There was nothing more he could learn and the hour grew late. His presence would certainly be missed at home and he did not feel like offering an explanation.

Whitmore tucked the paper back into his pocket and walked toward South Street, away from the scene. Chancing to look left he noticed something peculiar. A small pathway led between the buildings. The ground was littered with footprints, but not along the path; they were along the width, as if someone had been pacing. Comparing his own boot to the new prints, the man was slightly smaller in size than Whitmore and he had had a clear view of the murder. If he was a witness he certainly wasn't eager to share what he knew with the police. If he wasn't, who was he?

[63] The train was quiet, almost soothing in its rhythmic tapping of the rails, offering Whitmore a chance to lean his head back and rest. It was an interesting little problem, bringing him back to a notion he had conceived previously. It now seemed apparent that someone was investigating the Malone case with singular gifts in the art of observation and deduction. It was also entirely possible that it was the same man who had been looking into the Holmes case in the beginning, forcing a conclusion that the two cases were somehow related. He could not help but wonder if his conclusions in London were right and that the mysterious investigator was now closing in.

The opening of the compartment door broke his concentration, causing Whitmore to look up at the old withered man entering midway through the stops, taking a seat opposite him. He walked with his back slouched with age and a large shawl over his shoulders, covering threadbare clothes. His floppy hat covered part of his face, but as he looked up at Whitmore, the man's careworn wrinkles and matted silver hair spoke of a hard life.

In his tired state, Whitmore found himself studying the figure before him, finding the exercise of unfathomable interest and stimulation. Perhaps the most interesting feature of the man was his hands, for though his face was finely aged and tired, his hands seemed smooth and strong; they were not young, but not as leathery as the man himself. Whitmore remained quiet, looking out the compartment window from time to time, not overtly looking at the man sharing his journey. The countryside did not seem to interest the old fellow any more than the book in his right-hand overcoat pocket.

At the Lewes stop the man stayed on, joined by a young man in his twenties with a newspaper. He was of decidedly less interest, though the old man eyed him intently for some time, watching him until he departed at the next stop. Along the last leg of the journey the old gentleman spoke.

'Travelling to the seaside?' the old man asked.

'Is that where you are headed?' Whitmore returned, refusing to grant a morsel of information.

'Checking up on an old friend. I've not seen him in a while and thought I would check in on him. He had some trouble getting on last year so I check in on him from time to time. And you?'

'On my way home.'

'Eastbourne is a nice place to live. It's very quiet and restful there.'

An uneasy feeling swept over Whitmore. He gave a pleasant nod in agreement, but there was something about the innocuous statement that bothered him. He leaned back in his seat for the rest of the journey and tried to put it from his mind, returning his thoughts to the alley behind the Red Lion public house. The growing evidence began to form a picture quite unlike that which had been painted for the public eye. One thought permeated Whitmore's mind, that all was not as it appeared to be. The key players in the unfolding drama kept to the shadows, striking unseen and at will for reasons unknown. Whitmore believed one man held the answers, like a puppet master, intimately aware of the movement of every string.

Watching the shadowy exterior begin to illuminate with the upcoming stop, Whitmore knew they were pulling into the brightly coloured Eastbourne station. It would welcome him with open arms, whether he cared to look or not. Collecting his samples from beside him, Whitmore opened the carriage door and made his way down the platform to the gatehouse, where the porter called him a cab. He had to get the samples to the lab and begin some preliminary examinations at the very least. A note sent round to Willow would keep the hounds from his door for a few hours. Willow was categorical on that point. If he could not instantly reach out to his family, the entire world would be sent in search of them. At that thought Whitmore suddenly felt a sense of secure satisfaction. Whoever or whatever he had been in his previous life, there were now people at home who would move heaven and earth to see him safe, back in the safety of the estate once more.

SESSION CASE

QUEEN'S BENCH DIVISION

LORD JUSTICE

HAROLD A. W. STRATFORD

FIFTEENTH SESSION,

HELD AT

JUSTICE HALL, IN SUSSEX COURT,

ON FRIDAY, THE 27th DAY OF OCTOBER, 1903,

AND FOLLOWING DAYS.

TAKEN IN SHORT HAND

(BY AUTHORITY OF THE CORPORATION OF THE CITY OF EASTBOURNE)

BY A. WAKEFIELD

Eastbourne :

PRINTED FOR J. H. WILLOW, BY A. WAKEFIELD,

No. 74, MEADS;

AND PUBLISHED BY G. HERBERT, COUNTY COURT

1904

[64] Whitmore dropped the samples at the laboratory and returned to South Lodge. He entered through the back and made his way along the corridor, minding the placement of every member of the household as he went. In the foyer, Whitmore looked around again. If his next actions were ever discovered it would not go well for him. The task would necessitate a breach of trust, but there was no other way. Whitmore opened the closet door and sifted through the contents, examining each individual coat for a match to the hairs found in Seaford. There was nothing. Most of the coats had been removed. Closing the door, he tried to think of where else they might be. When George appeared from a servant's door, Whitmore stopped him.

'George, I had a heavier coat in the hall closet. You wouldn't happen to know what became of it, would you?'

'The winter coats were put away, sir.'

'Have they been cleaned? I'm looking for the key to a drawer at work. I was wearing my winter coat the last time I thought I had it.'

'I believe only Mr Willow's winter garments have been sent out for cleaning thus far. Yours were placed in the armoire upstairs. Would you like me to retrieve it for you?'

'No, I'm sure I can find it.'

'Very good, sir.'

Whitmore waited until George had rounded the corner before pressing on upstairs. He took great care to proceed unseen into Stratford's room. Once inside he closed the door and looked around.

The room was adorned in dark woods, greens, and tans. The bed was thick and high with hunter green velvet curtains trimmed in delicate lines of gold. It was no surprise to see Pritchard's Law sitting on Stratford's reading table or its large cumbersome concordance. A maroon leather Bible lay tucked on the shelf below, well thumbed. His judicial robes hung on a fine mahogany rack in the corner and his wig neatly on its stand. A butler's hanger sat at the foot of the bed, awaiting his clothes for the night.

In the wardrobe a selection of conservative, well-pressed suits hung evenly spaced. His shoes were shined and symmetrically placed along the bottom. Sweaters were perfectly folded in the bottom drawer with socks and undergarments folded like new in the upper. Everything about his armoire, like his room, was arranged with perfection. Whitmore pushed aside the suits and shirts to the coats near the back. There, hung first in line, was a brown and silver sable overcoat.

His heart broke at the sight. On the bottom edge, barely visible, easily overlooked by anyone not looking for it, was a brownish stain. The stain was too old to determine for a fact that it was blood, but its general proximity and the matching hairs suggested that it was. Whitmore trimmed the edges with a pair of nail clippers where the substance had been thickest. Hesitant to press further, Whitmore started to close the door, but stopped short. Gathering his courage, he returned to the coat once more and rifled through the pockets and lining. There, tucked away in the left pocket, was a small knife. It did not take the aid of a glass to see the brownish substance on the blade was dried blood. Yet even as he struggled against the obvious clues he was careful not to leap to conclusions. He returned everything to where it was and placed the sample in an envelope. He placed it in his pocket, collected himself, and stepped out into the hall, closing the door after him.

Whitmore turned around to an unexpected face. 'What are you doing?' Willow asked.

'I was looking for the judge.'

Willow wavered at the answer, but said nothing about it. 'He's downstairs.'

[65] After Whitmore departed, Willow stepped inside Stratford's room and looked around for a moment, trying to ascertain why Whitmore had been inside. Seeing nothing amiss, he closed the door behind him, motioning for Nigel as he came out of Damon's room with a bundle of laundry.

'Nigel, do you know what Mr Whitmore was doing up here just now?'

'No, sir. I was unaware he was at home.'

Willow glanced back at Stratford's room and then put his arm around Nigel's shoulders, turning him towards the back stair.

'I want you to oversee Mr Whitmore's care from now on. I want to know what he is doing, but from a distance. I want to know where he goes and what he is working on.'

Nigel gave a nod of understanding and disappeared through the servant's door.

[66] It was a solemn task Whitmore had set for himself, but he had to know if Stratford was involved. His first task, which was no small feat, was to devise a conclusive, indiscriminate test for haemoglobin. Theoretically it could be done, but no one had actually published work upon the subject. By his watch it was already past five. Though it would not be dark for a few more hours, Whitmore made his way briskly back to the laboratory, fondling the envelope in his pocket. There were a handful of overachievers left, but they seemed to have stayed more for company and conversation than work. Whitmore glanced at Porter as he passed his workbench, noting the disappointed expression on the older man's face. He had been letting down his side. A month earlier he had been Porter's best man. In recent days, however, he had become obsessed with the Stanton case, pouring over it day and night without relief. He might still have been seen as an asset if Porter had felt the work would yield a cure, but doctors and chemists both had failed on that front. Whitmore watched as Porter shut down the last lamp and shuffled off the last man.

'Good night Dr Porter,' Whitmore offered.

The chemist gave him a curt nod and closed the door behind him

Whitmore turned up the gas and retrieved the envelope from his pocket. It would be some time before he could test it, but it would not do to have it found on his person. He looked at it for a moment or two, contemplating the task ahead, and then locked it away in his drawer. Slipping a cold beaker of coffee onto the open flame, he got to work. Removing the Malone samples he had put away, Whitmore extracted a small sample and placed it in a test tube. Adding various elements before he placed it on a low flame, he then pulled out several sheets of paper and a pencil.

By seven he had formulated his first draft on the theoretical compounds needed to perform an age-indiscriminate test and had set up four samples of blood and tissue. Finally ready to begin, Whitmore turned up the flame on the burner and sat down. He sliced a small portion of tissue and dropped it into the liquid over the flame and then a thinner slice onto a slide. His focus was so great that even the gentle caress of Helena's delicate hand did not divert him.

'I brought you supper.'

To Helena his silence invoked a sense of insecurity and doubt new to her. He had turned dedication into obsession, forgetting about her and the family who had come to care for him. It was a side to him she had never seen and wasn't wholly sure she cared for.

'Is that still the Stanton case? Have you made any progress?'

All attempts to invoke even the smallest response were met with cold indifference. Helena put down the basket and turned away.

'I'll leave your supper on the table.'

[67] Hearing her close the door between them, Whitmore paused briefly at the distraction and then returned to work. It would be hours, if not a day or two, before there would be any results, and so he picked up the file and began again. By the eleventh hour, Whitmore turned down the burner's flame and poured a sample of the clear liquid into a test tube. Holding the pipette steadily over the opening, he carefully measured out three drops and then poured the solution into a cultured Petri dish. His task completed, Whitmore covered the dish and waited, drawing a blanket over him as he lay down on the cot for the night.

SESSION CASE

QUEEN'S BENCH DIVISION

LORD JUSTICE

HAROLD A. W. STRATFORD

SIXTEENTH SESSION,

HELD AT

JUSTICE HALL, IN SUSSEX COURT,

ON FRIDAY, THE 27th DAY OF OCTOBER, 1903,

AND FOLLOWING DAYS.

TAKEN IN SHORT HAND

(BY AUTHORITY OF THE CORPORATION OF THE CITY OF EASTBOURNE)

BY A. WAKEFIELD

Eastbourne :

PRINTED FOR J. H. WILLOW, BY A. WAKEFIELD,

No. 74, MEADS;

AND PUBLISHED BY G. HERBERT, COUNTY COURT

1904

[68] After days of experimentation Whitmore had solved the problem and was eager to test his hypothesis. He pricked his finger, drawing a fresh sample to analyse. The test was positive. Taking a sample of his own blood upon a cloth he had prepared earlier and he ran a comparison. It was a perfect conclusive match. Not allowing fatigue to dissuade him, Whitmore placed a few strands of the matted coat fibres into the solution and began his distillation. A cloudy liquid collected in the flask, then clarified. Whitmore released an unsteady breath. The test had proved out. It was a devastating find, but hardly proved that the judge was a murderer.

The blood could have come from any source. To prove the blood on the coat came from Malone he would need a blood type, which could be had if Malone had been sampled at any point by hospital staff. Porter kept records dating back years. His system of recordkeeping was first rate, allowing for any patient's records to be retrieved in a matter of minutes, and Malone was no exception. Retrieving it from the drawer, one glance confirmed the findings. Yet, even in the face of cold fact, Whitmore was unwilling to face the answer. As he started to close the drawer his eyes rested upon another file, this one for Stratford. Whitmore paused a moment for strength then he forced it open.

The file revealed a light scattering of notes and tests, surprisingly few for a lifetime. However, the large cluster showed a recent trauma over the past year, stemming from a badly broken shoulder, collarbone, and two upper ribs. An order of morphine had been prescribed by the doctor at hand, and later laudanum was prescribed to replace the heavy doses of morphine. Skimming down the list of dates and tests, Whitmore stopped short at the last entry before snapping the file shut. He drifted over to table and turned off the burner, dragging his weary body over to the cot. It was with deep regret of the wasted day that Whitmore drew the covers up over him and shut his eyes again.

The problem swirled around in his brain until after only a few hours he sloughed back to the table and pressed on. He pored over the bubbling mixture of chemicals and solutions until he no longer required the lamp for a primary source of light. He stretched forth his hand for the sickening thick brownish concoction at the other end of the table and put it to his lips. Over-brewed and lukewarm, the bitter coffee still granted the much-needed fortification required for his concentration. Before he could put the murky container to his lips again, a hand took the cup and replaced it with a fresh one.

Porter glanced over what Whitmore had scribbled down throughout the night, giving a nod of interest. He did not need to ask if Whitmore slept, for the messed cot and his dishevelled state spoke of a few hours here and there, but nothing sufficient. Porter had come to know him well enough not to insist on rest, for Whitmore had a unique power of focus and dedication, and Porter admired it, although with less than total approval.

Porter took an ungracious stance at the wreck before him, unimpressed at the amount of progress for such dedication. 'What is it this time, Stanton's stool samples, a discussion of rigor mortis, or a cure for meningitis?'

'There is no cure for meningitis,' Whitmore returned. 'However, I did manage to improve on the detection of mature bloodstains. The test is now age-indiscriminate.'

'Age-indiscriminate,' Porter echoed. 'Can I take a look?'

Whitmore struggled to his feet, hobbling to the desk where he had left his notes. Handing them to Porter, he sipped at the refreshing coffee and eagerly awaited Porter's opinion.

'Not bad, but what can it be used for? With the amount of time you have been spending here I would have thought you had cured half the diseases in Sussex.'

The less than enthusiastic response did not sit well with the overtired chemist, who snapped back the file.

'Do you understand that we can now clearly determine whether the substance is coffee or blood, and that distinction can save a man or convict him?'

'You've spent too much time in that house up there.' Porter came back, refreshing his coffee. 'I know his lordship has a job to do, but so do we. We haven't been idle all this time. Stanton cannot be cured. Whatever she came into contact with has dissipated in her bloodstream and we cannot isolate it. There is no evidence that someone poisoned her or that a crime has been committed. Put it aside and help us treat the ones we can still cure. You're a fair chemist and I would be lying if I led you to believe we don't need the help. Now go get some sleep. We'll talk tomorrow.'

Porter clearly was not about to let the matter go, as he picked up Whitmore's coat and handed it to him. Seeing he had no alternative, Whitmore slipped on his coat and made his way out into the warm blue day.

[69] Glancing at a bit of paper he had hidden away in his pocket, Whitmore checked the address and headed to Bourne Street. Standing at the foot of the stairs, Whitmore paused to outline in his mind what he would say, and then made his way to the dull grey door with a tarnished brass knocker. Several raps upon it brought an elderly gentleman in a cardigan sweater to the door, opening it with a less than enthusiastic welcome. His face was careworn with dark circles under his eyes, suggesting he had not been sleeping well. His gruff demeanour reflected his state of exhaustion and sense of guilt, confirmed by the distinct odour of gin.

Virgil Stanton wrapped the cardigan tight around him, looking suspiciously at Whitmore. 'What do you want?'

'I wish to speak with you about your wife's condition,' Whitmore opened bluntly.

'Who are you?'

'My name is Myles Whitmore. I am a chemist at hospital laboratory. I have taken over your wife's case.'

The man stared for a moment or two, as if sizing up the stature of the man leaning heavily upon a black wooden cane with a silver handle, marking him no ordinary chemist. He took a breath, as though he were about to say something, and then replaced it with a simple, 'Go away,' moving to close the door.

'I do not believe the poisoning was deliberate,' Whitmore quickly put forth, causing the door to suddenly stop in its path. 'If I had a sample of the poison, I am sure I could find a cure.'

The old gentleman opened the door, retreating within with no more invitation than that. Stepping inside, Whitmore closed the door and followed him inside, where a short foyer opened into a dimly lit sitting room with drawn curtains. It was remarkably clean and well kept with every piece of furniture neatly arranged in perfect order.

Even the pictures on the mantel were dusted and straight. Stanton showed Whitmore to a chair by the fireplace and then proceeded to disappear into the kitchen to tend a boiling teakettle. A few minutes later he returned with a tray of tea and biscuits. Whitmore took the cup out of courtesy but held it in his hands the whole of the time.

'There is no cure,' Stanton finally said.

'I have rarely found a substance that could not be counteracted. Perhaps if I knew how she had come by the poison,' Whitmore led him, receiving nothing in reply. 'I see you have an apothecary shop downstairs. Might she have come by an unusual mixture of some sort? I beg of you, Mr Stanton, for the love your wife, please help me to find the answers.'

'You are John Willow's boy, aren't you?' he asked. A relaxed look momentarily overtook his face at some undisclosed thought, but quickly reverted to his former expression. 'I think it is time you left, Mr Whitmore. I regret I cannot help you.'

'Why do you persist in hiding the truth when it can only harm your good wife? I know you love her. You sit with her every day. I also know you have been trying to cure her yourself.' He had gained the full attention of his host. 'The needle marks on her arm, you put them there in an attempt to cure her. I believe we can cure her, but not the way you are attempting it. You need my help. Tell me what it was that caused her condition!'

'I can tell you nothing,' Stanton insisted, 'for I know nothing.'

'You cannot find the antidote alone.'

Stanton stood up and motioned toward the door. 'I regret to cut this interview short, Mr Whitmore, but I am a very busy man.'

Unable to move him, Whitmore made a bold attempt to bluff his way into information. 'I have seen this chemical compound derivation before. Sherlock Holmes came to me before he died. I am in possession of his notes and have been working on it. I am quite confident, if I had a small sample of the extract, I could find an antidote.'

For a moment or two, at the mention of the name, Stanton looked as if he were going to speak, but in the end would not relent. 'Please see me no more,' Stanton persisted, gesturing toward the door again.

Whitmore could see there was a distinct suggestion of fear in the man's posture. 'Your life is in danger? From whom?'

'I really am exceedingly busy, sir,' Stanton insisted, holding open the door.

Without the actual substance, Whitmore could do little but attempt to continue on with his experiments on Malone's tissues and the woman's blood, trying to isolate the individual elements, but there was more to the case than Stanton being unwilling to help his own wife. He clearly loved her, which left the resounding question of why he would not do all he could to help her. What could possibly overshadow such a love? Only one thing came to mind, a name he could not bring himself to speak for the sorrow of it.

SESSION CASE

QUEEN'S BENCH DIVISION

LORD JUSTICE

HAROLD A. W. STRATFORD

SEVENTEENTH SESSION,

HELD AT

JUSTICE HALL, IN SUSSEX COURT,

ON FRIDAY, THE 27th DAY OF OCTOBER, 1903,

AND FOLLOWING DAYS.

TAKEN IN SHORT HAND

(BY AUTHORITY OF THE CORPORATION OF THE CITY OF EASTBOURNE)

BY A. WAKEFIELD

Eastbourne :

PRINTED FOR J. H. WILLOW, BY A. WAKEFIELD,

No. 74, MEADS;

AND PUBLISHED BY G. HERBERT, COUNTY COURT

1904

[70] At South Lodge, a friendly game of billiards began to wind down as the hour grew late. Faulkner put up his cue. The laughter and the pleasant conversation were amusing and distracting, but in truth it was designed for one purpose and one purpose only, to wait for Helena's return to the house. The barrage of legal interpretation, one case after another, was interesting only to a point, but it did not fill the young barrister's heart as it did the judge's. For a young man, pressed by his father to marry, spending time with his lordship played a secondary role to his primary function. It had been a week since her return from London and Faulkner's patience seemed to be rewarded only with her increasing insistence that she was busy.

A brief comment about her absence did not appear to disturb either her father or Willow, pressing Faulkner's frustration. Insistence to know her whereabouts resulted in a light-hearted, extremely intense and aggravating discussion.

Stratford put up his cue and finally gave his full attention to the boy. 'She was not expecting you. She is probably working late or has gone out with a friend. I think she mentioned going over to Eileen's to see the baby.'

'It is getting warmer, she could be down at the marina,' Damon added.

A sudden wave of concern struck Faulkner at the thought. 'You don't think she would take the boat out this late, do you?'

Stratford laid that to rest. 'Oh, don't be absurd. You don't fool with a boat alone after dusk.'

'Really, sir,' Faulkner said with a fair amount of frustration at the aloof attitude about the missing girl. 'If you cannot control her...'

'Control her?' Stratford snapped around in surprise, both at Faulkner's tone and his attitude. 'My dear Mr Faulkner, outside of the traditional parental role, she is not mine to control. She is a fully-grown woman with a mind and will of her own. There is little I can do to control anything she does. I may advise, even dissuade on occasion, but hardly control. I am afraid the fear that stirs your young heart and angers you every time she goes off on her own, or directs her attention to any other man, will be lifelong should you marry her. It is not I who need control her; it is you who needs to learn where and how to apply authority within your own household.

Helena will never be controlled, she will never yield to force, or allow herself to be dictated to, but she will yield to the man who holds her heart.'

'That is extremely difficult of late, for she neither allows me to make appointment or to drop in on her spontaneously. This trip to London has made her worse. I might be persuaded to believe she is avoiding me. There have been other occasions I have endeavoured to see her only to find her work has apparently taken her outside of the office for many hours on end. What am I to do? How am I to trust her?'

'Trust is earned my boy; it cannot be coerced,' Stratford replied.

'When have I ever given her cause to distrust me? She has asked for my patience and I have given it. She has asked for my understanding and I have granted it freely. She asks me to wait, but for how long? My patience grows thin.'

'A forced marriage,' Willow finally interjected in quiet reserve, 'is no marriage at all. If it is meant to be then time will see it so. If she cannot resign herself to spending the rest of her life at your side, nothing you can say or do will make it so. Even Harry's empathy and personal desires cannot overturn what has been written into law. England no longer recognizes a marriage without consent, even if it is approved and ordained by the highest of authority.'

With that one short the poignant message, Willow ensured that no one in that room could have a rebuttal, for to do so would undermine everything that house stood for. Faulkner closed his watch, replacing it in his waistcoat pocket, and took his leave. Walking down the long green corridor, Faulkner was quickly joined by Damon, who walked along quiet and solemn. Faulkner's anger and frustration dictated his pace until finally the pair stepped into the cool night air and he felt free enough to slap his gloves against his hands. He had not got the response he had expected. His greatest ally seemed to be taken over by the man formerly content to keep his opinions to himself.

'Where the hell can she be?'

'I think you know where she is,' Damon said. 'You did notice another conspicuous absence this evening, did you not? It is funny how Willow designs these accidental meetings between Helena and

Whitmore and ensures a lengthy stay. What is he after, I wonder? He knows you and Helena are to be married. Why does he insist she tend to this crippled man's every need? If he is so debilitated, why not hire him a nurse? I tell you true, my friend, if Willow has his way that will be no marriage.'

Damon's cruel, harsh words weighed heavily on Faulkner's mind, for despite all the reassurances given by Stratford, it could not be denied that Willow's strong silent hand could now be felt. Helena loved her father, but there could be no denial that her love for Willow trumped all. For all Faulkner's efforts to remain dispassionate, his desire for the girl swelled his jealousy. It was not only his father who maligned his manhood at the inefficiency of his ability to marry, but colleagues and peers. Faulkner climbed in the awaiting motor, ordering the driver to go by way of the hospital laboratory to see for himself.

[71] Stratford looked at the clock on the mantle; it was getting on in the evening and his own concerns were being raised.

'The boy is right, she is rather late tonight. It used to be that if she were going to be out late, she would let us know ahead of time. You spoil her, John. It's dangerous for a woman to be out late at night, alone.'

'She is not alone.'

'Whitmore,' Stratford said with an air of disappointment.

'Why do you dislike him?'

'I do not dislike him.'

'You disapprove of him spending time with our Helena.'

Stratford threw down the spent match in his hand, frustrated at Willow's persistence in ignoring all conventionality. 'It is not that I dislike him. In truth I like him very much. He fits in here very well. It is not about Whitmore. You know what is at stake here, John! Would you tear down everything we have built, everything we have invested?'

'Would you condemn her to a loveless marriage? She does not love him and she does not want him. She wants distinguished maturity, not impetuous youth.'

'We are old, John. She needs to settle down with a husband, have children, and get on with her life. To be selfish, I would like to hope for grandchildren before my days are too long into decline. Wouldn't you?'

'Of course, but it should be her choice who she spends her life with. She doesn't want Brandon.'

'Should she be resigned to spending her life alone?'

'You cannot guarantee her security by mating her to a man you happen to think is a good social match! She doesn't want him!'

'No, because she wants you!' Stratford blurted out before he considered the repercussions.

Stratford regretted it the moment it escaped his lips, but any chance to minimize the damage had passed the moment he turned away. It was the first time in forty-one years Stratford was unable to look upon the man closer to him than any living soul.

Willow stood for a moment too overwhelmed to say or do anything. The undercurrent of the longstanding argument between them seemed insurmountable despite their desires to let it go. With his heart burdened beyond endurance at the continued arguments and distrust, Willow dolefully reached into his pocket and removed a tattered old picture from his billfold. He caressed it tenderly and then laid it affectionately on the table, pausing one last time before making his way down the hall to a hidden door melded into the woodwork and plaster.

[72] Willow took out a small key and slipped it into the hole, turning the lock and pushing on the wall to reveal the outline of a door. The room was dark. Even striking a match afforded very little light, swallowed up by the dark wood and antique artefacts.

Willow lit two candles and took care to close the door behind him before looking around the room in reverence. Removing his coat, he laid it neatly over the chair. A small altar sat near the rear of the room, housing a matched sword and dagger of gold and silver sheathed in ivory, rich with symbolism. A bowl rested before it for a single flame. Lighting it, he dispelled the match and took fervently to prayer, praying continuously for some time in Latin. Retrieving a small pinch of incense from the dish, he placed it over the flame and picked up the dagger, raising it to the heavens. He held the dagger horizontal to the angles of the ground and paid homage to each of the four corners of the earth. He brought it again to its vertical position, continuing to pray until the room filled with incense. The heavy draperies of rich brocade muffled all sound, accentuating the silence. He raised it to his lips and kissed its cruciform magnificence. He spoke the ancient prayer as he raised the dagger back toward the heavens only to find his hand suddenly halted by Stratford, who removed the dagger from Willow's hand. Stratford knelt beside him and laid the discarded picture before him. With the care one might afford any precious object, Willow picked it up.

'I love you, John. God forgive me, I love you so; but it hurts me,' Stratford revealed. 'There barely seems a time when you were not part of my life, never a time you were not there. For you to have her, though...' He stopped, unable to render the words causing his pain. 'But if it will keep you, I offer even that,' Stratford finally uttered; trying to retain what dignity he had left as he stood and made his way out.

Willow stared at the photograph. At the close of the door Willow jumped up and grabbed his coat. He doused the candles and paused only long enough to reseal the room.

'Harry!'

[73] Just as Stratford and Willow reached the stairs, Damon stepped out of the library with several files in his hands. 'Where did you put the Balanchine case?'

Stratford felt more than a little annoyance with the boy at the intrusion. 'I don't know, probably in the study.'

'I've just come from there,' Damon replied, holding up the files. 'The case is tomorrow and you said you were going to finish it.'

'I said no such thing. I told you to verify his facts.'

Damon shook his head. 'And then retracted it, telling me you would handle it personally. I put it in your hand and you threw it on the desk in chambers. Don't you remember?'

The question made Stratford uneasy, for it touched on a weakness he preferred not to reveal. It mattered little that Willow would have sided with him no matter what the situation. Stratford preferred it never come out, least of all in front of Willow.

'I remember telling you specifically to work on it today. I assumed you had it done!'

Willow waved them off. 'It is easily solved. We will go retrieve it. Is it at the office or court?'

'I handed it to him in chambers,' Damon replied, 'but I don't know where he left it.'

'I did not leave it!' Stratford insisted.

'It's all right, Harry. It doesn't matter who left it. If we need it we will go get it,' he said, patting Stratford on the back.

'To start the research now will take all night.'

Willow shrugged. 'Not with a little help. Get your coat.'

Willow rang the bell and had the footman make ready the coach as Stratford made his way back to the study. Outside, Willow soaked in the warm breeze until Damon broke the mood.

'He's not well, you know. I just saw him nearly collapse in the study.'

Willow did not wait, but started back for the door, held off again by Damon.

'He doesn't want you to know. He told me not to say anything.'

Willow put his hand on Damon's shoulder, turned on his heel, and went inside, stopping at the study doors to assess Stratford's condition for himself. Stratford looked tired, but he diligently rifled through his desk as if looking for something.

'What's wrong, Harry?'

'The keys are missing. I know I put them in here this afternoon.'

'Perhaps Damon took them. He wants to go. He probably just pre-empted you.'

'That boy is going to drive me to distraction,' Stratford huffed, rushing around the desk in haste, knocking into it as he tried to manoeuvre around the chair.

'Harry,' Willow started before being cut short.

'Don't!'

'I was only going to say you should stay for Helena. She should be back soon and if she found you gone she would be upset. Why don't you stay here and wait for her?'

'Where is she?'

'She is working on a legal draft with Paul Faulkner.'

'Paul? Why didn't you say so earlier?'

Stratford knew he would receive no answer. They both knew the truth of it, and to bring the matter back to the surface would only set them back to arguing.

Stratford grabbed his coat. 'I have to fix this.'

'Stop being so stubborn and wait for her. She has been distant lately. She needs you.'

Stratford stopped short at the prospect. 'Do you think so?'

'I do.'

'You don't mind, do you? Damon can handle it.'

'Of course he can. Get some rest. We'll be back in a couple of hours.'

Willow paused outside the study door, glancing back long enough to see Stratford walk steadily back to the chair. Pressing on, Willow took Damon in hand and headed to chambers.

[74] It was well past nine before Willow's stamina had begun to wane.

Taking the opportunity to break, Damon put down his pencil. 'I'm a little tired. I was thinking of going back to the apartment. Do you need me for anything else? Will you be all right? I will come back to the house with you if you're not. We can finish it up over breakfast.'

'No, no, you go on. I'm just going to finish this last document and then I'll go home. I don't want to leave Harry for too long.'

Damon collected his things and turned down the light on his desk, tucking a few files under his arm on his way out.

Typing the last document in the pile, Willow slipped the injunction into the folder and turned out the light. Standing in the doorway to the outer rooms, he checked his watch, finding it just past nine-thirty. Stepping into the front waiting area, Willow finally picked up his coat, fumbling for the sleeve when he heard a sound out of place for the hour. It was a knock upon the outer door. Damon had a key, so it would certainly not be some forgotten task. It could only mean someone passing by saw the lamp lit above. Willow withdrew the small firearm within his desk drawer and slipped it into his pocket before opening the door.

To his astonishment, it was a young woman, common and plain, but handsome in her own way. She was shy, revealing her tender age. Eager to learn her plight, Willow offered her a seat, taking her coat. Her story was all too common for her age, keeping her in squalid conditions, forced to accept any condition that might be put to her for her lack of means. In this case, the landlord had failed to fix the broken pipes in her lodging, causing the young lady to live without running water for some months. It was bad enough to have to deal with life outside of parental protection, but to do so with no education or assistance of any kind filled the brothels to bursting with these young women, often saddling them with an unwanted child or two before sending them back onto the streets.

'I am sorry for the late hour, but Miss Stratford told me to stop by after work and she would give me something to force the landlord to fix the water. I can come back at a more convenient hour. I don't mean to keep you from your family.'

'I am sure they can manage without me. I insist you do not leave this office without the papers in hand.'

The young lady turned her eyes away. 'You are very kind.'

'Not at all. It is a matter of typing a few papers and requiring your signature. I will personally file the petition in court tomorrow and you shall see water restored in your lodging within a day or two at most.' He took her into his office and reseated himself at the desk.

In half an hour the necessary papers were typed, with a host of pleasant conversations between to ease the passing of the time. She was quite charming and rather intelligent, given her poor education. Like most young women in her position, her life would have been dramatically altered with the addition of a few extra shillings each week.

'Your papers, Miss Valetto,' Willow said, placing the papers on the desk and handing her a pen. 'I will need your signature here.' He pointed.

To his surprise, she did not sign the papers, but leaned down and kissed him passionately upon the lips in a manner not befitting the deed or his position, taking him aback. The words she whispered in his ear found him staggering backwards in his chair, stumbling with fear at the thing. Attempts to dissuade her found her strategically placing her hand to override his pleas. She had made her intentions clear. Why she should do so he could not fathom at the time, his mind too preoccupied to think clearly.

It was not out of propriety or virtue that he resisted so vehemently, but that a demon long since tethered and caged into submission now began to rage in its anticipated release. Anger, fear, and contempt wrenched his soul back nearly fifty years, returned in an instant to those memories long since forgotten. In Miss Valetto's innocence, she could not understand his rejection, but she was unwilling to yield to it. Willow knew full well, however, the price of losing this battle. His father had spent years trying to tame the demon within his son to no avail.

Unable to kill the demon within him, Nathaniel Willow had sent his only child into the mechanized abattoir of a vicious war praying that it would allow Hell to reclaim its own. He never foresaw the possibility that his son might survive and return, the demon strengthened by what it had seen, what it had feasted upon. The tortures of that day now came flooding back in the instant of fear gripping him as he gazed into her lovely, innocent face. To lose this battle would be to lose his very soul, and unprepared for it, he had little hope of surviving. But it was too late. Willow felt his control slip away as he was borne under.

The demon pushed forward, wallowing in its justification and its unquenchable need. The need to feel her deepest flesh tear and see her innocent blood shed upon its throbbing weapon filled it with dark desire. The demon smiled and reached for her. It would feed and, oh yes, it would drink deep of the darkness.

SESSION CASE

QUEEN'S BENCH DIVISION

LORD JUSTICE

HAROLD A. W. STRATFORD

EIGHTEENTH SESSION,

HELD AT

JUSTICE HALL, IN SUSSEX COURT,

ON FRIDAY, THE 27th DAY OF OCTOBER, 1903,

AND FOLLOWING DAYS.

TAKEN IN SHORT HAND

(BY AUTHORITY OF THE CORPORATION OF THE CITY OF EASTBOURNE)

BY A. WAKEFIELD

Eastbourne :

PRINTED FOR J. H. WILLOW, BY A. WAKEFIELD,

No. 74, MEADS;

AND PUBLISHED BY G. HERBERT, COUNTY COURT

1904

[75] It was still before light and sleep had not come easy to the old barrister, troubled by his demon. A clanging noise seared into his brain, which responded by making a weak attempt at recognition. His leg, flaccid and sluggish, slid off the sofa and dangled over the side. Again the intrusive noise rang out, its tone resolving into a reasonable approximation of a small bell.

Reaching for his watch, Willow opened the tiny clasp to release the lid, eyes straining to focus on the hands. It was thirty-nine past five and the telephone on his desk continued to ring. Sitting up, Willow reached for a coverlet to wrap around himself, making his way over to the desk and sitting in the chair staring at the infernal device in contempt. Another ring found him fumbling for the receiver and picking the base up with his freehand.

'For God's sake, Harry, there is a law against raising the dead at this hour! Do you have any idea what time it is, old darling?' Willow addressed his faceless tormentor with familiarity. He was confident and sure that only one soul in the world insane enough to be up at so ungodly hour. 'Why, what has happened? I'm on my way. No, I'm on my way now!'

Settling the receiver back on into its cradle, Willow returned the telephone to the desk and scrambled for his clothes. He glanced back toward the sofa with a momentary thought of regret and then pushed it from his mind. Drawing on his coat, Willow rushed out the door into the brash cold morning. Winding through the streets the town looked like a desolate stage just before the opening of a play. He headed towards Hartington Place, but the police had Devonshire and Hartington closed, forcing him to head back toward South Lodge.

Willow barely had the carriage at a stop before he departed and scrambled up the stairs. Willow was a neat man by habit, so when he tore off his overcoat and thrust the crumpled mess into George's arms, it spoke greatly of the tormented state of his mind. George acknowledged him with a nod of acknowledgement, but Willow was distracted.

'Where is he?'

'Mr Whitmore is upstairs in his room with the doctor.' George barely got the words out before Willow headed for the stairs.

'Inspector Sanders is waiting for you with his lordship in the morning room, sir. I believe he wishes to speak with you before you go up.'

Willow stopped short and hesitated, debating which was more important.

'If I may,' George added, 'Mr Whitmore seemed annoyed more than injured. It was his lordship who insisted Dr Stoner have a look at him.'

'He wasn't burned? Cut? Any broken bones?'

'Nothing obvious, sir.'

Willow gave a sigh and turned back toward the morning room. 'Could I get some coffee?'

'Right away, sir.'

Willow composed himself, straightened his clothes, and proceeded towards the morning room, entering with an air of confidence. Sanders stood up, taking an official stance, but it was the pitiful figure huddled on the sofa near the fireplace, unmoved and quiet, which caused Willow to close the doors behind him. Stratford made no attempt to speak at Willow's entrance; keeping is head low, even as Willow approached. Sanders made a move to speak, but a demanding, short, sharp wave of Willow's hand had Sanders withdrawing in obedience.

Willow chose to take a seat on the sofa next to Stratford, rather than the chair opposite him, in hopes of easing his friend's plight. Sanders took the time to sit in a nearby chair and withdraw his notebook. Stratford looked up at the gesture, grimacing at the thought of his every word being recorded, prompting Willow to wave the notebook. Sanders complied, though with some reluctance.

Willow put a reassuring hand on Stratford's arm. 'I need you to tell me, in your own time, what happened.'

Stratford composed himself and took a deep breath. 'There was trouble and a fire at the laboratory. Nigel is dead.'

Willow sat up and turned towards Sanders.

Sanders gave a nod and Willow collapsed back onto the cushions of the sofa, his eyes tight shut.

Willow slowly sat up and prepared himself for the rest. 'All right. So Nigel was killed in the fire.'

Sanders shook his head. 'Nigel didn't die in the fire, John. He was murdered outside in the hallway. We are not sure yet whether the two incidents are related, but we are sure that Nigel was murdered. He was stabbed and the knife is missing. We found Mr Whitmore lying outside in the garden, unconscious. When he came to, he insisted we bring him here, against my better judgment. He should be in hospital. But then again, if he was shielding someone...,' Sanders looked over at Stratford.

'And you think Harry did it? Why, for heaven's sake?'

Sanders put his hand in his coat pocket and pulled out an elegant cuff link. 'We found this clutched in Nigel's hand.'

Willow motioned for him to hand it to him and then proceeded to examine it carefully. On first inspection there seemed little doubt as to the owner. The monogram was clearly Stratford's. Retrieving a small magnifying glass attached to a chain on his waistcoat, Willow went over the cuff link with absolute scrutiny before handing it back, albeit begrudgingly.

Taking out his cigarette case, Willow walked over to the fireplace, removed a cigarette from the case, put it in his mouth and closed the case, replacing it back in his pocket. Lifting the cover of the silver match box, he struck it and purposefully lit the cigarette before thrusting the match in the fireplace. The exercise afforded him a moment to puzzle out the problem in his mind.

Then, turning to Stratford, he made his move. 'Harry, did you kill Nigel?'

Stratford's expression was one of horror. 'No. When you left I waited up for Helena until after ten and then retired to bed. I never left the house.'

'Well,' Willow said, turning to Sander's, 'there's an end to it.'

Sanders dropped an expression of disbelief. Willow didn't have to elaborate. He had correctly assessed the situation and advocated for his client to the best of his ability. In this case it required no more argument than to point out that Stratford was a High Court Judge, a full representative of the crown. Once Stratford had stated that he did not commit the crime, to continue to accuse him was tantamount to treason. Sanders stood and put the cuff link back into his pocket.

'Would you see me out?' Sanders asked, taking his leave as George came in with coffee.

Stepping into the hall, Sanders made sure they were well away before saying anything.

'Do you want me to bury this? Is that what you are asking? Nigel all but told us who his killer was.'

'No, Nigel gave you a clue, which you interpreted incorrectly. Now I suggest you find out what he did mean by it.'

'Will you accept the answer if I do?'

'Some have it in them to kill, others do not. Harry is not a killer. Even when we were in the war he couldn't do it. If a man can't kill his enemies, he certainly cannot kill his friends, or his servant.'

'I went to war, too. I was in South Africa and I saw just how easy it was to turn an ordinary man into a killer. It takes less than you think. Nigel's knuckles weren't bruised or damaged, which means he didn't defend himself. He was stabbed in the front, which means the killer was less than a foot away. He knew his killer and wasn't afraid of him. Whoever it was walked right up to him and stabbed him. Nigel was close enough to grab hold of the man. Who is this man you brought back with you? Might someone want him dead?'

Willow stood unmoved at the question.

'You have a choice,' Sanders said, putting on his hat to go. 'Either someone wants Whitmore dead or someone wanted Nigel dead. Why don't you think that over and let me know which one you think is more likely and I'll start from there.'

Sanders tipped his hat and let himself out. Willow turned the problem over in his mind as he closed the door and made his way back into the front foyer, where George stood with a cup of coffee for him.

Willow tried to give a reassuring smile, but he knew his concern showed through. 'When was the last time Harry had his gold monogrammed cuff links on, the ones Helena gave him for Christmas?'

'I cannot be sure, but I believe I laid them out for him the other day.'

'Did he have them on yesterday?'

'Not to my knowledge, sir.'

'What was he like when I was gone?'

'Like, sir?'

'Did he hold his own?'

'Yes, sir.'

Willow took a sip of coffee and then downed the rest, returning the cup to the saucer and handing it back to George.

'Why don't you serve breakfast in about half an hour, and then write a letter to Nigel's family. He has a mother and a sister, doesn't he?'

'Yes, sir.'

'Make arrangements to have him sent back to them, or if they want him down here, arrange for their accommodations. Whatever they might need, take it from my personal account. Make sure they want for nothing. I'm going to go check on Myles. Can you look in on his lordship?'

George gave a nod and turned to go as Willow started up the stairs, but he offered one last consideration to lift a small weight from Willow's shoulders.

'If I may be permitted an opinion, sir,' George began, stopping Willow on the stair. 'Capable is not better, nor is holding one's own. I think his lordship found the house lonelier for your absence. I believe we all did, sir.'

'I understand. Thank you for that, George.'

[76] As the morning wore on, tensions rose swiftly. Sanders was making a nuisance of himself, continually asking questions of the staff and around town, an intrusion unsuitable for the guests due to arrive the following evening. Willow put off going to the office to keep an eye on matters at home. With the upcoming meeting there could be no remnants of the previous evening or its consequences. Sanders had returned, but confined himself to talking to Avondale for some time in the garden. To his credit, Avondale continued to work diligently, understanding the urgency of perfection both within and without the estate walls.

'He's still here, I see,' said Stratford, seeing that Willow stood unmoved, watching from the window.

'He has been in and out all morning. This is his third time talking to the gardener,' he remarked without prejudice, sipping his tea as a captain might aboard the deck, watching over his men. 'Odd, don't you think? Why did you hire him? I was not even aware you were looking to add to the staff. We have a gardener already.'

'Avondale? George felt we needed the help. He is actually rather good. I hardly ever see him walking around, yet he always seems to be there—like George, I suppose, invisible until you need him. Don't worry; he comes with the best of references. George would never have hired someone unsuitable, or someone who would place this house in jeopardy. If George wanted him, he has a very good reason for it. How is Whitmore?'

A gentle ease over took Willow's demeanour at the mention of the name. 'He's fine, just a bump on the head and a right nasty headache. He's a tough one.'

'I'm glad,' Stratford replied.

'Are you?' Willow said as he turned back toward the window.

Stratford slunk away at the question. 'Of course. He is in this house and under my protection, isn't he?'

Willow gave a nod and patted Stratford on the arm before returning to the window, intent on the comings and goings of the people below. Time and time again as they stood there, Stratford tried to muster the courage to say what was on his mind, fumbling for the words. It was an unspoken truth that without Willow's help the morning might not have gone as well. Stratford was waning fast, unable to hold the steady line he had once held, which could now turn into a problem as the monthly dinner was scheduled for the following night. As it was an annual meeting there would be more seated at table than usual, all looking toward the east, to Stratford.

Willow abandoned the exercise of watching Sanders fumble around for answers and set down his cup. 'I'm going out for a while. What are your plans? Can you stay with Myles?'

'I have to be in court in an hour, but I should be home early. Sam is downstairs.'

Somehow the thought was less than comforting, but it would have to do.

[77] The quarter hour bell saw Whitmore in the hall, ready for breakfast. Like Stratford and Willow, Whitmore found the customary procession down the stairs with Miss Stratford comforting in its routine. This morning, however, he found her looking down at the front walk. Whitmore had only meant to welcome her home, but all attempts to converse seemed to go unheard. His touch to draw her awareness served only to disturb her, causing him to look down at the view. Willow stood on the walkway talking to a man, an elderly gentleman who gestured with his hands as if describing something.

'That is Judge Martin Crampon, late of the Queen's Bench, down there talking to John,' Helena told him. 'He retired last year, making a fine speech. In truth, my father made him retire. King Edward and his actress were not the only scandal to hit England. Father and John helped to break up a legal syndicate of crime. Some of the men were highly placed and friends of ours. Crampon had associated with ... well, characters he ought not to have, but someone very high took great pains to have all ties summarily removed. My father was furious. He asked for Crampon's resignation.'

'Or he would break him, like Malone.'

'That is very harsh. Father did not break Mr Malone. He did it to himself. Father tried to help him. He gave him money to live when he had a difficult time finding employment and eventually worked something out with a few of his friends to hire Malone. Malone just didn't want it. He'd rather do nothing and blame my father for it.'

'They used to be good friends, Judge Crampon and your father?'

'For a long time. It broke Daddy's heart to know that Judge Crampon was involved. He trusted him. He always said what a good man Crampon was. Judge Crampon would never tell Father what his part was in the matter, not even after all was said and done. But you know Father. The law—' she started before Whitmore took over.

'Is the law, uncompromising and unyielding. Willow is more forgiving.'

'I'm not so sure of late,' she said, kissing him on the cheek. 'I'll be away again all day, possibly two. Will you be all right?'

'I assure you I will be fine. I have a mountain of work to do.'

'With the laboratory destroyed?'

'Yes, well.' Whitmore sighed, trying to think of how he was going to finish his work. 'I'll think of something.'

[78] Willow grabbed his coat and headed to Hartington Place. From the news he had expected a larger turnout of the fire brigade, but one pumper wagon and a hose team were all that were on the scene. The damage looked quite minimal from the road, giving some hope of answers.

FC Welford, seeing the unmistakable landau pull to the curb, stood and waited for him to cross.

'I didn't expect to see you here. I wasn't aware fires interested you.'

'Do you have a cause yet?'

'Now you know I can't tell you that.'

'So it was deliberate.'

'You keep pressing on matters you know I cannot speak of and it's going to cost you.'

Willow grinned at the reference. 'Send me a bill. I want to know what happened here.'

Welford motioned for them to walk on and he took Willow around to the back, talking as they went. 'What's your interest?'

'Myles Whitmore is in my keeping. He was the one in the laboratory last night. If it was deliberate I need to know.'

'You already have a client?'

'Not a client, family. If someone is trying to hurt him I need to know. I've already lost a good man on this one. I'll pay whatever price you want, just tell me what I need to know.'

Perhaps Welford saw the seriousness in Willow's eyes; he took him inside.

'There were two in it. One stayed outside and the other went in, probably to knock your boy out to keep him inside. That's why he wasn't killed right off. They were going to let the fire kill him so it looked like an accident.' Welford pointed to the cot Whitmore slept in. 'Your arsonists are amateurs. We're lucky the whole place didn't go up. There are thirty-eight beds upstairs. It could have gone badly, very badly.'

Welford headed back out of the laboratory, but as Willow turned, his attention on the devastation of Whitmore's table and section, something caught his eye. Leaning down, Willow moved the debris and files and picked up an ash-covered knife. It was a queer-looking knife, not one typically found on a chemistry table. Wiping it off confirmed the sinking feeling now overtaking him. He recognised it all too well. It was a Scottish dirk, the same dirk he had given Stratford when they were young.

'Are you coming, John?'

Willow wrapped the dirk in his handkerchief and slipped it into his pocket as he turned, catching Welford up at the door. Walking down the hall, Welford continued to explain the events of the evening, taking him back outside and around the side of the building.

Welford frowned and handed Willow a large bolt with scratches. 'We found this. They used an ordinary plumber's wrench to loosen the bolt to the gas line leading directly to the laboratory. It would have taken some time to fill the room, so one man could have done it, but it looks like he was too nervous. Maybe he was talked into it.'

'Why do you say that?'

'There are two sets of footprints near the outside wall near the gas line. One stays and paces back and forth. One set leads off around to the back door that leads to the laboratory hallway. The one at the gas paces from the gas to the corner of the building, like he was waiting for someone. Your inside man doesn't pace, he goes right in. He's not nervous; he goes right in the door and down the hallway. We figure your boy's asleep because there's no sign of a struggle. The guy sneaks up, whacks him on the back of the head, sets a small fire in the rubbish bin, and slips out, but instead of walking out easy as you please, he runs into Nigel. Nigel obviously knows him because they are standing close when they talk. That might be all right in the day, but we're talking about two in the morning. Bottom line is, when the fire breaks out, Nigel is going to know who was there and who did the deed. Your guy can't let him go and, because he knows him, he can't let him live. He gets in close, pulls out a knife and, in a panic, kills him. He walks out trying to act calm, but his pace is quick. It's not running, but it's quick.'

'How did Myles get out? I understand he didn't regain consciousness until the fire brigade arrived, and they found him in the garden.'

'As I said: amateurs. They don't account for nothing. Someone comes along, sees Nigel on the floor, tries to help but realises he is dead. They see the fire, grab your boy, and take him outside before calling us.'

'Does that someone have a name?'

'I'm sure he does, but he wasn't your killer.'

'That's some pretty fancy detective work, Horace. How do you know all of that? You can't tell me that comes from fire investigation.'

Welford looked away. 'A little bird told me.'

'A bird, ay? This bird have a name?'

'He does, but let's just say he's a little shy.'

'A shy detective. Now there's a first.'

'Well, I'm sure you can appreciate I afford all my friends the same anonymity as I afford you. He doesn't want anyone to know he's here, if you take my meaning.'

Willow's humour at the thing dimmed. His own words began slowly to take on a different tone from the innocence in which they were spoken. There was one detective, so called, that could effortlessly observe and deduce the clues with such precision, though it was not customary for him to leave the Diogenes, nor was it customary to keep his arrival from Willow.

'Do you have names for me?'

Welford pulled out a rag and handed it to Willow who fondled it. Taking a whiff to determine the identity of the faint odour emanating from it, Willow noticed it had remnants of oil and creosol on it. Returning it to Welford, the pair returned to the landau, Willow climbed in and took up the reins. 'I owe you one,' he said as he slapped the reins and headed down the street.

'Make sure it's a large cheque,' Welford called after him.

SESSION CASE

QUEEN'S BENCH DIVISION

LORD JUSTICE

HAROLD A. W. STRATFORD

NINETEENTH SESSION,

HELD AT

JUSTICE HALL, IN SUSSEX COURT,

ON FRIDAY, THE 27th DAY OF OCTOBER, 1903,

AND FOLLOWING DAYS.

TAKEN IN SHORT HAND

(BY AUTHORITY OF THE CORPORATION OF THE CITY OF EASTBOURNE)

BY A. WAKEFIELD

Eastbourne :

PRINTED FOR J. H. WILLOW, BY A. WAKEFIELD,

No. 74, MEADS;

AND PUBLISHED BY G. HERBERT, COUNTY COURT

1904

[79] Stratford closed the massive wood and glass door of his chambers behind him and removed his coat and hat. He placed them on the stand more due to ritual than by any desire to maintain a sense of order in his rooms. He gazed resignedly about and regretted for the first time that his duty beckoned. He drew on his robes, caressing them with the same gentle hand that one would use to caress a fine lady before drawing her close. Stratford stood in front of the mirror, adjusting the shoulders evenly and ensuring that his wig was set perfectly on his head, no less than a fine soldier ready for inspection.

Today, however, he felt unworthy of them, and replaced them on the hook before walking over to his desk. There was far too much to do to sit quietly at work among the duties he cherished and loved so much. To sit in judgment of others, while he sat judged for his failures, seemed criminal. The law was not the only thing in the world that Stratford cared about or loved, nor was it his only obligation. He was a part of a greater whole. Yet that whole was now threatened in every aspect of his life. His failures were more than his shame; they would see the crumbling of everything he held dear. Looking up at his reflection in the mirror, he saw his aging face staring back at him. It used to be easier in younger years, having the strength and stamina to ensure all corners were well protected, covered, and secure. Now, none of them seemed to be. His family was falling apart, as was his health.

The meetings to commence that evening would hold the seeds of new beginnings, indeed the world, if he could only make it through until then, to see to fruition the fruits of all their labours. Pulling out a pair of gold spectacles, Stratford took pen in hand as he opened the first file. He had no more than dragged through the first lengthy paragraph when an unexpected knock came upon his chamber door and an unlikely face appeared.

Stratford took off his glasses as his heart lifted. 'Johnny! Please, come in!'

'I need to speak with you,' said Willow.

'Of course, of course! Have a seat,' he motioned eagerly.

'I need your help.'

Stratford relaxed back in his chair. 'Good heavens, John, you had me worried for a moment. You are very welcome to my help, always. You hardly need to come down here to ask for it; you should have said so this morning and saved yourself the trip.'

'It is more complicated than that, and I fear it may tax our friendship to the limits.'

'I can imagine nothing which would break what a lifetime has built. If our argument could not break us, rest assured, nothing on earth will be able to.'

A strained look swept over Willow's face. 'This may.'

'Pray, tell me about it. Let me ease your mind.'

'No, not here, and not at South Lodge. Come to my house in Friston and tell no one that you are coming.'

Stratford gave him serious attention. 'That sounds very ominous.'

'Will you come?'

'Of course, but can you not tell me anything now?'

'Walls have ears,' Willow said, taking his leave as quickly as he had come.

The portentous request weighted heavily upon the old jurist, having been so formally asked so simple a favour, until by the afternoon he was quite unable to concentrate for the agony of the thing.

[80] Stratford arrived in Friston alone after fulfilling his duty at court. Willow paced nervously as Stratford propelled his coat and hat onto the table.

'Now tell me, old friend,' Stratford pressed, 'what is so terrible that you await my arrival with such trepidation.'

The answer was not an easy one, for in the duration of their long and trusted relationship Willow could cite only one other instance when he had deceived his friend. To date this betrayal had never been revealed, nor could it be. Such an exposure would render all trust annulled and cause a falling out of such devastating proportions that it could hardly be exaggerated. It had been the case in the past that even when directly ordered to hold faith with no one, he would seek out Harold's council and Harold his, secure in their trust for one another. It had been a good and kind relationship, granting survival in the worst of times. Seeing the look of deep concern on Stratford's face, Willow found it difficult to face his oldest and dearest friend now. The evidence suggested clearly that everyone, including a man utterly pure in the law, fell under suspicion of involvement in this murderous plot.

His opening was slow and unintelligible, floundering about an issue he preferred not to face, easing in a morsel of fact now and again to build a gentle case. He held back the truth, like a storm building behind a seawall that, if that bulwark failed, would sweep through their lives with terrible force, rending and destroying all they had built.

'Harry,' Willow began, 'we have had our differences of late but I should hope you know that you can trust me implicitly. I would never let any harm come to you, you know that. I never have and I never will allow it.'

'I trust that,' Stratford granted.

'I need you to tell me about David Malone.'

Stratford turned away, shrugging off the request. 'There is nothing to tell.'

'Nothing? Time is short; indeed, it has run out and you have nothing to say?'

'I know no more than you!'

'There was a time, not long ago, that you would not lie to me. Have we fallen that far? A man, a detective, paid a visit to Sanders. He worries me. He worries me a great deal. Everyone seems to deny his existence, but my sources say otherwise. After he was content to accept your word as judge, Sanders left, but you saw he returned, suddenly wanting to have a look around the estate. I found out what it was about. He has hair fragments taken from the blood at the murder scene in Seaford. They are strands of brown and silver hair belonging to a sable coat, found imbedded in scrapings of the blood on the ground near Malone's body. Where is your coat, Harry?'

'In the foyer closet! Would you like to see it?' Stratford burst forth in angered reproach. 'I did not kill him, John. I wasn't there.'

'You sent him to Seaford, to the alley behind the Red Lion,' Willow rebutted, stepping over to Stratford and facing him intimately.

Stratford turned away without answering, for more reasons than a desire not to answer. Willow's suggestion that he was somehow involved spoke too loudly of the broken trust between them. It had broken his heart to argue with his oldest and dearest friend, to learn truths he would have preferred remained buried. Willow's return gave hope to reconciliation, but it could not be had without trust, not after so intimate a betrayal.

Willow pleaded with him for honesty. 'For God's sake, man, if matters are bad enough for you to be implicated, or worse, if Mycroft is looking into these matters, you need me in your confidence! I cannot shield you if you are not honest with me!'

Stratford returned the offer with impertinence. 'Shield me? I need no protection, not from you, not from the police. If you have claims upon me, let it be handled by the law. I will put my trust there!'

'You blind, ignorant fool! Your own hand says that you sent him to his death!'

Willow removed a note from his pocket and laid it upon the desk in undeniable confirmation. He waited for his friend to give acknowledgement, but Stratford continued in his silence. Willow knew it was yet another slap, as the item came from Harry's locked desk, but it could not be helped.

'You left early and did not return until after eight, well after dinner. You deliberately took your own motor and drove yourself. It suggests a desire to conceal the fact that you went. You were seen on High Street near the time of the murder. Nigel says you were extremely agitated upon your return. I tell you, it doesn't look good, Harry. One might believe Nigel needed to be removed because he was the only one who could have given testimony.'

Stratford turned to him in evident disgust. 'So now you and Mycroft are together on this against me? Yes, I made the appointment', Stratford reluctantly conceded. 'But that doesn't mean I killed either one of them. I didn't meet Malone. He was not there upon my arrival. I waited for an hour for him, but he did not come. I was upset. We had things to discuss, important things. I was put out that he stood me up and felt the trip was a waste. I hurried back so as not to waste any more time. I am telling you the truth, Johnny!'

'Did you go to the laboratory last night?'

Stratford's frustration began to show through. 'I never left the house!'

'Please, if you have done something, let me help.'

'I didn't go to the laboratory last night and I didn't kill Nigel. You told me to stay and wait for Helena, but you knew she wasn't coming home, didn't you? You knew all along she wasn't coming home and yet you made me wait up for her. Sam came in around ten or so, but not Helena and not you.'

'I didn't leave the files which insured that Sam and I would have to spend most of the night working on them exclusively. It insured we would be out of the house. And what about Myles? Why are you so angry with him? What do you have against him?'

Willow watched as Stratford, turning away in astonishment and suppressed anger, tried to regain his composure.

'You favour him too much, John, too intently, obsessively so. You've lost all objectivity with him. You tend to Whitmore as if he were your—'

Willow scowled the attack, but took Stratford head-on. 'My son? I do favour him. I will not deny it. There is something about him, something that warrants a father's love. He has become like a son to me, dear to my heart in the ways of a father for a child. So I must ask you, as a point of honour: what happened last night?'

'I swear to you that all that I told you is true. It was not me who sent you and Sam from the house. If you recall, it was me who insisted I go with you. Sam was supposed to stay. I hardly say that is a well-contrived plan to get rid of all of you. I have never lied to you; Johnny, never, and I have never betrayed you. I do not know the full facts of what happened last night, but I know what I did and did not do!'

'If you weren't there, what is Sanders looking for at the house? Why is he talking so much to the gardener?'

'I don't know.'

'Does he know about your meeting with Malone? He knows something, and if he finds anything, make no mistake, he will arrest you.'

There could be no argument, but Stratford would not tell him the truth. Willow stood, watching Stratford stare out of the window, knowing Stratford was concealing something from him. Attacking a lion, even an old one, was foolish head-on. Aggression would achieve nothing except for continued silence, but Willow's heart was at stake every bit as much as his friend's life. They had never had secrets between them before, but their falling out had cost much.

'Do not force me to compel you to answer, Harry, I beg of you,' Willow threatened, clearly placing the king in check. 'Why did you send Malone to Seaford, and where were you when he was killed if you were not there? Answer me!'

Stratford mustered the last of his strength to stand and face his friend. 'Don't! Stop here, John. This I beg of you. On our friendship, leave this alone.'

'You were at hospital the night Ian Doherty died. I saw you there. Why were you there, Harry? What were you going to do? What did you do?'

'I tell you I wasn't there!'

Stratford stepped back, too angered or too overwhelmed to speak, but Willow had had enough of silence. Grasping Stratford by the arm in the strong grip known only to his Masonic brethren, Willow insisted.

'Harold Arthur,' Willow rasped out, hoping during the small pause that Stratford would stop him by agreeing to speak, 'Winston Stratford, on the square, I compel you to answer me!'

Stratford ripped his arm from Willow's hold in aggravated disgust. 'I will never forgive you for this,' Stratford choked out in loathing and disgust. 'How could you think I would murder my own friends? I don't know who you are anymore, John. I don't think I want to know you.'

Willow took the blow in stride and continued with calm insistence. 'Tell me what you were doing in Seaford meeting Malone secretly. Don't make this more difficult than it already is. You have been my closest and dearest friend for over forty years. I ensured your seat on the bench and I nursed you through a broken marriage, through broken dreams and broken hearts. I did more for you than I have ever done or could ever do again for any living soul. Tell me the truth!'

Stratford thought the matter over, still wanting to walk out, but there was too much holding him. It was more than the fact that Willow had been there for him at every turn. Willow had been a steady rock, always stable and always there. He knew, that no matter how angry Willow became with him, Willow would always forgive him and find a way to set things right. Helena had been the only quagmire they seemed unable to pass. Helena had seemed to be Willow's saving grace. However, in that grace, Stratford felt Willow should remember his place. In the thinking of it, Stratford wondered if it were not the true question in the matter and all else window dressing. And there was another reason, one that Stratford could not ignore.

'You don't leave me much choice,' Stratford remarked with less than subtle admonition. 'Malone was,' Stratford hesitated, 'blackmailing me.'

Willow's anger suddenly turned to surprise and confusion. This was an unlikely scenario, for to blackmail someone, one must first have a victim performing a questionable deed. Stratford could no more break the law than he could cut off his right arm.

'How?'

'The night before you came home from London, Malone came to see me. I told him it was not in either of our best interests for him to come, but he didn't care. He was anxious, nervous; I could barely get out what he wanted at first.'

'What did he want?'

'He wanted me to restore his right to practice law. Of course I told him I could not oblige, even if it were in my power to do so, but he seemed under the impression I had made some promise to him. I didn't, John. I swear I gave no such word, but he threatened to go to Mycroft and tell him I killed his brother. He also, and this is what made me set up the meeting, he said he knew Simon Ballard was at that house.'

'Ballard was there?'

'Malone said he was the one murdered at hospital.'

Willow sunk to the chair. 'No, but would explain much,' he said under his breath. 'How could I have been so blind? Tell me, how did Malone come by this information?"

'There is only one way he could. He was there, John. He was there. What frightens me is that he made it sound as though I were there also. The panic of Malone's words had dulled my wit or I should have pressed him for more at that very moment, but in the next moment the door had opened and Sam felt he needed to come to my defence, hearing the shouting. Malone left disgruntled and I had to think. The presence of Ballard explains much, such as us not being able to learn the identities of the men. They were Ballard's men, but why they should mean Sherlock harm I have no clue. I needed to learn more. I needed to meet with Malone again, to learn what he knew. That is why I arranged to meet him.'

'For heaven's sake, why did you not let him go to Mycroft? There would have been an end to it.'

'I could not. I could not place you or Helena in danger with the mention of Ballard's death at my hands, true or not.'

'Harry,' Willow sighed.

'There was a place in Seaford that Malone and I would go sometimes in our early days. It was quiet and we could speak freely, without the fear of eavesdroppers. I made the plans and wrote them on a note, sealing it with my insignia on red wax to insure no one but the two of us knew of the meeting.'

Willow turned the matter in his mind, hoping for flaws that could redeem his friend. 'How was it delivered?'

'I had Sam take it. I could trust no one else, not even a discreet telegram. I had him wait for a reply, instructing Malone to say nothing to Sam outside of giving a yes or no.'

Willow paced, lighting his pipe and giving the matter due reverence before choosing a course of action.

'This man, this detective, makes me nervous how he moves. I am afraid Mycroft is here and he knows about Malone. I understand why you would wish to meet Malone, but from everything you are telling me, you had a motive to kill him, and you set up a time and place.'

'I didn't kill him.'

'Harry, he ended up dead at the very hour and place you set up and you cannot seem to account for your whereabouts. Where were you?'

Stratford fidgeted, reluctant to reveal all. 'I did not kill him. I waited in the Inn for an hour and then left.'

'You were gone all day! You arranged to meet him and now he is dead! Where were you? You didn't come home until after eight-thirty!'

Stratford struggled, clearly embarrassed. 'I got lost on my way back from Seaford. I had arranged to meet him at five, but by six he hadn't shown up. It's all rather hazy, but I ended up leaving. I don't remember, but I must have gotten lost because I did not recognise where I was until well after Birling Gap. I figured that Malone had changed his mind. I was upset and angry because he knew how important it was for me to meet him.'

'Lost? It is one road and you only drove to Seaford! No jury in the land will believe that you got lost.'

'Don't you think I know that!' Stratford exclaimed. 'I became disoriented, confused. I did not know where I was. I was frightened, unable to find my way back home, to Seaford or even back to Seven Sisters. I could not read the signs, nor understand them. I sat on the side of the road too embarrassed to ask for help. There you have your answer! I hope you're satisfied.'

Looking at Willow with abhorrence, Stratford stormed out of the house slamming the door in a final denunciation. Willow sank into the chair, despairing at the sad truth, revealed too late to make any difference. Stratford was six years younger than he was, but showed clear and distinct signs of progressed deterioration that Willow had managed to avoid. Now he had forced Stratford to confess, not to the crime of murder or deception, but to the terrible truth that he was growing old and losing control of all he had formerly mastered with such ease. That, more than anything else, crushed Willow to the very core. He had deprived his closest and dearest friend of dignity.

Seeing the bent and sombre figure of his dearest friend walk past the front window, Willow found himself wishing Stratford really had killed Malone rather than to be guilty of growing old. It would have been easier for both of them. If Stratford had slipped in his mind enough, it was quite possible he could do things without remembering them. Taking the dirk from his pocket, Willow opened his desk drawer, placed it within, and locked the drawer.

SESSION CASE

QUEEN'S BENCH DIVISION

LORD JUSTICE

HAROLD A. W. STRATFORD

TWENTIETH SESSION,

HELD AT

JUSTICE HALL, IN SUSSEX COURT,

ON FRIDAY, THE 27th DAY OF OCTOBER, 1903,

AND FOLLOWING DAYS.

TAKEN IN SHORT HAND

(BY AUTHORITY OF THE CORPORATION OF THE CITY OF EASTBOURNE)

BY A. WAKEFIELD

Eastbourne :

PRINTED FOR J. H. WILLOW, BY A. WAKEFIELD,

No. 74, MEADS;

AND PUBLISHED BY G. HERBERT, COUNTY COURT

1904

[81] Whitmore spent what remained of the morning sifting through the rubble of his work. Two months of unrelenting effort had been destroyed in a careless instant and Mrs Stanton might pay for it with her life. Police had been curtailing his access to parts of the laboratory, but he felt sure their interest lay strictly with the cause of the fire and not what was actually contained there. It therefore begged the question of why many of his notes were missing. The table containing them, along with his experiments and Holmes's Bradshaw, remained largely intact, covered by debris. His initial notes and work on older samples of haemoglobin remained near his table, yet the folder showing his tests and the results on Malone's blood and the blood found on Stratford's coat were missing, along with Stratford's knife. The knife may or may not have been a curiosity, but the Bradshaw contained nothing of particular interest to anyone, or at least it shouldn't have. It only interested Whitmore because of the partial formula and solution written in the margins.

He had spent hours tearing apart his room, lest in the commotion he had left them at home, but it was to no avail. He had taken them to the laboratory and someone had removed them. He struggled through his remaining notes and flawed memory only to suffer through two more hours of failed attempts. It was impossible to focus. Too many questions ran through his mind, begging for answers. Someone had been following him and someone had been looking into the murders. Was it one man or two? Was he after Whitmore's work or the judge? If it were any man other than the one he feared, Whitmore might have let it go. The vague clues were hardly a trail of breadcrumbs laid out for anyone to follow. The clues were disjointed and made little sense. Even Whitmore could not entirely be sure of what they meant.

However, Whitmore thought, one man could discover their meaning. One man could find enough evidence to implicate a high court judge and take him down.

It was a puzzle, but one that had taken on remarkable odds of being true.

If it were true, Whitmore wondered, where would he be? Where could he remain elusive, yet accessible? He had to be close by, for he seemed to know everyone's movements. Equally, he could not be too close, for someone might recognise him.

In some perverse way it seemed as if this ghost wanted Whitmore to understand, to seek out that which was concealed and would be unveiled. Why he should do so Whitmore could not fathom. Had there been some understanding between them in the past? Was he trying to lead Whitmore to an answer this ghost, for whatever reason, could not reveal himself? By lunch he had been consumed by the possibilities. There was only one way to find the answer. He had to go to that place of horrid imaginings and tolls of death, that place he dreaded with all his being, that place they had gone to together and none survived.

Whitmore took to the street to hail a cab. The cabbie gave him no more than a puzzled look of morbid curiosity before setting off for the road leading out of town, up past Beachy Head and toward Birling Gap. Turning down a thin overgrown trail two miles between any residences, the sprightly carriage made its way to a dreary spot, which declined in appearance as they drew near.

Stopping at the top of the crest, the driver insisted he would go no further, suggesting that his fare do the same. His mind made up, however, Whitmore departed the carriage and handed the cabbie his fare and a sovereign for the trouble to send Willow word, but only after the end of his shift. Willow would be less than pleased if he knew Whitmore had gone out and would, most certainly, have attempted to stop him, especially if he knew the reason for the visit. Whitmore was no longer interested in the notes, but the hand behind why they were missing. He had to confirm or deny his theory and there was only one way.

Making his way down the path, the topology mirrored the waves, dipping and rising in a synchronous fashion. It was misleading as one looked down toward the channel from the hill above. Dark clouds hung above the water and an uncertain breeze buffeted the white cliffs. A storm perhaps, he thought as he gazed seaward. It almost looked as if the grass of the Downs pressed right into the water. It tempted a ride from top to bottom on bicycle, forming images in one's mind of a hot summer day and the cool breeze flowing through one's hair along the journey down to plummet into the cool waters at the end.

In truth, the grass ended suddenly at the cliff's wall, sending an uninformed visitor to the rocks below. For a place of such beauty it was a place that often ended sorrow and regret with one step. Many ventured to Beachy Head and the cliffs along the coastal path to end their morose existences, for the beauty of the landscape and serenity of the view spoke of a world unlike that in which all lived.

There was nothing between the summit and the lighthouse, save two miles of wave-like Downs and two houses, one of which was the Snowden house. As the wind whipped up over the soft white cliffs, the feeling that some impending doom waited ahead until he stopped altogether. Even at a distance there was something portentous about the house. It was a horrid place that soon revealed itself to be burned on the left side and putrefying everywhere else. Voices rang in his ears of the ghosts and shadows, through the low howling winds whistling through the charred cinders.

His attention was repeatedly drawn to the barn, some distance from the house and largely intact save the normal dilapidation of time. A cursory inspection of its contents proved hardly worth the effort to examine, and yet some inexplicable sensation obligated him to open its doors and step inside.

A dark feeling of dread filled him, causing his head to mercilessly ache as he approached. Softly, growing in the distance of his mind, he heard sounds that seemed familiar yet indeterminate. It echoed of water, dripping and pouring. There was a cold sensation that rushed upon his face as if the water had been poured upon him. Popping sounds echoed strangely in some forbidding manner, screams of pleas gone unanswered, the cold against which there was no protection. Whitmore walked cautiously up to the front view. Whatever hallowed imaginings the name of the house conjured in his mind, they were dispelled by its ominous dark presence. There was an air of death about it, like an odour that filled the senses until it manifested itself into taste, nauseating and sick.

The wood carried a peculiar sickly sweet smell of rot mixed with burnt mortar and ash as he made his way around the barn. The weathered grey wood and perforated ceiling rendered an image of dilapidation to the point of condemnation. The doors were a pair, but only one of them actually functioned. Inside was dark and dreary with only the far broken window affording any light. The other windows had dulled with dirt and grime over the years of disrepair. It even smelled dirty, damp and unhealthy. The roof was full of holes, the light blocked by the second level of beams and superficial flooring. One small glimmer of light managed to reach the inner temple, following with it a nagging continuous drip from former rain stuck between the slates.

Whitmore stood watching each individual drop as it fell from the hole in the rafters and made the long drop into a barrel. The gentle optical sensation was compelling and hypnotic. There was just enough light to see the each drop slap upon the water and ripple toward the outside, dissipating as it reached the very edge of the barrel. It was only after some time that he realized it was not the dripping of the water, per se, that caused him to hesitate. His conscious mind finally forced him to recognize where he was. Trying to coerce his brain to manipulate the calculations of the problem was not unlike forcing a rusty wheel to turn upon its axle after so long a time unused.

He moved toward the barrel as if its tangible presence could somehow aid him in recovering some lost ability to think. Stretching forth his hand to touch the ripples as they rose and swelled within, he looked down at his feet and around the sides of the barrel, the shelves, and the abandoned rags. The rags, he noted, were clean, as nearly as one might expect for rags found in an abandoned barn. Two were thrust carelessly alongside the barrel. Whitmore picked them up, stood in front of the barrel, and proceeded to turn toward the door and thrust them as if he were about to bolt in a long sprint. They fell very near the spot he had found them.

Turning to his rear, he looked around the dust-ridden barn with scrutiny. He found another oddity, which nagged at him: undisturbed footprints. They were made from the type of shoes worn by the military and police, save one pair that strode alongside the others. The second pair went to the back, came forward, and wandered aimlessly about the barn in circles and indistinguishable patterns. However, the pair leading away from the barrel was deliberate. Following the path led him to a back stall once used for a horse. It contained old stale hay and worn bridles long since unusable. The compartment appeared to contain nothing of value, nothing that might prompt someone to seek it out, yet he was sure it had to contain something. Worrying not for his appearance, he knelt down on his hands and knees, crawling through the straw and dirt, thrusting it to either side and behind him. It was in the very corner that his hand came upon something soft, yet which contained something hard within.

Pulling it out from its hiding place, he noticed through the dim light that it was a shirt, wrapped in a bundle and tied at the top. It contained some other type of cloth and something very hard within. Rushing to the door for assistance from the sunlight, he plunged to the ground and opened the bundle. A slow realization moved through him as he unravelled a pack containing a revolver and dirty shirt, unmistakable in its design, and a gold pocket watch. The watch was notable, even without the aid of a glass, in that the chain was broken near the third link. It was very old, British in style, unlike the modern French and Italian designs most popular at present. Opening the watch, its ownership could not be denied, and the sole purpose of its concealment. The articles had been cleverly hidden, but someone had found them, only to return them.

While the barn remained intact, the house itself had been reduced to burned beams and floorboards, charred walls that discoloured the outside paint. Facing his fears, Whitmore turned back toward it, approaching with trepidation as his anxiety grew. Strolling around the grounds, he began to see how the gruesome crime must have played out, ending in the death of all of the men with little to no struggle. The notion that such a crime could be committed without a fight stood out prominently in his mind as a queer thing, but he could make no more of it, especially with that dark threatening house looming over him, grimacing in the impending darkness. The path brought him to the front of the house once again, his heart beating wildly within his chest. He endeavoured to move ahead, trying to mask his growing feeling of panic, which now gripped his soul like a thousand dead men walking upon his grave.

He stepped up to the door and pushed it open. Standing in the doorway, a sickening feeling took hold of him, filling his being with an almost overwhelming urge to turn back. It was against all reason, as the very idea of spiritual survival after death was alien to his rational sensibility. Pressing on past the threshold, he stepped gingerly over the rubble and debris cluttering the entrance hall at the foot of the stairs. Surveying the worm-eaten wood of the grand staircase, he marvelled at how something once so majestic could become the very embodiment of menace. He paused at its foot, gathering himself against a growing sense of unease as the light seemed to fade. He tried vainly to focus his attention, but other voices filled his mind, drowning all light and sound as he collapsed to the floor, hearing only garbled, disjointed sounds reminiscent of gunfire as the light faded from his eyes.

[82] 'Welcome back.'

The familiar voice echoed through the darkness, becoming attached to a face as Whitmore opened eyes and started to focus. 'I thought only children rummaged through old burned out houses,' Dr Stoner teased him.

Turning his head, Whitmore saw a giant of a man painted against an azure sunset sky, quite unamused at the day's events, while a concerned old barrister tried to keep steady and dignified. Handing him over, Stoner put away his bag, assisted by Damon helping Whitmore to his feet. Whitmore found himself some meters away from the house. By the lack of soot-laden marks on their clothing and shoes, it was clear that the four men standing before him had not removed him from the rubble. The sky had not yet entirely darkened, marking the elapsed time to be no more than an hour, so the note sent by way of coachman could not have reached them, leaving the outstanding question of who had pulled him from the house and raised the alarm. There was the strange odour of gunpowder lingering in the air—faint, but distinguishable. For a long time Willow stood unmoved and silent. He then brushed off Whitmore's coat like a dutiful father, prompting some sort of explanation, though not expressly elicited.

Whitmore forced out an uncomfortable apology. 'I am sorry. I did not mean to trouble you.'

'Do you think that is all I care about, being troubled? You foolish boy,' Willow uttered, rubbing his temples. 'What would possess you to come here?' He turned his voice to an almost inaudible level, turning Whitmore from the rest of the company. 'You could have fallen through the floorboards or broken through the rotted beams. Without my protection you could have been killed! Anything could have happened. If anything had..." Willow shook his head, turning away, and walked back to the motor.

[83] The warm comfort of South Lodge dispelled the horrors of that house, like the morning sun washing away a nightmare. The relaxing exercise of a hot bath removed all evidence of the visit, clearing his mind as he sunk deep within the healing waters. Not more than a minute passed before Whitmore sat bolt upright, an annoying thought gripping him. The bundle of evidence—the gun, shirt, and watch—he had it upon his entry into the Snowden house, but did not have it on the journey home. It was far too important to leave out in the open, if it were there now at all. Leaping from the bath, Whitmore flew to his coat, rifling through the pockets. It was not there. For a moment he entertained the hope that he had put the paper back into the bundle, but reason dictated he had not. There were four men in attendance, fully capable of understanding the significance of the find. Yet, even in this reasoning there was a flaw. He had gone out alone and four came to assist him, but none of them had removed him from the house, so who had raised the alarm?

[84] At first light Whitmore saddled the chestnut mare and made his way back to the house. If all went well, he could retrieve the articles within the hour, before the house stirred for breakfast. It would not do to have Willow discover him there again, so it would have to be done by seven. Only then would he be allowed sleep and to forget that awful place. Making his way swiftly over the Downs, he thought of nothing save his mission to put matters right, pressing the mare to the limits of endurance. Coming upon that hideous site of evil, it seemed to beckon him to its cold dead arms of burned boards and hollow screams.

Sitting up in the saddle and turning round to view all sides, Whitmore found himself pressing against an irrational fear. The horse fidgeted and swayed, turning perpetually away, having to be turned back to the forever calling winds. Shrugging off the feeling, Whitmore slapped the horse on, causing it to whinny at some unseen phantom, rendering feelings of regret at the decision to disturb the dead.

Dismounting close to the house, Whitmore made his way directly to the place he had fallen in hopes of a quick retrieval. The morning winds howled through the broken boards and damaged old wood, urging him to make haste his task and depart. He did not think about it, but made the journey back onto the porch to search the spot on which he stood the previous day. He searched vehemently for the objects, but found nothing. They were gone.

Mustering all the courage he could, he stepped in closer, to the very spot in which he fell, but the items were not there. For a moment or two he convinced himself he had placed it elsewhere in his haste. Thus concluded, he searched the barn feverishly from top to bottom, leaving no bale of hay unturned or object unmoved. The only thing found were a second set of footprints, though not following his of yesterday. They seemed designed to be hidden, always coming to rest behind a corner or a post. The wet ground made the path easy to follow, coming in from the east to the house, concealed from his placement in the barn.

Kneeling, he noticed something wedged into the soil. Three spent cartridges from a flare gun lay just below the surface. It had been the sound he heard just before losing consciousness. Someone had followed him, but protecting him made no sense. Whoever his protector was, he knew the significance of the items. Someone knew what he was doing there, and by the few paths walked in parallel, he knew all.

Whitmore sunk to the floor a broken man, beaten down by events he could not recall. The little talent he possessed for observation came too slow. Someone had an unprecedented talent for the art of detection, and his little hypothesis was shaping into a theory. Theory without confirmation, however, was nothing more than a guess. His head ached at the thought, as if it somehow infringed upon a painful past he had put away to survive. Remounting the horse, he headed swiftly back to Stratford's estate.

The watch was the only tangible link to the crimes. Like a good officer, Doherty had taken great pains to keep it at the scene of the crime, yet equal lengths to conceal it until he was sure of his facts. It would be only a matter of time before this unseen hand found the watch and the shirt, if he did not have them already. Even in death the haunting phantom of Holmes's memory would throw wide the vile truth. Whitmore knew what he had to do. It would not be legal, but it had to be done. Whitmore could not take the chance anyone else would complete the investigation, taking down a virtuous man on false assumptions. He had to get the watch and the Bradshaw, but to do so required too much information he currently did not possess.

[85] By the time he had returned the morning sun had broken completely over the Downs to signal the lateness of the hour. Relinquishing the mare, Whitmore checked his watch to confirm the time, making the necessary calculations of time and effort, pressing quickly to catch a cab to the seven-thirty-five, and boarded the train bound for London. A small note left for Willow would hold him off for the moment. Making use of the time to study, if not memorise, the scanty autopsy report of Sherlock Holmes obtained from Stratford's desk, Whitmore concluded that no resurrection of the poor soul would be forthcoming. As the train paused just outside of Victoria Station, allowing the outbound trains to cross before proceeding, Whitmore checked the hour once more. He had about eight hours before dark. He would need every hour of that time to prepare.

A hansom cab took him swiftly to Whitehall where he spent the rest of the morning and part of the afternoon researching birth and death records of the house of Holmes. The location of Holmes's grave had been undisclosed to even the most influential of family and friends. They had made a public viewing on November 2, but the ground had been too hard for burial. It was customary in such cases to hold the body in a cold house until April, when a formal burial could then be made.

As it was already the second week in May, Whitmore speculated it would have already taken place, but no more than within four or five weeks, for it had been a hard winter.

From all accounts, Watson would have been present for the solemn occasion, but Mycroft Holmes would have abstained. The last report of him was that his health, both physically and mentally, had deteriorated past any hope of public appearance. Being so celebrated, Holmes's grave would not be within the city limits, lest any morbid aficionado seek it out for some last memento, requiring a guard to ward off grave robbers. It would also be doubtful that they would inter him next to his beloved father, for it would certainly be the first place an obsessed devotee might look. He would be placed inconspicuously among his own people, but not necessarily following the traditional paternal line. A comprehensive process of elimination left Whitmore with two likely candidates: the first was Holmes's grandmother, who was a direct descendant of the French artist Vernet. Her grave was an hour out of the city in a small Welsh town. It seemed the more reasonable of the two.

It was after four by the time he made his way among the headstones and burial mounds of the quaint churchyard, finding no less than six of Holmes's ancestors, but none of the graves were recent. It was evident that no one had visited the site for many years. The sun had declined well into the eastern horizon, marking short the available time. The second choice, upon reflection, was perhaps a more likely spot, for it was two hours out of London, but only half an hour from South End, a place Whitmore felt sure Watson had made reference to for his retirement. The clues had left little doubt, and coupling it with the cemetery being so close at hand, he chastised himself for not making it his location of choice.

Unfortunately, taking into account the return trip and train schedule, he did not arrive at Brentwood until dusk, making it difficult to see the condition of the ground, and making it hard to read the names on the stones. It forced him to acquire candles and lanterns before he made his way among the bleak unattended graves and marble markers of long forgotten friends. He had only one advantage in his favour. The hard winter had made it difficult to prepare the ground and breach the deep earth.

After nearly an hour of winding paths and the reading of obscure, weathered stones, he came upon a newly dug grave, for the grass was still patchy and bare in places. A grin of satisfaction escaped his lips as he held the lantern up to the writing on the insignificant stone bearing a solitary name and date. It read simply: HOLMES, 1854 -1903. A year or two would see the grave entirely forgotten, with no more reference to the celebrated detective than a surname and a reference to his young death, preserving his anonymity.

The cemetery suited Whitmore's needs rather well, with a tool shed near the entrance and a mausoleum some meters away. Breaking the lock on the shed, he procured a shovel and pickaxe by which to dig. Setting one lantern on a branch of the tree at the foot of the grave, he placed the other near the head and removed his coat, thrusting the pickaxe into the fresh earth.

It required nearly three hours of continuous digging before the surface of the coffin was reached. It was well past ten and his strength had left him, precluding any hope of carrying the body to the mausoleum to examine. It would have to be examined on site.

Clearing away the dirt from the sides of the lid, he pried open the coffin and straddled the corpse, readjusting the lantern at the head for better visibility. They had preserved his body rather well, dressing the wound to minimize the impact of its viewing, thus preserving the condition of the corpse to analyse. The bullet had entered in the rear of the upper left occipital lobe, exiting between the lower parietal bone, shattering the upper cheekbone and steering most of the damage. A strong Anglican jaw held a perfect set of teeth completely intact and a small scar just above his chin. His features were not unlike the characteristics described in Dr Watson's many accounts of him; tall, thin, middle-aged, and in good physical condition, all of which Whitmore had expected to find. The body certainly looked the expected part. Without further reverence to the dead, Whitmore unbuttoned the frock coat and pulled it away from the body, followed by tie and shirt until the entire upper body was exposed.

Hoisting the body in his arms and turning it over, he found the back to be clear, further substantiating his hypothesis, but confirming nothing. Laying the body back in the cold, unearthed box, Whitmore brushed the dirt from his hands only to note a peculiar residue affixed to his fingertips. The consistency was strange and colourless. Straddling the coffin, leaning up against the wall of dirt for support,

Whitmore leaned close to the lantern and examined his hands, finding a substance his mind puzzled over. It was theatrical makeup. The powder-like substance adhered to the skin with tenacity, causing a gentle prodding of suspicion in his mind. What cause would a man have to wear makeup? Grabbing the lamp and holding it close to the torn and inflicted head, Whitmore watched carefully as the shadows fell upon the crevices of the face, noting an odd discrepancy along the nose. The lantern flickered in the slight spring breeze casting shadows over the quiet and sullen face of the dead, fooling his senses.

The face looked lifelike, but possessed a disturbingly surrealistic quality. The small line of shadowing granted a distinct difference in texture between the various places on the face. The burns made it difficult to track the pattern of shadows. They were in varying degrees across his face, neck, and shoulder where he lay exposed to the flames. He had already been dead at the time, but the fluid in his body had caused the skin to melt. Continuing to gaze down from the hairline to the shoulder, he noted the degrees of texture changing, stopping repeatedly at the base of the nose, where the shadow continued to fall out of place. Searching his person diligently for the small pocketknife Helena had given him some weeks earlier; he opened it and gingerly scraped over the shadow of the burn. To his satisfaction, the skin moved, revealing a smooth patch of skin underneath. Holding the small membrane up to the light he found it to be opaque. A thorough search of each section of the face revealed several of these anomalies, primarily around the nose and forehead. With some prodding, the skin tore loose. With a smile of satisfaction, Whitmore turned his attention to the man's chest, noting that it was clear of any marks or old scarring, save a five-centimetre scar directly over the heart. Checking the hands, he found them free of cuts or scars, though there were numerous stains on his right hand. He sat back in infinite fulfilment, allowing himself to rest before returning the unfortunate soul to peace.

'Watson, you missed it,' Whitmore said to himself.

The hour had grown late, precluding any hope of a full return to Eastbourne that evening, and Whitmore was only half done with his search for the truth. There was something in London he wanted, and he no longer cared for the reverence or sanctity of the dead.

[86] Catching the last train, he made his way to the Marylebone station and walked up Melcombe Place to Baker Street. No longer taking care to avoid detection, he broke the lower corner windowpane on the door and turned the lock. With little more than the light of the street lamps outside pouring in the front windows, he made his way to the hall, stepping over the stack of mail still piled upon the floor.

Bursting into the upstairs rooms he lit a candle and made his way across the room to the table, sifting through the notes scribbled on several sheets of paper. Having obtained the object of his quest, he looked at his watch, which now read half past the hour of one. It would be five more hours before he could take a train back to Eastbourne. In a state of total exhaustion, he entertained the idea of facing the elusive proprietor, hoping in some tired, irrational way to confront the unfeeling monster who had deprived him of any semblance of his former life, not to mention the numerous lives given to save his and the total mental collapse of his own brother. Even Watson had been so severely affected by the detective's death that he closeted himself away from the public, retiring quietly to his country house.

The loathing for such a callous insensitive wretch began to well in Whitmore until all other thoughts dissipated from his mind. Examining himself in the mirror he shuddered at the frisson of disgust. The stink of the grave was upon him, but a great weariness overtook him and he sank into a fitful sleep upon the sofa until morning light broke like an alarm of realisation.

Whitmore struggled to his feet, rubbing the sleep from his eyes as he walked toward the front windows, looking out over the increasingly busy street below. There was a warm, almost familiar feeling about the view, giving rise to a sense of comfort he probably should not have lulled himself into, for the hour drew ever late. Still, the day promised to be warm and comfortable, easing the bursitis developed in recent months. He would at least be spared that pain, though the prospect of returning home to betray the trust placed in him was not a pain he could avoid.

Doing his best to clean himself up, Whitmore walked over to Kensington and hailed a cab to Victoria. It was with a heavy heart that he returned to South Lodge, which had become his home, to face the man who had opened his heart and home to him without reservation. More than once during that long train ride across the picturesque landscape of the countryside, Whitmore convinced himself that he could leave matters alone, let the pieces fall where they may without him. Let someone else take the burden of invasion and indignity.

But who would see to the proof of Stratford's innocence against an unbeatable man set against so esteemed a lion and lawmaker? Sherlock Holmes would again destroy any life Whitmore might dare to dream of having: a nemesis without feeling, a calculating machine, positively inhuman. There was no easy way to investigate the judge, no easy way to invade his deepest and most private secrets and, no excuse worth the betrayal needed to save his life. If only it were not Sherlock Holmes, the consummate unstoppable machine. From all accounts of him, the man was nothing if not unrelenting when he got the bit between his teeth, as it were. He was reckless, proving the truth to the detriment of any life around him.

[87] It was already past nine by the time Whitmore had arrived at South Lodge. Stepping inside he slipped the paper he had been fondling into his pocket and hung up his coat. Stratford, upon hearing the front door, stepped into the hall, sipping a cup of coffee. He greeted his guest without question or reproach as to his late arrival or questionable appearance.

Stratford put the cup in its saucer and gestured toward the door. 'John is in the study.'

The offer was given in a soft mild tone, but it was, not to put too fine a point on the matter, a command. Willow had been up all night, as a good parent or watchdog, protecting his investment. Some amount of concern was expected, but to learn that Willow had not spoken a word since the reading of Whitmore's note suggested a fair amount of anger. It was at this prospect that Whitmore gave up the idea of bathing before the confrontation, going to Willow directly.

Willow sat quiet and unmoved in his customary wing chair near the fireplace, but without his customary pipe. His staunchly expressionless face hid any hint to what was going on in his mind, though Whitmore had come to know it meant the very opposite of its appearance, prompting him to close the study doors. Willow continued his silence, though looking over his charge with a fair amount of scrutiny, if not curiosity. The tension rose sharply.

'It was important,' was all Whitmore could muster at Willow's obvious disappointment. 'I am sorry. I missed the last train back.'

Willow, taking it under advisement, stood up and slowly walked toward Whitmore, stopping at his shoulder. 'If you ever defy me again, I will kill you myself,' he rendered in a strong tone, suggesting he was entirely serious.

It was on Whitmore's mind to explain. It surely would have gone far to ease tensions, but without any more proof than a few scars and a tooth, Willow would not be convinced. This particular household would not be so willing to believe Sherlock Holmes had counterfeited his own death to solve a case, especially when it meant the death of others. Whitmore took the solemn warning to heart, but let him pass.

Out in the hall Willow motioned to Helena to draw nigh when he saw her exit the dining hall.

'I want you to go back to Chichester this very day and work closely with Brandon Faulkner, taking care not to let him out of your sight as you complete your work there.'

Brandon had been assisting his father in a proposal of new law, adding additional privileges for women in law. It was an excellent opportunity for Helena to work with Judge Faulkner, but considering recent events it hardly seemed appropriate to send her.

'I can't,' she said, almost pleading. 'I won't!'

Unlike Stratford's hold, which was slipping with his declining health, Willow knew his grip on Helena was as firm as ever. 'You would disobey me, as well?'

'Don't put it like that. You know my heart.'

'You will leave within the hour,' Willow ordered her, moving to go.

'Is it to punish me or Myles?' she asked, halting Willow.

'Neither! I need you there and all your senses intact,' he added with a soft tender touch that eased the reprimand. 'Trust me.'

SESSION CASE

QUEEN'S BENCH DIVISION

LORD JUSTICE

HAROLD A. W. STRATFORD

TWENTY-FIRST SESSION,

HELD AT

JUSTICE HALL, IN SUSSEX COURT,

ON FRIDAY, THE 27th DAY OF OCTOBER, 1903,

AND FOLLOWING DAYS.

TAKEN IN SHORT HAND

(BY AUTHORITY OF THE CORPORATION OF THE CITY OF EASTBOURNE)

BY A. WAKEFIELD

Eastbourne :

PRINTED FOR J. H. WILLOW, BY A. WAKEFIELD,

No. 74, MEADS;

AND PUBLISHED BY G. HERBERT, COUNTY COURT

1904

[88] It was not even ten o'clock and Stratford found his strength had left him. His hands were trembling, unable to perform the simplest tasks. His stomach felt queasy and his mind was sluggish to the point where even he could not ignore the obvious. His heart choked up into his throat until it was difficult to breathe. Reaching for the chair, Stratford barely found his way there before collapsing within its embrace, his head spinning through the pain. Damon stepped into the study, briefs in hand, ready to head to court.

Damon set the briefs down on the desk in contemplation of the problem. 'It's almost time to go. Are you going to make it?'

Stratford lifted his head and tried to muster a smile. 'I'll be all right.'

'How is the pain? Does your shoulder hurt?'

'No, it doesn't hurt. I just have a headache. I probably caught it from Myles,' he tried to jest.

'Do you want something for it? We have a long day.'

'No, no; I'm all right. Let's go.'

'Don't be stubborn. You have a full day of court and then the meeting tonight. If you let the pain get out of control you will never get ahead of it. It's just a little laudanum. Teixeira said it is as harmless as brandy and it can help you to think.'

'There is that,' Stratford conceded.

Damon walked over to the desk. Before Stratford could protest further, he unlocked the drawer and returned with a vial and syringe in hand. Stratford sat back feeling unworthy of his post for having to supplement his stamina. He had little choice. If he declined it would surely be noticed. He could not afford that. It was but a little prick and the deed was done. Stratford sat back in the chair and allowed the drug to surge through him, revitalizing him.

'Are you ready?' Willow asked, sticking his head in.

Stratford rolled down his sleeve. 'Just coming.'

Damon had been quick to put away the paraphernalia, but not before Willow caught the action.

By the close of court, however, Stratford's stamina had waned. He felt tired and unwell. Typically the arrival of distinguished guests each year found him at the top of his game, excited and sharp at the prospect. This evening, however, he dreaded the very thought. He sat in his room, sweating and uncomfortable. His chest felt heavy and every small detail seemed to annoy him. He paced back and forth full of regret, having to play host to an ungrateful crowd, It pained him to maintain a political stance when everything in him shouted to set the record straight.

His under butler knocked, waited, and then opened the door when there was no response. 'Forgive me, my lord, I did knock. Are you all right?'

'I am fine, other than to suffer through a thousand disturbances. What do you want?'

'Miss Stratford left word that she would be late tonight. She will be travelling with the Faulkner's.'

For whatever reason, the intrusion, the news, or both, Stratford did not take it well. He shouted for the man to get out and thrust the nearest book at him, striking the door as it closed.

[89] Hearing the commotion, Willow stepped out into the hallway.

'William, is that his lordship shouting?'

'Yes, sir.'

Willow wiped the shaving soap from his face and tossed the towel over his shoulder. 'What is he on about?'

'I believe he was not pleased that Miss Stratford will be late in this evening.'

Willow nodded in acknowledgement as he waved the man on and stepped across the way, gently knocking on Stratford's door.

'Now what do you want? I said to leave me alone!' Stratford shouted through the door.

Willow turned the knob and stepped in. Stratford had his back turned, but the fact that he could not stand still in the attempt to dress was telling. It was not difficult to see Stratford was at his wits' end. His demeanour adjusted slightly when he turned around and saw Willow, but his restraint could not hide the state of his health.

'I want you to stay upstairs tonight,' Willow announced.

Stratford tried to put on a brave front. 'I can handle it.'

Placing his hand on Stratford's back, Willow spoke softly. 'Tonight is very important. There are undercurrents, Harry, which could carry us away if we do not have a care. You cannot afford to show any weakness, especially in light of recent events.'

'I know that.'

'I didn't say you didn't. I am merely pointing out that we will be watched. You will be watched.'

'What are you implying?'

'I am implying that very question, spoken in that very tone, shows clearly the state of your nerves. I am on your side, Harry. I have your back, but you need to trust me.'

Stratford turned away for a moment before finally turning back to him. 'What do you want me to do?'

'I want you to play the role you were born to play, but in turn, let me play mine. Stay in the study whenever you are feeling tired. When you have the strength, make an appearance in my presence. I shall play opposite you. When someone asks for you I will say you are attending your guests elsewhere. When you approach me, let me offer the suggestion of where you were before you take the conversation over. When Helena arrives, keep busy elsewhere.'

The suggestion suddenly invoked suspicion. 'Why should I do that?'

'Because, old darling, she knows every facet of your face and bearing. She will be the first to know you are not feeling yourself and she will make a fuss. She will inadvertently draw attention to your condition when she fusses over you.'

Willow was relieved when Stratford sighed with a nod. One false move this evening could cost Stratford everything.

[90] Guests began to trickle in as early as five o'clock. Stratford granted an occasional and strategic appearance, which prevented anyone from noticing his frequent respites away from the crowd. Distinguished guests such as Pushkin, Woolrich, and Bacolor walked through the doors feeling the strength and power that had always prevailed at South Lodge. The streets teamed with hospitality and warmth seen but once a year. Carriages lined up along Darley Road waiting to enter. It generated a swarm of make-works, boys and young men offering ad-hoc services to gentlemen waiting in line, anything from opening a door to a last-minute buff and shine. Such

was the liquid nature and expectation of the event that one could even find a make-work for mild hemming and button replacement, sword polishing, and sheath repair.

As dusk fell over the waves at the marina, moving in towards the coastal line of hotels, pebble beach, and the brick walls of the estate, the great hall was opened with feast and festivities. Smells, sights, and sounds filled the estate with high hopes for the coming year. Tensions fell to the wayside in favour of laughter and cheer. Even young Faulkner had put away his thirst for blood in favour of Helena's companionship, happy to see her without her customary escort.

So beautiful was she as she stood atop the stairs that not one eye failed to gaze upon her in complete rapture. She paused at the landing to look down upon the guests in the hallway. Her eyes settled with a gentle smile near the doors to the ballroom where a proud father watched as his choice of his daughter's suitor bounded up the stairway to offer her his arm, escorting her down. Each step, each move held more grace than any other woman might hope to achieve. She was the picture of perfection. They looked a handsome couple, pleasing many of the old world elders, hoping to see the young couple carry on the grand traditions set down before them.

Faulkner released her long enough for Stratford to grant her a kiss on her cheek. It seemed to give him strength to see her confirming to constraint, approving of her with immense pride, which went far to dispel his disappointment in the tardiness of her arrival. He didn't even seem to mind when Willow took her over.

Pulling Brandon aside, Stratford whispered both reassurance and a warning.

'Have a care tonight. I do not want a scene, so hold yourself in check.'

'You mean because of your guest.'

'He is not going to be here tonight so behave yourself. Whatever happens, show restraint and allow her latitude. Remember, the bonds she forms will either make or break you.'

The reassurance that Whitmore would not be in attendance seemed just the balm Faulkner needed to relax. The two men followed into the ballroom where Helena quickly became the centre of conversation. Stratford was the perfect host, always watching and mingling properly with his guests, taking part only peripherally in the festivities, so that he might never appear neglectful. The young legal minds, akin to their older counterparts, grouped together in a conversation of the law, eager to hear the extraordinary insight of so beautiful a mind and body. It was not law, however, that occupied Helena's mind through the laughter, debate, and music. Her attention was repeatedly drawn towards a single hope of relief, which did not come. She looked for her father for a word, but he no longer seemed to be in attendance. A sudden fear swept over her at his absence. If Brandon Faulkner convinced her father it would be advantageous to propose to her in public, he might play along in hopes of forcing the issue. Desiring to speak to him before he did something foolish, Helena filtered through one crowd after another, in polite conversation, until she finally made her way out into the hall and back to the south wing.

Going through each room, she found her father tucked away in the corner of his study, curled intimately with a fourteenth-century book. Helena stole in like a bashful child.

'Daddy?'

Stratford gave a proud smile at the sight of her.

'I wanted to talk to you,' she said gently. 'I didn't mean to disturb you.'

Waving her in, Stratford stretched forth a hand for a kiss. 'Of course you are not disturbing me. They have been dead five hundred years,' he chuckled, waving the book. 'I think they can wait a little longer. What is on your mind? My word, don't you look the picture,' he remarked again.

'Can we talk about Brandon? I know you spoke to him and he told you his intentions. I also know you intend to announce an engagement between us tonight.'

'No,' Stratford said quickly. 'I only agreed to allow him the floor. I will announce nothing until you give me the nod.' Stratford put down his book and gave his daughter another kiss. 'But I will not say I am not delighted. He will make you a fine husband. I trust him implicitly, both with your welfare and the welfare of this estate.'

Helena cast her eyes away, knowing her next statement would not be well received. 'You asked me to think about it and I have. I would not disobey you for the world, but I cannot marry Brandon. I do not love him and I do not believe I shall ever come to love him, not in that way.'

'You want to marry someone else, don't you? It is not like I do not know your feelings for him,' her father replied, 'but you know my views on the matter. It is more than his age.'

'You make him out to be ancient and yet you approve of Dr Stoner, who is not all that much younger.'

'He is not half a century older than you. Dr Stoner is considerably younger and far more appropriate.'

'Do not exaggerate his age, Father. He's not that much older than I am. I am well aware you have objections. Let us speak of this rationally,' she found herself asking, slipping into debate before pulling back. 'I thought age did not matter? It didn't matter with Mother,' she blurted out before seeing the look on his face.

'She was not young enough to be my daughter!'

'Why now would you object to him? Was it not you who insisted I marry?'

'Why do you have to choose him?'

'Have you not said many times what a good man he is?'

'That is not the point.'

Putting her tender fingers to his face she turned his head, forcing him to look at her. 'I love him and I do not desire to live my life without him.'

'You don't know him as I do.'

With a smile she gave a nod. 'I believe I do. I have been in his arms and'—she hesitated for a moment, trying to gain the strength to reveal the news to him—'in his intimate embrace. I can accept no other.'

Stratford could feel his insides wrench into knots until a heavy hand pressed upon his chest, squeezing the breath from him. His teeth clenched so tightly that it was impossible for him to speak, though there was little he could say. He had told Willow he could have her if he would stay, but to hear his daughter speak of their intimacy filled him with scarcely controlled rage.

Desperate to mediate her father's violent reaction, Helena wrapped her arms around him and held him tight.

'I know it is hard for you. I know you had your heart set on your son-in-law replacing you on the bench, but—'

'Oh, I'm sure he expects to take my place. Has he asked for your hand yet? I can tell you he has not asked me!'

Helena pulled back at the harsh ingratitude of his tone. 'No, he has not asked me yet, but I am hoping he will shortly. And no one, Daddy, no one can take your place, not on the bench and not in my heart. But I love him. Can you not find it in your heart to love him too? I know he was not what you expected and you worry about him spending so much time in his laboratory, but I do love him so. He is so much like you.'

Stratford snapped back, taking her by the shoulders. 'Laboratory? Whitmore?' he questioned, trying to force his brain into adjust.

Turning away in despair, Helena picked up her wrap. 'Oh, Daddy, not tonight. I only told you so that you would not make a scene. I love you, but sometimes I wonder what it is you really want. Obviously it is not my children at your feet,' she rebuked him, and stormed out the door.

[91] Stratford longed to follow her, eager to clear the misunderstanding, but without warning an invisible hand reached up and clutched his chest, sinking him into the chair. At the earliest moment he could bring himself to rise, Stratford poked his head out of the door and looked for Dr Stoner. Teixeira might assist, but his discretion could not always be counted on when he took too much drink.

Seeing him in the corner, Stratford motioned to have a private word. Stoner eagerly took his leave from the prime minister who had been knee-deep in the explanation of why commercial industrialization was the key to domestic policy, and followed after.

Rounding the corner, Stratford ducked into the drawing room and closed the doors after Stoner was safely inside.

'I owe you a debt for relieving me. I thought I was going to die of boredom.'

'I need your help—and your discretion.'

'You are very welcome to both. What can I do?'

Stratford stood for a moment, wanting desperately to withdraw, but as he felt the sweat pour from him and his countenance waver, he pushed himself to speak.

'I need you to give me something to get me through the evening.'

Stoner suddenly looked at him through a physician's eyes, noting the obvious symptoms exhibited by his prospective patient. Where a cursory glance might have shown Stratford to be himself, he clearly was not. Even without an examination it could be inferred that Stratford was bordering on collapse.

'You don't look well, Harry. What has been going on? Come, have a seat. I need to have a look at you.'

Stratford pulled away. 'Ah, don't start that! I need something to get me through this evening. We can fix the rest later. Do you know what is at stake out there? Everything we have worked for, everything we have built. If I falter there will be nothing left. Just give me something to keep me going for tonight.'

'Are you in pain?'

'Considerable, at the moment.'

'What are you taking for it? Be honest. I can't help if you don't trust me and confide in me.'

'Laudanum, four times a day.'

Stoner made the calculation in his mind, stacking it up against Stratford's appearance. 'What else?'

'Nothing. Al, I can't do this on my own. I have no energy, I can't think, I'm faltering. Just do something.'

'Harry, you have to tell me.'

'I am telling you the truth! Why does everyone doubt my word?'

'All right,' Stoner appeased him. 'Take a seat. I'll go get my bag, but I want your word you will be in my surgery tomorrow. If you don't, count on me being here by supper.'

Returning with a small black leather bag, Stoner looked over at his patient with a fair amount of reluctance.

'I am going to give you a medicinal dosage of cocaine. You will feel yourself become flushed, but don't be alarmed. It will allow you to focus, give you more energy and some strength. If you notice anything unusual—'

'Just do it,' Stratford insisted.

Stoner was reluctant, but weighed against Stratford's power, especially in terms of getting to see Helena and spend time with her, Stoner was required to keep his own countenance. If his objections were not compelling, it would be wise to yield.

'Roll up your sleeve.'

Placing the needle to the skin, Stoner pressed gently inward and pierced the vein. Depressing the plunger he watched Stratford's face relax and drift momentarily away. Withdrawing it, he cleaned the needle and tucked it neatly back in its leather case, wrestling with the wisdom of his decision. In a few minutes Stratford's composure shifted dramatically, and he stood and rolled down his sleeve. Patting Stoner on the back, he straightened himself and made his way back to the activities as if nothing had transpired.

SESSION CASE

QUEEN'S BENCH DIVISION

LORD JUSTICE

HAROLD A. W. STRATFORD

TWENTY-SECOND SESSION,

HELD AT

JUSTICE HALL, IN SUSSEX COURT,

ON FRIDAY, THE 27th DAY OF OCTOBER, 1903,

AND FOLLOWING DAYS.

TAKEN IN SHORT HAND

(BY AUTHORITY OF THE CORPORATION OF THE CITY OF EASTBOURNE)

BY A. WAKEFIELD

Eastbourne :

PRINTED FOR J. H. WILLOW, BY A. WAKEFIELD,

No. 74, MEADS;

AND PUBLISHED BY G. HERBERT, COUNTY COURT

1904

[92] For nearly an hour the young lady mingled, listened, and intently searched the crowd for one face that remained conspicuously absent, informing her that her father had stacked the deck against her. Excusing herself from the gathering of men trying hard to sound intelligent for her benefit, she made her way across the room to safe shores. She clung to Willow's arm for the much needed strength to persevere. His presence kept the feeding sharks at bay, for even the boldest was too insecure to approach him. In his care she was not required to make polite conversation or paint on a smile mindlessly. She could catch her breath and allow herself to think.

A shadowy form passed by the window in the distance and Helena bestowed a thankful kiss to her watchdog before breaking free. Though warm in heart for the reassurance, it alerted the keen old barrister to piranhas in the water. Much to his dismay, she disappeared around the corner into the crowd, leaving only the sight of his old friend, watchful at the door. An unsettling feeling swept over him. His mind raced as he glanced over the many faces in the room. Brandon Faulkner had also disappeared, heightening his anxiety, even without open trouble.

The smoking room was the most popular, offering to its guest a wide variety of tobaccos and spirits for relaxation. If ever a man could be pampered, this room and its contents would provide the means. Paul Faulkner favoured it, but his son favoured another room, a room away from the crowd. Getting there, however, was not as easy as taking a flight of stairs. Many members found the occasion an excellent opportunity to speak to him privately, detaining him at every step. Stratford had put him up for an important position, and if approved, it could open many doors for him. Brandon could hardly cast the others off, making him that more the eager to see Helena when he finally escaped.

Brandon took off up the stairs the moment he was free and found Damon standing at the end of the hall outside of her room, as if waiting for him. At Brandon's approach, Damon slowly pushed back the door to reveal a large, clean, airy room, devoid of occupants. The bed was in perfect order and the room tidy, save for a pile of clothes draped over the chair to be collected for laundry. Faulkner sauntered in dejection around the room, hoping to find comfort, if not some clue, as to her whereabouts.

'Where is she? When she left I thought she came upstairs.'

'I don't know. She left in a hurry, though. I see that Mr Whitmore has gone out as well,' Damon poked. 'It seems to be the pattern these past few months. They never seem to be apart anymore. Perhaps she is in his room.'

'Not tonight, Sam. He is not here and I'm not in the mood for your prodding.'

'He was. I saw him come out of his room looking a bit untidy.'

'Leave it alone, Sam,' Faulkner scorned, making his way back down the hall to the stairs.

No more than one step down, Faulkner was recalled by four simple words. 'Now that is odd.'

Faulkner turned around to see Damon standing in the doorway to Whitmore's room.

'What?'

'It is nothing,' he shrugged. 'We had best return.'

Faulkner slowly made his way back to Whitmore's room, glancing in to understand the comment. A disturbing sight caught his eye. It was enough for him to break protocol and enter Whitmore's room irrespective of permission or propriety. He saw something that froze his heart.

It was a small heap of indistinguishable cloth lying haphazardly on the floor, its presence notable only in its soft delicacy contrasting sharply against the marked bachelor setting of Whitmore's room. He shambled into the room, his mind screaming at him to simply turn and leave as quickly as possible, but still he moved forward like a man transfixed. Stepping up to it with curiosity, Faulkner stared at the mound for a moment or two before bending down to pick it up, its shape finally taking form in his mind.

It was a simple garment of silk, strewn carelessly on the carpet. He fondled it in his hands, its soft silky texture pleasing to the touch, smooth and free-flowing. Drawing it to his nostrils, he took a deep breath, for the subtle hint of lilacs called to him. It breathed of her, that soft delicate child he waited for, dreaming of her until his passions could not be quelled. The anger began to well in him like an awakening volcano, but it was the bed that turned him cold. It was dishevelled with impressions of two people. Such a simple thing, how could it ruin a man? How could it eviscerate and ruin him utterly? Devastated beyond words, Faulkner threw the garment on the floor and burst out into the hall.

Damon took care to pick up the woman's garment and replace it in the laundry hamper in Helena's room before making his way slowly, but amiably, past the old gentlemen and friends downstairs.

[93] Outside of the smoking room, Willow approached his old friend casually, without drawing attention, concerned that Stratford's expression showed too much agitation. He felt sure it was no small matter, for Stratford was not easily disturbed, even when ill. Given Stratford's natural containment, to let loose even a shadow of emotion suggested a matter of significance.

'What is wrong?' Willow queried inconspicuously, diverting his inquiry with a nod for a glass of wine.

'I don't see Helena.'

'She has had something on her mind all evening. No doubt she is overwhelmed by all the attention of the little boys. She'll come around when she is ready.'

'Was that a reproach?'

'Just an observation, dear boy. Don't lose your composure. She probably stepped out for some air. She'll be back.'

'I told her to stay put,' Stratford retorted with some amount of frustration.

'Don't work yourself up. I'm sure she simply needed a moment to herself.'

'To hell she did,' Stratford muttered under his breath, gulping the last of his wine. 'She went to Whitmore after I expressly told her not to. I told her to trust me.'

'It's not the end of the world. Mind your temper,' Willow warned, trying to lower Stratford's tone as he raised his glass to a most keen observer of their conversation across the room. Paul Faulkner had a sharp eye, with a reputation for missing nothing. It made him a formidable enemy in the courtroom, and often he would take it upon himself to overrule findings on a subtle observation made during proceedings. It was wise to raise a glass that all was well, lest he make it his business to know the details of the conversation.

'Not tonight, John, please. Appearances are everything. She should remember her duty. She gave me her word.'

'Calm yourself. Let us see how the matter falls out, and remember, we are being observed.'

Stratford would have done well to heed the words of his dearest friend, for it did not take Judge Faulkner long to observe that all was not as well as Willow had professed with a raised glass. A circulation of inquiries of his own told him quickly that the girl was not in attendance, but he held fast in hope since his son had also gone missing. He had minded well, over the prior months, how Stratford's hold on his household was slipping. For a man in Stratford's position, any sign of weakness meant his enemies would quickly set upon him. It would go far for Stratford's guests to become aware of Helena's absence, if she were to be found in the company of Brandon Faulkner, a couple in love escaping the eye of the general public. Public opinion was a powerful force, persuading the most stubborn of men.

Paul Faulkner was being too agreeable and Willow had become nervous at the thought. Stratford was not in control and it would not take long for it to become widely known. The entire court hung as if by single threadbare strand. One minute disruption would cause total collapse.

Motioning to Stratford for a word, Damon subtly took him aside, speaking quietly to him for a moment in the hall before Stratford made an unprecedented outburst.

'I'll kill him!' was heard coming from Stratford as he immediately tore off out of the room, disappearing into the corridor. Willow stood helplessly, caught in a mob of conversation and interest. Though he pressed through the crowded coats and elbows to reach the judge, he arrived too late. Stratford had gone, with no clue as to his direction. All Willow could do was wait, anxiously, fearfully, regretfully, for the next move.

At first it seemed as if the unfortunate statement was hollow, for by his watch it had been twenty minutes or so and, outside of Stratford's absence, nothing seemed amiss. Giving a short sigh of relief, Willow took up a glass of port and struck up a conversation with Bridgewater.

[94] It wasn't hard for Brandon Faulkner to find them. Helena always headed to the stables when she wanted to escape. It was not too far a leap of the imagination to believe she now wanted to escape with that deformed creature Faulkner was fast coming to despise. Rounding the corner, he stopped short at the sound of their voices.

Pressed to his limits of endurance, Faulkner would not be put off in making his intentions clear. He wanted Whitmore's life extinguished in his hands. The image of his perspective fiancée entwined in heated passion with a man such as Whitmore was beyond any human endurance and would not be tolerated.

Faulkner stopped short outside the stables. Seeing her sweet face, even in the presence of Whitmore, he found himself unable to continue. Even without being able to hear their conversation, her close proximity to Whitmore could not fail to further rouse his protective, if not possessive, nature towards her, but he held fast. When she reached out to touch Whitmore's arm in so loving a manner, Faulkner could stand it no longer and started inward when Helena suddenly departed through the rear gate.

Waiting until Whitmore was alone, Faulkner took him by surprise. 'I warned you before to leave her alone.'

The challenge instantly turned the mood, causing a subtle but unmistakable grin to escape Whitmore's lips as he stood fast.

'You can't have her.' Faulkner continued. 'Do you honestly think all it takes is to bed her to make her yours? You have no idea what you are playing at. She is mine, and there is nothing you can do to change that. Lord Stratford will never allow it.'

Whitmore could say and do nothing without incriminating the young lady, but Faulkner's temper rose sharply anyway. 'Come on, man; do you stand there and deny it? Admit it!'

'I will do no such thing,' Whitmore replied, moving to go.

'I warn you, old man, leave her alone. You've already worn out your welcome with the judge.'

'And Willow? You say you have Stratford's backing, but how is it you discount Willow? I noticed your relationship with him is, shall we say, strained?'

'Willow is nothing.'

'On the contrary, Willow seems to have a greater hold on the young lady than her father. Her affection toward him is—'

'You hold your tongue. I should kill you where you stand! It is no less than you deserve.'

'Is that what you said to Sherlock Holmes? I understand you didn't like him either, did you?'

Faulkner suddenly backed off. 'I did not know the man.'

'He certainly knew you. Your name was prominently displayed in his Bradshaw beside an investigation of his into your affairs.'

Faulkner smiled with assurance. 'I don't think so.'

'You don't think he wrote it or you don't think I found it? I wonder what Lord Stratford would make of the matter. I'm sure your involvement of the man's murder would certainly interest him.'

'I wasn't involved in that.'

'Then you have an alibi for the evening?'

'Solid.' Faulkner's reply was overconfident.

'I think you did know Mr Holmes, and you also knew that Miss Stratford admired him, studied him, even came to model his methods and his celibacy in order to devote herself to her work, just like he did.'

'You are very much mistaken. I tell you, she could not abide the man. He mocked the law and for that she hated him. Her interest in his career was but a passing fancy, no more. What do I care that she escapes into a world of his adventures hidden beneath pages of folly? He was no threat to me.'

'I think he was! He made specific mention of you in his notes. There was a note tucked in his Bradshaw that had a list of your suspect investments. He made a list while on the way down here and tucked it within the pages of his notebook. I found it whilst in London. If that investigation ever came to light, your prospects for marriage to Miss Stratford would be at an end. What a lucky thing for you it disappeared. I think his interest in you would have gone far had the results of his investigation reached Lord Stratford.'

Faulkner's face darkened and his voice took on a murderous tone.

'How dare you! You bastard.'

'It was not I who prevented your marriage these past years. Perhaps Mr Holmes created obstacles that you would prefer to have removed, such as his investigation into certain interests of yours in Ireland. His death seems to have solved those issues rather well, especially since the accompanying deaths took all notice and suspicion away from you.'

'Sherlock Holmes was no more than an amateur dabbling in the crimes of the upper classes. He presented no threat to me, or my marriage to Miss Stratford, no more than you do now.'

'It is only a matter of time before the truth comes out. Eventually, Mycroft Holmes will become involved, if he isn't already.'

'What now, chemist, do you fancy yourself a detective? I have a better idea: I give you a good thrashing and you crawl back to wherever it is you came from.' He removed his coat and put up his fists with a smile.

Eager to meet the challenge, Whitmore took a ready stance. Faulkner had been a thorn in his side long enough and this was a chance to get back some of his own.

Making the first thrust, Faulkner reeled to regain his balance, eagerly attempting the move again and again, only to be struck on every punch thrown by his opponent. His anger grew in close harness with his increasing humiliation. Whitmore was at least ten years his senior and partially crippled. For such a creature to be held in higher regard by the young lady than a young virile man of her father's liking could not be more unimaginable in Faulkner's mind.

Helena's stallion, unnerved by the fighting, kicked at his stall feverishly until it was more than the blows of an inexperienced boxer that threatened harm. Splinters of wood flew from the stall as Myth reared up and broke some of the loose boards. His disdain for tension could easily be lethal, had he not been so well confined.

After several rounds of unsuccessful attempts at degrading his elder and more experienced opponent, Faulkner reached for a thick riding crop and swung it at Whitmore. Grasping Faulkner's arm midway into the swing, Whitmore overpowered him with too much ease for Faulkner's comfort, but Whitmore grew tired of the game of juvenile revenge taken out in violence. He had had enough of bloodshed and carnage. Removing the crop from Faulkner's hand, Whitmore thrust it into the corner, infuriating the young subordinate to the last extremes of mortification.

'You think you've won, that you have succeeded in besting me,' Faulkner tried to berate him. 'If you take her, the only thing you will succeed in is making her your widow!'

Whitmore looked at him in disgust leavened with pity. 'Strong words for a boy who cannot even overcome a crippled old man.'

Faulkner could not hide his rage at the slight, taking a last swing at his opponent for his insolence. Whitmore met him head-on, and with a push sent Faulkner stumbling in disgrace. Arising in humiliation, Faulkner whisked up his coat, pulling it on in haste to leave. Reaching for his own coat, Whitmore stood for a moment, reflecting on the implication of Faulkner's words. They had been said in anger in an attempt to discredit him, but had there been a ring of truth to them? Faulkner was a jealous man with a flash temper. He clearly had no love for Holmes, and the implication that Faulkner would not have liked the outcome of one of the detective's side investigations gave Faulkner more of a motive to kill than the most obvious suspect. His obsession with the judge's daughter, coupled with his ideas of success, made for a dangerous combination.

Faulkner had no more than turned away when suddenly, without warning; he lunged at Whitmore with a pocket-knife, which had been concealed in his coat pocket. Slicing open Whitmore's coat, vest, and shirt through to the skin, the moment of surprise dulled Whitmore's senses so thoroughly even the pain was unable to register.

'I warn you, Whitmore, don't ever turn your back on me.'

Faulkner left him standing there, his hand clutched to his chest in reaction more than physical pain or injury. Pulling his hand away revealed an amount of blood which suddenly seemed to throw the horse into a wild frenzy, bursting easily from the open stall, quite mad, rearing up and trampling everything in his path. Cornering Whitmore with no escape, the horse fiercely waved his forelegs at him as if Whitmore were the ultimate threat. Crushing the mirror and loose fittings in the way, Myth presented a clear and present danger.

Whitmore was trapped, for the area of the barn which held him had no means of escape, save past the wild horse. Striking Whitmore smartly on the arm, Myth had torn Whitmore's shirtsleeve and scraped off several layers of skin, marking well the danger he was in.

Hearing the wild cries of the angry horse from the back of the house and knowing full well that the horse had been a danger in the past, George dropped what he was doing and rang out the alarm bell, wasting no time in rousing the grooms to assist. Though assistance was fast in coming, the horse did not allow enough passage to render it captured. Myth bolted wildly about the barn as if trapped, unable to realise that his own panic had prevented his easy passage out. Everything in his path, including Whitmore, was a threat to him in his panicked state.

Each passing minute presented more peril, yet every attempt to restrain the poor beast, or to clear passage, was met with one thousand pounds of raw muscle trebled by panic. The calamity had captured the attention of the guests, who immediately rushed to the scene. George made an attempt to make his way around, but was crushed against the sidewall, breaking two of his ribs. There was no way out. Myth was beside himself as if wildly possessed, willing to die in panic to get out, rather than accept any human intervention.

Willow looked frantically for Stratford to assist in a plan, but Stratford could not be found, pressing on a raw nerve Willow tried to dismiss. Forcing his way to the other entrance of the stables, Willow came up over each stall until he was in the adjoining room, an arm's length away. An arm's length was as good as a mile, for every attempt to assist his charge met with more panic from the distraught stallion. It had been a long time since Willow had prayed in hopes of an answer, but a whispered prayer seemed to come at no better time, for no sooner had he looked up to God when he found his counterpart staring back at him through the window opposite ready to help.

Helena pushed her way to the front to reach the horse, feeling sure that a friendly voice would see him calm, bringing him back to reason. It was then that Helena saw for the first time that Whitmore had been pinned without escape, blood staining his white shirt. The horse quieted until her voice quivered, triggering the horse to bolt with even more brutality than he had before. For an instant her heart leapt from her breast in terror at the thought of harm coming to the man she had come to hold dear in her heart.

She screamed for her father to intervene, pleading with him with the confidence of a child, finding him now at the forefront of the commotion. His great heart broke at the sight, seeing her as she was as a little child, heartbroken at too painful a sight, knowing as he did then that it would have to be his hand to take something precious from her. He looked around for some agent of mercy to assist him, feeling powerless to ease the suffering. Then, from across the room, a voice called to him as if sent by God himself.

'Harry, the gun!' Willow called out over the commotion.

The manager's rifle hung over the riding crops and saddles near the window. A clear shot would see the animal down. It would not be an easy feat to obtain, but it seemed the only choice. Stratford stretched through the window and made for the gun. His fingers brushed the butt, moving it only slightly on each attempt. He was not tall enough. Calling for something to stand on, Stratford felt his chest tighten again until he could hardly breathe, forcing him to pause out of sight against the side of the wall for a moment. Whitmore was running out of time.

Reaching in one more time, he snatched up the rifle secured to the wall by two hooks. Myth seemed to take particular offence to another intrusion, adding to the panic, which caused him to thrust wildly about at the window, jolting Stratford back. Planning his moves carefully before executing more, Stratford blocked out all but what he had to do.

Coming round the outside window, which gave a clearer view, Stratford took careful aim. With shaking hands he put his finger on the trigger, struggling to force himself to squeeze. He stood for a moment or two holding the gun, trying to dispel the image of his four-year-old daughter witnessing him putting down Myth's mother, Helena's little tears streaming down her face as she pled for her father to stop.

Stratford held the rifle to his shoulder and looked down the barrel between the sights to the beast, now quite mad. The individual voices of the crowd began to pass from his ears, hearing only the echoes of the past and the throbbing pounding of his own heart. Time slowed as if to capture each horrific moment. The steel barrel felt cold as death and his heart beat ever louder in his ears. He looked up, facing Myth eye to eye, passing some indescribable message to the animal, and knowing what the next moment would bring. The horse seemed to settle for an instant, as if he knew somehow, and Stratford did not look back, prepared to take the shot while he had it. Stratford drew a breath and squeezed the trigger. The crowd waited in breathless anticipation for the startling explosion of the gun, but it never came.

Mumbling some profanity to himself in ultimate frustration, Willow scrambled up the wall with deliberate intent, ignoring the risk to intervene. As he breached the top, one leg nearly over the other side, Myth bolted straight for him. Just as the horse reached the wall a shot rang out from above and the horse fell dead. All eyes turned toward Avondale, who stood masterfully behind a smoking revolver.

The explosion seemed to strike the girl's heart as if it were her own, causing her to leap forward only to be held back by a strong arm. Brandon took her in arms like a delicate flower and in the next moment the crowd had closed the gap between her and the door. Brandon Faulkner was adept at many things, but seeing a woman outside of conventional roles could not be counted among them. To him, she was a tender rosebud in need of protection, and so he took the lady back to her room with his heart as warm for her as ever.

Willow set the staff to tending the injured and the removal of the horse, drawing Whitmore to his feet, while Stratford took the nearest available seat awaiting the repercussions of yet another failure, now on the grounds of his own home. He had failed to secure and failed to protect, and it was not for the first time. It did not matter what the reason was. He had failed in his duty. Ensuring that Whitmore was taken in hand by Avondale and Dr Stoner, Willow came around to Stratford, who looked pitifully up at him. Willow offered him a hand and they strolled up toward the house, Willow putting a hand on Stratford's back on his way, guiding him in procession. The long walk was taken in silence, leading away from the commotion of the house, taking the path to the study doors.

Inside, Willow latched the doors closed, turning around to face his old friend, trying hard to put away any preconceived notions or appearance of doubt. However, he now also had to set himself in a position outside of those realms, for he had made the same vow as Stratford with regard to the estate. As Willow placed the rifle on the desk, he tried to remember his failure with Stratford before.

Stratford took a seat in the chair beside the fire, awaiting the verdict with anxious trepidation, keeping only his own countenance. Standing for some time, Willow finally returned his attention to the rifle. Picking it up, he slipped the release, bending the handle back from the barrel. Finding it devoid of shells, he gently forced it closed and replaced it back on the desk. Without a word, he walked over to the doors leading into the hall and stepped out, closing them after him to leave Stratford in peace. A repayment for the embarrassment he had unwittingly visited upon his old friend, or a subtle sign of contempt? That he would keep forever to himself.

SESSION CASE

QUEEN'S BENCH DIVISION

LORD JUSTICE

HAROLD A. W. STRATFORD

TWENTY-THIRD SESSION,

HELD AT

JUSTICE HALL, IN SUSSEX COURT,

ON FRIDAY, THE 27th DAY OF OCTOBER, 1903,

AND FOLLOWING DAYS.

TAKEN IN SHORT HAND

(BY AUTHORITY OF THE CORPORATION OF THE CITY OF EASTBOURNE)

BY A. WAKEFIELD

Eastbourne :

PRINTED FOR J. H. WILLOW, BY A. WAKEFIELD,

No. 74, MEADS;

AND PUBLISHED BY G. HERBERT, COUNTY COURT

1904

[95] Whitmore's injuries looked far worse than they truly were, superficial in nature and easily tended to. At the deepest point, one cut had possibly needed a stitch, but no more. George's ribs, however, would have to be tightly bound, for at least two of them were clearly broken.

Standing in the doorway, Willow observed everything, waiting patiently for matters to settle. His silence, however, could not be taken as distance. Someone had stepped out of bounds, harming not only the man Willow had taken in hand and heart, but in disobeying the primary rule of the estate. If the argument between the two men had been witnessed, no one was quick in coming forth. From the divulged information from his sources about the incident, the tragic scene in the stables could take many forms in terms of guilt; one, unfortunately, was not in Stratford's favour. Additionally, Willow had noticed the bolt had been released from the stall and several key players that should have been first on the scene were last. 'Amnesty and Protection': to break this rule was to face a punishment far worse than any court could bestow.

Complete in the task of dressing Whitmore's wounds, the myriad of doctors and assistants departed to leave only Willow and Judge Faulkner, while Brandon waited without for his enemy to bring his career to a close. Willow stepped all the way inside and nudged the door closed.

'Does it hurt much?' Willow opened with a half-hearted smile in an attempt to reassure his friend.

'It's like old times,' Whitmore jested back, and Willow broke into a full smile.

'It doesn't look so bad,' Willow offered, examining the wound. 'You're lucky; you could have been killed. Any ideas on how Myth came to be out of his stall?' Willow asked, knowing full well Whitmore knew far more than he was telling.

'It was my own clumsiness. I cut myself and did not depart soon enough. I should have been more careful.'

Willow stood for a second or two trying to figure out why Whitmore was holding back. He knew there was more to it than clumsiness. The arched cut was clearly not from any awkwardness. It was distinctive. Rumours had already circulated which placed

Brandon Faulkner on the scene and in the heat of an argument with Whitmore. And it took more than clumsiness to deliberately open the door to the stall of a mad stallion. The bolt was designed to require a deliberate action to unhinge it. However, without confirmation, any decision would fall to Stratford. Willow took his leave and gave a nudge to Judge Faulkner to depart with him.

[96] In the hall Brandon waited anxiously for the verdict. His fate would not be lightly handled and he knew it. At the time his actions had seemed justified, but now seemed foolish. Brandon would have to tell his father what he had done, but how much others knew or how much Whitmore had told them, he would have to wait to discover.

Brandon tried to hold his countenance in his approach, careful not to inadvertently reveal too much. 'So, what did he say?'

Paul put a hand on Brandon's shoulder. 'Apparently Mr Whitmore is unaccustomed to being around horses. It appears his own clumsiness was to blame. I only thank God that's all it was. There has been too much violence of late and we are all too sensitive to any more goings on.'

Brandon Faulkner looked up at Willow for confirmation, but received none. Willow's staunch expression revealed nothing of his thoughts on the matter. For the moment all was well, but as Brandon and Judge Faulkner went to descend, Stratford held him fast at the top of the stair.

Stratford stood as a judge to a prisoner. 'Is it true you fought with Mr Whitmore out in the stables?'

'Who told you this?'

'Is it true?'

'We had words,' Brandon reluctantly conceded, knowing this path could lead nowhere pleasant.

'You threatened him, and I know, though he denies it, that you cut him. In this house, on these grounds, you threatened him, cut him, and moments later his life was in mortal danger. Did you open the stall?'

'No! On my word I did not!'

'Your word no longer has meaning in this house,' Stratford said with the utmost condemnation. 'You were witnessed coming from the stable just seconds before the alarm was raised, directly after you argued with him and threatened him.'

'Harry,' Willow intervened, much to Brandon's surprise. 'Myles backs the boy's story. He does not accuse Brandon of anything outside of the argument.'

'I tell you, I did not try and kill him! Do not judge me without law. Yes, we argued, but that is all!'

Stratford spoke with sorrow in his heart. 'No, Brandon, that is not all. Even if I were to concede that you did not pull the bolt on the stall, you did more than have words. You violated this house and attacked a man under my protection. Turn over your knife,' he demanded, holding out his hand.

Reluctantly, Faulkner reached into his pocket and handed Stratford the knife, knowing it might well mean his position. Though he had wiped it, a small stain of Whitmore's blood still clung to the tip. Closing it, Stratford handed it to Paul Faulkner before continuing.

'I was too late to stop you, and for that I must pay my own penitence. I held great hope for you, but this house must stand fast. This house is a sanctuary and we vow to protect those within its walls. In your jealousy you violated those terms and I must, therefore, withdraw my backing on your behalf and banish you from these walls hereafter.'

'No,' Brandon rasped out in horror, putting a pleading hand on Stratford's arm. 'Not that, I beg of you. I did not try and kill him. Please!'

'Even if I believe that, son, you harmed him on these sacred grounds. If you had done this outside of these walls I might have been able to help you, but being that your crime was committed here I can do nothing. At the close of the meetings I must ask you to leave.'

'But Harry, if you ban me, what of Helena? What of our children, your grandchildren? Do you know what you say?'

Stratford lifted his head up high and looked Brandon straight in the eyes before turning away from him, departing without another word.

'He knows, son,' Willow imparted at last. 'He knows.'

[97] Whitmore leaned back on the pillows. Things were getting out of hand. There could be no doubt that his slight brush with the Holmes case had set the killer on the scent. He would not stop until Whitmore was dead, but it was not that which disturbed him. Lord Stratford was somehow caught up in the web of death, trapped by what he could not see. Willow seemed somehow immune, but Whitmore could not count on that remaining true. He needed help, from the very man he felt sure was gathering evidence to hang Stratford. Somehow Whitmore needed to find him before the next turn of events, or before Sherlock Holmes returned to indiscriminately tear down the noble halls, which he had come to call home.

Reaching for his bag of tobacco and a pipe, Whitmore heard a soft knock upon his door and watched as the handle turned. Helena stepped inside and looked over to see if he was still awake.

Seeing him well, she relaxed her shoulders and moved toward him. 'Are you all right?'

With an odd mixture of welcome and discomfort at her tender concern, Whitmore put the matter off with as much expediency as he could. 'Perfectly.'

'I heard Brandon stabbed you.'

'As you can see, the report was greatly exaggerated. A scratch, nothing more. Do not concern yourself over so trivial a matter.'

'I don't know what could have come over him. I've known him to be stubborn and occasionally aggressive, but never overtly violent. He usually leaves that to his contemporaries,' she added with an air of contempt. 'I'm surprised he had the stomach for it. Usually he stabs you in the back before you even know he's done so.'

His mind too full to continue with pleasantries, Whitmore eased in the conversation another direction. 'Helena, what do you know about Faulkner's investments in Ireland?'

Helena thought for a second and then nodded. 'I know he travels there from time to time, but I don't recall him mentioning anything in particular about his investments. Why, is it important?'

Whitmore shrugged it off, and in the next moment her father had stepped in.

Making his way over to the bed he put his arm around his daughter. 'How's our patient?'

One look at him showed Stratford to be unwell, concerning both Helena and Whitmore, who noticed a bluish tint to his mouth and fingernails. His eyes were dark against a pale complexion.

Whitmore knew he was running out of time. There was only one way to stop the madness and only one way to save Stratford's life.

'It has been a long night and I'm sure we are all tired. Helena, why don't you see your father off to bed? I'm a little tired myself.'

Waiting long enough for them to close the door, Whitmore leapt up from his bed and grabbed his notebook as he thrust off the covering of his chalkboard, reviewing his notes on the poison. He was running out of time and only one man could help. After an hour with no discernable progress, Whitmore sank onto the bed. 'Where are you?' he murmured to himself.

Picking a collection of Watson's old stories, Whitmore read for hours trying to find something that would give him an insight into how Sherlock Holmes thought. 'A simple case … a simple case.'

Suddenly he sat upright and leapt from his bed. He made his way swiftly down the stairs and back to the servant's hall, stopping at the last door on the left. Whitmore no longer considered perception or civility; he threw back the door to face his nemesis. It would not be easy to stare down Sherlock Holmes, nor could he guarantee Avondale would admit to the deceptive disguise empty-handed. He would need more. A quick look around found the moment anticlimactic as the room was without an owner. He did not take long to think about it. He rifled through the bureau drawers and desk to find where Stratford's watch might lay hidden.

The contents of the drawers were meagre and there was no sign of hidden articles or false bottoms. The detective was nothing if not consistent in his assumed persona.

Fifteen minutes of intensive search proved to reveal nothing. Unable to press on, Whitmore sank into the chair and closed his eyes. The hour was growing late, exacerbating his irritability. Even the chair seemed uncomfortable. It poked at him until he was forced to readjust the cushion.

It was more than a loose spring or button; the object beneath him was cylindrical. With a grin of satisfaction, Whitmore pulled out a revolver. Opening the chamber, he noted two spent bullets. He recognised the revolver as the one missing from Holmes's effects, for its delicate design and well-worn handle matched perfectly with the description of it. His opponent was clever indeed if the placement of the revolver was any indication of his hiding methods. He would find nothing more on his own. The only thing he could do was wait.

Seated again, time slipped away without meaning until some indistinguishable noise brought him back to the present. Looking at his watch, it showed the hour to be past midnight. A coming storm revealed itself, coming up along the horizon, with a familiar figure sauntering toward the house. Whitmore watched as the lightning accentuated his opponent's arrival. It outlined the figure like a ghost coming from the beyond. The phantom detective shuffled into the room, preoccupied with some object in his hand, and made for the top dresser drawer with vigilance.

Avondale had been the man Whitmore had been inexplicably afraid of. The very presence of him gave off a strange sense of security and familiarity, yet it was tainted with disgust. It had all been a lie, designed for informational purposes only, without value or truth. The character, entwined in the pages of a book, reverberated with imaginative brilliance and splendour, but in person he gave a very different persona. The man was thin, but hardly the sick, gauntly figure portrayed in the good doctor's accounts of him. Other features of his unworldly appearance seemed exaggerated, as well, for the man appeared as normal as any that walked the streets of London. The moustache hardly covered as a disguise and the exaggerated grey could easily have been paint. The only thing true to form from the stories was Holmes's unadulterated focus. It was only the sound of the cock being pulled back on the revolver that caused the man to turn toward the chair in the opposite corner.

He reacted quite calmly at the sight of the readied revolver aimed squarely at his heart. He took out a pipe, took the time to fill it and light it, and then sat on the bed, all in his own good time.

Whitmore returned the favour of aggravated civility. 'The situation is an awkward one, Mr Avondale, as I find I am in need of your help,' he began. 'Or should I say Mr Holmes.'

'No, I don't think you should,' the man insisted.

'I do not wish to kill you, Mr Holmes, but I cannot allow you to continue your investigation for you could quite possibly hang an innocent man. Now, if you will be so kind as to return my papers and Lord Stratford's watch, I must further ask you to quit Eastbourne and leave matters to me.'

Avondale sat thinking for some time, drawing occasionally on his pipe. With a deep breath he finally spoke. 'You obviously do not know me by sight. I must confess I am somewhat disappointed in your ability to remember.'

Whitmore sat quietly, unnerved by the old detective who seemed innately calm and quite unreasonable.

'Might I ask what is so important about the poison? It is most singular in its properties, I will give you that, but it is hardly extraordinary in its purpose. What do you see that I do not?'

'A woman's life. Is that not worth the effort alone?'

'Of course, but you border on obsession over the case, making it more important than any other life, including Lord Stratford's.' He paused before adding insult to injury. 'And Miss Stratford's.'

Avondale took a long draw on his pipe, watching Whitmore's reaction.

'Are you in love with her? I cannot blame you. She is a woman of incredible beauty and intelligence. Any man would die for her. Worse, any man would kill for her. But you'—he took another draw on his pipe—'I would not have expected it from you.'

'The watch and the formula, Mr Holmes, if you don't mind.'

'Do you honestly think the watch is the only evidence against Stratford, or that an incomplete antidote to the poison will put you on the right path to a cure? There is nothing in the formula to suggest an answer. I know; I've worked on it for months. As far as Lord Stratford is concerned, Mr Willow is a man not to be reckoned with in court or out of it, therefore possessing Stratford's watch would do nothing. What is it you are really after?'

'You know that neither Willow nor the courts would ever question your word. If you said you obtained it at the scene of the crime and it had direct bearing on Stratford's guilt, it would be taken as true.'

'Then you misjudge Willow when it comes to Stratford,' Avondale said sharply. 'Have a care with him my friend. He is a man you do not want to misjudge. Virtually nothing is known of the man prior to his discharge from the army and little has been learned of him since. He is fiercely loyal and obsessively controlling. He remains in the shadows but his reach stretches over oceans. Mycroft said of him that he is unfathomably deep and it is best not to traverse those waters. Willow will go far to shield Stratford. If it comes to that, evidence will be the least of my worries. I am going to need your help to get around him.'

'I should see my way clear to go to the devil himself before I assist you. I mean to have the watch and the files on the poison even if it means your life. I won't risk you using any of it as evidence.'

'Admitted as evidence?' Avondale laughed heartily. 'You really have spent too much time in this house. I actually think if I leave you here much longer you will be entirely converted. It is absolutely astonishing how compelling Stratford is. It no longer matters to you if he is guilty or not, you would go to the gallows for him, wouldn't you? Stratford is a remarkable man. When we have more time I should like to tell you about him in detail. Like it or not, however, we must allow the exercise of making him the prime suspect in over nine murders.'

Whitmore looked at him with adamant loathing. 'He did not do it.'

'You speak from faith, which is hardly like you. No matter, all evidence suggests that he did and I am afraid faith, even from you, will not be enough to clear him. Killing me will not save Stratford, not this time. I might also point out that saving Mrs Stanton is predicated on the assumption that the reason she does not respond to treatment is that the treatment is wrong. Have a care that the objective is already being met by keeping her ill. What you must face is that everyone in connection with her case has been summarily removed, suggesting someone very highly placed, with limitless resources.

'Doherty found enough evidence to implicate Stratford in the murders. That is why he is dead. I should thank you for that, by the way. I knew he had hidden the evidence somewhere on the grounds, but it took myself and two police officers three days of searching to come up empty-handed.'

Whitmore felt his blood turn cold. 'You sent me to that house.'

'I am sorry to have put you through that, but it was important I find the evidence first. Doherty hid it to protect Stratford. He, like you, wasn't convinced Stratford was capable so he concealed the evidence, including Stratford's carriage tracks found at the house when they arrived. I also matched up the lanterns used at the house with the missing lanterns in his private stables.

'I am confident Malone was involved, as well. His coming to this house forfeited his life, and Charles Grace, as well. There can be no doubt that Virgil Stanton is involved. He was one of the two at the laboratory the night of the fire. I cannot be sure, but either our man or Stanton was in the alley the night Malone was murdered. You found the footprints?'

Whitmore gave a nod.

'Were you aware that Lord Stratford cannot account for his whereabouts during the time of Malone's murder? Oddly,' Avondale said more to himself than to Whitmore, 'it may be his saving grace.'

'Going for a drive does not make him a murderer.'

'No, you are missing the point. The motor being out so long—does that not suggest anything to your mind? And the blood you sampled upon Stratford's coat, which you subsequently found in his wardrobe. Does that not bother you?'

'There is no proof that the substance was blood. It could be clay.'

'Why do you persist in hiding from the truth? It is beyond madness! I know you found the coat, and you tested it for blood. You are so blinded by your love for him that you will see nothing else. In this case, however, love is the very thing that will hang him. He needs an objective view and I need those tests.'

'There are no current tests to prove conclusively whether a substance contains blood, not after a period of twenty-four hours. It cannot be proved.'

'You, of all people, know that it can! You are a proficient chemist, more so than I had realised. You could make it your profession. I was truly impressed that, without reference, you reproduced a conclusive test for the determination of haemoglobin, and in under a week. You saved a great deal of doubt and speculation. I must thank you for that, as well.'

'Save your gratitude. I will never testify, nor admit that I have the test.'

'You will,' Avondale remarked with arrogant confidence.

'To accuse Stratford of the murders would crush Hel—' Whitmore stopped abruptly as he realised the familiarity he had nearly used. 'Miss Stratford and utterly destroy Willow, leaving this house open to chaos!'

'That is not my concern at the moment,' his opponent came back, unaffected. 'You could solve the case if you wanted, far easier than I, and perhaps with better results. I have wondered why you have made no attempts and why it is that you chose to pursue the problem of the poison, rather than the murderer.'

'You really are heartless and cold! You should have stayed dead and left Watson to solve the case. Actually, the cases. They are all interlinked, you know. At least he would understand that there are people involved, not lifeless subjects in a laboratory.'

'Don't be too sure. I believe I can safely say that he would do the same thing.'

'No! You unjustly cut Watson at every turn. You use him as your footstool, giving him credit only when it suits you and denying him credit when it is truly deserved. Why are you so jealous of him?'

Avondale chuckled. 'Jealous? No. I doubt I could ever be jealous of Watson.'

'You think that what you do cannot be done by any other man, but you are so wrong. Neither Watson nor Mycroft gave up love to do what you did and they are the better men for it. For allowing other experiences into their lives, they have expanded beyond what you could ever hope to accomplish. Watson has everything you want. His life is full and extraordinary. How I envy him, every bit as much as I loathe you. No, I'm afraid you hardly measure up to the man who walks beside you and the man who walked before you. I wouldn't walk on the same side of the street as you.'

Avondale let out a boisterous laugh at the conclusion of Whitmore's great speech as if truly amused. 'I had not realised how heroic the doctor is portrayed in those stories and how pathetic the hero.'

'Quite the opposite. Dr Watson's humble nature and adoration for you allows for nothing save praising your name. A man so inclined to generosity is truly extraordinary.'

'And yet, without Sherlock Holmes, the good doctor would be ordinary. Did it ever occur to you that Watson is the man he is because of his experiences on Baker Street? How ordinary would his life have been had he not decided to share rooms with Holmes so many years ago? He would never reach so grand a life on his own. Watson can solve cases because he was groomed for it, not because it was in him waiting to come out, though I am curious: why do you trumpet Watson when he played only a secondary role in the cases?'

'Why do you discount him? And why do you have to continue to punish him? Is it because he let his emotions get in the way of finding you after you fell at Reichenbach Falls?'

The old detective's curious laughter suddenly dampened. 'I beg your pardon?'

'You fell, didn't you? You didn't fall all the way, probably only to a ledge. When Watson arrived he didn't see the clues. He allowed sentiment and emotion to cloud his judgment, leaving you there to crawl out yourself, or die. The great unemotional detective succumbed to anger and petty revenge.'

'How do you know this?'

'What is it you say? To eliminate the impossible and that whatever remains, however improbable, must be the truth? Your account to Watson was filled with holes and implausibility. What are the odds that you left there unscathed? And if Moriarty were such an expert shot, why did he continue to miss?'

The overwhelmed sleuth stood up, turning his back to Whitmore to hide his expression. 'Improbable as it may seem, it is not impossible.'

'My pity is not for you, but for him. Watson believed you because he sees you with love. He has been like a brother to you, ready always to give his life if necessary to protect you.'

'And yet he failed,' Avondale said softly.

'At least he would not be so cold as to ignore the devastating effects his investigation would have upon this household. He would take infinite care, like the excellent surgeon he is, to cut away only what is already dead and leave the living.'

'And in having such emotions he would prolong the investigation and the agony it causes in taking so many precautions. Do not fool yourself into thinking he could bring this case to a successful conclusion on his own. Emotions in this case only hinder progress!'

'This family will be crushed under the weight of the conclusion if you reveal what you know. Whatever it may look like, it is not!' Whitmore argued.

'This house is already being crushed under the weight of it. The murderer is in this house! But you already know that, don't you? You cannot dismiss the facts!'

Whitmore drew back in horror at the man before him, confronting what he had thought to be nothing more than an exaggeration of truth for the effect of publication, only to find it more than real. The anger welled deep within him, pressing through to his stomach, which turned sour, almost nauseous. It rose to his head, now throbbing in agony in the attempt to restrain himself until he could contain it no longer. Bursting forth with more emotion than thought, Whitmore poured out months of resentment and loathing, which had been building within him since his ordeal.

'You are worse than heartless. You are incapable of any human feeling. You really would destroy everyone around you in order to solve your case. You truly don't care who is hurt over it, do you? You have taken great care to ensure my safety, but you could care less that it is an entire family you destroy, and me along with it! You destroyed my life and robbed me of any past I may have had. I will not let you destroy theirs.'

'I care very much about your life, including your past, which is part of the reason the progress of this case has been hampered. But I did not wish to sacrifice your life in the solving of it. Your life is all that matters.'

'My life!' Whitmore exclaimed in bitter surprise, reaching for a handkerchief to wipe away the thick, warm red liquid beginning to flow from his nose once again. 'What about Mycroft? Your actions forced him into nervous collapse, from which he may never recover! And what of Watson? He must be beside himself with grief. How insensitive can you be? You are not helping them, you are destroying them as you have destroyed me!'

'I assure you, Watson is fine and Mycroft is hardly crushed. He is apprised and will understand when matters are once again in hand. My duty is here at the moment and Mycroft would agree.'

The look upon Whitmore's face must have revealed the true loathing he had for Holmes. He desired to pull the trigger of the revolver he now held tightly within his grasp. As if seeing that Whitmore was not faring well under the strain, Avondale walked over to his closet and pulled out a coat from the back, reaching into the pocket for a small packet. Pouring out a glass of water, he stepped up boldly to Whitmore and grasped the barrel of the revolver as if he were unconcerned that it was loaded and cocked. He removed it from Whitmore's hand as easily as if from a child, replacing it with the glass of water and the packet.

'This should work better than what you have been taking,' he said, settling back on the bed.

Whitmore leaned back in defeat, both from his nemesis and his headache, now raging out of control, pounding out each beat of his heart in his head.

'I had hoped your memory would have returned by now. It could have brought this case to a cleaner solution. But even with some facts out of place, you know why I am here and that we have some understanding or relationship between us. Yet, it took you until now to find me and you have conspicuously not asked what that relationship is or was between us.'

Whitmore allowed his eyes to close, no longer able to continue the fight. 'You were not an easy man to find.'

'On the contrary, it was a simple deduction. Who is the only member of the household here now that was not here seven months ago?'

'I am not sure I would say it was simple. Others were suspect. The cab driver with the city boots, the man following us in London, and later, the detective who impressed the Seaford medical examiner's office, and the man who has been beating me to every clue offered in this house.'

And a few others, like the old man on the train, all played by me, including the man who bumped into you on the pier, which confirmed your identity to me. One must conduct one's interviews in such a way that they are not seen as intrusive or revealing, one must never be seen, and one must gain entry to the house. That day, when I learned that you had not died in that house, I had to understand the situation and what part you were playing. You may have been on the investigation yourself, following your own leads in your own way. I could not take the chance of revealing your identity for it certainly would have meant your death. I had to learn what you knew, add it to my own knowledge, and pick up the investigation from there. I needed to be close at hand to protect you, once I found out your injuries left you defenceless.'

'Do not exaggerate my injuries. I am not defenceless,' Whitmore insisted.

'Without your memories, I am afraid you are! You need my protection because this murderer does not stop at killing a defenceless man, lest you forget those who died at the Snowden house for you.'

'For me?' Whitmore reopened his eyes and sat up straight. 'They died for you!'

'A matter of semantics, I would say. You had to be protected, and who better to protect you than a member of the house seen as a benign figure?'

'Touché,' Whitmore mocked. 'So I am not a detective. If I were, you might grant a request to hold off until I could solve the matter. How can I persuade you to end this?'

Strolling over to the right side of the bed, the false gardener leaned down and pulled back the carpet. Retrieving a pocketknife from his pocket, he pried up a floorboard half hidden in shadows. Procuring a box, he handed it to Whitmore. The old detective then sat back with his pipe, as if waiting for the full magnitude of the contents to sink in. Removing the lid revealed several bits of paper, a small notebook, a photograph, Stratford's pocket watch and his dirk cluttered among some odds and ends. After waiting so long for the watch and the solution, the other contents of the box suddenly seemed to take precedence. Almost hesitant to look, Whitmore pushed aside the watch and the knife to reach the papers beneath. Uncertainty gave over to anxiousness. Whitmore took his time, reviewing all of the notes before making any hasty conclusion, but what was contained within the pages was something he did not expect.

The evidence pointed in a singular direction, but his notes also pointed out the errors of that evidence, which provided an alternative conclusion. Putting aside the notebook at long last, Whitmore shuffled through the rest of the box's contents, though not entirely sure what all of it meant. A shard of glass covered in soot on the inner curvature suggested nothing to his mind. The significance of a flare gun wrapped in a handkerchief could be inferred. Yet, it was more than the notes and evidence that caused Whitmore to sit so still and quiet. At the bottom lay evidence of his true identity.

There was no other way to return the man to his former self, for the time had come for the two to work together once again and the knowledge locked inside Whitmore's head was in desperate need to solve the case. Whitmore grasped a photograph and withdrew it from the pile, examining it without emotion at first, refusing to allow its image to form a complete link. The young woman was handsome, with a plain purity about her that spoke of contentment as she held a young child in her arms next to an unmistakable man beside her. It was a face that called a memory to his mind, a face he could never again forget or walk away from, try as he may. Though the photograph was quite old, as it showed no signs of the man's loss of innocence and the rugged scars obtained over the years, the image was unmistakable. Inscribed on the back, written in pen, were the names of the subjects pictured: Simon, Nancy, and Rowan Ballard, 1884. The other photographs did little more than confirm the original, though he stared at them for what seemed an eternity.

No words needed to pass between the two men to confirm the significance of it, offering absolute proof of Whitmore's identity. Opening the door to this one conclusive piece of evidence forced the pieces of the puzzle to fall in their proper place, much to the great disheartening of the pitiable man who now sat broken in his chair at the revelation. No more could he take perverse delight in maligning his counterpart or offering blame to ease his own suffering.

Resigning himself, Whitmore looked up at the other man. 'So who are you?'

'Dr John Watson.'

'Of course.' Whitmore slumped back into the chair. It was some time in deep thought before Whitmore addressed his companion once more. 'It's not Stratford.'

'You can't prove it.'

'Maybe Simon Ballard can.'

'That's madness! You'll be killed. No, I don't like it. If Willow is in any way involved this could go very badly.'

'You were going to send a wire to Mr Holmes, were you not? Tell him to meet you here just before the meeting. And one other thing. I want Miss Stratford out of the house. I don't care how you do it, but I want her gone.

SESSION CASE

QUEEN'S BENCH DIVISION

LORD JUSTICE

HAROLD A. W. STRATFORD

TWENTY-FOURTH SESSION,

HELD AT

JUSTICE HALL, IN SUSSEX COURT,

ON FRIDAY, THE 27th DAY OF OCTOBER, 1903,

AND FOLLOWING DAYS.

TAKEN IN SHORT HAND

(BY AUTHORITY OF THE CORPORATION OF THE CITY OF EASTBOURNE)

BY A. WAKEFIELD

Eastbourne :

PRINTED FOR J. H. WILLOW, BY A. WAKEFIELD,

No. 74, MEADS;

AND PUBLISHED BY G. HERBERT, COUNTY COURT

1904

[98] The day began quietly enough, but there was an almost palpable tension in the atmosphere of the estate. The outward attempts on Whitmore's life may have been subtle and the offered explanations easily accepted by present company, but the house had now been unmistakably violated. Not one member of the household could lull themselves into thinking all was well. The house had been breached and in the most intimate fashion. All looked and felt as it always had, but nothing was the same. The staff and attendants were at their stations in every corner of the house making ready for the day. It would still be hours before the masters and guests of the great house would rise; all were still sleeping, save one.

Whitmore paused outside the door opposite his own and stood in solemn contemplation. It was hard to look at the house or its members in the same way again, for his new eyes saw everything from an angle previously unconceivable, rendering him uncomfortable and alone. Whatever way he made his path, there was one direction he could never go again.

[99] As the sun broke over the windowsill, Stratford made his customary rounds only to inconspicuously retire to his room as often as he could. Willow, with his quiet nature, stood in the background, ever watchful, always diverting any question of Stratford's absence. He would take no chances, make no mistakes. He knew the placement and conversation of every member of the house and every guest until the hour ultimately struck eight and the illustrious guests gathered once again.

This time they paraded out of the north wing like choirboys. They walked in unison to the chapel near the north gate and ascended to their respective positions in plush carpeted chairs along the sides, front, and rear. They came in full regalia, obeying ceremony and custom. The first bell chimed out to take their seats, while a host of staff stood invisibly by the wall like statues, ready to serve. George seemed uneasy to those who knew him best, perhaps exemplified by the fact that he was sweating, a thing his English nature and lifetime of servitude would otherwise never permit. Under these circumstances there were definite undeniable undertones. Never once, however, did he miss a beat, seating Stratford at the head, discreetly easing him into the chair to shield the fact that he was not well.

Stratford was clearly not himself, but to most he still presented a formidable front. He sat like a monarch at the head of state without wavering, but took the first opportunity to ease his stature after every man took his seat, a thing he was loath to do. Willow, as Tyler, armed with his sword of office, took his seat at Stratford's right hand, never once allowing his eyes to wander far from the man he placed above him. By the half hour chime of the bell, George stood in the chapel foyer, ringing a strange ornate bell in a mechanical manner that seemed to herd the last of the white-haired old men into the room. Each wore fitted robes of concealment, marked with sashes, belts, pendants, and jewellery in significance to position. The room had been particularly decorated with ancient artefacts, draperies and cloth in colours of black, light blue, gold, and silver, illuminated by torch. Stratford rose, displaying the dieugard and penalty, and all conversation instantly turned toward the order of the day.

It was at the precise stroke of nine that a knock came upon the great doors of the hall, the interruption quelling all conversation instantly. A plain dark- robed man arose and stood by the clock like an omen at the door until he received a nod of approval from Stratford to open. There, looming in the doorway was a hooded sojourner, marked in a similar fashion to that of another who had come to that house in similar garb some time before. The hooded figure turned toward Willow in respect and bowed, but it was Stratford who gave a subtle nod granting him entrance. Stopping at the nearest table he was greeted by the Master of Ceremonies, who insisted upon answers.

'Brother, by what intent do you come to stand now before us?'

The figure kept his head low. 'For the purpose of a man's life. For those who have come before and who now will never come again.'

'By what manner do you come?'

'From East to West and West to East, I travel in search of justice.'

'For whom do you speak?'

'I speak for the dead who came before to this house in seek of sanctuary, but received death.'

The ominous statement invoked both fear and curiosity, provoking low murmurs of conversation in the room, hushed only by the beating of a gavel.

Shaken, but determined not to break tradition, the Master of Ceremonies continued in established fashion. 'By what capitulus does the sojourner come?'

'By the house of succession,' he replied, stirring every member in attendance, including Willow, who suddenly gave more attention to the meeting than he had a moment before.

Every member, every chapter and house seated or represented in that hall, knew the meaning of his words. What had seemingly begun as an archaic prelude suddenly took a sombre and compelling turn, and now suggested something far greater and more terrible.

The Master of Ceremonies stood as speaker of the house, dropping all traditional speech and mannerisms. 'What is this?'

'Murder, power, and greed. To rob this noble order of its dignity and position.'

The edict could not have been more ill received, or more debated, for there were now several murders to be contemplated and one in which everyone sought truth. The room filled instantly with conversation, even across tables and jurisdictions, and the Grand Master beat the gavel again in a futile effort to bring the room to order.

The Master of Ceremonies spoke at the first availability. 'Do you speak of the Holmes murder and that of his companions?'

The figure gave a nod. 'I do.'

'If you can shed some light upon this dark puzzle, sir, we would be indebted to you, for the police in three providences and countless investigators have been unable to solve this matter.'

'I submit to you that the reason for it is that those in charge do not want this matter resolved. Indeed, investigation has been prevented by the very hand that has engaged it,' the man offered, causing great unrest within the congregation.

'That is a most serious charge, sir.'

'Murder and treason often are,' the cloaked figure rebutted.

'You speak of treason. Do you have proof of this?'

'I will give you the facts, and you can decide for yourself how the matter falls,' he conceded, placing a tattered box upon the table.

'The resolution to the murder of Sherlock Holmes should have been as easy as the killer believed his murder to be. It is the surrounding and subsequent murders that presented difficulty. The connection was but a thread, but a thread which led back into this house.' The dark figure let his audience simmer for a moment, chewing on the bone he had given them before opening the lid to the box Stratford had taken to London.

'We know from accounts of his landlady and partner that Sherlock Holmes was engaged upon a case at the time he left Baker Street October last,' he began, removing the billfold from the box. 'Contained within the billfold are three business cards, the first belonging to his partner, Dr Watson. The second belongs to Miss Susan Millhouse, a seamstress of Glentworth Street, London, engaged to repair a wool topcoat. The last card, gentlemen, could only belong to the man to whom Sherlock Holmes spoke last, the man who had engaged him. That man was Charles Grace, of Belgravia, London, a research assistant for the department of Egyptian antiquities. It is upon Grace's authority, and that of his superior, that any piece's authenticity is accepted.

'Grace was a shy bachelor, comfortable in his salary and a practicing Freemason. Grace was key to the Holmes murders. Grace hired not just any detective, but the only detective able to deliver the man and the artefact our killer sought. The ancient stone Holmes was hired to obtain has no pictures, but is legendary in name. Grace counterfeited a detailed drawing and accompanying history of it.' The man flung open a set of drawings showing a stone, marked and altered with notations crossed out and modified.

'Is this what it appears to be? Are we to believe Mr Grace hired Mr Holmes to obtain the Masonic Stone?'

'In essence, yes.'

'But it does not exist. Even in our tradition we only believe it to be a symbol. No one believes it to be a genuine stone. Why should Mr Grace fabricate this artefact and hire Mr Holmes to find it?'

'To allow his employer to be able to claim he had possession of it. If one were to produce the stone and two authorities verified it to be genuine, power as we know it would shift into his hands. But whether or not the stone actually exists is momentarily beside the point. In order for our man to lay such a claim there could be no one to dispute him. It also meant that the person hired to obtain the stone could not ever reveal what he knew.'

The Master of Ceremonies gave a nod, starting to understand. 'You speak of Simon Ballard.'

'I do, but Simon Ballard is as elusive as the stone he is believed to have possessed. He is a man of a thousand faces. His resources are supplemented by the government and to touch him is treason. I know of only two men who are capable of finding such a man: the brothers Holmes. The killer needed only the younger. He need not kill both, for the death of the younger would render the elder incapacitated by grief. By the time the killer took over the Masonic Order there would be no one to stop him.'

'Are you saying these killings were in some way tied to this organization?'

'I think the brotherhood is at the heart of it, yes,' he revealed, causing a great uproar and sparking numerous arguments among the assembly.

After several attempts to regain order, banging the gavel against the block on the table numerous times, the Master of Ceremonies asked the question foremost on every man's mind. 'Do you have proof of this?'

'Facts do not lie, Master.' The cloaked figured bowed. 'Whether you believe the stone to be real or imagined, it was the basis of Holmes's engagement. Unaware of the danger he was in, revealed by the accounts he gave to both Dr Watson and his landlady, Sherlock Holmes left Baker Street to conclude his investigation on the twenty-fourth of October last. His mood was fair as he headed out into the cold October winds, hailing a cab for a small shop in Merton, on Melbourne Road.'

The cloaked figure produced the old merchant's receipt, placing it before the Master. 'This receipt, found in the bloodstained frock coat belonging to Sherlock Holmes is dated the twenty-fourth of

October. The shopkeeper, a pleasant little man, was an old friend, often providing valuable information on a case. In this instance, the shopkeeper sent Mr Holmes to Rye with specific instructions on how to approach this most unusual and elusive man.'

Holding up the receipt, he pointed to each line as he recounted the instructions. 'Rye bread: go to Rye. Rice and high tea: right onto High Street. Curry powder: ask for a curried dish. I spoke with the landlord and his wife at the Inn. Both confirmed that he asked for the dish, but accepted the stew when told there was no place to obtain it. The woman said that Holmes had with him a small bag, which he sat on the table. She remembers it because she had to move it to set down his dinner, but that he replaced it on the edge of the table at the earliest occurrence.

The man paused for a breath and then continued. 'It was a few minutes later that he was joined by a man, a tall, thin, rough-looking man, who looked in the bag before taking a seat at Holmes's table. They talked for no more than five minutes before leaving together. Two men, who had walked in and sat down just prior, got up and left directly after Holmes and his companion. An examination of the inner lining of Holmes's coat pocket revealed traces of sugar and mint, along with fibres consistent with brown paper. It was the signal, gentlemen, giving the all clear to be approached. Such extremes could only mean he was meeting Simon Ballard. No one else would take such elaborate precautions just to meet a man over a simple transaction.'

The Master of Ceremonies looked up from the drawings, trying to piece everything together. 'But if the intent was to find this man, why did Mr Grace not go himself?'

'For two reasons: first, the shopkeeper would never have revealed the pass code to Grace. It was only his longstanding relationship with Mr Holmes that got him to reveal what he knew. Even then, the shopkeeper made every attempt to dissuade Holmes from going. It was only the fact that coincidence seemed more likely than treachery that convinced the merchant to trust that his friend could handle matters. Even then the merchant felt uneasy. The signal was a dual message: one to approach and the other that trouble was following.

'The second reason Grace could not go is trust. If Grace had sat down at that table in Rye, even with the signal, Ballard would most assuredly know something was amiss. A careful, distrusting man of extreme caution, Ballard would not approach just anyone. Grace, or at least his employer, knew that Sherlock Holmes giving the signal would throw the man off his balance just long enough to be caught. Once he stepped forward to find out why Holmes had signalled him, he would have revealed himself. The brother of Mycroft Holmes signalling him held its own curiosity. A short conversation revealed the trap and they quickly departed. Ballard's first concern would not have been for his own life, but for Mycroft's younger brother, protected by the brotherhood.'

Once again the present company roared in conversation and debate at Ballard's name. Inconceivable though it seemed, Willow showed no signs of flinching. His blank, expressionless face hid whatever he was thinking. Though Stratford showed no strong reactions to what was being said, the intent furrow of his brow said that he was scrutinizing every word, remaining out of debate or conversation.

The dark figure continued. 'Ballard knew instantly, the moment Holmes asked for the stone, that a trap had been set and both their lives were forfeit. He could slip away easily, but he could not guarantee that Holmes would not be captured and killed for any information his murderers might think he had. Ballard had sworn an oath to protect him, even if it meant his own death. He was trapped. Unfortunately Ballard made a fatal mistake. He trusted this house.'

At this Stratford clenched his fists, barely holding himself back.

'Time was limited to effect a successful escape, but Ballard returned to his room to retrieve something under the floorboard. Whatever it was, it was important enough to risk their lives to retrieve. General inquiries into a man leaving his rooms suddenly revealed Ballard's room, though he went by the name of Mr P. Phasma, an interesting little play on words. He was not a difficult man to find, as he left his room through the front window and a board in the floor had been removed. Taking the window instead of the door suggests their pursuers were coming up the stairs at the time. Ballard knew that all exits would be blocked and that an attempt at returning to London would see them in enemy hands. He had to get help, but who could he turn to? Who could he trust after so obvious and deliberate a betrayal? Unfortunately, everything he knew was against him. He headed directly for Eastbourne to find the one man who could protect Holmes and return him to London while Ballard made his escape.'

The Master of Ceremonies took immediate interest. 'Then you know how he came to be in Eastbourne? The police found nothing. No carriages were rented or found, no train tickets were on any of the men, and no motors were found.'

'They came by train,' the figure said with confidence.

'You are guessing! It's impossible to board the train without a ticket and the conductor does not remember any passengers matching that description,' said the Master.

'It is no guess,' the man calmly insisted. 'They had no ticket because they rode on top of the railway carriage, not inside.'

'On top?'

The revelation seemed to startle and amaze most, for no one had dared contemplate such a bold move, let alone put forth a theory to dispel the idea.

'It would explain everything. Three spent cartridges were found between stations suggesting that Ballard gave the signal of distress well before they arrived. He could not have given such a signal inside the carriage. He had to be on top. But in alerting his friends he also alerted his killer that he was on the way.

He continued, 'The autopsy of the body presumed to be that of Sherlock Holmes had one inconsistency. His leg was broken, consistent with a fall from the distance of the railway rooftop. It would also explain the presence of additional men, one being a physician. One might ask how difficult it was to identify these men when their funerals were not unattended. An injury of this magnitude would quite prohibit them from continuing on by foot. Dr Phillip Worth, the attending physician, was retired and did not own a carriage. The decision was made to send an emissary to their final destination: this house.

'Ballard had expected an army, but instead he received a carriage and instructions to go to the Downs, to the Snowden house. Ballard must have considered the matter first, deciding to trust, but only to a point. He decides the house would be sufficient, but before he does he gathers one more to his aid, an old soldier by the name of Maryland Holt. Holt served as a major in the army most of his life. His campaigns stretch as long as my arm. Though retired, the old soldier stood six foot two and weighed in at over two hundred fifty pounds. It clearly suggests Ballard expected trouble or at least suspected it.

'It confused me at first, for I was not present as the drama unfolded, but I was in a unique position with possession of facts not generally known. Facts would suggest that Simon Ballard wanted to ensure everyone survived that night and that his charge was returned safely to London. To that end, one man was removed, rendered unconscious, and hidden in the barn in order that the rest could claim Ballard had already gone. You see it was assumed that Sherlock Holmes and his two companions were of no consideration. None of them knew anything and Ballard would certainly never have revealed any additional plans to any of them if he had them, so keeping Holmes safe was the primary objective. A search of the house and grounds would show Ballard to have departed, and a party sent on ahead over the Downs would show him long gone. When the killer and his partner, David Malone, arrived, three men greeted the man who promised sanctuary, and not one of them offered a true account of whom they were. To this day only one man knows each identity and who it belongs to—me.'

The account could hardly be taken lightly. Questions rose faster than they could be answered, overwhelming the pounding of the gavel until the entire room was enthralled with the possibilities.

'The level of treachery, however,' the hooded man continued, 'was unexpected, and the old soldier's arm must have lost its vigour, for the man they all took great pains to remove and hide in the barn had regained consciousness. Hearing the commotion inside the house, he rushed headlong into the hands of a monster. It was near ten when the first three were murdered. It took another hour to torture the fourth to turn over something he could not give, for he did not have it to turn over. By eleven no one in the world knew where they were or what had happened. It would not serve the killer's plans to leave them undiscovered, or discovered so late that identification could not be made. Without his prize, the murderer had to resort to an alternate plan. He wanted certain people to know who these men were, at least the part about being Masons and being in the company of Sherlock Holmes, stirring already taut tensions.

'To ensure that all appeared as if everything this estate stands for was undone, the killer steps to the highest point in the yard and fires three red flares, to denote all lives were in danger. He then sets the house ablaze and promptly departs, while Malone sets the lights, which Stanton discovers almost immediately. The killers knew that the army Simon Ballard had expected earlier would soon be on its way. Sergeant Doherty was first to arrive. He pulled a survivor out of the wreckage, barely alive. What he discovered in those few moments ensured his own death and those of Constable Carter and the nurse. He discovered Holmes's identification, his clothing, notes, and Bradshaw, and something else.'

The dark, ominous figured walked slowly over and stopped in front of Stratford. 'Could you please explain to me, my lord, how the watch that has never left your possession in thirty years came to be at the Snowden house on the night of the murders?'

If the man's presence and precept had not stilled every tongue with its ominous opening, this singular question did. All eyes diverted from the dark cloaked figure to the judge, who sat unruffled in the chair as if he were presiding on the bench.

'No, sir, I cannot,' Stratford answered.

'Then could you tell me how your carriage came to be there?' he asked, moving Stratford slightly. 'I examined the tracks before the police made too much of a mess of things. The right front tire has a flaw, a small chip from the metal on the inner side. I took the liberty of comparing it against the tracks found at the house on my first visit here.'

'No,' Stratford returned, 'I cannot.'

'Then perhaps you can explain your flare gun being there? No,' the man answered for him at Stratford's silence. 'There were two revolvers used that night. One proved to belong to Sherlock Holmes, but not the revolver that was used to shoot at the last man, lying unconscious after falling through the floorboards. You missed, by the way, but then you knew that when Sergeant Doherty informed you that a man had survived. The bullet was lodged in the wood next to where the man rested on the beam. The floor collapsed and you had no way of getting to him to ensure he did not survive. In the dark you took your best shot, coming within inches of his head. You left him for dead when you saw that he was not moving. Four lanterns were found at the house. They were first used as light and then to set the house ablaze. I noticed that your stable has new lamps. Your manager told me it was to replace ones that were stolen back at the end of October. The theft was not reported, other than to you, because you told him it was probably wayward youths. Do you remember that?'

Stratford returned to a judicial position. 'Yes. The loss was a minor one, not worth a police investigation. Many young men from college sneak off to the top of the hill, which overlooks the town, often in the company of a young lady. You see evidence of it all the time: a forgotten blanket, shirt, or lamp left in the darkness. It is so popular a location that we have taken to placing a bench at the overview, in fond remembrance, for some of us. I saw no reason to bother.'

'But Sergeant Doherty did bother, didn't he, my lord? He bothered to come to you first, before returning to the police station that morning. He was so bothered that he lost his shirt! It was a puzzle to me from the first, until I realised that in finding the shirt I would find the secret behind Doherty's death. I felt a modicum of relief when I heard that the survivor was being well guarded by two policemen and no one was allowed to visit without the permission of a judge. Whoever tried to kill him would have to reveal himself to try again. Unfortunately, I learned the following morning that he was dead, along with his guards. Coincidence?'

He shook his head in defiance, assuring the company that he had proof to the contrary before resettling himself in front of Stratford once more.

'You had ordered Doherty there, away from the investigation and continuously on duty. After more than a week he was tired, and his guard was down. My application to see the patient told you that you could wait no longer. If the unknown man regained consciousness, he would reveal all. You had to kill them all. You waited until late, until your daughter and the rest of the household had retired, and then went to hospital. Only someone whom Doherty trusted implicitly would have kept him seated. It is inconceivable for it to have been a stranger. Doherty knew his killer, and did not rise until Carter had been slain. He rose quickly, realizing his mistake, determined to protect the patient against you, but it was too late. He fell at his post, protecting the patient to the last. Without Doherty's notes and the watch, the investigation began to die. Mycroft Holmes slipped into despair, as you knew he would. You knew he would take your word as fact. That is why you went in person. At the funeral, you stood at his side to be sure he was of no threat to you, for having to murder so old a friend I think would weigh even on your conscience.'

Stratford spoke softly, anguished, but allowing the man his say unhindered. 'That is not fair.'

'No one knew about Grace, a man who died alone and without the mourners his companions had in the wake of this tragedy. It was easy to hire him. He was a young up and coming Mason who would have done anything for a Grand Master of so prestigious a lodge as South Lodge. You could manipulate him and discard him without anyone knowing there were relations between you save a few well-placed endowments to fund his research. It was easily explained, wasn't it? You had never met the man, not to anyone's knowledge. A smart man like you would have sent a representative. Malone was in it, too, hoping that in pleasing you his career would be restored. You set up the meeting with him in Seaford.'

The man produced the hand-written request, which took Willow by surprise, having taken pains to conceal it.

'Your coat has Malone's blood on it,' he continued, producing Whitmore's tests and Malone's file to damn the judge further.

Turning to the congregation, he continued. 'When I visited Grace's apartment I also found black marks on the fireplace stoop and Cavendish blend tobacco in the fireplace grate. When I saw Lord Stratford's habit of placing his foot upon the stoop to clean out his pipe and that his favourite tobacco blend was Cavendish, I could conclude nothing else but that Stratford was there, and when he left, Grace was dead. Grace's landlady confirmed my facts by describing the man last to see Grace. The brown and sable coat was unmistakable in its description. With everyone involved dead, all evidence of a plot to seize power of the Masons had been erased.

'I suspected, but did not confirm my suspicions until I walked into your house. I had not been here for more than five minutes before I realised I was standing in the very heart of the Masonic Order, the house of Protection and Amnesty—of sanctuary,' he announced, causing even more uncomfortable looks among the present company.

'It was this secret society which gave me my first clue to this little demonstration, for it can hardly be called a mystery. The demonstration of power is hardly mysterious. You failed, my lord! You failed because you left Simon Ballard alive and Mycroft Holmes suspected as much, which is why he sent your oldest and dearest friend to snatch him from your grip before you could do any more.'

Willow sat bolt upright, as if somehow he could withdraw the words before Stratford could hear them, but it was too late. Stratford accidentally let a look of anguished surprise escape him before regaining his composure. He said not a word, but it took all the power he possessed not to let a single tear of anger fall from his eyes. He looked over at Willow, who could not bear to look upon his friend's face for the shame of it. It spoke volumes of their recent distrust of each other. Even if Mycroft had bid him silence, had there been enough trust, not even Mycroft's orders could put them at a distance. Shame quickly turned to anger mixed with curiosity as Willow now gazed intently at the dark figure before them, for such an account was not rendered easily. The man ignored Willow's gaze and continued to hammer away at Stratford.

'Malone knew about Ballard and he came here to use it against you. He was going to tell all, wasn't he? You had to kill him. You sent a note with the arrangements, making sure that no one knew of the meeting. You discounted, however, that he left the note with his wife. When you murdered Malone she confronted you, yet you were still confident. You knew he would meet you. He would do anything to be restored, and he felt safe as long as he had the Snowden house murders over you. You went to the alley and waited for him in the centre. He approached you without reservation and you stabbed him as he came close to you. His blood dripped upon your brown sable coat and the bottom of it brushed against the pool of his blood as you stepped over him.'

Stratford sat staunchly in the face of reason, unable to speak even in his own defence, staring at Willow in astonished shock at the revelation he had not expected and the horrors of the truth. Walking down to the end of table, the dark, cloaked figure stood directly before Stratford, this time leaning on the table to bend closer to him.

'How far did Malone go, my lord? Whose hand actually beat Simon Ballard half to death with such vicious cruelty that it deprived him of his memories and any life he had ever known or could ever have again?'

The slight pause seemed an eternity to Stratford, who sat reeling from the unexpected revelation. It was there in front of him all along. Willow had been working against him for the first time in their lives. The benign, pitiable chemist he had come to care for was the very man everyone sought. It was not so much that Willow brought him under the protection of South Lodge, but that he did so alone and under the guise of a lie. Stratford had hoped his actions against Willow had not destroyed their love and trust, but to sit in full view of the public gaze and be told his partner and friend had distrusted him rendered Stratford utterly quiet.

'You tortured him for nearly an hour, growing more ruthless as time ran short. Malone demanded that the torture come to an end, for no information had been derived in that entire time and your very lives were now being put to exposure. Malone knew he had taken on more than he had bargained for at the sight, even in your name's sake. If discovered now, it would be a hanging job. Finally, Malone insisted they draw off, beside himself with fear at the consequences, unable to reason that he was already well in it and leaving a man behind alive would mean certain death. With him broken and bleeding, you used a pocketknife to cut Ballard's hands free of the ropes binding his hands. It was the same knife that killed Malone, for the markings were unmistakable.

'Exhausted, Ballard fell, huddled on the floor in pain, hoping for death to take him. You stepped up to him casually, the tips of your boots stepping in the spots of blood on the floor near his head. Enflamed with rage, you picked up a lead pipe from the floor and raised it to him. With all the strength he could muster, he knelt before you, raising his hand to shield his face, and spoke. "Will no one help the widow's son?" he quoted, moving in close to Stratford, driving the point home by sharply slamming his fist on the table, causing Stratford and others to jump at the force. 'Writhing in pain, he raised his other arm to shield his face from your wrath again. "Oh Lord, my God, will no one help the widow's son?"' The old detective shouted rather than spoke, again slamming his fist into the table to accentuate the point, causing an unsettling jump in the present company. 'And with no hope of defence he faced you, spitting up from the depths of hell from which you had sent him, and spoke those inevitable words: "So mote it be". He rebuked your insolence, and for this you struck him down, fracturing his skull, sending blood dripping into his eyes to blind him. He crawled from your sight, inching away in tortured agony only to hear you follow. He could not see, but he could still hear. He heard the boards begin to buckle under the weight as you followed him, eager for death to take you along with him. He knew his death was imminent. He prayed for it now, hoping only that he could take you into the bowels of hell along with him, but the floorboards gave way, unfortunately with only one poor soul taken.'

Stratford put his head in his hands. 'Please, no more.' Stratford barely managed to whisper for mercy, unable to free his mind of the images, trying to hold back the emotion. Willow leaned forward in an attempt to rise, ready to take on the entire congregation if need be to come to Stratford's defence, but a calm soothing hand upon his shoulder from behind held him at bay. It would hold, but not for long.

'You killed them.' The hooded figure spoke more calmly now, as if knowing he had won. 'Didn't you?'

Stratford looked up at the figure as if looking upon the face of death, the long hooded cloak covering the manner by which he had been undone. Stratford opened his mouth to speak, but Willow could abide no more. Even the steadying hand keeping him in his seat could not hold him. He glanced up as he began to rise, seeing for the first time who held him, but motion, once in play, could not be stopped.

'Harry, don't say anything. They cannot hold court here,' Willow insisted before returning to Stratford's accuser. It was only then that he saw how matters were playing out. Turning then to the dark cloaked figure, Willow's patience wore thin. 'Enough of this. Who the devil are you, sir?'

The question drew a hush over the crowd who eagerly looked on to see if the demand would be met. And as the man put his hands to the hood, Willow glanced back once more to see Mycroft's response. It was as he thought. The two were working in unison.

Removing his hood, Watson stood facing the order, allowing a moment for the pieces to fall into place.

'Dr John Watson, and you are quite right, we cannot hold court here. Master Speaker, would you fetch the police.'

As the unstoppable wave of passionate debate began, the speaker beat the gavel again in attempt to bring the congregation back into order. It was not the gavel, however, or Willow's confusion at the presence behind him, that stilled the noise of the room, nor the repeated requests for silence and order. It was only when one man rose, laboured and riddled with obvious pain that a hush came over the crowd. He caressed his forehead using one hand and steadied himself upon the table with the other, waiting for the room to quiet enough to speak.

'With all due reverence for your talents, Dr Watson,' he began, the pain in his head obviously gripping him to distraction. 'I must compliment you on your deductions. They were, in nearly all incidences, completely accurate. You do your friend much credit. You are correct in saying that Malone protested the extreme treatment and that it was thought Sherlock Holmes and his companions were safe. My arrival on the scene proved we were all out of our depth. However ...' He paused, stopping as if too pained to go on.

'I assure you, the facts as I have outlined them are the exact and literal truth, and in light of your absent memory it is beyond debate.'

Whitmore wavered in his stance, causing Willow to place a concerned hand upon him to steady him. Placing his hand over his forehead, Whitmore ran his fingers down his temples, stopping over his eyes and nose. 'Nevertheless,' Whitmore insisted, now wavering. A few small drops of blood from beneath his hand fell onto the table in demonstration that the condition had grown worse. 'I remember.'

Willow held him tighter just in time to find his charge sinking. Guiding him gently to the floor, Stratford called out quickly for a doctor as Willow cradled him in his arms. At Stratford's insistence, Dr Watson was sent through the pressing crowd like a bucket of water along a brigade line.

'I want him lying down. If we could manage his room it would save a move later, which might be more harmful in his condition.'

'What condition?' Willow asked frantically, repeating his query more ardently upon the pause.

'His blood pressure is extremely high and his heart rate is too fast. I was afraid of this. The prospect of exacerbation of myocardial ischemia could lead to acute myocardial infarction, a cerebrovascular accident, or renal failure.'

Willow's frustration showed. 'In English, doctor!'

Watson looked up at Stoner for a moment and then translated. 'If we can't get his pressure down he could suffer a heart attack, a stroke, or his kidneys could fail. His medicine is in his room.'

Watson waited anxiously for Stratford to set the plan into motion, but no one, not even Stratford, would now make a move without Willow's authority.

'Take him.' Willow motioned for Damon and young Faulkner to come forward.

'I will be fine.'

'No, son. I'll have no argument,' Willow insisted.

[100] Whisking out the doors of the chapel, they helped him across the yard and back into the house and up the stairs. Half the congregation seemed to follow in utter captivation, teeming with conversation both upstairs and down. It did not take long before loyalties turned into factions and sides were drawn, each strongly voicing an opinion.

Inside, Dr Watson took up a small bottle and a syringe, extracting a measure of clear liquid and administering it into a thin vein.

'What are you giving him?' Willow asked, monitoring the procedures intently.

'Phenytoin sodium. It is used in the treatment of seizures.'

'I know what it is, Doctor,' Willow croaked out gruffly. 'I don't see how it applies. You said it was his blood pressure.'

Watson held fast for a moment, putting away the syringe as he formulated a more acceptable answer.

'It's all right, John,' Dr Stoner intervened. 'It is common to use with patients suffering his symptoms. It's just new, that's all.'

'It is absolutely paramount, however,' Watson added, 'that the dosage be precise and that he sleeps.'

'Can he not tell us first what he had to say?' asked Willow.

Watson shook his head. 'The mixture I have given him is very tortuous. It must be administered slowly or it could have fatal results. Given in moderate doses, he will be fine by tomorrow. What he needs is rest. I'm sure, whatever it is, he can tell us in the morning.'

As the two doctors began the procession out along with the Master of Ceremonies, Willow held Stratford back. For an instant, at the thought of what might be said or left unsaid in the light of truth, Stratford wanted nothing more than to withdraw from him. He recoiled ever so slightly, but Willow held fast, allowing the others to leave.

'Harry, I am so sorry. This is my fault. I should not have left you. You are my brother and I should have taken greater care. On my love, I give you my word I will fix this, all of this,' he added, leaving Stratford with a strange, uncomfortable feeling.

In the next moment Willow turned his attention to the growing fracas in the hall. The Grand Royal Captain requested with some intensity that Stratford be confined to his room under guard. The notion rousted an army of voices against the action. It was not an easy matter to keep Stratford from anything, especially in his own house. Stratford was well liked and highly supported by all levels and factions. Even in the face of strong evidence against him, there were many loyal constituents that would refuse to abide by the verdict.

There were others who felt no one was above the law, even Stratford, and they would fight wholeheartedly against the other. In the best of times and situations it took great pains to keep the collective whole. To have so distinguished a man as Stratford at the heart gave rise to aggressive unrest. For every man who tried to lay hands on him, there were two to contain the restrainers, quickly resulting in physical altercations. The company had become so embroiled in taking sides that Willow's presence had not been noticed until he spoke.

'Desist!' It was all Willow needed to invoke to quell the argument, his hands raised in the air as if to lord over the feuding masses.

[101] It is here that it must be proclaimed and understood that John Willow was a man known for his passive nature. He was a man of mystery, if ever a man could lay claim to such a title; no one, not even his closest and dearest friends, knew the whole of him. There was no doubt that Stratford held the supremacy of Sussex, controlling everything in the highest position in that most secret of societies, the Masonic Order. There was equally little doubt, upon seeing him, given his bearing, his height, and his manner, that Stratford could exact punishment on anyone against the law or in the Masonic Brotherhood. Stratford's title was a simple one, yet reflected his persona accurately. He was the grand king, the Second Grand Principal.

With his strength sapped by worry for the man he might otherwise call his son, and the mounting evidence against the man he had taken as brother who now stood before him accused of such atrocities against the former, Willow stepped into the volatile tensions in the hall to face an angry mob against the man accused of betraying him. He stood, facing his brother with shaking hands, unable to find the words to confront him. It was the saddest of all betrayals when brother set himself against brother, tearing at the heart with the intimacy of lovers without the ability to walk away.

So quiet was the house in those few moments that the voices outside on the road could almost be heard with clarity, watching and waiting with baited breath for the hammer to strike down.

Turning to Dr Stoner, Willow quietly gave his pronouncement. 'Escort him to his room. See to his health and comfort. I want him well cared for.'

With this Willow gave a small but distinctive nod towards George, who in turn gave several silent commands, sending the men with him in different directions, one to the post outside Stratford's door and another to Willow's room.

'If I may suggest,' Watson interjected, 'that I sit with Lord Stratford in his room, if you wish to continue downstairs. He doesn't look well.'

Willow turned to Stratford, seeing the upheaval had already taken its toll. Stratford said nothing, but turned away from Willow and went to his room, shutting the door behind him as if to shut it against Willow.

[102] 'Do you think Ballard will clear him?' Damon asked

Willow gave him a pat on the arm. 'It will be all right, Sam. I will see to it.'

Reluctantly, Willow motioned for the lagging members to return to the north hall, waiting patiently behind for the man George had sent into his room. Appearing with a magnificent sword of St John, exemplifying the image of a knight and a cross, the man bowed before Willow, who put his arms out to be fitted.

The sword affixed, the servant bowed again and made his way down the back stairs. Willow stood for a moment facing Stratford's room. Alone and in the quiet, he thought of the unpalatable task that faced him.

'What are you going to do John, kill them all?' A familiar voice rang behind him.

'Go home, Mycroft. You've done enough. I should have seen your hand was behind this,' Willow retorted, brushing past him.

'You should have told me about my brother.'

Willow whipped around with contempt. 'And you should not have asked me to betray my brother,' Willow snapped back before turning on his heel and trotting back downstairs.

SESSION CASE

QUEEN'S BENCH DIVISION

LORD JUSTICE

HAROLD A. W. STRATFORD

TWENTY-FIFTH SESSION,

HELD AT

JUSTICE HALL, IN SUSSEX COURT,

ON FRIDAY, THE 27th DAY OF OCTOBER, 1903,

AND FOLLOWING DAYS.

TAKEN IN SHORT HAND

(BY AUTHORITY OF THE CORPORATION OF THE CITY OF EASTBOURNE)

BY A. WAKEFIELD

Eastbourne :

PRINTED FOR J. H. WILLOW, BY A. WAKEFIELD,

No. 74, MEADS;

AND PUBLISHED BY G. HERBERT, COUNTY COURT

1904

[103] It was a long night, leaving many unable to sleep for both excitement and worry over the drama unfolding before them. Sherlock Holmes had become a legend of infallible detection and it was well known that his partner intimately shared his methods. There were few that did not know his name or reputation, though the distinguished guests in the house were generally unaccustomed to needing his services in a criminal matter. To see events unfold before them held a certain morbid curiosity, providing a passing frisson to season their dull lives. Willow, on the other hand, had had enough of death and drama, and retreated to the inner temple behind closed and locked doors in solemn prayer until he fell asleep, sword in hand, too exhausted to go on.

Watson opened the clasp of his watch, turning the face of it to the window, which afforded the only light in the room. It displayed twenty past the hour of four, accounting for the decline in his stamina, which was exacerbated by the lack of movement. It found him dozing off in the chair from time to time. It was an unusually quiet night both inside and out. Only Stoner's excessive snoring roused him long enough to check on their charge. Stratford lay quiet in bed, unmoved since he first laid his head on the pillow. It was good for him to sleep, for all could see his strength had left him, overburdened by recent events. Shutting his eyes, Watson placed himself once again in a meditative state.

[104] At the half hour chime a slow and unobtrusive turn of the doorknob to Whitmore's room allowed a dark, shadowy figure to cast a silhouette against the moonlight. Once inside, the figure moved stealthily to the bed, leaning over the prostrate sleeper, who was surrounded by a mound of blankets and coverings. Picking up the small bottle and syringe placed on the bed table, the figure moved to the window for light, injecting the needle into the bottle and withdrawing a full complement of the solution.

Moving back to the bed, the vague form set down the bottle and gently rearranged the coverings to expose the midsection of his victim's left arm when he turned back the sleeve of the dressing gown. Making a gentle but precise insertion into the vein, he depressed the piston to its full depth, holding the arm fast to the bed despite the lack of struggle. Withdrawing the needle as gently as it was inserted, the agent was unprepared for the hand that reached across his body and grasped his wrist firmly with one swift motion. Startled, the perpetrator attempted to move away, but his victim followed, the man's fingers still firmly attached to his wrist as his victim threw back the covers and stood before his bold executioner.

An instant found the room lit with the use of the electric light switch, illuminating the room to reveal the truth. The agent of death now gasped in full horror as he faced the last man he expected to see holding fast to his arm. Equally, his captor's expression was one of surprise, though of disappointment, anger and betrayal toward his captive. Lord Stratford slowly rose from the bed, too stunned to speak, no less so than the man who stood firmly in his grasp. Stratford had replaced Whitmore in bed to lay a trap for the agent of death he knew would come. But never in his darkest dreams would he have supposed that Samuel Damon, who he had nurtured as his own son, would be that man.

[105] Whitmore, who had been diagnosed at the edge of death, now stood masterfully at the light switch along with Watson, who stood like a watcher at the gate. Sanders and several key members of the meeting stood along the wall like an audience ready for a spectacular finish while Mycroft stood, watching keenly at Whitmore's side.

'Why, Sam?' Stratford demanded, broken at the Damon's betrayal. 'You were going to kill him, in this house? My own ward, practically my son, was going to kill the man in my keeping? Did you kill those other men, too? And David? Did you drag David into this in my name?'

Damon stood too dumbfounded for words. 'Harry, I filled the syringe. You need to counter its effects before it is too late,' Damon addressed with passionate regard for the judge, who had taken the poison for its intended recipient.

Stratford slapped the syringe from Damon's hand. There was no need for him to elaborate; it was unmistakable that he should prefer the poison in the syringe to the poison of betrayal within his own household, by the boy he took in as his own child.

'Don't be a fool. It will kill you. Let them counter its effects. Please; I don't want you to die,' Damon implored.

Stratford shook his head. 'I thought Dr Watson mad when he proposed the idea of the murderer being in this house, a member of my own family. No, said I. No member of this house would dare betray me. We shall see tonight, said Watson, for the killer cannot risk Ballard's testimony and when he tries again we will have our man. May he forgive me; I thought it was John. I let you poison me with your lies about him. How could you?'

'I didn't lie, Harry.'

Stratford tightened his grip until Damon winced in pain. 'It is you who stand here before me, the blood of your deeds still upon your hands, not him!'

Damon cast his eyes down and repeated his request, 'We can discuss this after you have taken the antidote. You are not meant to die.'

Stratford let go of him as one might let go of a serpent, reaching into his pocket for a vial of laudanum. 'Not meant to die? It was you who tainted my laudanum in that very hope!'

Damon looked up at him in earnest. 'No. It was never meant to kill you.'

'It is difficult for us to take you at your word,' Watson interjected. 'What did you think would happen if you exposed him long-term to its effects? Drugs act and respond differently when they are combined. You must also take into account his age and medical history. You added cocaine to an opium-based drug along with a substance I have never seen. It put enormous strain on his heart and the unknown substance has been denying his body the oxygen it needs to live. When he took additional cocaine to keep him going, it was too much for his heart. When you told him about Mr Faulkner's intent he went to stop it and suffered a mild heart attack.'

'That was never meant to happen, but nor is this. Harry, please, take the antidote.'

'Don't worry, son.' Stratford berated him with the sarcastic use of the word. 'Dr Watson has been countering your concoction. Nothing was in that bottle save vitamin water. Would he have let its poison surge through my veins I would have been the gladder for it.

I should welcome it to your betrayal. Dr Watson would never place his own brother in harm's way as you have placed me and those in this house. Did you torture Mycroft's brother with your own hand? How could you do that?'

'I didn't touch Mycroft's brother. We needed the information Ballard had. He wouldn't yield.'

'You didn't even bother to find out who you were torturing. It wasn't Simon Ballard you tortured, it was an innocent man. What kind of monster have I raised that would allow you to torture an innocent man to death? Answer me!'

The new information suddenly shifted Damon to an unsteady footing. 'I had to. He wasn't innocent. I was there in Rye. Ballard had the stone, and with Willow he was going to destroy everything, you and this house included.'

'You stupid, stupid boy,' Stratford came back. 'You don't know John any more than you knew what you were doing at that house. You killed the wrong man and then tortured a man who knew nothing!'

'You never give me credit for anything. Nothing I ever do is good enough for you.'

'Possibly because you can't get it right! There sits your proof. You didn't kill Sherlock Holmes, you killed Simon Ballard and then tortured the wrong man for information he didn't have.'

Damon looked over at Whitmore, trying to take it all in.

'They switched places on you. But like always, you rushed through the details, this time resulting in the torture of an innocent man. Ballard thought you would leave Sherlock and the other men alone if they knew nothing of your plan. He couldn't give you anything, but you killed him anyway. In your greed and ignorance you stilled the very voice you needed to take your prize.'

Damon stared in disbelief, finally quiet.

'It's true,' Watson said. 'It was Simon Ballard who fell from the train and broke his leg. He sent Holmes for help, but Phillip Worth did not have a carriage. That is why they did not go back to his house. Holmes was sent here by Ballard to retrieve Lord Stratford, but he met you first. Outside the gate?'

Damon nodded his head. 'At the South Gate. It was dark and he was lost. In my defence, the two could pass for brothers.'

'Ballard saw that, too. He was a man accustomed to disguise and Holmes was an easy one. It required very little alteration. It is one of the reasons the identification could not be entirely accurate. Though I was intimately aware of what Holmes looked like, the fire made it impossible to remove the theatrical alterations.'

'So you came to Eastbourne to see the patient. To confirm your hypothesis?' Sanders asked.

'Exactly,' Watson said. 'The only way to be sure was to identify all the other men. When I viewed the body of the patient afterwards I did not know Willow had removed Holmes just prior.'

Stratford gave a nod. 'And so you assumed it was Sherlock; very reasonable.'

'I didn't know he was alive until the day on the pier. I approached him several times, but when he failed to recognise me I took the investigation on myself.' Watson chuckled to himself. 'I have to commend Willow for his plan to protect Holmes. We can see the tragic consequences had he failed.'

'Yes; I did underestimate our dear Willow that time, but I wasn't wrong about him in Rye,' Damon said. 'I had it all planned. I let everything calm down and waited until Doherty had gone for days without sleep. I knew Father would have him there day and night. I just had to wait. We made sure the laudanum was given regularly so Father wouldn't show up at the wrong time.'

'And then walked in wearing his coat, hat, and boots,' Mycroft added.

Damon smiled. 'It was perfect. Unless there was proof, no one could question a high court judge. It's treason.'

Mycroft found Damon's attitude disconcerting. 'Willow managed it by knowing what he was doing. Unlike you, he is not an amateur. He had Doherty in his confidence and thus was able to take my brother out and substitute a cadaver.'

'You can imagine my surprise'—Damon gave a small chuckle—'when Whitmore came back from London and I realised who he was.'

Stratford's shock began to pass, rekindling his anger at the light tone. 'Why, Sam? Do you despise me so greatly that you would tear down this house to shame me? You have been like my own son!'

Damon suddenly lost the smirk fastened to his face like a prize. 'Despise you? I could never despise you. Quite the contrary. I admire you more than any man I have ever known. I admired you so much that growing up, all I ever wanted was to be you,' he offered with genuine sincerity.

'I marked you for the bench.'

'The bench, Harry? Dr Watson was right. Possessing the stone, I could have taken the Lord High Chancellorship. I could have made or broken South Lodge.'

'My God, you've taken leave of your senses.' Stratford reeled back in horror.

'Mad? No,' Damon came back. 'Not everyone sides with you, Harry. I love you; by everything I hold dear I love you, but you can be so blind. You started this. You betrayed us! You betrayed the brotherhood, and you betrayed this house! When a judge can no longer perform his task to rule without emotion, without judgment, without personal belief, he has ceased to be judge, ceased to be king and grand principal, and we have the right and obligation to overthrow him—at the cost of lives, if necessary! You betrayed this house and the brotherhood when you struck Willow and drew the first blood, banning him from this house without trial or reprieve! And what was his crime? If I am guilty, I demand that you stand in the docks before me,' he screamed at Stratford. 'Where do you think I got the drug I have been using? Who do you think found other purposes for it? How do you think I was able to hire Grace, hunt down Ballard, control Malone, and bring everyone to their knees? You think you can stop us, but you can't. Nothing can stop it now.'

'Your power came from me. It was in my name you did those awful things. I will stop you. It ends here and now.'

Stratford motioned for Sanders to arrest him, and Sanders took him and led him from the room. It was only then that Stratford saw Willow standing in the doorway. How long he had been there and how much he had heard was unknown, but his undemonstrative expression hid a multitude.

Rushing past the crowd, Brandon Faulkner walked them out. 'Say nothing, Sam. They can't use what they have as a confession. I will see to it.'

Damon stopped and, facing his friend, he laughed.

For a long time Stratford stood quiet, staring at Willow out in the hall and allowing everyone else to leave the room. Who could say if the feelings he had were borne of freedom, weariness, or drugs. His life seemed shattered, not entirely unlike the moment the mast snapped on the ship and the boom thrust into his shoulder, shattering the bone and throwing him into the sea half-conscious. In those moments, the water swirling around him, rocking him in wet, cool sensation, the pain was too unbearable to feel anything.

Watson was right. There were secrets in his house, too dark and deep to reveal to the light of day. He had left Stratford-upon-Avon to build an empire from the bricks of law. Every stone upon the estate was made holy by virtue of the blood spilt in reverence to the law, but at the expense of being irreparably torn from his family. Now an entire life lay as shattered as his shoulder, drifting in the currents, not knowing if he would drift toward life or death.

One singular thought stood out in his mind as the image of Willow's face was seared in his brain. Willow had come to care for his charge in a manner unlike Stratford had seen in years. There was a spark in his old friend's eyes that had been long extinguished. Suddenly, standing in the dimly lit hallway, Stratford started making connections his mind had never considered.

'You gave him your son's name,' he whispered.

'Yes,' Willow said.

'John, I...' He paused, not knowing where to begin, not knowing how much Willow had heard or what Willow was thinking. 'You had every right to distrust me. If I could beg for your forgiveness....'

'I told you before, Harry; there is nothing to forgive.'

[106] It had been a long and solemn night for everyone, and many were relieved in the morning to learn that they no longer had to pass judgment on the Lord Justice. The prospect of that great estate crumbling into ruin was unpalatable to every man there. Though still terrible, the fact that the great duo of detectives had been on the case from the start and had found the murderer to be Samuel Damon was of immense comfort. The lesser blow allowed the great estate and its integrity to remain intact. The esteemed old gentlemen

could return to more important matters of politics, recounting their encounter with the great Sherlock Holmes and Dr Watson to children and grandchildren to come as if they were a part of the great case.

For some, however, the interaction would not hold such pleasant memories.

Willow took his time dressing, standing at length looking in the mirror and tying his tie, away from cheers of success mixed with business in the north wing, standing quiet as the morning light began to illuminate the room. But even as it did so, it could not override the shadows within. Stratford stepped in with a soft tap, putting a gentle hand on Willow's shoulder in support.

'Mycroft is waiting downstairs to take his leave.'

Willow continued to primp in front of the mirror, and then turned to other business in his room, delaying his departure.

'John, please talk to me. You haven't said a word all night or this morning. Please, tell me what you are feeling.'

For a moment, Willow stopped what he was doing and looked at his friend. His composed blue eyes revealed nothing of what was behind them. Stratford waited for a reply, preparing himself for any eventuality, save for the one that came. He readied himself to be sympathetic to grief or supportive to anger, but instead, Willow turned and walked out without a word or an expression.

[107] Downstairs Mycroft waited outside with his brother and Watson. The concept of home had taken on a new meaning for the once famed detective, who had become content to leave the problems of crime and the police courts in Baker Street without him. He had removed the art of detection from his world, replacing it with warm coastal breezes and long summer walks, basking in the problems of chemical conundrums rather than criminal ones. The adventurous machinations between mastermind and detective were best left to the man who picked up the gauntlet as his saviour. Yet, to remain in that house would serve little purpose outside of giving him the peace he so desperately desired. However, it was highly doubtful that the world could continue to see him as a simple chemist, content to keep his hand out of crime. His name alone would precede him.

The argument to stay had dwindled to a slim one, left for posterity to read about in books Watson would someday write.

It had been a long seven months, weighing heavily upon the shoulders of some more than others, who were glad to see an end to them, but sad to let new friends go. Mycroft extended welcoming arms to Stratford, now struggling against the poison in his body to perform even the simple task of host. It was time to return life to its former state, setting back into balance the gentle tides of the ocean before Stratford could begin the long, arduous task of ridding himself of the poison inflicted upon him to the point of addiction.

Watson would return the detective to Baker Street to settle him in before returning to his home in the country. There would be no more chemical conundrums, no walking down to a quiet breakfast of newspapers and briefs of the day. The Spijker, that lovely machine, would speed over the downs now without him and the skiff would be set to sail burdened with books of escapism, but for only one. Sherlock Holmes did not belong in this world, filled with absolute law and chess games. He belonged among the soot-covered buildings and dark murky streets of London, seeking out danger to fulfil his life. Sherlock Holmes remained transfixed in one spot, for all of time, unable to choose his own path.

'What will you do now?' Mycroft asked Willow, who stood staunchly on the stairs.

'I will take Harry away for a while, until he is well again, and put this business behind us. And you?'

'Same as you, I suppose. Help Sherlock put the matter behind him.'

Unable to bring himself to say anything, Willow looked intently at his former charge for a while and then took himself back inside.

SESSION CASE

QUEEN'S BENCH DIVISION

LORD JUSTICE

HAROLD A. W. STRATFORD

TWENTY-SIXTH SESSION,

HELD AT

JUSTICE HALL, IN SUSSEX COURT,

ON FRIDAY, THE 27th DAY OF OCTOBER, 1903,

AND FOLLOWING DAYS.

TAKEN IN SHORT HAND

(BY AUTHORITY OF THE CORPORATION OF THE CITY OF EASTBOURNE)

BY A. WAKEFIELD

Eastbourne :

PRINTED FOR J. H. WILLOW, BY A. WAKEFIELD,

No. 74, MEADS;

AND PUBLISHED BY G. HERBERT, COUNTY COURT

1904

[108] The journey north to London took place in complete silence. Any attempt at conversation was met with a disturbing distance, which was taken by Mycroft as no more than his brother returning to the old habits of his former disposition. In truth, it would be a hard and uncertain journey back to the life his mind had rejected, back to surroundings familiar to everyone except himself. Watson's assurance that his memories would return gave little comfort, and Sherlock Holmes was acutely aware that there was much more to the mental rejection than the horrors based in the old house upon the Downs. A chill of trepidation passed through him as the train paused outside Victoria Station, growing as the hansom took them through London to Baker Street. It culminated in the awakening of absolute dread upon the carriage arriving outside his door.

Watson pushed back the stack of mail barring the door, bundling it together for future sorting. Mrs Hudson had gone to her sister's house after the funeral, greatly affected by the loss. Watson had occasionally tried to sort through the correspondence, writing back to businesses and subscriptions, informing them of Holmes's death, but for the past month he had been working strictly on the case. Watson offered an apology for his neglect of the flat, allowing the brothers Holmes to pass. Jogging up the stairs, Watson opened the windows to air out the rooms, returning to find his old partner sifting through the mail on the chemistry table.

'I'll have to let Hawkins and Lestrade know you're back. They have kept an eye on everything since Mrs Hudson left.'

'Ah, so that is who it was?' Holmes chuckled to himself. 'I am curious.' Holmes turned to Mycroft. 'Why have my rooms been kept rather than being let out? Surely you would have spared yourself the expense if you truly thought me dead.'

Mycroft tapped a tiny snuff box on his hand. 'It was John's idea. I should have realised then that he wasn't telling me everything. He told me he thought dismantling it might disrupt some overlooked clue. I believe he offered Mrs Hudson a handsome settlement to keep it intact.'

Seeing that Sherlock gave no emotional response Watson continued on with brushing off the furniture.

'It's a little dusty, but I am sure we can manage until Mrs Hudson returns. It will take her some time to settle matters enough to come back, but I am sure she will be happy to return without delay. In the interim I will have someone come in and stay with you when I have to be away, someone to clean up and run errands. I can see if Albert is available, unless you think otherwise.'

'Carry on, Watson,' Mycroft insisted. 'I should really get back to Whitehall.'

Holmes stopped what he was doing and waved at both of them to desist. 'I do not require maintenance, Doctor. I assure you my maladies are minimal.'

The formality unsettled Watson, but to his credit he said nothing. He ceased his incessant attempts at tidying.

'Forgive me, I meant no offence. It is just that I know how you don't like being alone.'

'Ah, well,' Holmes said, embarrassed. 'I'm afraid I must yield to your superior knowledge of my own affairs and person.'

This peculiar wording made Watson refrain from pressing further, and at the earliest convenience he made some excuse to take his leave gently.

'I have to make a telephone call to my wife.'

Mycroft rose ponderously from his chair. 'If you are leaving, Doctor, I'll come with you. Will you be all right, Sherlock?'

Holmes waved them on, too engrossed in the study of curiosities to look over his shoulder.

'The tobacco is in the Persian slipper, though it may be somewhat stale. I will pick some up while I am out,' Watson went on, as if to a guest staying for a fortnight, not meaning anything by it outside of offering ease and comfort to an old friend. Yet it did feel uncomfortable, standing in those rooms once more, for both of them. Each knew that it would never be the same again.

[109] Holmes sat patiently in his usual chair beside the fireplace. Nostalgia swept over him in his study of the room, causing him to reach down, as he had done only weeks before, and pick up the pipe lying on the floor, hidden beside the chair. The tobacco was old and musty, unfit for use, but the pipe itself felt comfortable in

his hands. Reaching around for a pipe cleaner, Holmes leaned over the fireplace grate and cleaned out the dusty briar pipe, reaching almost instinctively for the Persian slipper. Refilling his pipe full of tobacco of a brand he must have smoked countless times before, he pressed it firmly into the pipe bowl, drawing out a match from the matchbox in his pocket. The tobacco was indeed stale, having not been touched for more than seven months, but it would suffice until better could be had. Drawing his legs up onto the chair and wrapping them tightly in his arms, he began to smoke and to think in favour of reliving old times.

Over the next couple of days, Watson came and went, but Holmes remained steadfast in that room. Though it was somewhat frustrating to Holmes for someone to be continually cleaning, disrupting his chain of thought at every opportunity, the subsequent days were spent in one continuous effort to restart the sluggish processes of his mind. Try as he might to force himself to turn away from all thoughts of Eastbourne, it crept in at every inopportune moment. He had, for so long, been content to leave matters of crime and puzzles to the professionals and turn to more rewarding pursuits. Striking the notion from his head, it always brought him back to the singular conundrum his faulty faculties had left unsolved. His concentration was so complete that it was not until a booming voice behind him spoke his name that he broke from his thoughts to address his visitor.

'Sherlock!' Mycroft Holmes stood at the door, thrusting his hat and gloves onto the sideboard. 'What is this I hear that you are refusing to eat or sleep? What is wrong?'

Without looking up, Holmes replied, 'He said "you."'

Mycroft walked across the room and sat down with interest, waiting curiously for the boot to fall.

'What are you talking about?'

Holmes looked up but briefly. 'Damon said "you were not to die," with an emphasis on "you." And of course the reference to "us" and "Willow". He said he did not lie about Willow and that Willow would bring South Lodge down. We have to go back.'

'No,' Mycroft insisted before seeing his emphatic answer drew attention. 'Give them a month or two to recover.'

'If I am right, at least one more person will die.'

'It's a long leap from one to the other. Besides, John has probably already taken Harry abroad. What's this all about? So the boy misspoke. What of it?'

'I don't believe he did misspeak. Watson deduced the plan most cleverly, but he failed'—he glanced at Watson—'to give an explanation of why I took the case in the first place. He also failed to mention the note Damon intercepted from Ballard.'

Mycroft perked up. 'What note?'

'The one Damon decoded mentioning both Stratford and Willow. It was something Damon said that bothered me. He went to Rye because he thought Stratford was going to meet Willow. I believe he was meant to, but never made it. The night I went to see Ballard in Rye, Ballard told me he was late. He was expecting someone. I suspect it was Willow, but I cannot be sure. Ballard had obviously sent a note to Stratford to come to Rye, but though Willow seemed to react to it, Stratford seemed to know nothing about it when mentioned. I therefore concluded that the note was intercepted. Perhaps it is this that caused me to take on such an obviously inaccurate case at the onset.'

Taking a seat in curiosity, Watson took out his pipe. 'Inaccurate?'

'The clues, pinned to the board, the ones you removed to write the formula.' He pointed across the room. 'Miss Stratford first proposed that the answer to the case was at the beginning, the reason why I professed it to be so simple. She asserted that the answers were here on Baker Street for I would not have entrusted them elsewhere. She makes a terrible detective, but her argument is sound. In every account you have recorded of me it is stated that mental stimulation was the driving force in my selection of cases. As I must yield to your expertise in matters of my own person, I must conclude that the obvious chore of purchasing an artefact in a prearranged meeting would not have interested me unless there was more behind it.'

Watson's expression suddenly sank. 'Before you left you asked me if I had ever heard of Lord Stratford. It was that clue that told me I was on the right track in finding you.'

Holmes sat up on the edge of his seat at this, giving his full attention and encouraging Watson to offer more.

'You said you were disappointed in the investigation until Stratford. You said you had been in Sussex all week and that you were disappointed in the investigation until that day.'

'I wouldn't have happened to mention where in Sussex, perhaps?'

'No, but you said you had new information that convinced you that there was something in it after all.'

'What was that?

'I don't know. You didn't say. In the next minute Grace was at the door and you insisted on handling the case alone.'

Holmes leapt from his seat and paced the floor. Then, inexplicably, he stopped short and turned back to them. 'Damon,' he directed towards Watson. 'When the lights went on and you saw Damon, you seemed surprised.'

'Not really. It made sense.'

'But it was not who you expected. So who was it?'

'I'm embarrassed to say.' Watson might have stopped at that, but Holmes waved him on with insistence. 'Brandon Faulkner.'

'Faulkner? Why not Willow?'

'It was Faulkner who was seen leaving the stables just before the horse bolted from the stall. It was Faulkner who continued to disappear just before every incident of trouble. I also could not confirm his whereabouts when Malone was killed. There was that, and the fact that Willow was with you in London.'

Holmes shook his head. 'No, he was not with us. He left shortly after our arrival in London and we did not see him until the day before we left. And Damon never confessed.'

'What puzzles me is Damon. If you are right and I have missed something, it has to do with the stone and power over the Masons. But how could Damon have seized power if Lord Stratford were still alive? Surely he would have to die in order to for Damon enact his plan to take South Lodge, yet we know Damon wanted him alive.'

Mycroft slapped the arm of the chair. 'He would have to kill more than Harry. He'd have to kill John, as well, or he would leave no stone unturned to find Harry's killer.'

Holmes turned away. 'I wonder.' Giving it thought, Holmes repeated his assertion. 'We need to return to South Lodge. If Stratford's life is in danger we must discover the source.'

Mycroft sat uneasy in his chair. 'If they haven't already left. I'll look into the matter, but I'm afraid we must leave Stratford in Willow's hands. John's not going to let anything happen to Harry. I can guarantee that.'

Holmes turned away in a huff, walking to the window and staring out.

Moving to go, Mycroft paused at the door. 'I'll see what I can find out. In the meantime I want you to remain in London. I'll check on you in a few days.'

Holmes waved him on, and guessing that he would get no further on the matter with him, Mycroft departed.

SESSION CASE

QUEEN'S BENCH DIVISION

LORD JUSTICE

HAROLD A. W. STRATFORD

TWENTY-SEVENTH SESSION,

HELD AT

JUSTICE HALL, IN SUSSEX COURT,

ON FRIDAY, THE 27th DAY OF OCTOBER, 1903,

AND FOLLOWING DAYS.

TAKEN IN SHORT HAND

(BY AUTHORITY OF THE CORPORATION OF THE CITY OF EASTBOURNE)

BY A. WAKEFIELD

Eastbourne :

PRINTED FOR J. H. WILLOW, BY A. WAKEFIELD,

No. 74, MEADS;

AND PUBLISHED BY G. HERBERT, COUNTY COURT

1904

[110] Samuel Damon listened as the outer lock on the gate clicked, and the clank of keys slapped against the iron bars, echoing through the sterile walls. It gave him a perverse sense of satisfaction to hear, knowing that they paraded in to see him, each hoping to get out of him the information their predecessors had failed to derive. They had failed to gain a confession. Even more disheartening, Damon refused to reveal any more of the particulars leaving unanswered questions.

Damon had become proficient at determining how many were coming by the clop of shoes against the stone floor. There were two of them this time, a policeman and a gentleman of breeding and means. Their stride and step fell distinctively. Their footfalls finally slowed and Sanders's face filled the small window into the cell, confirming the identity of the policeman. It now remained to see who the gentleman was. The keys turned in the lock and the door swung aside. John Willow stepped inside.

'Stand outside, Robert, and close the far door after you,' Willow insisted with quiet reserve. 'And take the guard with you.'

Willow stood tall and quiet, saying nothing until he heard Sanders turn the key to the outer door down the hall, the squeak of the gate, and a second clank of the keys turning. It was difficult to say whether Willow's years of courtroom presentation automatically put him in the mode to unnerve his opponent by his stance and silence, or if it were out of some preparation to speak, for Willow was known for getting straight to the heart of the matter, dispensing with formalities. Whatever it was, it was extremely efficient.

'Get me the hell out of here,' Damon insisted. 'You don't want me saying anything in court.'

'No, that would never do,' Willow replied with disturbing calm. 'We could not allow our shame to be publicized to the world.'

'So get me out of here.' Damon turned and hung his feet over the edge of the cot.

'All right,' Willow conceded with a nod. 'I have prepared a shower for you.'

'Why?'

'To get off the stench of this place. Then we are going to have a little chat.'

'And then what? Where are you going to take me?'

'Take you? I am not going to take you anywhere. We will go our separate ways, you and I. I will not see you again. You are to be set free.'

'Free? You aren't going to just let me walk out of here without some punishment. Your little friends must have their playtime. Didn't you bring your candles and silk robes?' Damon taunted him. 'Harry should be in here, not me!'

'Be careful of what you say about the next Lord Chief Justice, laddie.' Willow's tone suddenly shifted. 'Anyway, we can hardly put it to a trial, or let you blackmail us. It will be understood, however, that all Masons will ostracize you for all time with no hope of reprieve. You will leave here, never to address another Mason in any capacity again. You are to be excommunicated.'

'And that is it? I will walk out of here a free man, just like that?'

'Not just like that. You leave here half the man you were, disgraced and denied by every brother in the world. They will look the other way, and turn their backs on you, even in death. Not one Mason will ever again speak your name or acknowledge that you existed. There will be no acknowledgement of your life ever, wiped clean by the wrath of God.'

Damon's scepticism showed, but Willow's expression remained sincere. Willow opened the cell door and patiently waited for Damon to gather his things. The traditional posts and sentries were absent, leaving a clear path to the shower area, consisting of six showerheads affixed to a ghastly sick green-tiled wall entered through an archway. A bath sheet had been laid out for him along with towels and a shaving assortment. There were no guards or awaiting thugs, no ritual sword or candles, just a pail and mop propped up against the far corner wall, left by the janitor, and a clean set of clothes neatly folded. Willow motioned that the bath waited, turning his back at Damon's continued hesitation, lest it be for modesty.

Damon removed his clothing; placing them over the bench, glad to be rid of them, for it had been days without a change of clothes. Stepping into the shower he noted Willow's continued observance of privacy, easing Damon's mind that Willow would not suddenly present some unforeseen threat. Willow remained genuine and soft-spoken, without recrimination. A sense of clean dignity washed over him as the water struck his naked body, running over his face and washing away the stench of confinement. He could no longer see Willow, who remained against the wall supporting the showers. The odour of burning tobacco told Damon precisely what Willow was doing, allowing him to freely set himself under the flowing water until the tension began to disperse. Willow's voice in the silence startled him, but its calm gentle tone raised no alarm. Rather, there was satisfaction in the subject matter.

'I am curious,' Willow started without threat. 'The young girl who came to the office.'

'Miss Valetto. Did you like her?' Damon asked, giving Willow time to adjust to the truth.

There was a long pause, lagging to the point where Damon felt a need to glance out of the shower to see what Willow was up to. He had not moved, still leaning up against the wall smoking.

'Yes,' Willow whispered, almost unintelligible, and Damon ducked back under the water. 'I liked her very much.'

'I knew you would. I chose her myself, as a gift.'

Again there was a long unnerving silence as Willow adjusted himself to the answer.

'Honestly,' Damon continued, 'I wasn't sure for a long time how your tastes ran. At one point I even thought you and Harry were'—he paused—'well, intimate.'

'Intimate?' Willow sounded surprised.

'Well, you must admit, you were not very forthcoming in your affections towards women. I eventually figured it out,' Damon came back. 'Do you remember the bad storm, the year the north wing roof had to be repaired? It was the night of the legal conference. Helena, though still quite a child, was developing into a stunning woman. You and Harry had been gone all day. You came home rather late, but did not bring Harry back with you. I forget why now, but you were talking to George about how horrid the weather was. You were drunk, so drunk you could barely stand. You hobbled up the stairs, and even with George's help you barely made it. I don't think anything could have awakened you once you fell into bed. Do you remember that night?'

'I remember.'

'I'll tell you what I remember. I remember being woken up very early in the morning by an ungodly commotion. Harry was holding you down in your room. Helena was crying hysterically in the hall. George had a syringe with something to calm you down. You were saying the strangest things. You had broken your wrist putting it through the wall. I noticed the scars on your hands. It wasn't your first time,' he grinned, an awful grin. 'Funny thing about Harry, when you think about it. He is intelligent and observant on the whole, but with you, he hasn't figured it out. It would never even cross his mind. Even now you could tell him and he wouldn't believe you. But I figured it out. You could not be sure, in your intoxicated condition, what you might have done to his daughter, or more to the point, what you would have enjoyed doing to her. She was so young and innocent, yet so ready and willing to explore love. The storm had frightened her. It always did. Harry wasn't home, so she had gone to her other father, curling in so softly, so tenderly. She would have, you know—given into you. Lovely dream, isn't it? Sweet Helena, there in your bed, wanting children with you, wanting to have a life with you. Harry has been afraid of that prospect for years.'

Damon smiled inwardly at the toll this must be taking on Willow. "Did you fuck her? I couldn't be sure,' he jeered. 'Miss Valetto, on the other hand, that was a treat not meant for marriage. You judge yourself far too harshly, John. Of what use are they if not to surrender under our desires? I almost had her myself, but then I didn't want to spoil her before she came to you. You would not have liked her then, if she were sullied. Consider it a gift in honour of our'—he paused, trying to find the right word—'relationship. No hard feelings.'

[111] Willow stood, no longer against the wall, but in front of the archway facing a different kind of demon than the one inside; this was a shadowy reflection of himself, if left unchecked. Samuel Damon, though a beast by any other name, still paled in comparison to the evil he had unwittingly unleashed with his game. Willow had his answer, though it changed nothing. The gates of hell had been

opened and the demon released, loosed upon the quiet streets of an unsuspecting world. He was too old this time to chain it down. It was too late for regret or careful inspection of the locks. Thirty years of sleep and confinement had been undone. Damon had not noticed that Willow had removed his coat, but he had; nor did he notice that Willow had meticulously rolled up his sleeves.

They stood, devil and fiend, face to face: the energy and enjoyment of youth and the calm dignity of age.

'It was the blood,' Willow put forth as a matter of fact as Damon washed the soap from his face.

'Blood?'

'The thing that induced my fear the night my daughter came to me. It was unfortunate timing on her part, still young and inexperienced in becoming a woman, and mental impairment on my part, having had too much to drink and too many wild dreams as a result. You are right; I could not be sure of what I might have done. She was in my arms and her blood was upon me nonetheless, and I was...' He stopped for propriety's sake, but decided to clarify, being honest in return for honesty. 'The blooding: the smearing of the first blood, when a boy becomes a complete man through understanding of his acts, having been marked with the blood of his prey,' he explained, stepping into the shower and tightening down the water nozzle to a small flowing stream, watching the water pour into the drain like a river flowing out to sea.

'See how the water ebbs and flows, even without the tide,' he mused. 'I do not permit anyone to put my family in harm's way, let alone do them an injury. You should have remembered that,' Willow said as he turned around to face Damon, who suddenly felt a sharp pain across his midsection.

It was an unrecognisable pain at first, but quickly growing in severity. Willow's expression remained unaltered, as if he was unaware of any affliction. Yet, looking down at the flowing water, it was now tainted bright red, washing into the drain, back into the sea. He had been cut, marked in Masonic fashion, though no dagger or knife could be seen. It hurt, stinging in the cold away from the warmth of the water, but if that was all Willow had in him, it would suffice as payment for release. Before Damon could force his mind into accepting what had happened, Willow forcibly, yet without inflection of any kind, thrust his fist through the last layers of skin and opened the incision, bursting out a portion of intestine and entrails, lifting them casually and unaffectedly up for Damon to view before scattering them against the north wall.

Whatever Willow was chanting or saying no longer registered in Damon's mind. He was too shocked and too much in agony to grasp the significance, even as Willow stretched forth his hand to grasp the second and third fistful of organs, innards and bowels, scattering each handful to another point of the compass, even as Damon's hand weakly clutched at him to stop. He slumped against the wall of the showers, watching his own blood pour into the drain as his innards were scattered to the four points of the earth.

'In retrospect, Sam'—Willow picked up the conversation as if nothing had transpired, collecting a towel after running his hands under the water—'though Miss Valetto was most satisfactory, it might have been best not to have opened those gates.'

Willow put his hands in the light stream of water, cleansing more blood from his skin as he squat down to face Damon once more.

'And I will tell you a little secret, in appreciation for your kind gift. You were after his power, but Harry does not hold the true power. He is a figurehead in a meaningless society created for the very purpose it serves: to protect us. And I'll tell you something else, about the stone. It wasn't meant for either Harry or me. It was only to remind us of what we had forgotten. The stone can never break the true Masons, only our illusionary faction. Searching for the word of God never ends. Ballard didn't ask me to come to Rye to collect the stone, but rather to meet Harry. Ballard wanted us to mend our differences and thus mend our power. The Templar and the Mason, the true power of the Brotherhood,' he explained.

Willow then leaned in close, seeing that Damon had but moments to live, coughing out those final gasps of air. He took Damon's head in his hands gently; caressing his hair much like one would a lover's. 'Would you like to know the name of the true First Grand Principal, who rules England under the hand of the Grand Master Builder, the one who guides the hand of their majesties and the rest of the world?

Or better still, the next Grand Master Builder, who will bear the stone and change the world?'

Leaning in closer still, drawing his lips softly against Damon's ear, he whispered the name and then drew his hand tenderly, as a father would to his son, across each of Damon's cheeks, marking him with blood. Damon's eyes grew wide at the hearing of it, glazing over in horrific revelation as he sank into death, with the truth the entire world sought to know. Damon had indeed received the Blooding, bringing him from boyhood ignorance to the knowledge of manhood, even unto death.

[112] Willow stood up and stepped out of the flowing river of water and blood, wiping the blood from his hands and thrusting the towel onto the bench. Rolling down his sleeves he called out for Sanders, who quickly unlocked the outer gates and doors, making his way down the hall and into the showers, just as Willow drew on his coat and straightened his tie in the mirror, as if unaffected. Sanders, on the other hand, rushed into the shower stall only to be confronted with the sight of Damon's body. He instantly vomited where he stood. It seemed too inconceivable for Willow to have stood so, collecting his cane and replacing his hat on his head, before turning to Sanders.

'Finish cleaning up your mess,' he ordered with profound reproach. 'And pray I do not ask for an accounting of why Doherty was there instead of you. It was a damn waste of a good man!' he barked, turning mechanically and exiting in the manner in which he had come.

[113] It began to rain, and Holmes paced the floors between his rooms. He took but momentary breaks to sift through files and pictures of an old life. They had once contained a life, an entire story behind each and every page, now lost in the chasm of his mind. Hints of distant memories were all that seemed to be left, and his mind always returned to Watson's formula on the chalkboard. It might have gone better had his brain not been otherwise employed, mulling over facts he could not press from his mind. Try as he might, the questions resounded in his brain. Something inexplicable pulled him time and again back to the chemical compound.

Spending unrelenting hours experimenting with various possibilities, Holmes continued to alter the dynamics of the substance, hoping to see something he missed. As he stood mesmerised by the various components, Holmes began to see the same error over and over again. Rushing to the board he exchanged two variables and stood back for a moment to read it over.

'It's a hallucinogen, Watson,' he said with a smile as it began to come to life. 'It's not a poison, it's a hallucinogen.'

With this one revelation more pieces of the puzzle began to fall into place. It would explain why Lord Stratford was sluggish in mind. It would also explain his physical deterioration with the prolonged use of the drug. The cocaine masked some of the lethargy, but eventually it would collect in the tissues and begin to break down the cells. It made him susceptible to suggestion while making it appear, at times, that his mind was remarkably clear. With the oscillating symptoms it would be next to impossible for Stratford to be entirely sure what he had said or done, all of which explained Stratford but not Mrs Stanton. What was her role in the unfolding drama? Was she nothing more than a test subject or did Stanton really care about her as much as it appeared? In either case it seemed cruel to keep her in a coma-like state, slowly deteriorating.

And then there was Damon's reference to another person or persons. Stanton would be the logical choice, for it was his wife affected and he who had the facilities to alter chemicals. Watson also believed Stanton was responsible for the fire in the laboratory. But if Stanton were involved, what did he want? Why keep his wife ill and what motive could he have for assisting Damon in killing anyone who could dispute a faked artefact? There were too many unanswered questions and everyone seemed too eager to be rid of him the moment it was learned who he truly was, or at least the name.

Finding his coat and hat, Holmes rushed out the door, nearly running down Mrs Hudson on his way.

'But where are you going?' she asked.

'Eastbourne. To stop a murder,' he replied with excitement, nearly forgetting the note he had hastily written. Turning back to her he begged one thing. 'Take this to the telegraph office at once. There can be no delay,' he added, climbing into the hansom and tapping the driver on.

[114] Willow stood on the steps of the police station putting on his gloves as he ran over every detail of Watson's account. Waving on his driver, Willow climbed in and ordered the coachman to Bourne Street. The dull grey door was not unfamiliar to him, though it had been some time since he had last visited. Striking the tarnished brass knocker, Willow waited, looking up and down the street in acute observance. It was only at the turning of the latch and the creak of the door that brought him back to his business.

The colour flushed from Stanton's face as he saw Willow standing upon his doorstep. 'John,' he managed to get out in a nervous little voice.

Tipping his hat, Willow gave a courteous nod to the old gentleman. 'Virgil.'

There was no need to ask whether Stanton could spare the time. Willow's presence alone moved the anxious old man to the side, allowing Willow free passage. Willow removed his outerwear and placed it over the back of the nearest chair, making himself at home in the small sitting room. Stanton followed him in, growing increasingly unnerved as Willow looked around the room. Willow gave only a cursory look at the chemistry table near the window, but Stanton found himself wishing it were in another room, sure Willow knew everything Stanton did there.

'Do you want some tea?' Stanton asked. 'I have a pot on.'

Willow gave a pleasant nod, releasing Stanton to the kitchen. Stanton tried to keep his mind on the task at hand, but Willow's unceremonious presence unnerved him. Stanton found himself continually peering around the doorway and looking over at the chemistry table. Willow ran his fingers across the little bottles perched on the edge. He picked up a vial or two, examining it in a curious fashion the way any inexperienced person might do. There was nothing he lingered over. Moving on, Willow showed the same interest in the pictures on the mantel, relieving Stanton's nerves. Stanton shuffled into the room and sat the tea tray on the small table between them, pouring out for Willow first.

Taking the cup, Willow looked up at Stanton. 'How is your wife?'

'She's doing well,' Stanton came back. 'There is hope.'

'I am so glad. Our loved ones are so important to us. We try to protect them, but still they come to harm. Katherine is such a beautiful and virtuous woman.'

'Yes,' Stanton agreed in a begrudging tone, again before he realized it betrayed his true feelings.

His life had been open to his closer friends, who knew the truth of it. It was true his wife was both beautiful and virtuous, but Stanton had long since grown tired of her modesty.

'And the business, doing well, is it? I see you have closed it, save for the first part of the week.'

'Yes. I only have Percy part-time, and with Kathy in hospital I cannot always be there.'

'Of course. If it would help I could send you someone to help out in the shop.'

'No,' Stanton came back quickly. 'No, I have it. I mean, there is not a lot going on during the week and my customers know they can always reach me if they need anything special.'

Willow leaned back and took a sip of tea. 'I hope your rejection is not over the concern of money. You are our brother. We will take care of all expenses. I think our intervention is long overdue. You must give all attention to your wife, Virgil. Spare nothing in her care and rest assured we, your brethren'—he paused—'will take care of you.'

Setting down the cup, Willow retrieved his hat and cane and took his leave, leaving Stanton to reflect upon the offer. He had smelled fear on the man. Willow smiled to himself. Yes, the man had taken his meaning.

Heading to the station, Willow checked his watch as he closed the door to the railway carriage and drew the inner curtain. The hour and a half to London would be traveled in silence and alone. Careful to lay his parcel on the seat next to him, Willow leaned back and prepared himself. It was just past one, and taking into account that it would be at least fifteen minutes to traverse the crowds out to a cab, travel another two and a half miles or so from Victoria Station to the Inner Temple, and walk the rest of the way, he could count on it being past three when he arrived at his ultimate destination.

It was well past the hour when Willow walked through the doors and stood reverently on the white marble floor. Clutching the heavy parcel, Willow made his way down the long corridor to a dark thick oak door halfway along. Inside, the room was sparsely furnished, and an old man sat in the chair facing the window. He was attended by a servant who disappeared into the next room when Willow closed the door.

'You have it then?' the old man asked.

'Yes,' Willow acknowledged, remaining where he was until the old man motioned for him to bring it forward.

Placing it in the man's care, Willow took a step back and watched as the old man gently, and with trembling hands, opened each layer.

'Still arrogant and resistant to ceremony, I see,' he said in reference to Willow's refusal to kneel or even bow in respect. In the next moment his attention was diverted to the tablet as he peeled away the last layers of cloth. Running his fingers along the ridges and crevices, the old man smiled at his treasure. 'Ahhh. Well done; well done, indeed. Your predecessors would be proud.'

Giving a thought to the cost throughout the years for the hardened clump of minerals, Willow gave a silent sigh as he looked through the window at the opposite building. The great pillars and noble architecture echoed those same words and symbols in a constant remembrance, but they were overlooked.

SESSION CASE

QUEEN'S BENCH DIVISION

LORD JUSTICE

HAROLD A. W. STRATFORD

TWENTY-EIGHTH SESSION,

HELD AT

JUSTICE HALL, IN SUSSEX COURT,

ON FRIDAY, THE 27th DAY OF OCTOBER, 1903,

ND FOLLOWING DAYS.

TAKEN IN SHORT HAND

(BY AUTHORITY OF THE CORPORATION OF THE CITY OF EASTBOURNE)

BY A. WAKEFIELD

Eastbourne :

PRINTED FOR J. H. WILLOW, BY A. WAKEFIELD,

No. 74, MEADS;

AND PUBLISHED BY G. HERBERT, COUNTY COURT

1904

[115] Sherlock Holmes found himself hanging out of the window of the carriage as the train pulled into the Eastbourne station, opening the door even before the train had come to a complete stop. No more than cleared, he took off for the left side of the station, where cabs and motor carriages awaited passengers, bounding with energy toward a familiar and reassuring face.

'Whitmore!' Stackhurst called out, taking him in hand. 'I'm sorry, dear boy. I meant Holmes. You must forgive us. We are all still getting used to calling you Mr Holmes. Even now I can scarcely believe it.'

Sherlock Holmes said, 'I know how you feel. Did you get it?'

'You didn't give me much time,' Stackhurst said, reaching into his bag for a folder and handing it to the former detective. 'So what is the urgency?'

Holmes flipped through the file, oblivious to Stackhurst's attempts at conversation. When he slapped the folder shut, he could feel the bright twinkling sparkle in his eyes as he turned to Stackhurst. 'Do you have the motor?'

'I am a schoolteacher, Holmes, not a high court judge. I regret to say you will have to make do with the school's old trap.'

'It will suffice,' said Holmes, taking Stackhurst by the arm and turning him toward the exit.

Climbing into a small cart drawn by a tired-looking mare, Stackhurst took the reins. 'Where are we going, back to the estate?'

'To see Virgil Stanton.'

Stackhurst's expression dropped. 'You haven't heard then? No, you wouldn't have. Stanton committed suicide about an hour ago.'

Holmes sat for a moment in thought and then turned to Stackhurst with firm conviction. 'What do you know about the Stanton's?'

'I really shouldn't tell tales out of school,' Stackhurst began, but Holmes glared at him. 'It was Mrs Stanton. She was, well ... distant.'

'Distant? In what way?'

'In her duties as a wife. Oh, she was a marvellous housekeeper, meticulous in habit to a fault. They both were, he more than her sometimes. Neither could abide a mess. It was just in areas of the marital union, if you take my meaning.'

'Is it common knowledge, this picture of the Stanton's?'

'Common enough when Stanton had a few pints in him. Katherine Stanton was never one to openly show emotion, but she was even more reserved with Virgil. It is speculated that they married because she was with child. It was never presumed that the child was not his, but some speculated.'

'She didn't marry him for love.'

'I've known Virgil Stanton ever since I came here. He has been in love with her since the day he met her, but she did not return his love, not the way he wanted. She went away for a while and when she came back they had married. It caused a raised eyebrow here and there, but it passed. Oddly, and perhaps most unfortunately, they seemed to be doing better just before her accident.'

'Better in what way?'

Stackhurst shrugged his shoulders. 'I don't know, just better, more at ease, more agreeable. Mrs Stanton had a way about her, you understand. She meant no ill respect, but she often came across a little gruff in her manner. I don't know what changed, but in the few months before her accident she seemed'—Stackhurst tried to find the right word—'I don't know, more agreeable. It did a world of good for him. I never saw him happier, until her illness.'

'Which he may have caused,' Holmes muttered to himself.

'Look, I know your reputation as a detective, but—'

'Former,' Holmes emphasised, 'detective. I make no such claim now.'

'You really don't remember, do you?' Stackhurst's tone softened.

'Head to the police station.'

'Why?'

'To check on our murderer,' Holmes replied.

Holmes tried to fit the pieces together in his mind and formulated a plan along the quiet route to the police station, running through what he would pose as an excuse to see Damon. The moment Stackhurst stopped, Holmes jumped down and made his way up the stairs with all due haste. Seeing Sanders coming down the hall, Holmes turned away to let him pass without notice, pushing Stackhurst around the corner. He would take no chance that instructions had been left to deny him access. A portly old constable sat behind a desk in the main hall and did little more than point the way to the office down the hall.

'I would like to apply for permission to see Samuel Damon. My name is Sherlock Holmes and I am working with the London police on a case.'

The officer shook his head. 'I'm afraid that's impossible.'

Dismayed at the rejection, Holmes pressed his luck. 'I have permission from Inspector Lestrade from Scotland Yard. Damon is wanted for questioning in the murder of Charles Grace.'

'I'm sorry sir, Mr Damon has been transferred.'

'Transferred? Where?'

'Up north, I think.'

The vague undemonstrative answers told him there was little point in pursuing the issue. He was sure Damon was dead. Stackhurst followed after Holmes, who took to his heels down the hall, not stopping until he reached the steps outside.

Seeing his friend disgruntled and staring off, Stackhurst gave a pat on Holmes back. 'I'm sorry, old man. I suppose it was a bit much to expect they would leave him here. He did murder nine people. They probably took him to Chichester, out of reach.'

'I'm sure you're right, but someone is going to great lengths to remove all evidence to this case.'

[116] The short attempt at investigation was instructive, and helped to put together a picture that began to worry him. It was not only wise, but also prudent, to send Stackhurst back to the Gables. It was not time to take on an apprentice or to have to worry about a partner's safety. The opponent he faced was far too formidable. It would take all of Holmes's powers to confront him, with only a small hope of succeeding.

A slow walk took Holmes back to South Lodge, back to the borders of the life he yearned to embrace, but was forced to reject. Its walls still towered and protected with warmth and comfort, making the task at hand more difficult to bear. Stopping a block before the estate, Holmes waited until the streets were clear before revealing his direction. It would not do to have his presence revealed before he was ready. There were those that might hide the truth, for good or ill, if they became aware that matters were in the hands of Sherlock Holmes. It was best to wait and discreetly make his way in through the stable entrance, keeping his inquiries subtle. The gym and pool houses were adjoined at the back of the house, concealed from the front road, making it a perfect place to enter and conduct his investigation.

He turned toward the brick fence, moved toward the large iron gates, and found them unexpectedly chained and locked against him. Taking the lock in his hands to dispel his disbelief, he let it fall from his fingers at the possible reasons. At first he contemplated the idea that he was too late, that Willow had already taken Stratford abroad to recuperate. Looking toward the house all seemed closed and still, causing him to pace anxiously in thought, for it was not only unexpected, but did not fit with his premise.

However, there was an obvious error in the picture before him, which now served as a thorn to irritate him. Holmes studied the intricate details of the windows as he moved along Darley Road, following the same process. He ran his eyes slowly and observantly over the house, sure that there was something in it. The curtains were drawn, making the house look dark and deserted. It was an odd thing to do if one was going abroad. Surely they would have left most of the servants behind. Even if they hadn't there could be no purpose in drawing the curtains if the gates were locked. An intruder would find it more enticing than an open window, where his presence could be seen, and drawing sheets over the furniture would have already spared the colours from the sun. They were concealing something.

Circling around the estate, Holmes made his way up the slope of the outlying village and waited at the archway into the stables. Two sentries covered the grounds, which further suggested concealment, but it begged the question of why. Slipping inconspicuously through to the stables, Holmes watched and waited for the guards to move across the lawn as he peered around the corner and looked toward the adjoining garage, confirming his suspicion. Both the motorcars were inside. Only the landau was missing, suggesting a local trip by Willow. Slipping into the alcove of the main doors, he looked for anything that could tell him what was truly going on, taking advantage that there would be few obstructions. The actual house seemed relatively deserted, allowing him to steal inside without hindrance.

He slipped through the passageway to the main house and made his way through the halls to the west wing, knowing that at any moment he could come face to face with a member of staff, or worse, Willow. It would be better to be confronted by the master of the house than the man he had set his sights on. He was starting to see that Willow, despite his sadness at Holmes's departure, was the hand behind his quick dismissal from the house. Finding that Holmes had returned would not sit well. However, forcing the reattachments of old connections in his mind did not come as easily as he thought they would. His brain was slow to form mental connections. The west wing seemed deserted, taking him through empty corridors and deserted rooms.

It was a short distance to the study with a clear passage just past the main hall. He checked again to see if it was clear and whisked inside, closing the doors behind him. Bookshelves lined every wall from floor to ceiling. A ladder, attached to a bar at the top and wheels at the bottom, allowed for easy access to every corner and shelf. It was an excellent place for concealment of parchment or a small box, prompting his first point of active investigation, looking for anything that could lead him to the truth. With no more than a vague outline of investigation comprising of 'anything out of the ordinary,' it was difficult to know what to look for or where to look. Quite literally the vital clue could reside on a scrap of paper or be staring him in the face larger than life. The old instinct and intuition for detection still eluded him, forcing an old-fashioned approach, but that, too, failed to yield anything.

Concluding his search of the bookshelves he turned his attention toward the furniture, opening drawers and sorting through cupboards. Moving onto Damon's desk, Holmes seated himself and sifted through the various drawers, running his fingers along edges and seams, finding little more than normal files, supplies, and appointments in a book. Reaching the long upper drawer, he found it to be locked, taking him aback. It was odd to have only one drawer in Damon's desk locked, while the others remained free. Surely they would have unlocked all of them or have locked all of them. In an effort to find the key, he looked through the other desks in the room, but few minutes of intense effort found him no further along. The lock, like the desk, was of superior quality, not easily undone, even with the aid of a knife. Flopping back into the chair in defeat, Holmes let it go, unable to see around the problem.

It was on his mind to turn his investigation upstairs when his exit presented a singular alteration in the walls. He had lived on the Stratford estate for months, walking down the front hall from the foyer to the morning room every day, onto the sitting room, and finally the study and dining room. Only the halls and passageways were ever past that point. All the rooms were to the right as one passed from the foyer to the servant's hall. To the left had been a solid wall, ornately decorated with pictures, portraits and elaborate trim. He had assumed it abutted a large kitchen, for the dining hall was extremely large and would have required a large kitchen close at hand. However, to his complete astonishment, the wall was not solid at all. Two double arched doors opened to reveal a hidden room within.

[117] Curiosity over wisdom found him inching toward the opening. The open doors led onto a pulpit overseeing a great room, which looked very much like the structure of a chapel. The azure ceiling supported by cerulean and navy blue beams trimmed in gold accented the cream-coloured walls, making the dark woods of the room less obtrusive. As he stepped to the entrance he saw that the altar sat prominently in the centre of the pulpit draped in blue, facing out toward three pillars on the square, the blue carpet flowing down the length of the room over a dark wood sea. The three candles on the pillars were still lit though their height had dwindled to the stumps. Two rows of cushioned seats lined half the length of the room where two triangular desks picked it up. The chandeliers seemed almost dwarfed by the great hall, necessitating the reading lamps. Banners hung from the balcony overtop a light blue cloth draping, pinned with gold posts.

A handful of elderly gentlemen sat in various chairs at the far end, undisturbed by his entrance. The occasional rustling of newspaper was the only sound, barely rising above the vastness of the room. It was a singular experience, to observe so distinguished a company as these illustrious men, ancient as the artefacts and relics around them. An inspection of the faces proved Stratford and Willow to be absent, momentarily leaving him safe. It was curious to see a meeting taking place, when the north wing remained empty of its original occupants. This time, however, the meetings were different, with secrets and locks added to the proceedings. It was out of place, disjointed from the basic facts.

Not a single face among the quiet old gentlemen was familiar, save perhaps for a likeness or two in the newspapers. These were not the same men who had been there only a week before, nor did they act in any similar fashion. Where the previous congregation had flaunted ceremony and power, eager to display pomp and circumstance, these men exuded power without ceremony. They seemed unaffected by his entrance, as if entry to the house was sufficient for entry of the room, even if entered without explicit permission. There were no guards, no heated conversations or offence at his lack of membership.

Stepping down the long carpeted pathway to the far side, Holmes found his journey stalled. 'Sherlock Holmes, isn't it?' A soft wrinkled hand on his arm accompanied by a care-worn voice made him pause.

Holmes turned to see a silver-haired old gentleman well into his late eighties or nineties. 'What a surprise it is to see you here,' said the old gentleman with a smile. 'We heard you had been here, but I thought you left. Do you know you look very much like your mother? Yes,' he echoed to himself, 'definitely your mother. Are you alone, or is the good doctor with you?'

'I expect him later,' said Holmes.

'And Mycroft, is he well? I was sure we would not see anything of him this trip. This horrible business has taken a toll on so many. But come, you look lost. Tell me how it is we may assist you.'

'I was looking for Lord Stratford.'

'I'm afraid he isn't here. He went out with Sir John.'

'For long?'

'Not very long, no. You look troubled,' the man noted, offering Holmes a seat opposite him. 'I'm sure they won't be very much longer. John is anxious that these proceedings conclude quickly. I believe, just between you and me, he would have preferred to have dispensed with us altogether. He doesn't like us very much, you know.'

'Why?'

'The answer is as varied as the members of this room. I suppose we are not without our blame for it. John has given everything without question, asking nothing in return. He has hope, you see, that someday Stratford will be proclaimed Most Grand Masterful Mason and it ultimately guides his actions. So he tolerates us. There are many of us who agree with him, yet others of us would see another take the position. Willow might be better suited. He might have taken it once, but when his son died...' The old soldier paused at the thought. 'What a horrible thing that was. John has led such a sad life. He has lost so much and so much was taken from him. Little Myles was his life. It changed him. Some say it even tamed him while others say it broke him.'

Holmes slunk back in the chair at the chord resonating in his brain. 'Myles? Willow had a son named Myles?'

'A bonny little fellow with blond hair, blue eyes, and a wonderful intellect. He was an observant little one with a heart of gold. He would have made a fine successor to his father's legacy. John was worried we would make a Mason out of him, but he took after his father. The sword of justice was in his hands. We encouraged Willow to have another child. Perhaps we pressed too hard.'

'And his wife died in childbirth,' Holmes concluded.

The old soldier hesitated for a moment. 'A month or so prior to her date. After that John never smiled again, not like before. I have always maintained there was more to that story than we know. He has mellowed somewhat over the years. Harry has been a good influence on him. And then there is Helena. What a pleasure and comfort she is to him.'

'Why was it so important that Willow have a child? Of what possible difference could it make to anyone?'

'Look around you,' the old man instructed him with more than an air of rhetorical request, prompting Holmes to truly take notice of the men in the room. 'There comes a time when you become acutely aware that there are more days behind you than lay before you. To a solitary man it means nothing more than the number of his days, but to the brotherhood...' He stopped, as if unable to relay the importance of this in any just manner. 'We are the balance of the world, you understand. We prevent the world from tearing itself apart, controlling those greater issues that mortal men themselves cannot regulate on their own. While some men eagerly seek self-enlightenment by way of religion, we fulfil religion. We are guided by the word of God alone. No higher authority dictates our action. Yet,' he fell back into morose silence for a moment, 'we are but mortal men. We distrusted too easily. We are old, son. Our time here is quickly coming to an end. We have not taken care to trust or to accept, and we have found ourselves wanting. We are dying without replacement. Some deaths might be accepted, while others cannot be allowed. Many held much hope in John Willow. We still do. The time has come, and for good or ill, we must proceed.'

'But surely you have younger members that are viable? Brandon Faulkner and Samuel Damon?'

Brandon perhaps, though I do not think John trusts him very well. And as for Mr Damon, do you think, if he were the sort of man to conduct himself in such a manner, that we would ever have considered him in the first place? Whatever you have been led to believe, he was not one of us, nor would he ever be. He was but a cursory member in the outer order.'

'Unless he was to marry Miss Stratford.'

'Only the pure of heart may enter the temple. Only those who have been raised in our ways can understand. Leave a man out in the world too long unchecked and he becomes hard, like stone. We must chip away at him to sculpt him, but it takes great precision and one slip of the hammer can ruin him. Rear a child to emulate his father and he is worn, like water over a rock.'

'You keep referring to Willow as not a part of you. It is something Mycroft said, as well. Is he not a Mason?'

'He is a Templar. He guards and protects our journey, as we guard and protect the sacred order which lies in wait.'

'You make it sound as though you are awaiting old legends to come to life.'

'What are legends if not old truths waiting to be discovered?'

'Thank you,' Holmes added, taking his leave before he overstayed his welcome.

In the old gentleman's conversation, Holmes began to remember something Ballard had tried to tell him. He could see it clearly now, slipping past the barriers he had set to keep them out. Striding past the altar on his way out, Holmes chanced to see an old book, more ancient than the relics seated among the antediluvian artefacts. It was turned to a delicately drawn image of a dream or ancient prophecy.

Turning the thin membranes of the pages, he found the inscriptions to be written in an ancient dialect of Hebrew. In the illustration, a dead king, whose sign was the Royal Arch, rested on an altar lying in wake. In the foreground a boy king was being crowned. Carved in the altar was the Ark of the Covenant, a symbol of divine presence; the letter 'J' for Jachin, meaning 'God will strengthen and establish,' and Tetragrammaton, the sacred name of God, represented in Hebrew by its 'four-letter word' or symbol YHWH, meaning yod-ye-vau-he. Tetragrammaton, Eve, represented the Mother of All Living, which was not only represented on the altar, but in the depiction of a garden surrounding the floor and entwining itself around the servant and the two kings. The two guarding pillars stood in the front, the left bearing the letter 'B' for Boaz, meaning 'in strength,' 'smiter,' total obedience, that God would chase enemies, shield and protect. The right pillar bore the letter 'J,' as on the altar and the right sleeve of the boy king.

The strength and majesty of the thing was overridden by the sadness of its encompassing ruin. Its only hope lay in the boy, who was being crowned in mighty power at a tender, delicate age, older than some monarchs who took the throne, but younger than one would expect for so esteemed a position. In the boy's right hand was the power of God, represented by a stone of light, and in his left hand he held the staff, again reiterating the awesome power being bestowed upon so young a boy. The pillars, once mighty and unbreakable guarding the temple, now lay crumbled before the garden. The garden was brown and dead, stemming from a dead tree, which had borne two fruits, one on the left branch and the other on the right. They, too, bore the letters of 'J' and 'B'. A servant in long black robes adorned with a small beehive stood between the dead king and the boy king, to the right, opposite the tree, as if passing power from the old to the new. The vines of the garden favoured the dark-robed figure most as their dead leaves and twisting vines clung to his feet. The servant's head was bowed low, and though his face was not shown, it seemed he was more overtaken by sadness in his humbleness than servitude to the new king. It was an intense illustration with a multitude of symbols and hidden and antiquated references, marking it as old as or older than the book itself.

As he studied the picture, Holmes began to see connections not previously available to him, answering many outstanding questions. Just as he turned back to ask the old gentleman a question, the door opened and Stratford appeared with Willow, obviously embroiled in an intense tête-à-tête, unaware that the inner temple had been breached. Stratford stopped short as his eyes settled upon his unexpected guest.

His expression made it adamantly clear he did not wish to see Holmes there. Stratford was too stunned to say or do anything, fully aware of the ramifications and consequences of his guest's presence in those particular rooms, but he quickly recovered as he saw how his own plans and agenda might be furthered by the sudden change in affairs.

Willow, however, was not as forgiving. He knew, as did they all, that Holmes was ignorant of what he had done, but Willow had tried desperately to avert it at every turn, pleading with both Stratford and Mycroft Holmes to keep him away. In the end, Holmes did things his own way, this time finding himself drafted into something he could not step away from or control. The intrusion was an atrocity of intimacy, slapping Willow in the face with disrespect after his first stern warning that should Holmes ever disobey again, he would pay with death. This time it was not merely the intrusion into one's affairs, but an invasion of matters that did not concern him, for no purpose other than to prove a theory in his mind. Holmes had not entered those hallowed halls for reverence to God or the brotherhood. He wanted only to solve a puzzle, ignoring all warning and consequences, some of which he could scarcely contemplate, and this time he had gone too far.

Willow lunged at Holmes. Grabbing the lapels of Holmes's frock coat, Willow forced him backward until he pinned Holmes against the altar, sending candles and book hurtling to the floor. Snatching up the ceremonial dagger, his eyes never deviated from Holmes's face, as cold and detached as the man he held at bay, ready to strike without reservation. Willow had promised him death should he ever cross the line again, and his cold, steel blue eyes suggested he was prepared to make good on his word.

'You ignorant fool!' Willow reproached with vehemence, preparing to sink the dagger into Holmes's chest.

As Mycroft rounded the corner, barely in the door, he was confronted by the imminent danger his brother was in, and joined Stratford, grabbing Willow from both sides. It took the energies of both men merely to keep Willow at bay. The power and strength in his arms was but a small reflection of the power Willow held in his hands. Willow was a quiet man, easily underestimated, and one shove could find anyone at the wrong end of his wrath.

An odd collection of antediluvian artefacts were these gentlemen of indifference, for either they looked up in passing interest or did not bother to look at all, as if the outburst were so distasteful that to acknowledge it would be party to it. It was the law that any intruder breeching the halls of the temple would be summarily put to death without hesitation. With all confidence it could be assured that this law was practiced to its fullest extent. In Holmes's case, however, some were willing to make allowances for his genealogy and position in the house. The subtle old soldier Holmes had engaged at the end of the hall was among these, assimilation rather than extermination finding benefit beyond law for law's sake.

'Mr Willow,' the old soldier called out in a calm stately tone, seemingly unbothered by the violence taking place. 'A moment of your time, if you please.'

Though Willow would be loath to admit to the fact, it was a testament to the conflict within him to have been given those few seconds of hesitation, allowing Stratford and Mycroft to pull him back. It was undeniable that his anger was great and that he would have carried out the execution, agonizing over it later in private, but never showing it publicly. No man standing in witness would argue the point, so to hesitate spoke volumes of his reserve rather than of Stratford's intervention. Holmes's former arrogance, briefly borrowed for the occasion, still could not conceal his fear of the man lording over him with superior power. He knew, for all Willow's reserve, that Willow would do it.

For the moment, however, Willow withdrew, leaving Holmes to stand erect on his own, while Willow brushed off the tension along with the ruffling of his clothes. He clutched at the dagger in unreleased anxiety, arguing the point silently with himself before descending the pulpit stairs, composing himself as he strolled down the velvet blue bridge to face his company.

The old soldier waited until Willow and Stratford stood in front of him before speaking. 'You have interpreted the law efficaciously and your response just, John. However...' He hesitated, noting Willow shifting his stance. 'We should respect protocol. Lord Stratford opened these proceedings and, as such, must make the determination. Mr Holmes is no ordinary intruder, you must admit. Let us follow protocol and allow the Master of Ceremonies the final say,' he chastised with a delicate hand.

Willow turned his icy gaze onto his friend and a change passed over his countenance. In this place of all places, this sacred temple, form must be obeyed and the majestic protocols of true Masonry followed. Only one man held the power over life and death, of acceptance or denial, the worshipful master Lord Justice Harold Stratford, who stood in the east. In those small innocent words of the old strategic soldier, order had been restored, leaving Willow to realise his unforgivable sin in that brief moment of anger. He had lost control.

Stratford, seeing the value of such an ally as Sherlock Holmes, now coupled with the elder, more endowed, Mycroft Holmes, waved Sherlock Holmes to remain, once again overturning Willow's authority.

'Life is unpredictable,' the old soldier offered. 'In going about our business, each to his own ends, paths have crossed. It does little good to argue whether more precautions should have been taken or not; the fact of the matter is that our paths did indeed cross. The boy has questions, which he felt we could answer for him. He had been a resident in this house. Is he therefore to blame for utilizing the tools available to him? Does not the carpenter's apprentice pick up the tools of his master to finish the job asked of him?'

'Sherlock Holmes is no carpenter,' Lord Anderman offered, joining the discussion, obviously knowing Holmes's reputation. 'He is a detective and I, for one, question why he has chosen to investigate this house at this time. These proceedings are sacred and secured. Anonymity is paramount. The law is there to protect us in just such circumstances. Mr Willow acted justly.'

'He is harmless,' Willow offered in quiet calm, his eyes now cast low.

'He knows too much,' an anonymous voice from behind offered gently, knowing Willow's position. 'Letting him go is dangerous.'

Willow's barrister nature began to reveal itself as his eyes once again grew cold, like glass, and his head rose. 'Dangerous? He is no more dangerous to us than an ant crawling on the floor beneath our feet.'

'An ant can be more powerful than you think, and digs up the dirt to reveal what has been sown. His lips must be sealed.'

'And you think his lips are not sealed already?' Willow argued back abruptly. 'Do you mean to convince us that he has no feelings toward his brother, or Harry, or this house? If you mark him an obtuse man no oath will seal his lips, and if you mark him an intelligent one he already knows what is at stake should anything be revealed. You do not seek to bind him in hopes of sealing his lips, you want to use him.'

'What upsets you so?' Stratford turned to face his friend for the truth. 'This is not like you. You brought him here.'

'Not for this!' Willow answered with vehement conviction, almost revealing again more than he wished to, on the brink of losing control.

Willow saw it, no less than his two old friends standing before him, guessing too close to the truth until Willow begged to be excused. In a moment of recovery Stratford ran after him, not satisfied with a polite departure. Calling after him to stop, Stratford pressed his energies to catch him up.

'What was that all about, you arguing against me? It could have meant his life! For a moment there I thought you were actually going to kill him, or get him killed.'

Willow stopped, running his fingers along the brim of his hat in his hand, unable to look at his friend. 'There are worse things than death,' he remarked, 'If you love me you will send him back to London unhindered and seek him out no more,' he said as he turned and left.

Watching Willow stride the length of the corridor to the door, the strain, both physically and emotionally, had reached up into Stratford's chest and squeezed the breath out of him. Staggering to the wall for support, he found a strong arm securing him.

Stratford looked up into strong eyes. 'I did not know you were here.'

'I'm not. I am on my way out. You are playing a dangerous game, Harold. Be careful it does not come back to bite you.' Seeing George appear in the hall, the man waved him to come. 'Take your master upstairs. If anyone should ask, tell them he is tending to matters of state.'

The quiet hand behind the man knew the meaning of Willow's seemingly uncharacteristic behaviour, for he did not allow sentiment or desire to colour his judgement. Where Stratford found it inconceivable that Willow would cradle his charge in so fatherly a manner one day only to eagerly seek his death the next, this man found Willow's actions understandable and satisfactory. To Stratford, who only saw him from gentle eyes, Willow was like a calm sea, weathering the rocks around him to a smooth glassy finish, not a hurricane of violent altering emotions. Stratford was not accustomed to seeing his friend so out of character, and was too blind with pain to see that Willow was not out of character at all. Urging Stratford to withdraw abroad immediately with Willow, the man met with his own stubborn resistance, though for the moment a small compromise could be reached by Stratford retiring to his room.

[119] Life quickly resumed within the room. Servants appeared, as if by magic, to restore the room and disappear back into the

woodwork. Mycroft took his brother in hand and led him to the library, taking a bit of snuff from a tiny silver box before addressing the problem.

'I thought we agreed you would stay in London.'

'I agreed to nothing.'

'You don't know what you are playing at, Sherlock. I said I would look into it, but you must remain in London.'

'You knew they hadn't gone yet but you deliberately wanted me to think so. Why? Who are you shielding?'

'Yes, I knew. I also knew you couldn't just burst in here expecting that these men would welcome you. It's not like before. They are not like the former guests here. The lines you crossed today could well mean your life. You need to return to London and forget what you have seen here today, for your own good.'

'And sacrifice Stratford's life? He will die. Damon said Harry was not meant to die from the drug and that nothing could stop it now. This is not over.'

'Whistling in the wind, nothing more. I have found nothing to suggest Harry's life is in danger. Damon is behind bars and the plot is over. It makes little difference, however. John doesn't let him take a step outside these walls without him.'

Holmes sat back in his chair. 'Do you know how the Templars amassed their wealth? A traveller paid a fee to the Templars to guide his sojourn across the desert. He was not allowed to carry money on his person during the journey for reasons of safety. It was turned over to the Templars for a voucher, which could be redeemed when they reached the city. It was caution to safeguard them from thieves and Muslims. But there was a clause. If the traveller died en route, his purse was remanded to the Templar banks.'

'If that was supposed to be a reference to John Willow, you are chasing the wrong goose. John's no murderer.'

'And yet Stanton and Damon are dead, within days of our departure. You know as well as I that Damon was not transferred. He never made it out of his cell and Stanton had no reason to commit suicide, at least not on his own. If he did, and I am not convinced of it, he was led to it.'

'John would never harm Harry.'

'Damon was right about them fighting. They had been quarrelling for months, erupting into a physical altercation in the pool house. The blood is still visible on the baseboard. We do not yet know the cause, but it was enough for Stratford to break his vow against violence within South Lodge and turn Damon against him. You yourself called in Willow, feeling you could not trust Stratford.'

'I was wrong,' Mycroft insisted.

'Perhaps only about which one to distrust. Stratford is no killer, but Willow would have taken my life over entering that room.'

'He was just upset. You don't know him like I do. He wanted to protect you, to keep you out of all of this. His family means everything to him and Harry is his family. He would never harm him. I would stake my life on it.'

'You life perhaps, but are you willing to wager Stratford's life?'

SESSION CASE

QUEEN'S BENCH DIVISION

LORD JUSTICE

HAROLD A. W. STRATFORD

TWENTY-NINTH SESSION,

HELD AT

JUSTICE HALL, IN SUSSEX COURT,

ON FRIDAY, THE 27th DAY OF OCTOBER, 1903,

AND FOLLOWING DAYS.

TAKEN IN SHORT HAND

(BY AUTHORITY OF THE CORPORATION OF THE CITY OF EASTBOURNE)

BY A. WAKEFIELD

Eastbourne:

PRINTED FOR J. H. WILLOW, BY A. WAKEFIELD,

No. 74, MEADS;

AND PUBLISHED BY G. HERBERT, COUNTY COURT

1904

[120] It was upon Watson's arrival that Holmes was remanded to the upstairs. Once alone, Watson ardently sought out the reason behind his partner's obsessive behaviour.

'Good heavens, Holmes! What on earth would possess you to come back here, and unannounced? You don't know what you are playing at. You could have been killed!'

Holmes seemed dispassionately unaffected as he stood staunchly at the window looking over the garden. He watched as one by one the old men tottered out the door, congregating in the yard as carriages pulled up to retrieve them. Some he recognised, but most he did not know by sight. Then, out of nowhere, Willow appeared in the lower garden, walking towards the house. He approached just as Helena Stratford was returning home. She kissed him on the cheek and they spoke for a while. Willow ran his hands up and down her arms as if consoling her and then took her in his arms, kissing her on the head. He released her only to put his hand to her cheek and kiss her again, this time releasing her fully, watching her walk back the way she came.

William brought two trays upstairs for their supper, stating unequivocally that Holmes was to stay where he was, under the guard of John Watson. For a moment, however, it seemed as if fate had smiled upon him, for Stratford appeared before him, dressed and pressed and looking well.

'We are going out for the evening. We shall be back late,' Stratford announced, securing his cuff link.

Holmes shuddered at the thought. 'With Willow?'

'Of course; all of us will be going. We will be taking George, but William and the rest of the staff will be on hand, and Helena should be home momentarily,' he offered, as if to say Holmes was still under their watchful eye.

The notion that Stratford would be in public company seemed to abate Holmes's fears, but he found his mind racing at the possibilities.

'Have some dinner and get some sleep. We'll talk in the morning. Doctor, I rely on you to take care of him tonight. No more wanderings, I beg of you.'

With a nod of reassurance from Watson, Stratford descended the stairs. A moment later Willow stepped out into the hall, cloak and hat already on, giving a stern look toward Holmes.

'I want you to return to London, tonight, as soon as we are gone.'

Holmes shook his head in rejection. 'I will not leave the judge. You may now consider him under my protection.'

'Protection?' Willow echoed in disbelief. 'He is not yours to protect! Harry belongs to me!' Willow continued with a sense of deliberate force, turning abruptly to leave.

'Stratford or his daughter?' Holmes bated.

Willow stopped short, as if stunned by a blow he could not counter. Regaining his composure, Willow turned back around and spoke with firm determination.

'Do not meddle in affairs you do not understand. You have disobeyed me before and I have let it go. Do not disobey me again. Do as I say and return to London tonight, before you go too far,' he reiterated, exiting before any further altercation.

Holmes engaged his old friend the moment Willow had descended the stairs, challenging him to see the pieces falling into place. 'Do you remember my words to you just before I left for Rye?'

'I believe so. You said the case was a trivial one and that you did not need my help. But you were wrong, Holmes. I should have listened to my instincts and come with you.'

'No, Watson, I was not wrong. The case is a simple one, which is what put me off my mark. That,' Holmes emphasised, 'more than anything else, forged those deaths upon the Downs. What have I always said were the two greatest reasons for crime?'

'Greed and love,' Watson replied.

'Two forces that will tempt any man into committing any act, even murder. Damon was not interested in love. He wanted money, power, and position. He wanted South Lodge and everything it stands for, but even with her father dead Helena would not turn over South Lodge to Damon. If Damon thought South Lodge would, for all intents and purposes, be his, he had to be reasonably sure his accomplice would marry Helena. In either case Stratford has to die, but Damon could not run the risk of being implicated in his murder.

That is why he said Stratford could not die that night. He didn't mean any night, just not that particular night. Stratford would have to be killed at a time and place when Damon would not be suspected. If his plan was going to work he needed more than an eye witness for an alibi. Stratford's murder had to take place in public, where Damon would be ruled out as a possible suspect.'

Watson chuckled at the far-reaching theory. 'And how do you suppose he was going to assume power, even if he did have South Lodge? Do you think the Masons would just step aside and let him do it?'

'I think they might. Did you see the picture in the book downstairs? It is a prophecy which states that, in the wake of a dead king, a boy will be crowned in his stead and rule the Masons.'

'I'm not sure it was meant to be prophecy. You could just as easily say it was a variation on the ages of man, infancy to death.'

Holmes gave a wave of his hand. 'No, it is far too detailed for something so trivial. The image suggests a boy who is ordained, not by man, but by the word of God written in stone.'

Watson stopped chuckling at the implication. 'The ancient artefact: the Masonic stone.'

Holmes gave a nod. 'Damon was in that room and saw that picture. He not only saw it, he studied it. He was going to use a piece of history to claim the ultimate power. Upon the death of a king, God would choose a successor through His word, given to the boy.'

Watson shook his head in disbelief. 'Judging from the warm welcome you received upon entering that room, I highly doubt Stratford would let him waltz in there. I lived in this house for weeks and never knew the room existed. Did you?'

'Nevertheless, he was in there and he saw the drawing.'

Holmes retreated to the comfort of a chair, taking out his pipe and spending the time in thought as he refilled it, lit it, and brought it to a good draw before continuing.

Watson took a seat opposite. 'I am unconvinced.'

'Consider the facts. This estate stands for more than wealth. Stratford has made it the heart of the Masonic lodge and Stratford rules Sussex. My memory of the Masonic order is a little rusty, but does that not make him king?'

'I suppose so.'

'There are only two figures that stand out, the dead king and the boy. The other players are mourners: the one closest to the king, one who stands alone, and the older boy. They may or may not play a part. If Damon could convince enough people that the prophecy referred to this house, the imagery would place Stratford as the king and himself as the boy. If he then produced the Masonic stone with the Word of God carved into the surface, authenticated by experts to be genuine, no one would dare oppose him. Even with the stone, Damon could not possess South Lodge. He has no real claim on the estate and another man is in line to marry into it.' Holmes took another draw on his pipe becoming more excited at the thought.

Watson took out his pipe. 'But surely Brandon Faulkner would not turn over South Lodge to him. Once he married Miss Stratford it would be Faulkner who held the power in the south, not Samuel Damon.'

'But Faulkner was removed as suitor. At the sudden death of her father there would be only one man she would turn to, a man who doesn't need South Lodge to rule.'

'I am beginning to see your meaning. If you're right, Stratford could be in grave danger.'

'And they have already left. They are not going to hold this meeting in the Masonic Chapel. They are going to hold it somewhere they won't be seen or heard. Miss Stratford mentioned something about a ceremony honouring Willow. We haven't much time. We have to search this house.'

Watson suddenly grew nervous at the thought. 'If we are caught ... No, I don't like it.'

'We'll start in Damon's room. You can stand watch.'

'You're insane. If Stratford came back and found us, or worse, Willow found us...' Watson shuddered at the thought.

Holmes took on a serious expression as he faced his old friend. 'If I am wrong, no harm done. If I am right, Stratford's life is in jeopardy. If Damon's accomplice is Willow, every second we delay can cost him his life.'

Reluctantly Watson agreed and stepped out into the hall to peer over the banister for any signs of movement. At a clear view

Watson waved Holmes on to Damon's room. The room was simple and clean. His clothes were hung neatly, with pockets clean and jewellery removed. Damon had placed all personal effects in a small jewellery box on his dresser beside his shaving kit and brush. His barrister's robe stood on a special stand to keep it aired and fresh. His shoes were immaculately polished and his hat brushed, all signs of meticulous habits. His small writing desk was well maintained, the papers neatly housed in the top drawer.

Picking up the first few layers of paper, Holmes retrieved a charcoal drawing stem and a pocketknife from his coat and scraped the charcoal onto the paper, pressing gently to embed the dust into the indentations of the page. It revealed nothing of interest. It contained nothing but notes on briefs he had been working on in the last days before his confinement.

It confirmed his first hypothesis that Damon was a far greater adversary than anyone could have imagined. He neither put his plans to paper nor confided them to any living soul. It was an exercise in mental superiority almost unparalleled. His mind had been as meticulous as his room, allowing him to keep every step recorded in his mind. He thought ahead, calculating every possible angle before making a move, keeping all facts and changes in a mental catalogue. Had Damon's facts been accurate, he may well have risen to the highest height unchecked unless there was a greater mind behind his, telling him what to do. Crawling across the floor, Holmes looked for any loose floorboards or papers hidden under the carpet. There was nothing. Removing the drawers from the desk and dresser revealed nothing as well. Motioning for assistance, Holmes moved the dresser far enough for him to reach behind it. Running his hand along the back revealed nothing, but as his fingers slid along the top edge he felt something metal and cold.

'Well done, Watson,' he said as he pulled a small set of keys from beneath a section of adhesive.'

At the revelation even Watson had to agree Damon's access to the secret room was now not only possible, but probable. The keys held more than the peculiarly shaped metal key to the secret temple. It contained cabinet keys and another small key, which Holmes took to be to the mysterious locked drawer to Damon's desk. Slipping them into his pocket he pushed back the dresser and the pair made their way down the hall. It seemed a familiar, comfortable thing, passing the same images he had seen every day for half a year.

It appeared as if any remaining clues left behind had been summarily expunged. Collecting his thoughts and bearings on his theory, Holmes looked up and down until one room stood out above the others, laid open in unqualified temptation. Returning to the banister, he insured that the household remained engaged. To be caught in Willow's quarters would be a fate worse than death. Yet, without the effort, there could be no certainty. With all quiet, Holmes whisked back to Willow's door and turned the knob, glancing back one more time for the promise of free passage before setting Watson to keep watch.

Stepping within, there was a clear atmosphere of warmth about it. Unlike Damon's cold, sparsely furnished, and perfectly kept lodgings, or the judge's room with its bachelor-style perfection of well-worn years, Willow's room breathed reassuring comfort. It was clean, but well populated with furnishings. The soft browns mixed with dark burgundies and rich deep blues, all coordinated in perfect harmony. His toiletries were displayed on the dresser instead of being neatly packed in a bag, as if the owner could readily pick them up at any moment. His robe lay draped on the edge of his bed as if always waiting to be drawn on. Stacks of books were piled at every point, from his bedside table to the small reading table in the corner. Even the bench at the foot of his bed displayed a small stack of two, and unlike the rest of the household members, Willow's selection of reading was not confined to law. His drawers were tidy and meticulously arranged, indicative of a soldier long in service. Every drawer, every cabinet was put to inspection.

Moving the books from the bench chest, Holmes tried the lid but found it to be locked, the only thing locked in the entire room. Removing his pocketknife, he attempted to pick the lock, hoping it would come to him by virtue of intuition of years of practice. It seemed a thing one would not tend to lose, yet for all his efforts, memories of his past still remained largely blocked.

'Holmes!' Watson whispered loudly, urging him to hurry. 'Holmes!'

Just then the lock clicked, and with a gentle pull was released. A sigh of success had Watson peering into the room in some hopes of seeing what his companion had found, though minding that his primary duty was to give them enough time to escape. From the doorway not much could be seen, though Holmes had clearly found something of interest, for the expression on his face as he looked up toward his old partner was one of complete and utter disbelief. The waters indeed ran deep with Willow, but not even in his wildest imaginings could Holmes have foreseen the enormity of the ocean's depths. Replacing everything, Holmes took care to put all as it was, and then relocked the trunk. Scampering to the door, Holmes tapped Watson on the arm.

'We must get to them as quick as possible!'

Watson rushed to keep up, his heart pumping fiercely at his friend's expression. 'Why? What did you find?'

Half way down the stairs the front door opened downstairs, freezing them cold in their tracks. As if on cue, a large stout figure stood in the foyer, accompanied by Helena Stratford.

'Where are they?' Holmes asked.

'I presume you mean John and Harry. They're gone for the evening'

'We must get to them right away.'

'More of this theory of yours? I would trust John with my life, and yes, I would trust him with Harry's life, too.'

'I was wrong about Willow, but only because I thought he wanted to marry Helena. I now know he cannot.'

Before he could utter another word, Holmes saw the hard blow he had dealt without thinking. Helena Stratford stood brazenly for a moment and then cast her eyes down, hiding the pain of his words. He hadn't meant to be so blunt, but time was of the essence.

Holmes paused at his indiscretion, but then continued. 'If Willow was not in league with Damon he will be a victim, seen as a threat. You must tell me where they have gone. Mycroft! It means Willow's life!'

Helena put her hand on Mycroft's arm, pleading with him with her eyes.

'The Royal Pavilion, beneath the old church' Mycroft said.

Without ceremony or further adieu, Holmes took to his heels out the door, pacing outside for his brothers. Within minutes Mycroft had led them to a secret door in the old church. Holmes did not wait, but whisked down the half-lit corridors descending along a stone pathway. Visibility was slight, but the echo of his footfalls denoted some sort of surrounding rock. The temperature was a steady twenty-five degrees centigrade again suggestive of a cave rather than a man-made catacomb, but he could not be sure. The twists and turns could have led anywhere. There was a slight sound of water dripping in the distance, into a larger pool of water, filling him with a slight sense of discomfort, pressing him on ahead. Anyone could be lost, never for it to be known where they had lost their way.

[121] The long passageways of stone and locked doors deposited him in some large inner chamber. It was an amazing vision, an enormous chasm of religious regalia. It was lit with candles and adorned with elegant furniture and banners. Men were standing throughout, dressed in ornate clothes, sashes, jewels of office, and aprons. It was a magnificent sight, taken from a page of history without blemish.

Holmes crouched down behind various tapestries and flags trying to find Stratford or Willow. In the distance a soft sound grew into the sweet music of Mozart. He was too late. The ceremony had begun. Just as Watson came up behind him, a line of robed men walked in procession around the altar and great lights. One by one the four masters took their place, each in turn, in the majestic splendour of ceremony. There was no sign of Stratford or Willow. With a great booming rap of the Tyler's staff, the room grew quiet and the next phase began.

In the east stood an ornate gallery divided into upper and lower tiers. Set between a pair of massive mahogany pillars both above and below were heavy velvet draperies the colour of blood, concealing an antechamber. Two men dressed in the colourful livery of the King's Service stood to either side of these curtains in the upper gallery, and before them was the Master's throne. Three sonorous blasts from a ram's horn sounded within the vastness of the cavern, and Lord Justice Harold Stratford appeared in the east from behind the draperies of the upper gallery, seating himself in the magnificent chair.

'We pray to Almighty God', he intoned, 'the Architect and Master Builder of all Creation, to sanctify and bless our Brethren and our most sacred work.'

'So mote it be,' answered the brethren, their one voice thunderous in the cavern.

From between the great pillars of Jachin and Boaz, John Willow, dressed in the uniform of Grand Commander of the Knights Templar, strode purposefully toward the west, his face set in a grim mask. A large man carrying a sword accompanied him: the Tyler of the Lodge, there to protect against helots and eavesdroppers. As they came to rest the Tyler moved on alone and whispered a few words in the ear of the Senior Deacon in the west, who conveyed the message to the Worshipful Master.

'Sir John Willow, Grand Commander of the Knights Templar, prays for permission to array his Knights in Grand Parade and solemn encampment in the east.'

Stratford rose unsteadily and nodded. 'Permission is granted to our illustrious Brother.'

From the tunnel leading to the cavern marched eight columns of nine times eight knights each in full battle array, forming and parading in four concentric circles. The outermost circle wheeled counter-clockwise, the next clockwise and so forth, centred upon a circular island twenty-seven feet in diameter. Willow took his place in front of the altar at the centre of the island and faced the east, as the knights, their chain mail gleaming beneath their resplendent surcoats, revolved like the stars of heaven about the Great Lights arrayed upon it. Their steps rang out in unison and reverberated from the vaulted ceiling above. The knights wheeled about the altar nine times seven, finally forming rank upon rank to either side of the Worshipful Master.

[122] Willow regarded his friend keenly and frowned. Harry wasn't well; his face was pale and drawn. Was he trembling?

'Dear God', Willow muttered beneath his breath at the sight. Although he understood the importance of the Grand Convocation, this did not stop him from wishing his friend were at South Lodge instead, where he could look after him and care for him.

The company of Knights Templar was in place and, high above, Stratford rapped the gavel three times upon a stone plinth. The few murmurs of approval from the assembled brethren ceased. The vast space was deathly still. A commanding figure had emerged from behind the curtains of the upper gallery. He was still in shadow as his voice spoke the ancient words of invocation. The brethren rose as one, while Willow and the Knights Templar sank to one knee in reverence. The figure continued to speak as he moved into the light; he was Edward VII, King of Great Britain and Ireland, and of the British Dominions beyond the seas, Emperor of India.

As the King concluded, Stratford bowed deeply and accompanied him back through the curtains. They emerged together onto the floor with two royal attendants, taking their place to either side. The ceremony continued with great pageantry and ritual, commemorating the journey of the Templar and their assimilation into the brotherhood. It was of great interest that Holmes watched Willow approach the east. Stratford was sweating, though the caverns held a steady temperature of sixty degrees. His hand gripped the ceremonial dagger too tightly and his stance was too taut. Others must have noticed it for once or twice Holmes saw a man whisper something to him from behind.

Willow knelt before Stratford and then rose again, removing his gauntlets to receive the ceremonial handshake to welcome the knights home. Stratford extended his left hand, but did not clasp Willow's. Instead he placed it fondly upon Willow's shoulder as if to draw him into his welcoming arms.

'No, that's wrong. You don't shake with your left hand,' Holmes muttered to himself.

Not giving it another thought, Holmes leapt out onto the floor and dove headlong toward Willow. In a coordination of activity, Sherlock Holmes tackled Willow to the floor just as Stratford's right hand lunged forward at Willow with a long ceremonial dagger.

There was a sudden flurry of activity around the commotion. Chaos reigned and the knights, sworn protectors of the crown, drew their weapons and moved in three circles to safeguard Edward.

Deadly intent was written on every man's face. Watson quickly followed up behind to restrain Stratford, fighting against a warrior's stance and a strong arm. Stratford showed no signs of relaxing his murderous intent, but before he could move a step further, Mycroft took the other side to restrain him, reaching for the dagger.

Looking up from the floor, Holmes shouted towards them. 'Don't touch it! It's poisoned!'

Mycroft quickly pulled out a handkerchief and placed it over the dagger, removing it from Stratford's hand. But as Stratford continued to struggle against his bonds, the crowd reeled in anarchy.

The king wheeled about and roared, 'I command silence! Faithful knights, you are ordered to stand down!'

The knights instantly halted, sheathed their swords, and stood watchful and at the ready.

Holmes struggled to his feet, looking over to see that Stratford was firmly detained. Then, examining the source of pain in his arm, he separated the two halves of the tear in his coat. Though the wound was superficial it had already begun to bleed. Giving a short chuckle at his clumsiness, Holmes looked up at Mycroft and then fell unconscious to the floor. Willow gave a short shout of fear and rushed to Holmes's side and knelt on the ground, drawing the lifeless body into his arms.

[123] Unseen from above, a dark-cloaked figure looked on, now slowly rising and descending the stairs of the balcony. He was a tall man, dressed in a formal evening coat, covered by a cloak. He had no face. No, he only appeared so, as a flowing black cowl covered his entire head. The crowd parted slowly with each purposeful step he took, kneeling at the sight of the ring upon his finger. With a nod of his head, quite inconspicuous, Mycroft was taken in hand and moved strategically away with the others until only Willow remained in the centre of a large circle. As the man approached, a great stillness once again filled the lodge and a deep voice spoke from behind the hood.

'With your Majesty's permission.'

The spectral figure faced the king, who amazingly bowed deeply before him and withdrew several steps back toward the curtain.

Addressing Willow, the ominous figure needed no introduction. 'Well, well. Do my eyes deceive me or is this our troublesome detective, who lies at my feet, deep within the Masonic walls?' he asked with an air of distain, turning to look at Stratford as the source.

'Alex.' Willow looked up with hopeful relief to whisper the name.

The dark figure turned away with callous disregard. 'How far my children have fallen in my absence. You are, I fear, imperfect ashlars, unfit for The Great Builder's use. You were tasked and you were found wanting. What has led you here do these walls great injustice. A seed of doubt grows into distrust and distrust into argument. When argument turns to division, is it not easy to be led astray? These are the frailties of men. In my sympathy I send you guidance, but you kill my emissary, rise up against your master, and divide the brotherhood. My sword,' he said, motioning towards Willow, 'exacts swift punishment, but does so like a point chisel, roughing out and removing material quickly instead of using a tooth chisel to define the peaks and valleys left in the wake. On a soft stone, the point chisel can leave a bruise.' He paused, moving again to Stratford, who was still struggling against his restraints. He put his hand to Stratford's chin and lifted his head up and to either side before withdrawing his hand. 'In your haste,' he addressed Willow again, 'you have defaced the stone.'

'What does that matter now? Do something!'

The black, seemingly empty cowl turned to address him. 'You still do not see. Sherlock saw it. His friend, a mere layman in the art of observation and detection, saw it. Why can't you? Look at him.' He pointed toward Stratford. 'He is but an empty shell, the instrument of your murder.'

'I don't care.'

'You should,' the stranger returned gruffly. 'Your petty arguments divided you, and your enemies descended upon you both. Even before you left it had begun, but to ignore his anger you had to ignore his behaviour, blinding you to the truth. Malone was but a test to see if he was ready for this night, ready for you. Do you want me to wake him, so you may see for yourself, or are you still denying that you harbour your enemies? Do you recall that Stratford's alibi for Malone's murder was irrational?'

Willow shook his head in adamant denial. 'Harry didn't kill Malone. It is not in him to do.'

'I am afraid you are wrong there, brother mine. Do you honestly believe Malone would not have noticed the difference between Stratford and Damon, even disguised? Stratford was there, walking through the motions as he was instructed to do, just as he is now. Oh, Damon was there, to be sure. He hid in the shadows to see the unfolding of his play. He watched as Stratford killed Malone and then calmly got back into his motor and drove home without ever realising what he had done. His confusion, which you so eagerly dismissed, was his awakening. No doubt a sound he would inevitably hear along his route home or a smell he was bound to come by before too long. He awakes and is unaware of what he has done. And if he can kill one friend, he can kill another.'

'Why kill me now and not before? There is nothing in it.'

The dark figure moved intimately close to Willow, kneeling down to address him ever so softly. 'Your arrogance has made you weak, John. Amateur he may be, but not his friends. Look at the man you have loved and nurtured. Make no mistake, he would kill you if I released him.'

Willow looked at the faceless man with confidence. 'Damon had poisoned the dagger long before this night. It does not make me weak or inefficient that I should miss the means of his final stand. He admitted we could not stop his plan altogether.'

'Then tell me, who gave Harry the order to kill you tonight? He had not been supplied with the drug until his sweat released it from the handle. If Damon acted alone Harry would have been rendered benign. You can ready a man's mind to receive instruction, but you cannot trigger him to act merely with the application of a drug. He was instructed here, in this room. Your enemies do not merely surround you, they penetrate your ranks … Templar,' he added with an air of mockery.

'We do not have time for this. Save the boy.'

'Save him? Why should I save him? He has breached the sacred hall and desecrated these proceedings. Let him die. It is no less than the law prescribes.'

'For God's sake, Alex!' Willow forced out with all the air of contempt he held within. 'You can't let him die!'

'Such familiarity for so grand a request,' he said, rising and turning away with callous disregard.

'Damn you to hell,' Willow choked out. 'Save him or I swear we will die with him together. He is just a boy.'

'Of what consequence is that to this order? There is nothing more important. We hold the world in our hands.' The old man thundered around to face Willow's contempt with cold detachment.

Willow stood and faced him, anger welling in his throat. 'You are just like your father! There is not an ounce of feeling left in you!'

'But there is in you, and that is your weakness, my dear brother. You must learn! You must detach yourself from all personal associations in order to see and apply truth. Do not let emotions dictate your actions. If you want his life, kneel to me and offer yours to me in his stead. Do not whine to me like an old woman. Show me your strength, Templar. Make the ultimate sacrifice for your son.'

For a moment the two stood toe-to-toe, glaring at each other in an eternal struggle, as if good and evil faced one another, each waiting for the other to yield. As Willow stared at him, the robed man softened.

'You won't let him die,' Willow said in momentary victory.

With complete calm, his opponent spoke, never taking his eyes from Willow's face. 'I did not ascend to this position by holding emotion as a virtue. There is nothing on this earth that is more important than this order. If you value what we stand for, you must rise above mortality to embrace the greater whole. You must learn, John. You have become strong. I am well pleased with your progress, but you still allow sentiment to cloud your judgment.'

'Don't be a fool with his life,' Willow demanded. 'If you have the means to save him then do so; if not, let a physician through.'

'Can you not afford me a little respect, for my position, if not as your brother? You must let it go, without emotion. Do not falter in your strength or all is lost. Sentiment will bring such devastation as you cannot imagine, far more than losing Stratford or even the boy. Do not take this office lightly. You despise us, but we are your blood. Rise and take your place!'

'My God,' Willow growled. 'You're mad.'

'Which is the greater good: to sacrifice one to save ten thousand or sacrifice ten thousand to save one? You expect me to be what I cannot. All that I was has passed away for what I have become. If I yield, my enemies would descend upon me as your enemies have descended upon you for your failure to stand fast. The eldest of the household is named father, master, and ultimate authority. All who belong to him and claim their allegiance to him are his and must hold his values. The authority of father is extensive. His responsibilities include procreating, instructing, nurturing, and yes, even disciplining. You're the priest. Tell me, what must a father do if his son entices him from his loyalty to God? Prove your loyalty. Perform the Olah. The binding of Isaac as korban.'

Willow shook his head in horror. 'You're insane.'

'This office will stand without emotion, but not without respect!'

Willow's body tensed with distain as he turned away, trying to think.

'Come with me, John, and I will forgive you.'

Willow whipped around, brought to the breaking point. 'Forgive me? Like Father forgave me? I was a child. Did my sins warrant my abandonment? He took my brother and he took my life. There was no feeling in him then as there is no feeling in you now.'

'He did what he had to do, as I do now.'

'I was only three, Alex!' Willow shouted. 'Don't tell me he did what he had to do, and don't tell me that letting Sherlock die is what you have to do. Is there nothing human left in you? I hated him for what he did. Do not make me hate you, as well. What good can come of his death?'

'The lesson that it will teach you,' he returned unaffectedly.

Willow looked back at the life slipping away from his charge. 'What do you want?'

'You must show this office respect, for we cannot exist without it.'

Willow took a deep breath and gave a nod, kneeling before the cloaked figure in bowed respect. The old gentleman granted a smile of immense satisfaction, understanding the struggle Willow had with that one particular act. He placed his hand on Willow's shoulder in assurance of faith.

Removing a black leather case from inside a deep pocket, he knelt down beside Sherlock Holmes and laid the case on the floor. He opened it carefully and took out the contents and laid them out. Exposing the limp, sinewy arm of his patient, he thrust the needle deep into the vein, emptying the contents of the syringe. Taking a cloth and pressing it against the tiny wound, he withdrew the needle.

'Turn him over. We need to expose the base of his neck.'

At Willow's compliance, he retrieved a small glass vial containing a single bee, rousted by the ill handling. Removing a pair of tweezers, the old gentlemen held the jar up to the light and uncorked the top, inserting the tweezers inward to capture the bee. Still secured between the blades of metal, he pressed the bee to Holmes's neck until the bee thrust its stinger deep into the skin. Once injected, he carefully pulled upwards on the bee, detaching him from the stinger and returning him quite dead into the vial. The area reddened and swelled in reaction to the sting. It seemed an odd sort of remedy, but within minutes the ashy colour began to fade and the bruising slowed. Holmes's colour began to return and his breathing regulated until a smooth rhythm took it over.

Willow relaxed his shoulders and sighed in relief as he looked across Holmes's body to grant a thankful smile. Then, with one swift motion, a hand stretched forth from the dark robe and reached over to grasp Willow by the wrist.

The old gentleman pulled Willow over the body and whispered, 'You once said I could not understand you because I had never lost a son, never had him wrenched from my arms, never to lay claim to his life again. I know your pain, Johnny. I know what hurts you.'

Still holding fast to Willow's wrist, he shrewdly turned his hand, palm upwards to the light, and drew a dagger effortlessly across Willow's palm. Willow snapped back at the implication more than the pain, and recoiled in revelation, watching his counterpart repeat the same incision on his own palm, a centimetre above an identical scar. Grasping Willow's wrist again, he held it firmly in his grip, blood to blood, pain to pain. In the instant of Willow's shock, he took the dagger still stained with blood and made a three-centimetre incision across Holmes's left breast, never releasing Willow's grip, now struggling to break free.

'Don't look so shocked, Johnny. Did you honestly believe there would be no price for his life? ' he asked. 'I said I would take your life in return for his—and I have.'

Willow wanted desperately to curse him again to hell, but begrudgingly kept his tongue. He had been marked with the arc of succession, the one position Willow never aspired to. Willow wanted neither power nor to rule. He wanted to live out his life in peace, without fanfare or ceremony. He had been asked, and agreed to give up his own life for his love. Eager though he was to give up his mortal life, letting his blood flow from his body, he was not eager to be whisked away, dead to all who knew him.

Withdrawing his hand abruptly, Willow knew his opponent understood the meaning of the rejection, even if it made little difference. Whether out of age or stature, the slightest suggestion to rise found two previously invisible men, dressed in black and quite peculiar in their design, immediately appearing to assist him, calling the meetings to a close. Brushing out his robes, the old gentleman stood before Stratford and spoke three simple words to release him. 'Willow is dead.'

Standing disoriented before his master, Stratford looked at Alex and then over at Willow, still holding Holmes in his arms, trying to understand.

'The torch is now passed onto you, my First Grand Principal. Take care of John in my absence.'

The aged figure made his way slowly past the congregation, all straining to get a glimpse of the man who held sway over the entire world. They could see nothing of the ghost who walked through their midst. He would remain as elusive as the private exchange with Willow, hearing only an occasional word spoken out of context. Unobtrusively, the old gentleman reached out and brushed the hand of Mycroft Holmes as he passed.

SESSION CASE

QUEEN'S BENCH DIVISION

LORD JUSTICE

HAROLD A. W. STRATFORD

THIRTIETH SESSION,

HELD AT

JUSTICE HALL, IN SUSSEX COURT,

ON FRIDAY, THE 27th DAY OF OCTOBER, 1903,

AND FOLLOWING DAYS.

TAKEN IN SHORT HAND

(BY AUTHORITY OF THE CORPORATION OF THE CITY OF EASTBOURNE)

BY A. WAKEFIELD

Eastbourne :

PRINTED FOR J. H. WILLOW, BY A. WAKEFIELD,

No. 74, MEADS;

AND PUBLISHED BY G. HERBERT, COUNTY COURT

1904

[124] The mad dream of intense images within his brain at an end, Holmes opened his eyes to a soft breeze tickling the sheers from the small opening in the window. His surroundings were unfamiliar, though it was clear that he was in quarters that had been prepared for him, for his clothes hung on a fine cherry valet. His personal items sat smartly on the dresser, including his own brush and shaving supplies that, to his knowledge, were still back at Baker Street.

Drawing back the white eyelet comforter and soft down pillows that surrounded him, he sat upright between the curtains that hung from the canopy of the large mahogany bed. A robe and slippers had been set out for him in anticipation. He had not bothered to look out of the window, for had he done so he might have found his bearings, but his mind struggled to piece together the clues from within. It was all too familiar, like a dream.

Stepping into the hall, he pressed onward to the open parlour, noting at once that the furnishings were vaguely familiar. A chemistry table had been set up for him, complete with the latest equipment. A glass and cherry wood curio cabinet sat diagonally near the table with items from his Baker Street 'museum' contained within, neatly displayed. Stepping over to the desk, Holmes gently opened the top centre drawer. Contained within was the rest of his collection from Baker Street, including his black leather case and a picture of Irene Adler. A small key lay on the desk, which he took and tried in the lock of the upper drawers. Finding that it fit, he slipped it into his dressing gown.

Over the fireplace in an alcove hung, not his picture of Reichenbach Falls, but a family heraldry. On the wall to either side of this hung two smaller pictures: one of the sword pointing to the naked heart and the other of a beehive swarming with bees, the site of which returned him to the strange and terrible dreams which had begun the day. A small delicately carved tray of cards sat prominently upon the fireplace mantel, printed: Sherlock Holmes, Pure Honey, Violin Lessons.

As the idea of bees ran through his mind, striking vague chords, Holmes began to recognise where he was, confirming it as he looked out the window. A small but elegant sign reflected the same imagery of the bees. In the distance, barely but distinctly visible, were several beehives teeming with activity. In the corner, on the chair, lay gloves, a beekeeper's hat with face netting, and a scarf. Touching it, as he routinely did to everything, Holmes heard a small tapping sound, like a tiny mallet against a windowpane. It was coming from the corner of his chemistry table. Stepping closer he noticed a bell-shaped glass container, secured with a cork with a wire handle through the neck and an opening port in the bottom. Its occupant was a single bee, thrusting itself against the glass, which pinged it as it did so. A note was held under the glass, folded with his name written in an old calligraphy-style hand. Freeing the paper, he opened it to read its content.

> It might interest you to know that this humble creature saved your life. Keep well this Brother, lest his secret become lost forever.
>
> 

The inscription was intriguing, notably the capitalization of the B in brother, but more so was the small arrow at the bottom. In an attempt to ascertain its meaning, Holmes stood as if placing the note, and then looked in the direction of the arrow.

To his left he found his old blackboard beside the window. It was covered with the same cloth he had placed upon it in Baker Street, as if the thing, in its entirety, had been transported. Stepping up to it, Holmes drew a deep breath and pulled off the cloth, revealing the work he had begun nearly a year earlier. However, a few changes had been made to his formula, expounding upon it until it gave a clear and decisive solution to the problem.

As his mind began to wake and clear, the full enormity of what had transpired filled him. The sword had been tainted with the same poison affecting Mrs Stanton, the equation he had tried in vain to solve. Someone had known of its existence and had found the antidote, saving his life, but at a cost. He had been granted entrance into the celebrated secret society. What had begun as a quest to place a criminal behind bars had resulted in membership in an eternal brotherhood. Giving the idea due reverence to accept or decline, he decided he would not go back to Baker Street; he would remain on the cliff's edge to guard the southern coast. They had granted him a house. One look outside proved it to be the house he had admired on his walks. It had been transformed, as he had.

Hearing someone in the kitchen now pressing down the hall toward him, he felt an odd sensation of expectation run through him. Hearing footsteps draw closer, he arranged himself in a structured pose and grabbed a cold pipe, tucking it between his teeth to conceal any hint of pleasure.

'Mr Holmes! What are you doing out of bed?' Mrs Hudson exclaimed. 'I was given strict instructions not to let you out of bed for at least another few days. Dr Watson was most insistent upon that point.'

He discarded the pipe with dejection. 'Is he here?'

'No, sir. He left a couple of days ago.'

'Days? How long have I been out?'

'Oh, it must be more than a week now. You had us worried. Mr Willow thought you would be more comfortable here rather than in London, so he had some of your things brought down and asked me if I wouldn't mind coming along. Of course I wouldn't mind,' she said with an embarrassed smile. 'What a nice man he is. He stayed with you night and day until you were better. He said to tell you he and Lord Stratford had to leave, but he would be back as soon as he could. He left you a note over on the desk. Mr Mycroft is on an errand at the moment and Dr Watson said he will be back on the weekend. He said a telegram or telephone call can have him here straight away if you need him.'

'You said Mycroft is on an errand?'

'He had to stop downtown for something,' she said, straightening the pillows on the sofa. 'You look like you still aren't feeling well. You put up your feet and I will bring you some tea.'

'Mrs Hudson,' he called after her, just before she rounded the corner. 'Were there any other visitors?'

'Others? No, sir, not that I can recall. Is it important?'

'No,' he replied, crushing his last remnants of expectation.

Holmes picked up Willow's letter and turned his attention toward the inviting sofa as he opened it. It said little more than what Mrs Hudson had imparted, which was nothing. He found himself a little off his mark, disoriented and tired. Discarding the note, he picked up the newspaper from the table and leafed through it. There wasn't even a whisper of Damon or the affair at the estate. It was if it had never happened. Putting down the paper, Holmes leaned back on the cushions and studied the details of the room. It was almost unrecognisable from the rooms he had so admired only months before. One could only imagine the powerful hand behind its transformation in such a short time.

He was free. No one would follow him and his enemies would die away. Baker Street would remain in London, a fixture of the past where passersby would marvel at the once great adventures begun within. London would struggle on without him, as it was meant to be, while he nestled in the hidden acres behind the hills leading down to the single, slippery slope to the sea. He was free to perform his experiments and take up the tending of those most singular bees. The name of Sherlock Holmes would slip quietly from the lips of the everyday, leaving his enemies to pursue nobler tasks and adversaries. He would give himself over to that quiet serenity of the country, happy to free his slowing mind and body from the pounding of his former profession. Yet in his freedom there was a pervading sense of loss within the silence surrounding him. In his absence, life had gone on without him, without the need of him. The adventure was over, set now only in books to be read and debated for years to come.

Mrs Hudson put tea on the table as he stared out the window at the fading colours overshadowing the cliffs and waters below. Turning aside, he sat down to table and lifted the lid only to replace it again, the summation of his life falling before him. In spite of all the amenities he had been given, every wish that had been granted and bestowed, he was alone.